Trust

THE TEMPTATION SERIES III

ELLA FRANK

Edited by Mickey Reed

Edited by Candace Wood

Also by Ella Frank

The Exquisite Series
Exquisite
Entice
Edible

Masters Among Monsters Series
Alasdair
Isadora
Thanos

The Temptation Series
Try
Take
Trust

Sunset Cove Series
Finley
Devil's Kiss

Standalones
Blind Obsession
Veiled Innocence

The Arcanian Chronicles
Temperance

Sex Addict
Co-authored with Brooke Blaine

PresLocke Series
Co-Authored with Ella Frank
Aced
Locked
Wedlocked

Dedication

To Tate,

Before this, I didn't know you were essential for me to feel alive.

- Logan

Part One

Self-Reliance: The belief in one's own instincts, choices, and opinions.

Chapter One

THE BRIGHT CITY lights of downtown Chicago reflected in Logan's rearview mirror as he checked the lane behind him and merged to the left. With his window down and the breeze ruffling his hair, he floored it up an empty street, thankful it wasn't yet the coldest time of the year.

It was, however, four fifteen a.m.

Fuck. Tate was not going to be happy when he banged on his front door. But that was too damn bad. He'd made a deal with Mr. Morrison not so long ago, and if he recalled correctly—*and I know I fucking do*—he'd stipulated no dead silences.

Granted, at the time, he'd meant more of the days and weeks variety, but after the night they'd had—and the fact that he'd missed the opportunity to peel Tate out of his tux—the past three hours and fifteen minutes had felt like an eternity.

Earlier in the evening, it had made sense to drop Tate at home, especially since they both had separate places to be today. But when Logan had walked into his condo and crawled between his sheets, he'd discovered that his bed minus Tate no longer offered a comfortable place to rest. Instead, it had made him antsy and hyperaware of how much he desired the company of the sexy, pigheaded man.

God, I miss him.

In only months, he had gone from a man who ran from commitments to one who was in his car, speeding headfirst toward a bigger one. He'd thought of that and nothing else while he'd tried to exhaust himself on the treadmill, and while his feet had pounded out a steady pace, he'd had time to think about exactly what he wanted—and now, he knew.

His motto of "try, take, and top" had changed.

Oh, he'd tried Tate all right, and they'd both done a helluva lot of taking, but for once in his life, Logan didn't feel the desire to win. He didn't need to come out on top.

What he wanted was Tate's trust—his *absolute* trust.

* * *

TATE LAY IN bed and willed himself to go to sleep. Tonight had not gone according to plan—lying there alone was proof enough of that, but it was also damn depressing.

He'd had high hopes for the night. Ones that involved being introduced as Logan's partner, and he'd been looking forward to that. What he hadn't anticipated was Christopher Walker being as much of a problem as he'd turned out to be.

Tate had been almost positive that Chris wouldn't have the balls to walk up to Logan and confront him. So he'd figured they wouldn't really have to deal with him at all. *How wrong was I?* No, Chris hadn't confronted Logan exactly, but he sure as hell had found an effective way to get his attention…

"Mr. Walker, you're new to Mitchell & Madison and a guest here tonight, so maybe you didn't know, but please allow me to introduce myself. I'm Logan Mitchell, and this is Tate Morrison, and he is my partner."

Tate noticed the way Logan kept his eyes focused solely on the man in front of them.

"Mr. Mitchell, you say. Aren't you one of the owners?" Chris asked, very much aware of that *particular answer.*

"Enough with the bullshit, Walker," Logan said, while Tate continued to silently observe the other man.

Chris's eyebrows rose as he ran his eyes over Logan in a way that made Tate want to punch him in the face—hard. "There he is. The mouthy Logan I know."

The tension rolling off Logan's body was palpable as he grit out in a low voice, "You don't know me at all."

"Actually, I know you very *well."*

That was the moment when Tate's patience snapped. As the taunt lingered in the air, he muscled forward, snarling the words, "Shut your damn mouth."

Chris chuckled, and his eyes shifted to where Tate had stepped in between him and Logan. "Sexy and protective. Down, boy. I'm not after your man. I've already had him."

Tate pulled his fingers free of Logan's and balled them into fists. "Listen to me, you piece of shit. I'm not the least bit concerned about what you want."

A couple of people by the bar turned to face them, and Logan walked up alongside him and once again took his hand. Tate caught Chris observing the gesture before his eyes reconnected with Logan's.

"Please," Logan managed to say in a calm voice Tate barely recognized. "Enjoy your dinner and tonight's entertainment, Mr. Walker."

Tate's head snapped around, and he was glaring so hard that he practically drilled a hole in the side of Logan's. But it was clear that Logan was done talking and telling him, in no uncertain terms, to shut it also.

"Oh, it's been very entertaining so far," Chris replied, his tone slithering down Tate's spine. "I imagine it will only improve from here…"

What a nightmare. Chris's appearance at the function had been exactly that—a damn nightmare. Not only because of *who* he was, but also because he seemed to like stirring shit up.

Tate knew full well that Chris wasn't one to advertise

his sexual preferences, yet he'd shown absolutely no compunction while hitting on him and wearing his wedding band. That meant that, even *with* Mrs. Walker milling about somewhere, he'd been determined to get Logan's attention—at any cost. *Arrogant or stupid?* Tate had no idea, but he didn't like it one little bit. Add in the smug expression that had crossed Chris's face at Logan's interference and, yeah, it was clear that Chris had known full well what he was doing.

Tate had to give Logan credit though. He'd blown him away by how easily he'd recovered. Pity the same couldn't be said for his own reaction.

"Logan?" Tate asked as he was ushered away from Chris and directed toward their table.

"What?" Logan didn't spare him a glance as they continued through the throng of patrons, but when Tate yanked his arm free from his grasp, he soon came to a standstill.

"Would you hang on a minute?" he asked.

Logan's feet shuffled to a stop as he pivoted to face him. "What's the problem?"

"The... Are you serious?"

Logan's jaw hardened, still tightly wound after he'd dealt with Chris, and then he leaned in so they were only inches from one another. "Not now, Tate. It's neither the time nor the place." Logan's voice was carefully restrained as to not include any bystanders.

He could tell that Logan was trying to pacify him, so when he reached his hand out in a gesture of unity, Tate automatically took it. "Although I do love how you wanted to defend me. That's hot."

"Just…not now, right?" Tate asked, his voice low as he tried to temper his own annoyance.

"Yeah. Now isn't the time."

Tate gave a nod. "You're the boss. You want me to shut my mouth. Consider it shut."

"It's not that—"

"Yes, it is," Tate interrupted. But he was quick to add, "It's okay. I get it."

Logan's eyes moved past him, and Tate knew he was looking at Chris again. He wondered what was going through his mind and hated that he wanted to ask. Feeling insecure was not an emotion he was comfortable with.

Then Logan glanced back at him and gave a tight smile. "Why don't you go and sit down? Dinner's about to be served. I'll be there in a minute."

Tate sat up in bed and looked at the clock on the wall, groaning at the early hour. He had work later this evening, and he could never sleep during the day, so the fact that he was up at the ass crack of dawn was just fucking great.

After pushing the covers aside, he then walked out into the kitchen to grab a glass of water. Maybe, if he was lucky, he'd be able to fall back asleep for a couple of hours before the sun decided to rise.

When he was halfway to the kitchen, a quick rap of knuckles on his front door brought him to a halt. Thinking he must've been mistaken, he continued across the hall until, again, there was a firm knocking more urgent than the last.

What the—

"Okay, okay," he called and ran a hand through his hair.

Once he'd reached the door, he switched the light on and winced at the bright glow that reflected off the cream paint. With one eye closed, he pressed the other to the peephole and was shocked to see Logan standing on the other side.

He'd been expecting a neighbor who'd locked himself out, not the broody man who'd dropped him home and kissed him on the cheek. Actually, now that he thought about that…

He pulled the door open, and Logan's eyes widened in stunned surprise.

"The cheek? You kissed me on the fucking *cheek* when you said goodnight to me earlier. What was that about?"

* * *

LOGAN STUDIED THE road ahead, anywhere but at his

passenger, as he weaved through the traffic. "Do you want to talk about it?"

Tate shifted in the seat beside him, and Logan knew he'd turned to look at him. That was one thing he loved about Tate. If he was coming at you with the truth, especially the hard stuff you didn't want to hear, he never backed down. He always did it with his eyes on the target.

"I don't understand how you managed to just sit there for the rest of the night and act as if everything was okay. It was as if it didn't even bother you, seeing him or talking to him. I guess I'm just…confused by how easy you made it seem. That's all," Tate said into the dark confines of the car.

"It wasn't *easy. Acting like that," Logan said, thinking back to the way he'd forced himself to smile and greet everyone who'd stopped by their table. It was a miracle he'd even managed that much considering he'd wanted to find Chris and tell him to take his business and shove it up his ass.*

"It sure seemed that way."

"Well, it wasn't," he reiterated. "Tonight was supposed to be about you and me. I was simply choosing not to play his games."

"By letting him have the last word?" Tate asked, his tone rising with his incredulity.

"Yes. If the choice was between a brawl or a public retelling of my past, then yes, he got the last word tonight. Not me."

"Fuck that," Tate spat out, disgusted all over again at the

entire situation.

"What would you have had me do? I was one of the hosts. The people in that room conduct their business though my office. Tell me, Tate. Do you think they want to see me or my boyfriend in a fight with my ex?" Logan demanded, turning to see Tate's pissed-off expression before returning his eyes to the road. "They want to trust the person they pay thousands—sometimes hundreds of thousands of dollars, too—to protect them. What kind of message am I sending if I can't conduct myself like an adult for five fucking hours? Now, drop it, would you?"

The silence in the car was heavy, remaining that way for several minutes until Tate said, "Consider it dropped."

"Good." Christ, this is so not the night I had in mind.

"By the way," Tate added, his voice cutting through the tense space. "Your brother knows about you and Chris. Rachel told me earlier, and I thought you might appreciate the heads-up."

Logan pulled to a stop at a red light and turned his head on the headrest. "Tate?"

Tate's brown eyes found his, and as always, they made Logan's heartbeat pick up pace.

"What?"

"I'm sorry about tonight."

Tate didn't smile. Instead, he kept a steady gaze on him as he replied, "I'm not the one you need to apologize to. I knew what I was walking into. Cole didn't."

"Logan?"

Logan was pulled from his thoughts and brought back to the present as Tate crossed his arms over his chest.

He looked good. Hell, he looked better than that. He looked fucking amazing in his grey sweatpants and white T-shirt.

"I asked you why you kissed me on the cheek tonight. Is that some kind of punishment for losing my temper?"

Logan was positive that that wasn't supposed to make him happy, but he was rather pleased that Tate thought a kiss on the cheek from him was a bad thing.

"I don't remember you losing your temper. I actually think you held yourself together pretty well, considering. When I dropped you off, I had a lot going through my head. It was just an absentminded gesture. That's all. Not punishment. Do you really think I would do that?"

Tate let out an irritated sigh. "I don't know what to think. It's four thirty in the morning. I'm surprised I can think at all." He paused and then finally took in his appearance. "What are you wearing? You look like you ran a mile."

Logan glanced down to his black hoodie, grey running shorts, and navy-blue Northwestern University T-shirt. "Seven actually, but who's counting?"

Tate scoffed. "You, apparently."

"Well, I can't have you thinking I lack stamina."

Tate rolled his eyes and stepped aside. "That thought has never *once* crossed my mind. Are you coming in this time? I assume you're not here to stand in my doorway?"

"And I see that you're still a little—"

"Irritable?" Tate supplied.

Logan took a step forward and ran his gaze over the tangle of brown curls falling by Tate's face. "Yeah. Irritable seems about right."

Tate didn't move, but he did hold his ground. "Well, do you blame me? Tonight was—"

"A total fucking mess?" Logan finished, hazarding a guess.

"Something like that."

He walked inside and scanned Tate's apartment as he stuffed his hands in the pockets of his hoodie. "I couldn't sleep," he admitted. When no response came from Tate, he continued. "I kept thinking back to when Chris put his hand on you and all I wanted to do was kick his ass. But then…" He watched Tate close the door and lean his back up against it—silent and focused on him. "But then I remembered the last time I'd seen him. I'd been doing exactly that. Kicking his ass." He came over to where Tate was standing and—quite unexpectedly—confessed, "I have trouble sleeping without you."

Tate's mouth opened as if he were about to say something, and then he shut it and, instead, smiled.

"Does that sound like I'm punishing you?" Logan asked. He loved the way Tate's eyes darkened as they lowered to his mouth.

"No."

"No? Then how does it sound?" he asked, continuing forward until he was between Tate's legs.

"It sounds—"

"Yes?"

"Don't interrupt me."

"I'm sorry," Logan said, trying to appear contrite. "You were saying?"

"It sounds as if you like me," Tate said. Then he added with an arrogant smirk, "A lot."

Logan's heart thumped in his chest as he concentrated on what he'd come there to do. But when Tate reached for his hips and pulled him flush against his body, all of Logan's thoughts took a flying leap.

"Mhmm, I do," Logan said. "It's a little more than *like* though."

One of Tate's hands stroked its way down to his ass, and when he pushed off the door and placed his lips to Logan's throat, Logan wondered if he'd remember his own name in the next ten seconds.

Then Tate's voice echoed through the silent apartment. "But you sent me away with a kiss on the cheek."

Logan jerked his head back. "That's really bothering you, isn't it?"

"Yeah, it is. I understand that it was tense in there—"

"Fuck yes, it was tense," Logan stressed, trying to make Tate understand where he was coming from. "After seeing Chris and then dealing with Cole, it was *unbelievably* tense."

Tate's fingers left him, and he started to walk away, farther into the apartment. "But when we were in the car and heading home, you should've talked to me. Communicated."

Lightning fast, Logan snagged Tate's arm and halted him in his tracks. "Say that again."

Tate narrowed his eyes and began to repeat himself. "You should've communicated with me. How am I going to know—"

Logan shook his head. "Not that. Back up a little further."

Tate's confusion was obvious as he told him, "I don't understand."

Logan took his chin between his fingers and pressed a kiss to Tate's lips. "We were heading home. I like that. *Us*, heading home, together. That's why I'm here."

"Well, I'm pretty sure that bird has flown the coop, Logan. You already dumped me at the curb—"

"With a kiss on the cheek. *Yes*," Logan groaned. "I noted that down, and I solemnly swear to never do it again. Which, by the way, I *have* kissed you on the cheek before, and you have never complained quite so emphatically. But that's not what I mean."

Tate frowned at him. "Then what do you mean?"

"I mean—no. I *want*..." Logan paused, his stomach knotting as Tate's eyes widened and his hands rose as if pleading with him to fucking speak.

"What? What do you want, Logan? Because, personally, I'd really like a couple of extra hours to sleep—"

Logan swallowed, and before he lost his nerve, he heard himself say, "I want you to move in with me."

Chapter Two

TATE WAS SURE he'd misunderstood what Logan had just said.

It was early and he was still half asleep. That had to be it, because for one crazy minute, he was sure he'd heard—

"Tate? Did you hear what I said? I want you to move in with me."

Tate brought a hand to his face and rubbed his forehead. Then, without a word, he spun on his toes and walked back to his kitchen. He could hear Logan following behind, but he didn't trust himself to speak just yet.

He stopped in front of the fridge, opened it, and scanned the contents. Milk, water, and orange juice. Nothing that was going to help with this. After shutting the door, he remembered where something that *would* help was. Upon opening the cabinet above the fridge, he found a bottle of tequila.

Yeah, fuck it. This calls for a shot.

He poured a small amount of liquid into a glass before he picked it up and downed it.

"Wow," Logan said as he stopped on the opposite side

of the kitchen counter. "I didn't think my invitation would drive you to drink."

Tate placed the glass down with an unsteady hand and gripped the cool marble. "Quit joking around."

Logan raised his hands, palms out, and asked, "Who's joking? I was serious. Never more so."

"Then you're out of your mind," Tate muttered, pushing the glass aside as he made his way around to where Logan was standing. "This is how you ask me? This is *when* you choose to ask me?"

Logan's eyes scanned his face, and Tate could tell by the way his jaw bunched that he was getting annoyed. "What's wrong with now?"

Tate let out a sound of disbelief and walked to his bedroom. "Other than we had a terrible night, we were just arguing, and it's almost five in the morning?"

"Oh, come on. This wasn't really an argument," Logan pointed out. "Tate? Hold up, would you?"

Tate took a deep breath and turned back to lock eyes with the blue ones trying to gauge his mood. "I can't move in with you."

Logan gave a slow nod before he asked, "Can't or won't?"

He wondered what the difference meant to Logan, but he repeated, "Can't."

Logan's mouth split into a wide grin as he strolled over to where he was standing—tense as a fucking trip wire.

"What are you smiling about?" Tate knew that his tone was surly, but this was just like Logan. Impulsive, brash, and always picking the worst possible time to say shit. He hadn't once stopped to think about how his request might make *him* feel. He'd just figured that, since he thought it was a great idea, so would everyone around him.

The problem was that it had instantly made Tate feel…inadequate. Although he was sure Logan would kick his ass if he ever told him so.

"I can work with *can't*," Logan said as he pushed past him into the bedroom. "Now, would you stop arguing with me so we can get a couple of hours' sleep?"

Logan took his hoodie and shirt off before he walked over to the left side of the bed to toe his shoes off. He then pulled the quilt back, removed the rest of his clothing, and climbed inside as if it were his own bed. Once he was comfortable, he placed his hands behind his head and aimed his eyes toward Tate.

"Don't act as if you get any more sleep than I do when you're alone. I won't believe you."

Tate pushed off the doorjamb and moved to his side of the bed. "You're a cocky bastard. You know that?" He removed his shirt and sweatpants and slid back under the covers; the warmth of Logan's skin lured him in, and Tate automatically fit himself to his side.

"I may have been told that once or twice before. *Hmm,*"

Logan sighed, but the sound was one of satisfaction, not frustration. "You will say yes. It's only a matter of time. Now, shh so I can sleep."

Tate felt a small smile cross his lips as he pressed them to Logan's chest in a light kiss. He wasn't sure he could say yes to what Logan wanted any time in the near future, but for the moment, he was content to shut his eyes and finally get some rest.

* * *

IT WAS THREE hours later when Logan cracked an eye open and saw Tate's face pressed into the pillow beside his. His dark lashes were full where they lay against his cheek, his lips were slightly parted, and the stubble lining his jaw had thickened overnight. Logan had a hard time keeping his hands—and his mouth—to himself as he lay there.

"Stop staring. You're giving me a complex."

The gravelly voice made him smile as Tate rolled away. Never one to miss an opportunity, Logan shifted in behind him and nuzzled his nose into Tate's hair.

"Liar," he whispered before he kissed Tate's neck.

"God, what time is it? Your enjoyment of early mornings is truly disturbing."

Logan aligned the entire length of his body along Tate's and wrapped an arm around his waist to circle his navel. "It's not that early, but it is time to get up."

One of Tate's hands flattened over Logan's and held it in place as he shifted to his back and stared up at him. "You're already *up*."

Logan bent his elbow and put his head against his palm, all the while drawing a line up the center of Tate's chest. "I'm glad you noticed."

"Hard not to when something that big is digging into my back."

When his finger reached the base of Tate's throat, Logan took his hand away and rested it on his own hip. "That may be so, but don't try to distract me with compliments."

Tate laughed. "Is that what I was doing?"

Logan nodded, and when his hair fell in his eyes, Tate pushed it back from his face.

"I need a haircut," he commented.

"I kind of like it like this, longer on the top."

Logan touched his lips to Tate's, his hair flopping down around them. "Well, since you like it…"

"Yeah?" Tate asked, his mouth curving under his.

"I just might keep it. But don't think I'm growing it as long as yours."

"What's wrong with my hair? Are you saying I need to cut it?"

"No, I'm fucking not," Logan said as he fingered the hair by Tate's ear. "And you know it."

"What would you do if I *did* shave my head?"

"Kill you? And likely get away with it since I have connections to a very reputable law firm."

Tate chuckled and shoved Logan until he was on his back beside him. "Be serious."

Logan turned his head on the pillow and ran his eyes over Tate's full head of hair. Then he returned his gaze to the eyes watching him. "I would quite possibly cry. For days."

"Over my hair? It does grow back, you know."

"Yeah, but not for months," he grumbled. "Can you please stop talking so calmly about this? You're making me nervous."

Tate shifted until his long, lean body was stretched out above him, and Logan widened his legs to allow him to settle in between.

"Don't worry," Tate assured him as he lowered his head to kiss the corner of his mouth. He then moved those teasing lips to Logan's ear and whispered, "I like your hands in it too much to cut it off."

Logan threaded his fingers through the thick waves and asked, "Like this?"

With a groan, Tate rocked his hips against him, and Logan twisted his fingers tighter.

"*Exactly* like that."

"Good," he said as he wound his legs around Tate's. "Because this way, I can have a tight hold on you when you're *trying* to distract me. I'm onto you, Mr. Morrison.

Don't try to use your body against me."

He almost lost his willpower when Tate, *the cocky fucker*, placed his hands on either side of his head and rubbed their erections together.

"You don't want me to use my body on you?"

"Fuck you," Logan said, knowing full well that, if he didn't change the subject or get Tate the hell off him, he was going to roll him over and cease talking altogether.

Usually he'd love nothing more, but right now, he wanted to know why Tate had reacted so strongly to his question from last night—well, early morning.

"We need to talk."

"Then you should have gotten up, gotten dressed, and *then* woke me."

He had a point—not that Logan would ever admit it.

"Why are you so skittish about moving in together?"

"I'm not."

"Yes, you are. And sooner or later, you're going to tell me why."

As Tate was about to respond, Logan's phone began to vibrate on the nightstand and they both looked over at it. When Tate said that it was Cole, Logan immediately lost any desire he had to continue fooling around as he remembered his brother's words from the night before…

"Your ex-boyfriend is a chatty asshole."

Logan winced at Cole, who was holding a frozen, pink drink with a bright-blue umbrella. He was about to ask what he meant, but before the words could slip free, Cole continued.

"We can't spend the evening dealing with your shit, got it? There are too many important people in this room for a spectacle. Deal with it, Logan. I want you to walk away. If you're calm, then Tate will be calm. Do whatever the hell needs to be done. Or I won't be held responsible for my actions."

Logan eyed Chris where he was watching the two of them beside a tall, willowy woman.

"Logan?"

His attention was drawn back to Cole. He hated the thought of walking away but knew it had to be done.

"Fix it."

Logan was convinced that, after his and Tate's conversation on the drive home and his impromptu visit, he seemed to be relatively fine concerning the events from last night—Cole sure as fuck would be a different story altogether.

He reluctantly let Tate go, and when he rolled off him, Logan made sure to say, "We aren't done with this."

Tate pushed the covers away without responding and got out of bed. Then he walked into his bathroom and shut the door. *Okay*, so that was a subject he needed to approach with more caution.

How the hell was I suppose to know that?

Logan snatched the phone up, brought it to his ear, and barked, "What?"

The silence that met him at the other end was exactly what he'd expected. He'd known that this was coming.

Then Cole spoke. "Get up, and get your ass to my place. Now."

Closing his eyes, Logan counted back from ten, trying to curb the instinct to tell Cole to fuck off. "Good morning to you too, Cole."

He'd barely finished talking when Cole snapped back, "I'm not in the mood, Logan. Get over here, and make yourself useful—pick up some donuts on the way. Rachel's hungry."

"Rachel hates store-bought donuts."

"Not this morning, she doesn't."

He was about to ask if there was any flavor in particular, but Cole had already hung up. *Yeah, this is going to be ugly.*

Somehow, Cole had found out about his little—*okay, not so little*—secret, and Logan knew there was absolutely no way to avoid talking to him about it.

Unless leaving the country was an option.

* * *

TATE HEARD LOGAN through the closed door as he snapped at his brother. He didn't envy Logan's position in that moment. He knew how it felt to have been keeping something from those you loved, and when they found out—well, you better be ready for the fallout, whether it was good or bad.

In Logan's particular case, Tate wasn't sure how Cole would react. But judging by the cool reception they'd been subjected to for the majority of last night, he assumed that it wasn't going to be an easy conversation.

He walked over to the sink and turned the hot water on, letting the basin fill for his morning shave as he stared at his reflection in the mirror. There, looking back at him, was someone he was finally beginning to understand again. But it was also someone who had a long way to go.

For so long, he'd lived his life for those around him. Always doing what was expected of him. From a marriage that had been a young, dumb reaction to lust to *staying* in it because he'd thought it was the right thing for those involved—something he would never do again. He was determined not to make those same mistakes, especially with Logan.

The fact of the matter was that Logan Mitchell was an influential figure in the city of Chicago. As one of the partners in a prestigious law firm, he was wealthy, respected, and smart as hell, and when Tate thought about the things he could offer in return, he was realistic enough to realize that it wasn't a whole fucking lot. So when Logan had suggested he move into his condo with him… *Yeah, I freaked the hell out.*

After he shut the water off and drew the razor down his cheek, there was a knock on the door, and Logan pushed it open. Tate's eyes found his in the mirror, and he straightened, surprised to see Logan fully dressed in his clothes from the night before.

"No, don't stop," Logan said, running his eyes over Tate in a way that suggested he liked what he saw. "I just came to tell you I have to head out. Cole is on the warpath, and if I'm not there soon, he just might send someone to hand-deliver me."

Tate turned to face him and leaned his ass up against the sink, the razor still in his hand. "Okay," he said, and then he asked, "Do you want me to come with you?"

Logan shook his head as he walked over to him. "No, it's okay. This is my bed of lies, and I have to crawl out of it. I should have a long time ago."

Logan stopped when he was directly in front of him. Then he reached a finger up to run it over the skin he'd just shaved.

"Nice and smooth," Logan commented and lowered his eyes over Tate's naked chest. "Just like the rest of you." He brushed a kiss across Tate's lips. "Keep this razor on your face, got it? If these curls go anywhere, I can't promise my reaction will be kind."

As Logan lifted his head, Tate smiled at the shaving

cream that was now clinging to his chin. He swiped it free with his thumb and scoffed. "You're so bossy."

Logan's lip quirked, and as he headed out the door, he called over his shoulder, "And?"

And, Tate thought as he turned back to the mirror with a huge fucking grin, *I love it.*

Chapter Three

LOGAN WALKED DOWN the hall to Cole's condo like a man heading toward his execution. Apparently, Chris had decided that the best way to screw with him would be to inform Cole of their…*what? Past relationship?* No, he certainly wouldn't call it that.

It didn't really matter, though, what he did or didn't call it. Chris had lined the target up, aimed, and fired. He'd hit, too. Cole had been frosty for the rest of the evening after he'd informed him that his ex was a "chatty bastard."

Logan had been dreading this day—the day Cole finally found out about his extra involvement with Chris. And the worst part of it was that he still wasn't exactly sure how much he knew.

So there he was, a bag of donuts in hand and a grimace across his face. Deciding that it was better to just get it the hell over with, Logan knocked and waited to see how this would unfold.

When the door opened, he expected to see Cole's fulminating scowl. What he got was a wide-eyed Rachel. She didn't bother saying a word as she reached for the white paper bag he held and opened it to take a deep inhale of the yeasty, sugary goodness.

"Oh. My. God. This is exactly what I wanted," she moaned.

The bag crinkled as she peered inside, and Logan couldn't help the laugh that escaped him.

"What happened to the girl who wouldn't touch a donut from a store if she was starving and it was the last piece of food left on the planet?"

Rachel raised her head and pinned him with a feral look. "She got knocked up by your brother and is now a raging lunatic if her food requirements aren't met. I wanted it hot, cheap, and easy."

"That sounds dirty, Mrs. Madison," Logan quipped. "Does your husband let you speak that way to everyone?"

"Oh, shut it," she grumbled, pulling a donut from the bag to take a huge bite. As she chewed the mouthful, she gave Logan a glazed grin full of mischief. "You're in trouble."

Figuring she didn't deserve to have so much fun at his expense, Logan snatched the bag out of her hands and placed it behind his back. He got immense satisfaction when she gave a small growl of annoyance and then frowned at him.

"Give that back," she managed around another bite.

"Not until you apologize for—"

"Taking delight in your impending doom?"

Logan narrowed his eyes, and as she stepped aside and gave an impish grin, he asked, "Does Cole ever win with you?"

"Not if he's smart."

He leaned in and kissed the side of her head. Then he brought the bag back out and gave it to her. "Here. Take them now, or you may have to pry them from my cold, lifeless fingers once Cole's done with me."

She took them and rolled her eyes. "So dramatic."

"Well, do you blame me?" Logan searched the hallway and then gazed back to Rachel. "How angry is he?"

The way she screwed her nose up and shrugged didn't bode well for him. It had him wanting to tuck tail and run—something he never usually did.

"Okay. *Where* is he?"

She pointed to the second shut door on the left. "In the library."

With a nod and a tight smile, he muttered, "Wish me luck."

Before he got two steps away, he heard Rachel say his name. When Logan looked over his shoulder, she gave him a soft smile that made him think what a wonderful mother she was soon going to be.

"You won't need luck. He's upset because he cares. We both do. You deserve so much better than whatever Chris gave you. And now, you have it with Tate."

He swallowed and wondered if she was right. Did he deserve better than Chris? *Do I deserve Tate?*

He certainly hadn't been an angel, and he was the first to acknowledge that he hadn't walked away from Chris when he should have. He'd stayed and allowed years of meaningless nights push him to one night he would do anything to forget.

He couldn't find any words for her in that moment, so he gave her a nod and pushed the door to his brother's library open.

When he stepped inside, he expected to see Cole as he usually was—behind his desk, working on his computer. Instead, he had a phone to his ear and his back turned toward him. So Logan wandered over to the wall lined with books from floor to ceiling, pretending to take great interest in them, all the while thinking back to Tate's refusal to move in with him.

He said that he can't move in with me, but why? Because of this thing with Chris?

Logan pulled his phone out and opened up a new message. He decided to remind Tate that he hadn't forgotten what they'd been talking about, and it would only be a matter of time before the topic was once again under discussion.

He wanted Tate in his house, his bed, and his life twenty-four-seven. And if it took him hours of conversation and weeks of constant reminders as to *why* living with him was an amazing fucking idea, then that's exactly what he would give him.

* * *

TATE STOOD IN front of his mirror and tied his black work tie. He needed to be out the door in the next five minutes if he wanted to make it on time. He'd landed double shifts for the next two weekends after both he and Logan had traded with Amelia for his days off. So that basically meant he had no life for the foreseeable future. At least, not one that took place on the weekend.

He tightened the knot at the base of his throat before smoothing a hand down the front of the narrow material and raising it to tuck the thinner strip into his white shirt. Shrugging into his black vest with the words *After Hours* embroidered on the pocket, he was reminded of his first day on the job at the upscale bar.

The day I met Logan. The day that forever changed his life.

Tate could remember every single detail from that first meeting. From the confused way he'd felt and responded, to exactly what Logan had been wearing. It was unbelievable to think back now and realize that, in that precise moment, he'd met the one person who would turn out to be the most essential in his life.

Who would've guessed it? Two people from totally

different walks of life colliding and having that one moment.

There was a buzzing on his bathroom sink, and he glanced down to see a text from the man himself.

Logan: I'm here. If I don't make it out alive, I love you. If I do, you & I have something to discuss.

With a grin, Tate grabbed his cell phone and typed: **So it takes the fear of death for a proclamation of love in writing from Logan Mitchell? That's good to know. I love you too. And let it go, would you? You're like a dog with a bone.**

He shoved it in his back pocket and made his way out of his room, flicking the lights off as he went. Grabbing his helmet and jacket, he walked down the hall to the front door and snagged his keys from the side table before heading out. When he got to the elevator, the phone vibrated again. He reached into his pocket, fished it out, and chuckled at the message.

Logan: No…it doesn't take the fear of death. But thanks for the reassurance of my safety right now. Did you really just use the word 'proclamation' at ten in the morning?

Stepping inside the elevator, Tate pressed the button for the parking garage and then leaned back against the wall typing: **It's 10:13, and yes, I did. I *do* know some big words, Mr. Fancy Lawyer. I can even spell them.**

When the elevator reached the bottom floor and the doors slid open, Tate wandered out into the cool morning air and walked across the lot to where his motorcycle was parked. He got on and settled in the seat before he brought the phone up to check the text, unable to stop the grin that spread across his face.

Logan: Now that's something we should further explore. Can you also spell while distracted? This fancy lawyer wants to know how good you would be at taking down his *dic*-tation. You know, in case of emergencies.

That smartass mouth of Logan's would get him every time. There was something so insanely sexy about his quick wit and smirking face, and Tate could picture him saying those exact words to him.

Chalk that up as another thing he loved about the guy. Anything Logan wrote down or insinuated, he sure as hell wouldn't have trouble saying to your face. And *that* made Tate want to kiss those arrogant lips until Logan was groaning.

Since that option wasn't available right this second, Tate decided that teasing him would be just as much fun.

Am I being interviewed for a specific position I don't know about?

After he put his helmet on, he turned the key in the ignition and felt his phone buzz.

Logan: While there are many *positions* I'm sure you'd qualify for, I think I've narrowed it down. I'm after a very private and *discreet* PA. But I need a few more details

before I invite you to my office for a sit-down-get-to-know-you interview.

Tate pressed a hand against the erection he was now sporting. *Fucking hell.* He could just imagine what an interview with Logan would be like. Torture. Thirty minutes of cock-pounding torture.

Logan in one of those immaculate three-piece suits he wore like a second skin. That coal-black hair styled perfectly, and his strong chiseled jaw. Add in those sexy-as-hell glasses that framed his blue eyes and *hell*—maybe he should go pay him a visit on his dinner break this evening.

Before he started the engine, he quickly text back: **Gonna be late for current job. Text me where I should meet you for this sit-in-your-lap deal or let me go so I'm still gainfully employed, SIR.**

* * *

LOGAN FELT HIS cock stiffen at that final word typed in all caps.

Fuck. He wanted to hear that on Tate's tongue in person. He'd never been one to get off on role-playing before, but—

"Logan?" Cole's voice broke through his thoughts as effectively as a bucket of ice water.

Well, shit. Time to face the music.

Maybe, if he survived, he could convince Tate to come and—

"Hey," Cole said.

Logan turned to see him standing behind his desk with his arms crossed. His blond hair was sticking up in messy spikes where he'd run his fingers through it. *Probably in annoyance at me.*

"Want to maybe pull up a chair and tell me about this little fucking surprise Christopher Walker dropped in my lap last night?"

Not really…

"That wasn't a question," Cole informed him as though he could read his mind. "Sit down. Now."

Cole's tone left little choice but to do as he'd said, and Logan knew better than to argue with him when he was in one of his moods. So he sat.

Since he wasn't sure *what* Chris had spilled the night before, Logan remained silent as Cole glared at him, and suddenly, he found himself grinning.

"What on Earth could you possibly find amusing right now?"

Logan stuffed his hands into his pockets and slumped down into the chair. "You're acting very much like a father right now, about to send me to my room. And just earlier, I was thinking how motherly Rachel looked. This whole pregnancy is really bringing out the best in you guys." A chuckle escaped him as Cole's eyebrows practically hit his hairline. "What? You do. Not that I'd know. It's not like ours ever bothered with me."

Cole pulled his chair out and sat, appearing to think over his next words carefully. He opened his mouth, but before he could say anything, Logan spoke up again.

"Please don't give me some speech about how I didn't miss much. This I already know. But I bet he used to look just like you when he was mad, all scary and shit. He had your hair color and my eyes. I've seen pictures. Mom used to try to be strict with me, but really, with *this* face?" he said, pointing to himself as he gave his most charming smile. "She always crumbled. A bit flaky, she was."

Once he finally stopped talking, Cole sat back in his chair and asked, "You done?"

Logan made a show of clamping his mouth shut and waited for Cole to continue.

"Jesus. When you're nervous, you don't know how to be quiet. It's been so long since I've seen that side of you I forgot it even existed. Nice to know that that geeky school kid with the skinny legs, big glasses, and shaggy hair is still lurking in there under all of that sophisticated arrogance."

"Oh, fuck off. Like you're one to talk," Logan retorted, but he appreciated that Cole was trying to ease the tension in the room.

He *really* didn't want to get into this. Not with Cole—the one person who'd known him since he was a teen. The one person who'd witnessed the way Chris had treated him back in college. How could he admit to him that he'd…what?

Gone back for more as an adult? For years?

God, he was disgusted with himself.

"So, you want to go first?" Cole asked.

Logan's brow winged up, and he asked, "What is this, show-and-tell? Just ask what you want to ask and get it the fuck over with."

Cole regarded him as if he were deciding where to start, and then he asked something Logan hadn't expected.

"Does Tate know everything that happened with Chris? Or just the parts you *decided* to tell him?"

Typical fucking lawyer, went straight for the jugular.

"He knows everything."

Logan couldn't be sure, but he thought he saw a flash of hurt behind the shock that entered Cole's eyes.

Cole's jaw bunched. "So, it's just me who was left in the dark?"

Logan wondered how long he had until the temper that was rising in his brother exploded. Deciding he should just lay it all out on the table, he offered up the details before Cole asked for them.

"I told him about Chris when we were up at the cabin."

The hazel eyes drilling him appeared hard as stone, and Cole looked just as unmoving. But what was most disconcerting was that he *still* hadn't revealed what Chris had told him.

"How nice," Cole said, but his voice certainly didn't

match his opinion. "Did it ever occur to you when you found out that Chris would be at the function that it might be a good time to tell me you, oh, I don't know, had a fucking affair with him for two years?"

Shit. He'd figured Cole had known it all, but he wasn't sure he believed it since...*well, how did Chris even bring that up?*

"Logan?"

"What?" he snapped, growing more irritable by the second.

"Please tell me he was lying. Trying to piss me off for punching him all those years ago."

He wished he could tell Cole that that was the case, but as he sat there staring his brother head on, it became apparent he was not going to refute the claim.

"Fucking hell, Logan. When did you even see him? *Why* would you... You know what? That isn't important right now."

Logan offered no words. Now wasn't the time to apologize, and it certainly wasn't the time for a joke, so he figured his best course of action was silence because there was no way Cole was done with him yet.

"I need to know if working with them, *him*, is going to be a problem? LPCW Architecture would be a huge account. You aren't stupid." Cole paused for a moment as if he wanted to tack something on after that claim, but then, he kept going. "You know how much revenue this would bring in. But if you aren't comfortable working with Chris—"

"I'm fine," Logan said, cutting him off.

"If you're not, that would be understandable."

"I said I was fine, and I *am*," Logan stressed.

"Is Tate?"

The room fell silent as the question lingered between them, and Logan was appalled to realize he hadn't even considered that.

"Well?" Cole pushed. "Is he?"

Good fucking question…

Logan stood as if the seat were on fire, making it rock back. Then he pulled the phone out of his pocket and looked at the blank screen. Tate hadn't said that he was upset about him working with Chris…*but would he be?*

"I have to go."

"Logan, I'm not done talking to you."

"Too bad," he said, his tone clipped as he stepped around the chair and walked to the door. When he got there, he reached for the handle and turned back to see Cole frowning at him. "The CliffsNotes are: I met up with him a few years back, we, as you so bluntly put it, had an affair for two years, and then it ended. That's it. Nothing more and nothing less."

Cole stood and shoved his hands into the pockets of his pants, a look Logan despised entering his eyes—pity. "I don't need to know the details, Logan. This isn't college, and you aren't a kid anymore. But..."

Logan swallowed, not really wanting to hear anything else.

"Be careful. Firsts are always hard to forget and, as you already seem to know, the hardest to walk away from. You have something real with Tate, one might even say something of the forever kind."

Logan bit back the urge to tell Cole to butt the hell out, but as usual, he resorted to his normal ammo—sarcasm. "Thanks for that, Doctor. How much do I owe you?"

"Nothing right now, smartass. But I swear, if I don't think this is doing us as a whole any good, I'm terminating their contract. No matter how much money they bring in. It's not worth it to my family. Remember that."

Logan lifted his chin and locked eyes with Cole as he felt his own temper finally snap. "You need to trust me. When we first pooled our money from our illustrious father together, we decided it was us against the world. *Especially* dear old dad. Since then, we've proven that we could each be successful in our own right and built one of the most reputable law practices in town. I would never jeopardize you, Rachel, or your baby. You're my family, and so is Tate. And I'll be damned if I screw that up for Christopher Walker. I won't screw that up for anybody. *You* remember that."

And before Cole could offer a response, Logan walked out the door.

Chapter Four

IT WAS LATE when Tate rode his motorcycle into the parking garage and shut the engine off. Saturday nights at After Hours were always busy, but tonight, it had been even more so. They'd been slammed from the moment he'd walked in until he'd clocked out, no doubt due to the cold front that had rolled in. It always brought the customers by, reminding them that the snow-filled winter was just around the corner.

With his helmet tucked under his arm, he made his way up to his floor and stifled a yawn as he wandered down the hall. God, he couldn't wait to get into bed. He was beat.

He was almost at his place when he spotted Logan seated on the carpeted floor with his back pressed against the locked door. He had his knees drawn up to his chest and his arms resting on them as he twirled his cell phone in his hand. He'd been home, as he was now dressed in jeans and a black, lightweight sweater, but the fact that he was sitting on the floor had Tate asking as he stopped beside him, "Did you get lost on your way home?"

Tate stretched out a hand toward him as Logan tilted his

head up so he could look at him from behind his glasses. Without a word, he reached for it and got to his feet.

"No. I'm exactly where I want to be. I missed you today."

When they were both standing, Tate gave him a crooked smile and then lowered his eyes to the phone in Logan's hand.

"Yeah, sorry I didn't text much. We were busy as hell. I barely had time to breathe."

It was nearly two, and he'd been planning to call Logan first thing in the morning to set up a time for their Sunday pizza night. But this? This was a much better way to discuss getting together.

"It's late," he told him as he tugged Logan closer. "Couldn't wait to see me, huh?"

Logan kissed his lips, and his cock twitched when he whispered, "Maybe I just wanted to see this uniform of yours. I don't know what it is about it but…"

"Yeah?" Tate encouraged, knowing full well that Logan had a "thing" for his After Hours attire.

"It makes me want to strip you naked and do all kinds of indecent things to you."

After chuckling against Logan's mouth, Tate drew his head away. "Then come inside and I'll see what I can do about accommodating you."

"Will you now?"

Damn right I will. It didn't matter how late or how tired

he was—Tate always became interested at the teasing tone in Logan's voice. The man was sex on legs, and he wanted him, which made Tate feel like the luckiest fucker on the planet.

Licking his lips as he opened the door, he thought about their texts from earlier. "If I remember correctly, you wanted to know some extra details before you would even consider me for possible positions."

Logan's body brushed the back of his as they stepped inside, and when his strong fingers gripped Tate's waist, any blood that was left inside his head found the quickest route to his cock.

"Oh, trust me when I say that I've considered you in *every* possible position. The problem is narrowing it down to which one I'd train you in first."

Tate shut his eyes and leaned back against Logan as his arms wrapped around his waist and he lowered a hand down to palm his rapidly growing erection.

"Train me, huh? And exactly how long would this…training take?"

He heard his front door shut and knew that Logan had to have kicked it closed. Then warm lips were pressing kisses down the side of his neck.

"I don't know. A long time. But I don't want to wait outside your apartment every night for the rest of my life."

Tate angled his head to lock eyes with Logan. But before

he could say anything in response, Logan squeezed his fingers around his hard-on, causing him to drop his helmet to the floor.

"God, *Logan.*"

"Hmm. I might be persuaded to wait around for that sound. I used to dream about you groaning my name. It's so fucking hot. Like I'm already inside you. Do you want that? Me inside you? Right here? Right now?"

Tate tried to concentrate on what he was being asked, but Logan's voice was close to hypnotic as he continued massaging him through his dress pants.

"Yes," he managed, and then he brought one of his own hands down to push Logan's harder against himself. "I want that."

He could feel Logan's arousal against his ass as his other hand came around to the buckle of his belt.

"So do I. In fact, I think we should see what it would be like if you came home to me every night. I'd take good care of you. *Especially* when you're tired and worn out."

Tate closed his eyes against the persuasive suggestion and reminded himself that he had good reasons for declining Logan's initial invitation—even though, for the life of him, he couldn't think of any right now.

Logan kissed and sucked his way down to the collar of his work shirt, his cologne filling Tate's nose and clouding his senses as his black hair tickled his cheek.

"Well…what do you say?"

There was nothing he wanted more than to say yes, but… "I could always give you a key."

Logan lifted his head and flicked his tongue over Tate's lobe. "You could, or…"

"Or?"

"Or you could just move in with me."

Tate knew he was in deep shit. When Logan wanted something, he was relentless until he either got it or knew the reason why he was being denied. He'd been in that particular scenario with him when they'd first met. Logan had been hell-bent on getting him in his bed, and nothing had stopped him from going after what he wanted. Not even the words *I'm straight* had been a deterrent.

Now look at us, Tate thought as the button on his pants was undone and his zipper pulled down. He was finding it more and more difficult to keep track of the conversation as Logan slid his hand into his boxers, all the while making promises that sounded really fucking amazing.

"My bed every night. Waking up together every morning. No late-night trips. No more 'when will you be by' texts. Just us. Together. Always."

But as his words ran over and over in Tate's mind, he kept tripping over the same two.

"My bed. My bed." It's Logan's bed. Not mine.

"Logan," he said as warm fingers finally wrapped around his naked cock.

"Hmm?"

"I can't."

Logan's body tensed behind him, but his hand didn't stop what it was doing as he asked, "Why?"

Tate was close to begging him to either stop or finish him off, but—

"Why, Tate?"

Jesus, what's my reason again? He clenched his teeth together, biting back a curse of pleasure. "I… Damn, Logan. I can't fucking think when you're doing that."

He heard a strangled groan of frustration come from behind him, and then strong fingers twisted in his hair and pulled his head to the side. Logan's tongue traced a line up his neck to his ear.

"You sexy, *stubborn* man."

Tate remained silent as Logan walked them down the hall to his bedroom, and when they stopped and a light switched on, Logan told him, "Don't move a muscle."

* * *

LOGAN FUCKING *LOVED* it when Tate got like this. When he obeyed without question. It was a pretty good indicator that he'd let all other thoughts go and was just in the moment.

He'd been impatient all day to meet up with Tate, wanting to talk to him about what Cole had said. But as usual, the minute he'd seen him, he had wanted nothing more than to get close and remind himself that what they had—*though it was progressing at record pace*—was very real.

He hadn't been lying last night, and ever since he'd admitted to himself that he wanted Tate in his home, to share it with him, he'd wondered if Tate felt the same—or if he ever would. Walking around to stand in front of him, Logan ran his eyes over Tate, and *fuck,* he was thankful he was his.

Oh yeah. This man with the soft curls, unfastened pants, and fuck-me-now eyes. He is all mine…even if he is *being a pigheaded ass at the moment.*

He reached out and fingered the tie knotted at the base of Tate's throat before pulling it out from behind the vest. As the narrow strip of material came free, Logan wound it around his hand, tugging on it until Tate's mouth was only an inch from his own, and raised an eyebrow.

"I want to fuck you while you're wearing this."

Tate's Adam's apple bobbed as he swallowed. Apparently, Tate was as excited by the idea as he was.

"My tie?"

Logan released the material and stroked his palm down the vest covering Tate's chest, and then he wrapped his fingers around his rigid length and started to give him a slow hand job.

"*No*. This uniform," he said as he kissed the stubble on

Tate's jaw. "I want you on your hands and knees with these pants down just enough to see your perfect ass."

"*Fuck,* Logan."

"And your shirt and this vest? I want you to keep them on also. I want to feel them against my skin as I sink inside you."

Logan released his hold on him before he took the tie again. Pulling on it, he brought Tate's head forward so he could crush their mouths together in a demanding kiss, and when Tate's lips parted, Logan slid his tongue inside to taste the pliant man swaying toward him.

As a moan ripped from the back of Tate's throat, Logan pulled away and spun him around to whisper in his ear, "Get on the bed, Tate."

He silently watched as Tate kicked his shoes off, went to his nightstand to grab a bottle of lube and a condom, and climbed on his bed exactly as requested. Without question, he dropped them both by his leg and positioned himself on his hands and knees, waiting.

Logan stood at the foot of the mattress and took in the picture Tate made, all the while thanking God that he had permission to touch what he was seeing. *Because there is no fucking way I'd have the willpower to leave.*

"You look un-fucking-real," he murmured, reaching for his belt.

As he unfastened it, the metal sound of the buckle had Tate looking over his shoulder at him with fevered eyes.

Logan gave him a shameless smirk and slowly pulled the belt from the loops of his jeans before dropping it on the floor. After removing his sweater and tossing it aside, he kicked his shoes off and stood in only his jeans and socks.

Tate's eyes ran all over him, his skin heating as they went, and when he licked his lower lip as though he couldn't wait for whatever he was about to get, Logan felt his cock pound behind his zipper.

Fucking hell, the guy is gonna make me come before I even get close enough to touch him.

Tate must have noticed the effect his perusal was having, because his eyes lowered to the more-than-obvious bulge in his pants, and he watched with a ravenous expression as Logan unbuttoned and unzipped.

He pushed his jeans and boxers to the floor and took his socks off to stand naked. He then placed a knee on the end of the bed and asked, "You ready for this, Tate?"

If the way Tate pushed his ass in the air toward him was any indication, he was more than ready. But Logan wanted a verbal response before he went any further. Making his way up the bed, he gripped the sides of Tate's dress pants and boxers and pulled them over the curve of his ass.

"Perfect," Logan praised as he smoothed his palm over the tan globe of Tate's cheek. "I know I've said this before, but your ass is fucking perfect."

"Hmm." A deep rumble left Tate's throat as Logan dug

his fingers into his hip and pulled him back toward him. "Logan."

"Love the way you say my name like that," he confessed, and then he grabbed Tate's other hip so he could rub his throbbing arousal against all of that bared flesh. "Say it again."

Tate dropped his messy head of curls forward and rasped, *"Logan..."*

Logan drew a teasing fingertip across the base of Tate's spine, and when he reached the shadowy cleft, he flirted with it, pushing his finger down between the hot crevice.

"Yes, just like that. I want to hear it *just* like that when I push my cock inside you. Got it?"

Tate's body vibrated under his hands, and Logan gave a seductive chuckle as he lowered himself over him and brushed his hair aside. When he placed his lips to Tate's ear, Logan stroked his hands down the sides of his thighs and ground his hard-on against him, delighting in the harsh cry that left Tate's throat.

"You want it, don't you, Tate?"

When Tate didn't immediately answer, Logan jammed his hips against him—hard.

"You can have it. You can have *me* whenever you like. *However* you like. But it would be much easier if we were living together. Don't you think?"

"Jesus," Tate cursed, gripping Logan's hand where it rested on his upper thigh. "You're seriously asking me that *now?*"

"I'm just trying to make a point..."

Tate pushed up, and when they were both kneeling and the vest covering his back was against Logan's front, he turned his head to face him. "How about you make it *after* you fuck me?"

Logan bit Tate's bottom lip, then he grinned against that irritated mouth and shoved his shoulder so he was back on all fours. "You're a very bossy bottom, Mr. Morrison."

"Like you aren't," Tate mumbled, and then he grunted when Logan pinched his ass.

"We aren't talking about *me*," Logan reminded him as he grabbed the bottle of lube, opening it. With a slick finger, he traced down to Tate's hole and gently pressed it inside.

"Holy *shit*," Tate whispered, grabbing his cock and starting to work it.

"I believe we were discussing your penchant for being stubborn and, on occasion...bossy." Logan pulled his finger free of the hot hole it had found, and when he slowly pushed it back in, Tate let out a hiss of air. "When you get all mouthy like that, it drives me fucking crazy."

Harsh breathing filled the bedroom as Logan worked Tate over one finger at a time. He could tell by the way Tate's arm had started a more rapid movement beneath him that his arousal was getting to that breaking point. That fevered edge when, soon, he wouldn't give a fuck what was done to him. He'd just want to come—and that's exactly where Logan wanted him.

With his fingers buried deep inside, Logan made sure to widen and then drag them out, hitting that small bundle of nerves that had Tate dropping forward and pressing his cheek to the pillow. He crowded down over him and removed his fingers, to then plant both hands by Tate's head as he wedged his cock against his ass.

"Now you're ready, aren't you?"

* * *

"YES," TATE REPLIED without hesitation. "Hell yes, Logan. *Do it.*"

Tate was pretty sure that, if he were any more ready, he'd come all over his sheets before Logan's cock got even halfway inside him. Gritting his teeth, he closed his eyes and pumped his hips, sliding his dick through his closed fist as Logan's thick length teased and tormented him with each glide between his ass cheeks.

"Another perk—and I'm just adding this because, honestly, stopping for a condom right now is gonna just about kill me. If you move in with me, we could certainly discuss forgoing this step and be able to come all hot and sticky inside—"

"Oh, fuck…fuck!" Tate cried out, and there was no way in *hell* he could stop his orgasm as it hit and exploded all over

his hand and sheets. He felt Logan still behind him and was about to speak when a strong hand flattened on his shoulder and pushed him down to his stomach.

"You did *not* just come," Logan growled in disbelief.

Tate tried to hold back a laugh at Logan's shocked tone.

But when Logan's lips found his ear and he whispered, "You fucker," Tate lost it and a chuckle slipped free.

"Oh, you think this is funny do you?" Logan asked, clearly frustrated and aroused.

Tate bucked against the solid wall of muscle pinning him to the mattress and reveled at the hard length that was still rubbing over his ass. "It's not my fault you never shut up. I told you."

"You know what I think?" Logan asked before he pressed his lips to Tate's cheek when he turned his head on the pillow. "I think the thought of me coming in your tight ass made you so fucking hot you lost it."

He couldn't deny that. It *had* been that final visual that had sent him over the edge, but it had also been the thought of coming in Logan that had finally done it.

"Am I right?"

He couldn't resist teasing Logan as he rolled over underneath him and kissed his mouth. "You're half right."

"And still fully hard."

Tate widened his legs, and when Logan fit his body against him, the way he nestled their groins together made him arch his hips.

"Well, if you hadn't been so busy pushing your agenda, you would be inside me right now instead of lying here, frustrated."

Logan's eyes scanned his face, and after he leaned down and took his lips in a fierce kiss, he told him, "Don't you worry about me. I can work with this just fine."

Tate watched with complete focus as Logan pushed up on both hands and dragged the lower half of his body over his in a sensual rub.

With Logan naked and hovering above him, Tate was more than happy to lie there and enjoyed the view. He knew what Logan was about to do and had absolutely no problem being used by this man for his pleasure.

The muscles in Logan's arms bunched as he flexed his hips and thrust his engorged erection over Tate's sticky flesh, connecting their cocks on every stroke of his body. His eyes latched on to Tate's and stayed there as his full lips parted and he swiped his tongue over them.

Tate couldn't drag his eyes off him, and he wondered how Logan would react if *he* started talking. So, as he pulled Logan down to grind against him a little harder, he began to do just that.

"It's so hot when you use me to get off."

Logan's eyes darkened at his words, and his thrusts picked up pace.

"The way your face gets so serious, like you'll kill

anyone who dares to interrupt your pleasure. And so you should, because, Logan?" he teased, leaning up so he could sink his teeth into Logan's jaw. "You're so fucking sexy when you're turned on. The thought of your come inside me definitely made my balls ache, but it was the thought of filling your ass with mine that really sent me over the edge."

Logan's jaw clenched as his body tensed above him, and then his eyes shut and he shouted Tate's name so loud that he made his ears ring. As his cry of pleasure finally subsided, Tate felt warm fluid drip onto his lower abdomen.

"You dirty-talking tease," Logan accused as he lowered his body down on top of him.

"One of my best qualities, wouldn't you say?"

Logan's lips skimmed his chin as he agreed, "I most certainly would."

"I know," Tate said, feeling smug that he'd, in his own way, won this round with Logan. It was a rare event. That was for sure.

"Hey?" Logan asked, breaking through his thoughts.

"Yeah?"

"You trust me, right?"

The question was so out of place and so serious that it brought Tate out of his relaxed, sexual lethargy real fucking fast.

"Of course," he replied and sat up as Logan moved off him to lie by his side. "Why did you ask me that?"

Logan licked his top lip and looked beyond his shoulder.

"Logan?" Tate asked, waiting until he had his attention again. "Why would you ask me that? You know I trust you or I wouldn't be here with you." Then Tate remembered *where* Logan had been earlier today. "What happened at Cole's this morning?"

Logan rolled to his back and looked at the ceiling. "Nothing."

"You're a terrible liar," Tate told him as he undid his vest and shirt.

Logan shook his head on the pillow and said, "Fuck, I hope not. Most days, my career depends on that."

"On lying?"

"On being…convincing."

Tate moved to the side of the bed and stood to undress. Then he turned the light off and climbed back in. "Well, you've never had a problem being that. But you still didn't answer me."

"And *you* haven't answered me."

"Yes, I did. I told you that I trust you." Tate could just make out Logan's eyes in the moonlight—he was so serious.

"Not about that," Logan said.

They eyed one another in a silent battle of wills, and finally, Tate turned away.

"Can we talk about it tomorrow when I'm not half asleep?"

Logan moved in closer and placed a hand on his chest.

"Will you talk to me, or are you going to shut down and run?"

Tate thought about all the things he wanted to say and had no idea how he would even start. But he knew that, if he didn't say something soon, Logan would undoubtedly get the wrong idea altogether.

"I'll talk, but you have to promise to listen and try to understand. Deal?"

Logan's hand stopped where he'd been drawing circles on his skin, and then he kissed him. "Deal. But that doesn't mean I won't try to change your mind."

Tate closed his eyes as Logan settled in beside him. As he lay there, he tried to think of a way to explain to this self-made, confident man that he needed to carry his own weight. That he needed to be able to stand on his own two feet before he could even think about moving in and sharing that responsibility with another. But he was drawing a blank. How could he ever admit to a man like Logan that he felt as though he was starting from scratch and it scared him half to death?

He had no idea, but he had several hours to come up with something because there was no way in hell that Logan would ever let this go.

Chapter Five

LOGAN WOKE THE next morning to the muffled sound of music filtering in from behind the half-cracked bedroom door. He shifted his head on the pillow to see it had just turned eight thirty a.m. That was relatively late for him on a Sunday, but he knew damn well that it was early for Tate.

Someone can't sleep this morning. Interesting…

He stifled a yawn and ran a hand over his face as a loud clang came from the direction of the kitchen followed by a soft, "Shit."

Smiling, Logan got out of bed. He snagged his jeans off the floor and stepped into them, deciding he better get into the kitchen before Tate hurt himself *or* burned the building down.

As he opened the bedroom door and stepped into the small living space, he spotted Tate standing in front of his oven, wearing a pair of black sweatpants and a red T-shirt. With his feet bare and his back to him, it was the perfect opportunity to watch him unnoticed.

Leaning against the doorjamb, he acted the silent voyeur to the oblivious man in the kitchen. Tate was humming to the soft music he had playing, stirring something on the stovetop, completely unaware that he had an audience.

This was what Logan wanted more than anything else—moments just like this, where he saw glimpses of Tate that no one else did.

As one of his favorite artists continued to fill the room, Logan found himself unable to stay quiet any longer. "Peter Gabriel, huh?"

Tate's head whipped around, and when their eyes connected, he stopped singing and smiled. "Yeah. He's a favorite of mine, among others."

When he turned back to what he was doing, Logan pushed away from the wall and made his way over to stand behind him. He couldn't resist the urge to put a hand on Tate's waist as he peered over his shoulder to check out what he was mixing on the stove—a creamy gravy with sausage in it. It smelled mouthwatering, and as Logan nudged his nose into the hair by Tate's ear, he realized Tate did also.

"You're cooking me breakfast?"

Tate chuckled, the vibration rumbling against Logan's chest. "I figured I owed you."

"Oh…so this is a 'sorry I came before you' breakfast? Why didn't you tell me? I would have worn considerably less and really made you apologize."

When Tate turned his head, Logan made sure to lick his

lips and Tate zeroed in on them with obvious interest.

"Considerably *less* than a pair of jeans?" Tate asked.

Logan nodded and gave him a kiss. "Yes. But I didn't know, so alas, I'm now clothed."

"That's a shame. We both know how bothersome you find clothing."

Logan ran his fingers under Tate's shirt and around the waist of his sweats. When he started to flirt with the silky hair of his treasure trail, Tate fumbled the spoon in his hand.

"I find *yours* bothersome too." With a laugh, Logan stepped away and pointed to the stove. "But it's probably for the best. I don't want you to burn yourself—or *me* for that matter."

"Fuck you," Tate said with a slight frown, his lips twitching as he fought back a grin. "Go and sit down, troublemaker."

Logan wandered over to the small table in the dining area and heard Tate say, "Turn this up, would you? It's one of my favorites."

He grabbed the remote for the entertainment system and turned the volume up on "Solsbury Hill"—one of his personal favorites also. Taking a seat, Logan angled himself so he could watch Tate as he worked around the kitchen and found, for the first time in his entire life, that he was truly content.

* * *

TATE SANG ALONG to the lyrics as he opened the oven and pulled a tray of biscuits free. He didn't usually cook. Actually, he never cooked. But as he'd lain there thinking about what he wanted to say to Logan this morning, he'd become more and more nervous. So he'd figured the best thing to do was get up and *do* something—anything to take his mind off trying to explain what was running through his head.

"You know, for his solo debut, this was a damn good song," Logan said, cutting through his thoughts.

Tate reached for two plates and then walked over to put them on the table. One on his side, the other in front of Logan.

"Yeah. I've always liked it. Probably more so than any of his others."

"Oh, come on. He did some of his best work with Genesis."

Tate agreed and turned back to get the food. "There's just something about this one. I've been listening to it a lot lately."

"Have you?" Logan asked, and his tone had Tate facing him.

"Yeah. Why?" He carried a plate with biscuits and the pot full of gravy over, watching Logan closely.

"No reason in particular. I was just thinking of the

coincidence. In an interview, he was quoted as saying the lyrics were about 'being prepared to lose what you have for what you might get. It's about letting go.'"

After Tate placed the food down, he rested a palm on the table to lean over and brush his mouth to Logan's. "I love what I got," he said, and he slid his tongue across Logan's lower lip to slowly sample him.

"Do you?" Logan's eyes practically sparkled at him, and he stroked Tate's cheek.

"Mhmm," he hummed before sitting in the opposite chair.

He loved the way Logan was staring at him. It was like he'd just offered him the world—it made him feel like a fucking king.

"So…this morning I get to try your cooking, huh? Is this a prelude of something I have to look forward to?"

And with those few words, Tate was reminded of *why* he'd cooked. He'd been unable to fucking sleep, and why? Because he didn't have the first idea how to explain himself to Logan—and he deserved an explanation.

Taking a moment to think, he shoveled two biscuits onto a plate and then poured the sausage gravy over it before handing the plate to Logan. He took it from him with a quiet, "Thank you," and Tate knew he was waiting—waiting for him to open his mouth and start the conversation he didn't want to have.

How the hell do I even begin?

He smothered his own food in the creamy sauce, and when he placed the pot back on the table, he noticed that Logan was still watching him. But this time, the look in his eyes was…pensive.

"You not going to eat?" Tate asked, mentally kicking his own ass for being a fucking coward.

"I am," Logan said and picked up his fork. "You going to talk? Or sit there scowling at your plate?"

"I'm not scowling."

"Yes, you are."

"I'm thinking," Tate explained. "There's a difference. And I'd think you would be used to this face by now."

"Oh, I recognize it for what it is. I was just checking. Well, then. I'll just sit here and eat my delicious breakfast quietly until you're ready."

Tate smirked as he stretched one of his legs out in front of him. "*You* are going to sit quietly?"

"Yep," Logan told him before he brought a full fork to his mouth, pushing the food between his lips. He bared his teeth at Tate and dragged the fork free, giving him a grin. "I can be quiet."

"No, you can't."

"Yes. I *can*."

Tate didn't reply. Instead, he started to eat his breakfast in complete silence. He watched Logan do the same, and as the seconds ticked by and turned to minutes, Logan sat forward in his chair.

Tate reached for his orange juice and raised it to his lips. After taking a sip, he put it back down and acted as if he were about to talk. Logan's eyes widened a little, expectantly, but Tate started to eat again, enjoying the game immensely.

Noticing Logan's jaw bunch as though he were clamping his mouth shut, possibly biting his tongue in an attempt to keep it closed, Tate was about to relent until Logan lost it first.

"Okay, so apparently, I *can't* keep my mouth shut. Happy?"

Tate crossed his arms over his chest. "Nah. I rather like you with your mouth open. But..."

"But the answer's still no, right?"

* * *

DON'T LET ME be fucking right, was all Logan could think as Tate sat up straight in his chair and replied, "Right."

He barely held back the urge to demand why. As it was, he was trying his best to be patient, but Tate needed to talk. He needed to help him understand what was going on.

"Is it me? You don't think you'd like living with me?"

Tate's eyes found his as he adamantly denied that claim. "No. *No*. It's nothing like that. It's not you—"

"If you end that sentence with 'it's me,' I might kick

you."

Tate brought a hand to his hair and pushed his fingers through it. He seemed extremely uncomfortable, and Logan hated that, but at the same time, he wanted answers. Then, with a long sigh, Tate dropped his hand onto his leg and squeezed his fingers into his thigh.

"Is it because of Chris?" Logan hedged, wondering if maybe the reappearance of his ex had somehow made Tate doubt him just as Cole had suggested. *Fuck*, he hoped that wasn't the case. He'd done everything in his power to gain Tate's trust, and he wasn't about to blow it on Christopher fucking Walker.

"No. I don't like that he's back in your life. But I don't give a shit about him," Tate said and then met Logan's gaze head on. "Should I?"

Sitting forward on his chair, Logan put his hand over Tate's, where it remained on his thigh. "Of course not. You don't ever need to worry about him," he said, curling his fingers around Tate's. "If it's not Chris and it's not me, then what is it?"

Tate entwined their fingers, a habit of his that always reminded Logan of how far they'd come since their first coffee date at The Daily Grind.

"I…" Tate trailed off, and Logan waited, figuring that it was best to let Tate get off his chest whatever was making him feel so uneasy. "I'm not comfortable moving in with you because…" He looked up then, and the emotion in his eyes made Logan feel anxious.

"Because?" he encouraged.

"I have nothing to fucking offer you," Tate finally said on a rush of air.

Wait. What the…"What are you talking about? I don't need anything—"

"Exactly. That's *exactly* my point." Tate let his fingers go and sat back in his chair, rubbing a hand over his face. "You're *Logan Mitchell.*"

Logan was sure Tate hadn't meant for it to sound like a bad thing, but right then, that was exactly how it had sounded.

"And what does that mean?"

Tate abruptly pushed out of his chair as though he couldn't sit still and turned away from him. "It means you're thirty-four years old and own your own company, not to mention a cabin with practically an entire forest behind it. You wear the best clothes, drive the best car, and live in *and* own a fucking high-rise in downtown Chicago." Tate stopped talking and turned with a frown. "It just means that it's a little intimidating is all. I had so many plans for myself… I still do."

For once in his life, Logan didn't know what to say. He'd had no idea *that* was what had been bothering Tate. It'd never even occurred to him. But as he remained seated and Tate walked into the living room, Logan knew he needed more information.

If that was what was standing between Tate living on his own and moving in with him, then he needed to know exactly what Tate wanted.

"Tell me."

Tate faced him, leaning his back against the small windowsill and crossing his arms. "They're just ideas in my head. They probably won't ever happen."

Logan stood and walked toward Tate, but feeling as if he might still need his own space, he stopped by the couch and sat. "Tell me anyway."

"Well," he started and then gave a self-deprecating laugh as he shook his head. "You can't laugh at me."

"Why would I laugh?"

"I don't know. Any time I've ever told anyone this, they just kind of laughed as if it would never happen."

Logan cocked his head to the side and narrowed his eyes at him. "Anyone as in Diana?"

Tate said nothing, and Logan knew he was right.

"In case you hadn't noticed, there are a lot of ways in which Diana and I differ."

Tate's eyes roamed over him. "Believe me. I noticed."

"Good," Logan said. "Then you're also aware that my reactions to most things *also* differ from her. You once told me not to compare you to Chris. I'm telling you right now—stop comparing me to her."

Logan could tell that the tone of his voice had gotten through because Tate's lips pulled tight and he replied with a curt, "Okay."

He nodded once and relaxed back into the couch, putting an ankle across his knee. He tapped his thigh several times, waiting for Tate's next move, and when he came over and sat beside him, Logan said again, "Please, tell me your plans."

* * *

TATE ANGLED HIS body toward Logan and thought about his next words carefully. For years, he'd had an idea he'd kept on the back burner, waiting for the right opportunity, and it wasn't until recently that he'd really started to think of the possibilities.

"Well, you know how I've worked behind a bar most of my adult life?"

Logan's brow rose, and when his lips curved into a smile, Tate wondered what he was thinking. He didn't have to wait long though, because he told him.

"Yes, I seem to remember frequenting one just to see you."

Tate narrowed his eyes and reminded him, "You were going there long before I showed up."

"I used to go in once a week, *maybe* twice. I didn't start hauling ass downstairs *every* day until you arrived."

Tate dropped his eyes down to Logan's fingers, which were still tapping against his jean-clad thigh, and then he raked them over his bare torso and lightly-haired chest. "I used to watch the door for you."

"Did you?"

"Yes," Tate admitted. "At first, I thought I was looking for the man who gave me a nice tip, but now…"

Logan shifted his arm across the back of the couch—an invitation Tate couldn't resist when it came to getting closer to all of that naked skin.

"But now?"

"Now, I know I just couldn't wait to see you." He watched Logan's thick lashes sweep against his cheeks as he blinked, and then he leaned over to place a kiss by his ear. "I'm so glad you kept coming back. Did I ever tell you that?"

"You're being very sweet to me this morning. Not that I'm complaining," Logan laughed, turning his head so their noses practically touched. "But stop avoiding the issue and talk to me. Tell me what you want to do with your life so I can be a part of it."

Tate put a hand on Logan's chest and took his lips in a slow kiss. As his mouth parted, Tate slid inside and groaned at the way Logan's tongue tangled with his. The kiss was unhurried; it was familiar. And when Logan's fingers came up to graze his cheek, Tate relished the heat that simmered just beneath the surface. With Logan, it was always there, always the same, even when the emotion behind the action was different, and Tate wondered how he'd ever lived without it.

Reluctantly, he pulled away and put his head against the arm Logan had resting along the back of the couch. He then looked up into the blue eyes watching him and said, "I've always wanted to open my own bar."

He waited, almost expecting Logan to laugh even though he'd already told him he wouldn't.

"I know it would be a lot of hard work and probably more expensive than I could ever imagine. But I got my business degree specifically for that reason. I've always wanted to run my own place."

As Logan remained silent, Tate started to feel self-conscious. He didn't know what Logan was thinking. Since he worked closely with and likely represented people who owned such establishments, he probably realized what a pipe dream it was.

He probably thinks I'm crazy.

"I think you'd run a fantastic bar," Logan finally said, shocking the hell out of him.

"You do?"

The genuine smile that crossed Logan's lips had Tate returning the gesture.

"Yes, I do. You're incredibly personable, and I, for one, have seen what a good rapport you have with customers. Have you looked into it at all? Owning your own place?"

Tate knew he must have looked stunned because Logan laughed.

"Why are you so surprised?"

"I don't know," he admitted. "I—"

"Tate?" Logan interrupted, grabbing him and pulling him into his arms. "I think you could do whatever you put your mind to, but *this*? I can definitely see you doing this. By the way, how did I not know you went to school for business?"

Tate shrugged. "It never came up, I guess. I didn't want to go to a university straight out of school, so I got a full-time job and then paid my way through night school. When I turned twenty-one, I got a job at a local pub, and the rest is history."

"Huh. Any *other* secrets you're hiding away?"

Tate pretended to think it over. "Hmm. Not that I can think of right now."

"You sure about that?"

"Yep."

Logan settled deeper into the couch, drawing Tate down with him.

"So, you really think I could do this?" Tate asked, tracing his finger across Logan's chest and swirling it around his nipple. "I mean, I'd have a lot to research before I could even consider it plausible. Loans, licenses, properties… It would be a huge undertaking."

"It would be," Logan agreed, playing with his hair. "If you wanted…" he started but paused as if he weren't sure whether or not what he was about to say would be welcome.

Tate pushed up a little and asked, "If I wanted…what?"

"I was just going to say if you'd like some help, I'd be more than happy to, you know, help in any way." Logan gave a nonchalant shrug as if he would be fine either way, no matter what his answer was.

But somehow, Tate knew that Logan wanted to be more involved than he was letting on.

"I'd like that," he told him, and the expression that came into Logan's eyes was well worth all the nerves and any embarrassment he'd felt in telling him what he wanted to do with his future.

* * *

LOGAN COULDN'T HELP the grin he knew he was aiming Tate's way. When he'd finally told him what he'd been thinking about, Logan couldn't have been more excited for him.

He knew that Tate would make an excellent proprietor of any bar, pub or even restaurant he decided to open. The only question that remained in Logan's mind was if he would want to do it all on his own or if he would be open to some help.

My help.

But when Tate nodded and told him that, yes, he would be, Logan just about tackled him down under him on the couch.

"You would, huh?" Logan finally answered, trying to play it cool.

"Yeah. I mean, only if you want to, of course."

Leaning down, Logan kissed his lips. "I wouldn't have offered if I didn't want to."

Tate put both hands on his chest, shocking Logan by pushing him back on the couch so he could crawl over him. "You honestly think this is a good idea? You're not just saying that?"

Logan settled against the leather, placing his head on the armrest as Tate wedged his hips between his bent legs. "Yes, I really do. You know, I happen to be pretty good friends with a couple of people who know a thing or two about this business."

Tate tilted his head to the side, and Logan continued.

"You happen to be also. Especially one pregnant woman in particular who I *know* would be dying to talk your ear off about this."

As if it hadn't even occurred to him, Tate's eyes widened when he made the connection. "Rachel. I didn't even think about that."

Logan chuckled. "I know. But I can't think of a better person to ask since she and Mason run one of the hottest restaurants in Chicago."

"Yeah, but I don't want them to think they have to help me because—"

"Tate. You've met Rachel. Do you really think she would A: ever do something she didn't want to, or B: *not* be offended if you didn't ask her? She'd kill me if she knew you were doing this without talking to her."

Tate leaned down and kissed his chest. "Hmm, you might be right," he told him, and then he flicked his tongue over his nipple. "I should call her."

With Tate's mouth whispering over his naked flesh, Logan was starting to lose the thread of the conversation. "Huh?"

Tate lifted his head and met his eyes with a smile. "I should *call* her."

"Yes. Good idea," Logan agreed absently, and arched his hips when Tate opened his mouth and gave his pec a gentle bite. He was about to tell him that he should call later, but Tate pushed away and got off the couch. "Wait. You're going to call her *now*?"

Tate walked into his bedroom, calling out, "Yeah. Maybe she'll be free tomorrow, since I'm off."

Logan sighed in frustration as he sat up and pressed a hand to his jeans.

Me and my big mouth. Couldn't have waited until I had him naked and under me for my brilliant plan, could I?

"I'm sure she'd be more than willing to fit you in. I know

I always am. In fact, I'd be willing to fit you in right now."

Tate came back out, his cell phone to his ear, took a seat beside him, and laughed, mouthing, "I'm sure you would."

Logan tugged him back in close so he was practically lying across him, and when Tate stretched his legs out along the couch and put his head on his thigh, Logan ran his fingers through his hair.

Tate's warm, chestnut-colored eyes found his, and just as he opened his mouth as if to speak, his gaze shifted and he said, "Hey, Rachel. It's Tate."

Chapter Six

AS THE ELEVATOR reached Mitchell & Madison's floor on Monday morning, Logan checked his watch for the second time and cursed his bad luck. The damn traffic had made him late. Once the doors swished open, he hurried out and through the lobby, giving a quick wave to Tiffany as he headed straight through the glass doors toward his office.

It was bad enough that Cole was probably still pissed about everything that had happened Friday night, but add in that he was now late for the meeting Cole had scheduled for this morning and Logan would be surprised if steam wasn't pouring out of his brother's ears by the time they caught up with each other.

Maybe, if I'm lucky, I'll get inside my office before that happens.

When he reached his PA, who held several files out to him and wished him a good morning, Logan offered her a tight smile and reciprocated. "Morning, Sherry. Is my nine-o'clock here already?"

She gave a swift nod and took his briefcase from him, pointing to the files she handed him.

"That's all you need right there. He got here around ten minutes ago, so I set him up in your office with a coffee. He seems comfortable enough. Lovely man."

Logan glanced down at the file in his hand as he started to walk toward his office door and then stopped in his tracks. *LPCW Architecture. Damn it.*

Well if that wasn't a big "fuck you" from Cole, he didn't know what was.

Spinning back to where Sherry was now sitting, Logan asked, "Are both of the owners here this morning?"

Sherry shook her head, and as the words, "Mr. Walker," fell from her mouth, all other sound vanished.

Christopher Walker was waiting in his office for him right now, and of course, he was running fucking late. *Thanks a lot, Cole. And yeah, great way for me to establish the upper hand.*

"Mr. Mitchell?"

His name broke through his thoughts, and he caught the frown that was plastered across Sherry's face.

"Was I supposed to let him wait in the lobby? I just assumed you'd want him comfortable, knowing he was a new client of ours."

"No, no. You did the right thing. I'm just catching up. Running late has me a little unorganized."

"That's why you hired me, remember? Let me know if you need anything else."

An escape route, maybe? "Thanks, Sherry. I will," he ended up telling her. Then he turned to face the problem that was no doubt lying in wait, head fucking on.

* * *

TATE PULLED HIS bike into the small parking lot behind the address Rachel had given him yesterday and turned off the ignition.

Exquisite. It hadn't been hard to find once he'd looked it up. Located in central downtown Chicago, it was in one of the areas that, over the last few years, had undergone some serious overhauling to become revitalized, trendy, and, by the looks of their website, incredibly popular.

Mason Langley and Rachel Madison were the proud owners of a well-known and loved upscale bar and restaurant that had garnered rave reviews and a 4.9-star rating.

After securing his helmet to the back of his bike, Tate made his way toward the rear door, where Rachel had told him to enter. He took his gloves off and shoved them in the pocket of his jacket as the gravel of the parking lot crunched under his boots.

Am I really, seriously, thinking about doing this? He'd wanted it for years but had never really had the support to go any further than just thinking about it. But after talking it over with Logan and spending yesterday searching potential areas downtown with him, Tate was starting to believe maybe he could pull this off.

Stopping in front of the door, he knocked several times and then stuffed his hands into the pockets of his jeans to wait. The air was starting to get cooler these days, and it wouldn't be long before the bitter cold of Chicago returned.

He craned his neck to look up at the high-rises surrounding them, reminded of Logan's condo and his request that he move in. The idea of living with Logan scared him as much as it excited him.

He knew that, if he hadn't been through a divorce and seen his life turned upside down once before, he would have said yes in a heartbeat, but that wasn't the case. He had been through a messy relationship, one where trust was a major factor in why it had broken down, and even though he trusted Logan, he wanted to make sure he was capable of standing on his own two feet before he leaned on anyone else for support.

After the locks on the back door clicked and rattled, it was then pushed open and Mrs. Rachel Madison beamed out at him.

"Well, hello there," she greeted and held her arms out for a hug.

Tate walked up the couple of stairs and embraced the radiant woman who'd welcomed him into her family from the very minute they'd met.

"Hey, Rachel. Thanks for meeting up with me today."

She pulled back from him and playfully smacked him on the chest. Then she stepped aside and ushered him in. "Don't thank me, silly. I'm happy to help. This is so exciting!"

Her exuberance was contagious as he followed her down the narrow hallway and past several offices. They stopped in a large restaurant-sized kitchen full of stainless-steel appliances and counters.

"So," she said, rubbing her hands together with a huge grin. "Where do you want to start?"

* * *

LOGAN STEELED HIMSELF as he reached for the handle to his office door and took a deep breath. *You can do this. He's nothing to you. Remember, you walked away from him.*

Pushing through the door, he stepped inside and immediately scanned the space for Chris. When he saw nothing directly in front of him as he'd expected, he frowned—until a hand grabbed his from the side.

"About time you arrived," Chris said, his familiar voice filling the air.

Logan glanced down at the man who sat forward on the edge of the couch and looked up at him. His blue eyes were raking over him in a way that used to make Logan's temperature rise, but now, all he felt was stone cold.

Yanking his hand free, he continued over to his desk without saying a word and then dumped the files on it as Chris stood. He was dressed in a tailored, black suit, a navy-blue shirt, and a tie, and although he was as attractive as Logan remembered, the sight of him made him feel ill.

"Have to say, Logan, as far as first impressions go, being late isn't a good one."

Logan's eyes narrowed as Chris started to walk in his direction, and he ordered himself to stay fucking still. He didn't know what he would do if he moved, afraid he might launch himself at the smug bastard and punch him.

"Your appointment wasn't until nine. It's five minutes past. It's not my fault you came early."

Chris stopped when only a few feet separated them, lowering his eyes to Logan's mouth.

"That's certainly not how I remember it. You used to always be the reason I came early. You were so fucking sexy," he mused. "You still are."

Logan pushed away from his desk and straightened, telling himself to keep his mouth shut. No good could possibly come from engaging Chris in a visit down memory lane.

"You're so quiet this morning," he continued. "That's unlike you. You really have nothing to say to me after all this time? After the way you left things?"

Nausea tightened Logan's gut as he remembered the

way he'd ended things with Chris. He'd been lying in a hospital room—one *he'd* put him in. Then he recalled everything that had led up to that moment and defiantly lifted his chin.

"If I hadn't ended it that way, you would have. You'd done it before."

Chris took another step closer and ran his eyes all over his face, which made Logan's resolve to stay put fade real fucking fast. He wanted to get the hell out of there. Being around this guy made him feel like the weak, pathetic version of himself he used to be—not the self-assured man he was when he was with Tate.

Tate… God, what the hell did I do to deserve him?

When he stared back at Chris, he honestly had no fucking clue. He went to shove past him, but as their shoulders bumped, Chris grabbed his bicep, pulled him against his side, and lowered his mouth by his ear.

"You really don't think about me at all? Come on, Logan. Your guard dog isn't here now to bark at me if I get too close. When you saw my name on your invite list, how'd it make you feel? It made me…excited. Knowing that I'd finally get to see you again."

Logan's jaw ticked as Chris's fingers flexed around his upper arm, and then he turned his head so they were eye to eye. "Let go of me."

Chris jerked him closer and continued as if Logan hadn't even spoken. "Don't you miss the way we used to go at one another? You could never get enough. The more I roughed you up, the more you wanted it. Throwing you on a bed and pinning you to it was the quickest way to get you off."

"Get your fucking hand off me, Chris."

Instead of doing as he'd requested, Chris rubbed his erection against Logan's leg as he goaded, "Make me."

Logan was about to shove him the fuck away when a knock on the door captured their attention. Before either of them could react, the door opened, and Cole walked inside.

* * *

TATE STOOD IN the center of Exquisite's main dining room and let out a low whistle. The place was full-on sophisticated elegance. Cream tablecloths, perfectly folded napkins around silverware, and an array of wine glasses adorned each table, and on one side of the establishment ran a long, mahogany bar. It was very impressive.

"What do you think?" Rachel asked as she came to stand beside him.

He grinned and nodded. "This place is amazing."

"Thanks." She smiled and placed her hands over her swollen belly. "We like it."

"So you should. It's stunning and has nothing but rave reviews."

"Except for that one about the head pastry chef going

postal on a customer because they said her cake was dry. But Mase gave me a pass for that since I'm hormonal and all."

Tate laughed as they walked over toward the bar, and then he helped her to sit on one of the stools. She was wearing a purple shirt that had *F.B.I* written across the chest, and underneath, it read *Funky Baby Inside*.

That pretty much summed up Rachel Madison, with her black hair streaked with blue and her brightly colored clothes. *Funky*. It always amused him that she was married to Cole, because from what he'd seen of the guy, he was incredibly serious.

"I want to hear all about your plans. I remember when Mason first came to me about opening this place. It felt so overwhelming. You have to find the perfect property, then get the loan, then—oh my God—the name. That was stressful enough on its own. Then add in all the legal paperwork… But you have Logan, who can help you with that," she said with a wink.

Tate had taken a seat beside her and ran a hand through his hair as he thought about everything she'd just said. "Yeah, it is kind of overwhelming."

Rachel tapped her nails on the bar and leaned in. "I know, but don't let that stop you. You have me and Mase. Josh is in construction, Logan is good for all the licensing and legal stuff, and the others, well… They like to eat and drink. So see? You already have a whole team of people who would love to help you out."

Tate put a hand over hers and gave it a light squeeze. "Thank you."

"Stop thanking me. We're practically family."

He thought about that for a second and was surprised he wasn't at all freaked out by it. After all, the only way he'd ever really be family with Rachel would be if he were to marry— *Yeah, okay. I was wrong. That definitely freaks me out to think about.*

"And how is Logan?" she asked, changing the subject. "He seemed upset the other day when he left, and Cole didn't want to talk about it, so I'm assuming they're both being stubborn and butting heads?"

Logan hadn't said much about his visit to Cole's except that his brother was pissed off about the Chris situation. But Tate was also under the impression that, some way or another, Cole had planted a seed of doubt in Logan's head when it came to his trusting him—and *that* irritated the hell out of him. He did trust Logan when it came to Chris, and the last thing he needed was Cole playing big brother and screwing shit up.

"Tate?"

"Sorry. Yeah, I'm thinking they're still being…obstinate."

Rachel sighed and shook her head. "I swear those two argue worse than females. God only knows how they ever got their practice up and running without one of them killing the other."

Tate agreed as he thought about the two men under discussion. He'd seen them both in action, and both *were* equally formidable when they wanted to be.

"I'm sure they'll work it out soon enough. But for now, I plan to stay out of it," she said, perusing the bottles of liquor behind the bar. "It's a pity I'm pregnant. Otherwise I'd make you get up and mix me a drink or three."

"At nine thirty in the morning?"

Rachel's laugh filled the room as she nodded. "Hey, sometimes, living with Cole drives you to drink."

"Now that I can believe."

She bumped shoulders with him, then said with a conspiratorial wink, "I'm sure it'll be the same when you move in with Logan."

His mouth practically fell open as he turned his head toward her and thought, *That scheming asshole.* "When did he call you?"

Rachel sat up and put a hand to her chest, feigning shock. "I don't know what you're talking about."

"Bullshit," he fired back good-naturedly.

"I really don't know what you're—"

"He is unbelievable," he said under his breath. Then he smiled at her. "When did he call you?"

She tried her hardest to fight back a grin, but in the end, she lost it and admitted, "Last night."

"Of course the sneaky shit waited until he got home."

"So you're playing hard to get. I totally understand."

Tate quickly stood, unbelieving of where the conversation had gone. "I'm not… What? No, I'm not playing hard to get. He already got me. Obviously."

Still not quite comfortable sitting around and discussing his relationship, he crossed his arms and looked back through the restaurant.

"Okay. I'll leave you alone," Rachel relented and slipped off her stool to stand behind him. "So, when are we going to start staking out locations?"

* * *

LOGAN SWALLOWED PAST the lump that had formed in his throat when Cole had stepped through his office door and firmly shut it behind him. Chris still had his fingers wrapped around his arm and was standing much too close for his liking—and Cole's, if the fulminating expression that had crossed his face was anything to judge by.

"I hope I'm not interrupting anything," was the first thing out of his brother's mouth, and the message couldn't have been clearer than if he'd flat-out said, "I better not be interrupting any-fucking-thing."

Logan tugged his arm away, and this time, Chris was smart enough to let it go. "No, you aren't. Not anything important anyway."

Cole's eyes continued to shift from him to Chris, and they finally came back to him. "Good. I trust you got the files you need to go through with Mr. Walker."

Becoming more irritated by the second, Logan glared at Cole and bit out the word, "Yes."

"Good. And, Mr. Walker, do you have any questions?"

Logan wondered if Chris would be dumb enough to try anything with Cole, but he should've known better. It seemed as if his main purpose today was to provoke.

"No. So far, Mr. Mitchell is handling me just the way I like."

Never had Logan seen Cole lose his professionalism, but as Chris's words sank in, he thought he saw his brother's fist clench by his side. Deciding that it was best to move Cole along, Logan walked forward and placed a hand on his arm, turning him away from the asshole behind him.

"Everything is fine," he lied, walking him back to the door.

When they got there, Logan opened it for him. Cole's brow furrowed, the look bordering between annoyance and concern.

"I'm fine," Logan said, trying to reassure him. "We just have to run through the forms, then he'll sign, and everything will be ready to go."

Cole did *not* seem convinced, but without any more words, he left, and Logan closed the door. He stared at the back of it for several seconds before he pulled his shit together and faced the biggest mistake of his life. Chris was watching him, his hands in his pockets, and Logan ran his eyes down over him. As he brought them back up to collide with the conceited bastard opposite him, a sneer curled his lips.

"I don't know what delusions you're under, but the day I left you in your loft, this poisonous thing we had was *over*." Logan strolled across the room, gaining more confidence with every step he took, and when he stopped directly in front of Chris, he kept his eyes locked on the man he'd once stupidly thought himself in love with.

How fucking wrong was I?

"And just so we're crystal clear," he continued, "it wasn't the way you threw me around that got me off. It was the misguided belief that you gave enough of a shit to know what I liked. But you know what really drives me out of my mind, Chris? What I can't seem to get enough of? When the guy I love is strong enough to stand up beside me and hold my fucking hand but is *also* strong enough to pin me down and pound me into my mattress." Logan gave him his best "fuck you" look and stepped around him to take a seat. "So, if you're done trying to make my cock remember that it once—a very long time ago—wanted you, sit your ass down so we can go through this file or get the fuck out of my office."

Chapter Seven

LATER THAT AFTERNOON, Logan looked out of his office window, thinking back over the morning. Ever since Chris had signed on the dotted line and left with the documents for his partner to do the same, he'd had a feeling of unease churning in his stomach.

Once he'd given the ultimatum for him to either sit down or get out, Chris had sat, played along, and done as Logan had demanded. It wasn't until he'd been leaving that a look flashed in his eye that made Logan wary as hell—Chris appeared challenged, and his, "I'll be seeing you soon, Mr. Mitchell," as he departed only further solidified it.

It was just his fucking luck that, right as he was getting serious with someone, Christopher Walker had to show up and try to ruin it. Maybe this was karma and he somehow deserved it. He wasn't sure, but whatever it was, there was no way in hell he was going to let his past anywhere near his present.

It was just turning five, and he was about to pack up and head home when his cell phone started to buzz on the desk. Turning to grab it, he felt a smile cross his lips, and any discomfort he'd been feeling vanished. There, lighting up his day in the way only he could, was the one person he knew he'd do anything to protect—Tate.

"Good afternoon, Mr. Morrison."

Tate's warm laughter filled his ear, and Logan could picture his gorgeous face in an instant. "Afternoon, counselor."

Logan closed his eyes as the deep voice traveled through the phone. "Oh, so I'm 'counselor' today, huh? Why? Did you get in trouble and need one?"

"No," Tate said. "I never get into trouble."

"Is that right? Well, would you like to?" Logan asked as he relaxed back in his chair.

The jingle of keys came through the phone before Tate's voice was back, telling him, "I don't know. It's hard to find a good lawyer these days. Makes me think I should play it straight."

Logan couldn't help himself with that comment. There was just no way. "You definitely should *not* play it straight, Mr. Morrison. But I understand if you're not comfortable with my expertise. Maybe we should meet up and we can discuss what you need in more detail."

Tate's chuckle had every other thought vanishing from Logan's mind. "You might be right. Maybe we should set something up."

A pleased hum of agreement left Logan's throat. "I'm

about to leave my office for the day, and I haven't eaten yet. But I always find that meetings at restaurants make it difficult to really get down to the hard facts. So perhaps it would be best to meet somewhere quieter."

A silence stretched between them, and even though they were miles apart, the sexual tension thrumming across the airwaves had Logan anticipating the next words that would come from Tate's delicious mouth—and he didn't disappoint.

"Did you have somewhere in mind…sir?"

Oh fucking hell, with the 'sir' again. That teasing fucker knew he'd stumbled on something that made him crazy, because that word coming from Tate's mouth was *so* much more effective than in a text. Logan coughed, clearing his throat a little, before rattling off his address as if they'd never met.

"I think I can be there in"—there was a rustling sound, Tate checking the time on his phone no doubt—"twenty minutes? I can stop and pick up some food on the way if you'd like."

Who gives a shit about food? I want—

"What would you like to eat?" Tate interrupted in a tone that screamed he knew *exactly* what Logan wanted. "I mean, since you're agreeing to meet with me after work, the least I can do is bring you some food."

Logan turned his chair around and bent to pick his briefcase up. He wasn't about to wait another second before he got his ass down to the car and on his way over to *eat* his meal.

"Surprise me," he suggested as he stood to switch the small desk lamp off and make his way to the door. "Just know that, tonight, I plan to *savor* my meal. So I hope you're not in a rush and can show some patience."

The rumble of Tate's motorcycle roaring to life came through the phone, and Logan felt his cock stiffen at the visual of him on it.

"I'll be on my best behavior. I already told you I don't go looking for trouble, counselor. Sometimes, it just finds me."

With that, Tate ended the call and Logan punched the button for the elevator a little harder than necessary. When it arrived, he got inside so he could hurry and *find* Tate.

* * *

TATE ARRIVED AFTER Logan, as planned, and took the elevator up to his floor. Sometime in the near future, they really did need to exchange keys, but for now, this suited him perfectly. He'd picked up some lasagna on the way over, knowing Logan's preference for Italian food, and was now waiting on his lawyer.

When he'd finished up with Rachel around lunchtime, they'd grabbed something to eat and then he'd headed home to research the areas she'd mentioned and the licenses he needed to start looking into. That soon brought to mind his thoughts from the other day, of sitting down in a meeting with Logan, and he wondered again what it would be like to see him in "work mode."

Hmm. Yeah, the thought of that really turns me the hell on.

He checked his phone and saw that it'd been around thirty minutes since he'd ended their call. And his desire mounted as the fantasies he'd been having all afternoon continued on a loop in his head.

Several minutes later, the chime of the elevator echoed off the corridor walls and Logan stepped out into the hallway.

With every step Logan took, Tate drank in the sight of him—and what he saw was damn appealing. His charcoal-colored suit showed off his broad shoulders and trim waist, and as his long legs closed the distance between them, Tate almost wished he was walking behind him so he could see how well those pants fit his ass.

When Logan got closer, Tate noted the white shirt and light-blue tie that was perfectly knotted at the base of his throat, and his cock came to rigid attention. Add in those black-framed glasses and Tate was seriously close to overheating in the hall.

This sophisticated side of Logan got him just as excited as the uninhibited one that would strip down to nothing and pleasure himself. What always remained the same, though, was the sensual promise in those blue eyes, and when Logan finally stopped in front of him, Tate knew he would get to see both sides tonight—eventually.

"Good evening, Mr. Morrison."

Excited that Logan was still on board with his little fantasy, Tate inclined his head and replied, "Counselor."

"I trust you haven't been waiting too long?"

Tate lowered his eyes to Logan's mouth and then returned them to the devilish ones watching him. "Not long at all. But I don't mind. Like I said earlier, a good lawyer is hard to find."

Logan unlocked his door, and as he pushed it open and stepped forward, he gave him a sexy-as-hell once-over and winked. "Or just hard in general."

Tate swallowed back a groan as Logan flicked a light on. Logan then placed his briefcase down and his keys on the foyer table.

Hell yes, those pants fit his ass perfectly.

He could tell that Logan was trying his hardest to play it cool as he walked through his condo, but Tate could see the tense way he was holding his shoulders and the tight line of his mouth. Those were both clear indicators that Logan wasn't quite as relaxed as he was letting on.

"Why don't you give me the food?" Logan suggested. "I'll put it away until after."

Tate held the bag out to him, and when their fingers brushed one another, he caught Logan's eye and raised an eyebrow. "After?"

"Yes. *After* you tell me a little bit about what it is you need and you decide whether or not you want to use me."

Jesus, Tate thought as Logan's tongue came out to swipe his full bottom lip, *I've definitely found trouble.* And by the looks of things, he was gonna get a whole lot of it.

"Why don't you go and take a seat over there," Logan said as he walked around the kitchen island. "Make yourself comfortable. I'll be with you in just a minute."

Tate readjusted his jeans and moved over to the couch in Logan's living room. After placing his helmet down on the floor, he took a seat to not-so-patiently wait for whatever was about to happen next.

* * *

LOGAN REMOVED HIS jacket and made his way over to the kitchen counter, where he'd left his laptop plugged in to charge. The grin that he'd been holding back had finally broken through as Tate went and took a seat on the couch.

When he'd stepped out of the elevator and seen him waiting by his door, Logan had had to resist the impulse to approach him and pull him in for a kiss. He knew that it would be welcome, but for some reason, he got the impression that, tonight, Tate wanted something a little different. Something to lighten the serious mood that seemed to be following them lately—and *fuck,* he was more than happy to accommodate him.

Choosing to go with his daydream from the weekend, Logan picked his laptop up and crossed the hardwood floors to the single recliner. As he sat and opened the computer up, he noticed Tate angle his body toward him and stretch his legs out.

"Okay, Mr. Morrison," he began in the most professional persona he could muster and opened a blank page so he could pretend to type. He thought he was doing well too—until he looked up. Tate placed an arm along the back of the couch, and his black T-shirt inched up to expose a strip of his tan skin. "Let's go over a few things that I require of clients before I enter into a new relationship with them."

The heated gaze Tate ran over his body was so damn sexy that it had Logan shifting in his seat and aiming his own eyes on the screen in front of him in an attempt to draw this out.

"First," he said, "I think it's important to disclose all important information in an up-front manner so we're honest with one another. That way, I can give you my full attention when we finally get into the deeper issues—wouldn't you agree?"

Tate moved the hand resting on his thigh to the crotch of his jeans and nodded. "That sounds about right. Is this where I disclose the fact I've been thinking about you in your suit, just like this, all afternoon?"

Logan bit the corner of his upper lip and nodded, since that was easier than speaking.

"I should also tell you," Tate continued, "I really want to kiss the hell out of you right now."

Flirty fucker, Logan thought as he peered over the top of his computer at him. "I'm not sure how that correlates with what we're discussing, Mr. Morrison."

Tate gave a nonchalant shrug. "You told me to be honest."

"You're right. I did. But I'm not sure you understood."

"Oh?" Tate asked, sitting forward on the couch. "What didn't I understand?"

Logan widened his legs slightly, his hard-as-fuck cock making it impossible to get comfortable, and caught Tate's eyes lower to take a look. When he realized there was nothing he could actually see, the frustration on his face almost had Logan cracking—*almost.*

Instead, he waited for Tate's attention and then said, "I require complete access, Mr. Morrison. I need to know everything. All the naked facts."

When Tate's teeth sunk into his lower lip and a low groan left him, Logan felt a "game on" smile stretch across his mouth, and he settled back into his seat as if he were completely relaxed—a total fucking falsity.

"And how do you usually get those?" Tate asked, just as Logan had hoped he would.

He'd lit the match, and now, it was time for this flame to

burn.

* * *

TATE WAS SO turned on that it was a miracle he was able to string two words together. With Logan opposite him, peering over his laptop, he was about ready to end the game and beg to be fucked on the floor.

As it was, the sexy way Logan raised only his eyes behind those glasses of his and pinned him with a look that said, *When I finally get my hands on you, you're gonna get it,* Tate was shocked he'd had the control so far to keep his hands out of his damn pants.

Logan's expression was one of concentrated lust, and with each *tap, tap, tap* on the keyboard, Tate felt his dick pound in time. He didn't dare turn away from the sinfully attractive businessman stripping him with his eyes. Then Logan slowly closed his laptop and put it on the small table beside his chair, and Tate held his breath for whatever was about to happen.

"Come here," Logan ordered, crooking his finger at him, "and I'll show you how I get my facts."

Tate was off of the couch and standing in front of Logan without a second thought. He looked down at where Logan was lounged back in his seat and saw the rigid length of his erection outlined in his pants. *Christ, I want him.*

"Take off your shirt," Logan instructed.

Tate reached for the hem of his T-shirt and drew it over his head. Throwing it to the ground, he watched with interest as Logan unbuttoned the cuff of his sleeve and rolled it up his forearm. He then repeated the move on the other side, all the while acting as if Tate standing there half naked didn't bother him in the least. Tate, however, was having a difficult time remaining as unaffected and reminded himself not to lunge for him.

"Very nice, you see? Now we're starting to get to the real truths," Logan said, and aimed his eyes to the waist of his jeans. "Give me your belt."

Tate unbuckled his belt and slid it free, and when he held it out to Logan, he refused to let go and was tugged forward until he stumbled. He had to grasp the arm of the chair to steady himself, and as his mouth came close to Logan's and he leaned in to take it, Logan—at the last minute—pulled away and sat back in the recliner with the belt in his hand.

"Take off your jeans."

The orders were being delivered in the bossy, no nonsense voice Logan seemed to have perfected, and they had Tate's cock dripping. He knew that, once the jeans were gone, Logan would become extremely aware of just how excited this role-play was making him—and he couldn't wait.

He took his boots and socks off. Then he dropped his

jeans to the floor and stepped out of them, only his tight, white boxer briefs left. Tate stood as still as possible while Logan's eyes tracked over every inch of him. The emotion swirling inside them was so potent that he swore he felt it as if it were Logan's hands—the same ones he was currently using to rub his own stiff shaft through his tailored pants. Unable to help himself, Tate reached down and massaged his hard-on as he stared at Logan, who was fully clothed and getting off on him being close to naked, between his legs.

Breathing hard, Tate slipped his hand inside the cotton.

A ragged sound came from Logan as he demanded, "Take off your fucking boxers."

Tate kept his eyes locked with Logan's as he bent at the waist and removed the final piece of clothing. There was something extremely arousing about being totally naked while the other person remained clothed, and when Logan raised his hand again and gestured for him to come closer, Tate dropped to his knees in a heartbeat.

He smoothed his hands up Logan's thighs to massage the bulge he'd been eyeing then leaned in to take a kiss. Before their mouths touched, however, Logan's hand cupped the back of his neck and kept them just a whisper apart. "My tie, Mr. Morrison. Take it off."

Tate was practically panting as Logan's breath ghosted over his lips before he reached for his tie and tugged at the knot. When it was undone and he began to pull it free, he held Logan's stare and said the one thing he figured would get the strongest reaction.

"Anything else, sir?"

* * *

LOGAN'S CONTROL WAS close to non-existent as Tate knelt between his thighs, naked, with one hand milking his dick and the other removing his tie. Then the damn tease threw out the one word that, for some reason, was *really* flipping his fucking switch tonight.

He ran his hand up to grip Tate's hair and craned his neck back as he shifted forward to the edge of the recliner. When Tate's lips parted, Logan lowered his mouth and traced his tongue along his lower lip before he whispered, "Just this," and then slammed their mouths together.

Logan dived inside and rubbed his tongue against Tate's in a sensual caress. The hand between his legs squeezed him tighter through his pants, and Tate moaned into his mouth. He could feel Tate's other hand on his thigh, using it to balance, as he continued to devour his mouth in a hot, dirty, tongue-fuck of a kiss, and when he finally pulled his mouth off Tate's, he told him, "Undo me."

Logan lay back against the couch and watched Tate's hands move to the buttons of his dress pants. When the zipper was down and the material spread apart, Tate's eyes rose to his and Logan cursed.

"Fuck, you're a sight right now."

Tate's chest was rising and falling with each labored breath, and as his eyes lowered to Logan's groin, Logan knew he needed to get them into his bedroom before he fucked Tate on the floor where he was kneeling.

"Go and wait for me in my room. Head at the end of the bed, pillow under your hips."

Tate slowly got to his feet, and as he was about to walk away, Logan stood and reached for his hand. After turning him back, he took his lips again in a fierce kiss, and when Tate pulled away, he gave his fingers a tight squeeze.

"I love you. Now, go."

* * *

TATE WASN'T SURE how he managed to walk from the living room into Logan's bedroom, but somehow, he'd done it and was now lying as requested—with his head facing the foot of the bed and a pillow under his hips. He'd also snagged one for his head, and with his eyes trained on the door, he waited once again for Logan.

His patience was rewarded when, several frustrating minutes later, Logan appeared. He'd taken off every stitch of clothing and was gloriously naked as he strolled into the bedroom. Tate couldn't help but thrust his hips into the pillow his cock was nestled on, causing a wicked-hot smile to stretch across Logan's lips.

"Hmm. Do you like what you see, Mr. Morrison? I know I do. Do that again."

Tate held Logan's gaze as he fucked his hips down into the pillow again.

Logan wrapped his fingers around his cock. "Your skin against my sheets looks fucking amazing. From now on, I'm only buying white sheets. That was one of the first things I noticed about you. Well, after your sexed-up hair, gorgeous face, and tight ass."

With every word that left Logan's mouth, Tate continued to rock his hips. Then Logan walked around to the bedside table, and he heard the drawer open and shut. Soon after, the bed dipped, and Logan was climbing on top of it.

Tate was shocked he'd been able to hold off for so long as turned on as he was, but he'd be damned if he went off before he felt Logan inside him tonight. He'd been thinking—*hell, fantasizing*—about being taken all afternoon, and he would wait—even if it killed him.

"Spread your legs."

Logan's voice penetrated his lust-addled brain, and as Tate parted his legs, he felt Logan's palms smooth up the back of his thighs to cup his ass.

"Goddammit, Tate," Logan whispered as he spread his cheeks apart, and Tate shoved his hips back toward the reverent man behind him. "I want you so damn much."

Before he knew that it would come out of his mouth,

Tate said, "Good thing I'm yours then."

He felt Logan's cock between his ass cheeks as he crowded down over him, and when the sharp scrape of teeth dug into his shoulder, he bucked his hips back.

"Yes, with what I have planned, it's a very good thing." Logan pressed a kiss to his ear and asked, "See the corner of the mattress over there?"

Tate focused on the edge of the bed and wondered what he was getting at—then Logan told him.

"Feel free to bite it when I'm fucking you so hard your throat is hoarse from shouting."

Oh fuck. Trouble had most definitely found him, and its name was Logan Mitchell.

* * *

LOGAN GROUND HIS body against all of Tate's naked skin, and as he rolled his hips over the ones pushing against him, a low growl rumbled out of his throat. He'd wondered what Tate's reaction would be to the words flying out of his mouth, and with each raw, unfiltered promise he'd given, Tate's arousal had increased until he was practically fucking the pillow for some kind of release.

The sounds coming from the man writhing around under him were so fucking erotic that Logan's desire to wait any longer vanished. Moving back so he was kneeling between Tate's legs, he rolled on a condom and then grabbed the bottle of lube to pour a good amount down the crack of Tate's ass. When his cheeks clenched from the shock of cold liquid, Logan's mouth pulled into a tight grin. But Tate had nothing to worry about, because in around five seconds, things were going to heat up real fucking fast.

Throwing the bottle out of his way, Logan lowered down over Tate, stroked his finger along the slippery crease, and pushed the tip against the small pucker. A loud groan left Tate, and when he turned his head on the pillow, Logan's desire intensified at the look in his eyes.

"You like that, don't you?" Logan teased and inched his finger in deeper.

Tate's lips parted as he nodded. "Yeah."

Logan took his mouth in a hard kiss, and thrust his finger in all the way, causing a curse to escape Tate as his tight hole clenched around him. He slid his finger in and out of him several times. Then he pulled away to kneel between his thighs.

"Forgive my impatience, but it's your own fault." He paused when he saw Tate's arms wrap around the pillow under him and bring it up against his chest. "Not only are you the hottest thing I've ever seen, but I know you get super fucking excited when my finger is in your ass. So *this* time, I'm going to get my cock in you before you explode all over my pillow there."

A grunt left Tate as his head dropped to the mattress and

he jacked his hips back. Logan grabbed his hip to hold him in place and used his other hand to line his cock up. Then he gnashed his teeth together and slowly slid inside Tate's body.

"Ah, Jesus, *Tate*," he growled, and when Tate propelled himself backwards and he sank in all the way, a curse tore from Logan. "Fuck yes. That's it. Take all of me."

He ran his palms over Tate's ass cheeks, spreading them a little, and then up his back before planting his hands by his sides and leaning down to kiss his spine. Tate shifted and his shoulder blades bunched, and Logan smiled against his skin, knowing exactly what he needed.

With his body molded to every inch of the gorgeous one laid out under him, Logan started to move. He pulled his hips back and then began to drive his steely length in and out of Tate, picking up more momentum with each hard thrust.

He kissed and sucked the line of his shoulder as he tunneled deeper with every solid punch of his hips. Tate arched back and turned his head toward him. Looping an arm around his neck, Logan held him in place, spearing his tongue between desperate, hungry lips.

Never had he gone at Tate with such ferocity, and never had Tate craved it like this. But when their mouths parted and their eyes clashed, Tate issued his own request with one simple word.

"Harder."

* * *

TATE CLUTCHED THE pillow under him as Logan's cock shoved back inside him with enough force to propel him up the bed. A harsh cry left his throat and he reached out and clenched the corner of the mattress, just as Logan had originally suggested, pulling himself up toward it.

The rhythm of Logan's body didn't falter as he followed close behind and stretched out to clasp his hands over the top of his. He entwined their fingers and started to jam his hips against him at an unrelenting pace, and Tate could feel his hot breath against his neck as he panted and cursed with every fuck of his hips.

It was unrestrained, it was passionate, and as Logan's teeth sank into the skin of his shoulder, Tate thought that it was absolute perfection. Logan had finally let go and was taking him the way Tate knew he'd always wanted.

Every time before this, he'd always been careful, gentle, and somewhat considerate—but not this time.

The man who was plowing into him over and over had lost any decorum his suit and tie afforded and had morphed into a man who was taking exactly what he wanted, *how* he wanted—and Tate fucking loved it.

"*Yes*. Harder, Logan," he rasped and then did as Logan had advised earlier. He clamped his teeth onto the mattress as Logan tensed behind him and shouted his name with a final thrust of his hips.

The high of knowing Logan had just come so spectacularly had Tate pushing back, trying to get more. When Logan pulled out, he almost sobbed at the loss until he was flipped over and Logan wrapped his fingers around his cock.

Without a word, Logan lowered his head over him and took his erection down his throat, causing Tate to buck his hips up in an effort to get closer. His hands started to stroke Logan's hair, but when Logan's mouth slid up and down his cock, Tate lost the ability to think and white-knuckled the sheets on either side of him so he could fuck that wicked mouth.

The sounds of pleasure that came from Logan as he greedily swallowed him time and time again drove Tate beyond his sanity. He shut his eyes, letting himself get lost in the moment, and then he gave one final shove down Logan's throat and came on a thunderous roar. No one had ever come close to understanding what he wanted in bed—not the way Logan did.

Once the calm after the storm had settled, Logan moved up his body, and Tate wrapped his arms around him. As they both lay there, in the silence of the room, neither one of them said a word—because, really, there was nothing to add to such perfection.

Chapter Eight

"TATE?" LOGAN SAID softly from where he lay with his head resting on his shoulder. He'd been there for a good hour or so, and when Tate shifted under him, he rolled to his side to see sleepy eyes now opening. "Sorry. I didn't realize you were sleeping."

"Nah, was just relaxing. You wore me out."

He placed his lips against Tate's ear and gently kissed it. "Then my job here is done."

Tate's chest rumbled with laughter as he reached across to trace a line along his jaw.

Logan closed his eyes under his touch and then said into the quiet room, "I wanted to tell you before you heard it somewhere else… Chris was at my office today. Cole scheduled the meeting. Probably his way of seeing if I could 'handle' him as a client or if he'll end up being nothing but a nuisance."

Tate's fingers paused before he drew them down to his chin and gripped it tight, angling his face up so he was staring directly at him. Logan expected questions—why or what happened—but instead, Tate's eyes got a look in them that had his heart *and* dick responding. It was one of annoyance and possession.

And hell, if that doesn't excite me.

"Did he touch you?"

Logan thought back to that moment in his office and wondered if he should—

"Did he touch you, Logan?" The gruff question and the fingers on his chin were pretty clear indicators that Tate expected an answer—now.

"He grabbed my arm—"

Before he could even finish his thought, Tate interrupted. "And?"

"*And,*" Logan added, "that was all. He wanted to discuss our past. I didn't. End of story."

Tate sized him up as if trying to decide whether or not to believe what he was saying, and then he shoved him on his back and loomed over him. Logan felt his heart thundering as he waited for what felt like hours, and then Tate leaned down and pressed their mouths together.

The kiss was quick and hard, like a stamp of ownership, and when he raised his head, he promised, "If he touches you again, I'm going to be the third person to punch that fuck in the face."

Logan sank his fingers into Tate's hair and tugged him down to suck his bottom lip. "So possessive. Gotta say, I'm a fan."

"He wants you back, doesn't he?" Tate asked as if he hadn't even spoken.

Logan wasn't sure if that possibility worried Tate or just pissed him the hell off. Either way, he needed to make sure Tate was aware he didn't have anything to worry about.

He wrapped his legs around Tate's waist and gently nipped his way along his jaw to his ear. "If that's the case, then he's out of fucking luck. *You* are who I want, and that's all that matters."

"Hmm," Tate sighed into his neck. "I like that."

"Good," he said and smoothed a hand over Tate's back to his ass. "Because there's no question, no doubt. Actually, speaking of things we want…"

Tate raised his head, and when they were eye to eye, Logan suddenly lost his nerve. *What if I suggest this and he says no?*

Before he could garner the courage to voice his request, Tate fingered a piece of hair lying against his forehead and asked, "You want me to get tested, right?"

Logan sucked in a shaky breath at the question, not realizing until then just how much he wanted it. To be one hundred percent bare with Tate, to be inside him in a way he'd never been with another.

Fuck yes, I want that.

"Yes," he admitted, arching his body against Tate's. "Is that something *you* want?" He held his breath as Tate placed his forearms by his head on the mattress and rested his brow against his.

"Yes. I want to be inside you with nothing in between."

"Mhmm."

"You like the idea of that, huh?" Tate teased.

Logan crossed his ankles over his ass, locking him in place, and pushed up to rub their shafts together. "Oh, I like it all right," he assured him. "I can't wait to feel it when you lose yourself inside me. I want us stripped of everything, except you and me—and, Tate?"

This time, it was Tate's voice that was unsteady. "Yeah?"

"I'm gonna go out of my fucking mind when I get it."

* * *

TATE HAD ABSOLUTLEY no problem with that, and as Logan's hands continued to stroke up and down his spine, he couldn't stay still to save himself. His desire to be close to Logan, to give everything over to him, should have been alarming, but the fact of the matter was it felt fucking incredible. Being with and wanting Logan were becoming as natural as breathing.

He knew that with as far as they'd come in such a short amount of time, given these extra steps, these gestures of trust they were extending to one another and the connection they shared was just going to get stronger—and he wanted that more than he'd *ever* imagined possible.

"Tomorrow," he said.

When Logan's fingers found his hair and tugged his head up, Tate saw the question in his eyes.

"I'll make an appointment tomorrow. And you?"

Logan's face softened and an expression of deep affection—and a little shock—crossed his features. "Umm..."

Tate chuckled at the unintelligent response and repeated back to him, "Umm?"

Logan blinked several times and shook his head against the mattress. "I'm sorry. I think my brain stopped when you agreed so easily."

A grin hit Tate's lips, and he couldn't help but ask, "Why?"

"Wh...*why*," Logan asked, and before Tate knew it, he was rolled to his back and Logan was over him. "I'm surprised because I expected to have to argue all the reasons why this is a good thing for us."

"Oh, I see," he said and bit back a laugh, placing his hands behind his head.

Logan lowered his mouth to bite his bicep, growling against his skin. "Damn it, you're gorgeous. I'll call tomorrow too."

"I think that's a *very* good idea if your cock is any

kind of indication."

A gruff sound of agreement left Logan's throat as he nodded. "You too, I see."

"I think I showed you just how much I liked it the other night when you first suggested it."

"I do seem to remember that. Your lack of control was…"

"Yes?" Tate prodded.

"Promising to my plight, to say the least."

He spread his legs and bent them so Logan was cradled between before asking, "Have you, you know, ever been with someone that way before?"

Logan shook his head.

But Tate had to ask, "Not even with—"

"Chris?" Logan supplied, screwing his nose up with such disgust that Tate knew he had his answer. "Hell no. I've never been with anyone like that. I've never wanted to—until you."

The sincerity behind those two words was obvious, and when Logan laid his cheek against his shoulder, Tate closed his eyes and enjoyed the feel of his body pressed against him.

"I never imagined it could be like this. Not for me. And certainly not with you," Logan said.

Tate tightened his arms. "Me neither. I never would have guessed the first time we met that we'd end up here.

Not in a million years."

"Yeah, I seem to remember that. Didn't matter though. I had enough hope for the both of us."

"Hope?" Tate scoffed. "You, Logan Mitchell, do not wait around and *hope*."

Logan raised his chin and aimed gleaming eyes at him. "No? Then what do I do?"

Tate leaned up and whispered against his lips, "You take what you want."

"Yeah, I do."

Nodding, Tate bit Logan's lip like he had that first time in the conference room. Logan groaned and took his mouth, spearing his tongue inside for a taste and moving his body over him in a delicious rub that had Tate reaching for his hips.

They were well on their way to a second go-around when a loud knocking started on the door.

"Ignore them. They'll go away," Logan said and skimmed his mouth over Tate's jaw.

He tilted his head back so Logan could run his tongue over his throat, and as their cocks grazed one another, Tate pushed up again only to hear *knock, knock, knock.*

"Logan," he groaned. "They aren't leaving."

Apparently, that didn't bother Logan in the slightest, because he was working his way down to his nipple.

Knock, knock, knock.

"Oh, for fuck's sake," Logan cursed and finally rolled off him. "If that's Cole, I swear to God I'm going to kick his ass. I avoided him all day after he scheduled that stupid meeting. The last thing I want to do is deal with him."

Tate pressed a palm to his stiff dick and willed himself to calm down. "I'll go, okay? You stay right there," he said before he got off the bed to walk over to Logan's closet, where he kept his running shorts. After snagging a pair, he pulled them up and turned to see Logan on his back, checking him out. "Yeah, stay just like that. I'll take care of him and then…then I'll come back and take care of you."

Logan's eyelids lowered to half-mast, and Tate practically ran down the hall, wanting to get back in there as soon as possible. Just as he was reaching for the lock on the door, the knocking sounded again and he had to admit that, if this *was* Cole, he was about to tell him to fuck off—just as Logan had suggested.

Pulling the door open, he was about to do just that, but the person standing on the opposite side was not Cole—*no, she certainly is not.* Tate's eyes narrowed as the woman lowered her hand and admired his naked chest and shorts before flashing a mischievous smile.

"Well, hi there, handsome. I was not expecting someone like you to be answering the door."

Tate couldn't seem to locate his tongue as he stood in front of the lady, wondering who the fuck she *had* expected to answer the door. *Logan? If so, who the hell is she?*

"You're a lovely surprise if I do say so myself."

Tate wasn't sure, but maybe he'd fallen asleep and this was some kind of bizarre dream, because he didn't have the first idea what this woman was talking about.

"Who is it you're looking for?" he finally managed to ask.

The dark-brown eyes assessing him were intelligent, and he could tell by her perfectly styled, raven hair, her red coat, and her black stilettos that she was definitely someone who could belong in this building—but that still didn't answer his original question.

"Oh," she giggled as if she'd completely forgotten why she was there in the first place. "Sorry. I got distracted. I'm in town for a little while and thought I'd come visit my Hot Wheels. Is he around?"

Hot Wheels? What the...

"He can't possibly be asleep yet. He's always been a night owl, which I never understood. How does someone stay awake so late but then be up at the crack of dawn? It just isn't right to function on so little sleep." When her rambling came to an end, she cocked her head to the side and asked, "You going to let me inside, handsome? I don't really want to stand out here for the rest of the night."

And that's when everything fell into place.

The hair color, the age, and that final sentence delivered in almost the exact same way as—

"Evelyn?"

Logan.

Tate looked over his shoulder to see that Logan had come to a stop in the hallway with a towel wrapped around his hips and his glasses back in place.

Yep, Tate thought, *it has to be.*

He rounded back to face the woman, who'd raised a hand to give an impish wave of her fingers. Logan's mother.

* * *

WHAT THE FUCK is she doing here? Logan thought as he marched into his bedroom. *And how can I get rid of her?*

He opened his closet and yanked the towel from around his hips, throwing it in the corner before reaching for his robe to wrap around himself.

"So," Tate said from behind him.

He turned and saw a shit-eating grin spread across Tate's face.

"You *do* come from somewhere. That's a relief."

"Don't be ridiculous," he grumbled as he tugged the belt of the robe tight. Then he ran a hand through his hair. "Everybody comes from somewhere."

Tate sat on the mattress and crossed his arms over his chest. "Thanks for the biology lesson, smartass, but you never talk about your family, so I was starting to imagine maybe you just arrived on Earth all perfect and shit."

Logan grabbed a T-shirt from his dresser and walked over to Tate, pressing it against his chest. "I'm nowhere near perfect, as you're about to find out. Put that on while she's here, please." He walked past Tate to go and deal with the woman who was no doubt already rifling through his liquor cabinet.

But Tate joked, "I hardly think your mother is going to be caught up with the sight of my chest."

Logan stopped in the doorway and turned back to eye Tate. "No, but I might be. And I need my brain fully functioning when she's in the room."

Leaving Tate to finish dressing, he walked out to find Evelyn exactly where he'd expected her—at his kitchen counter, pouring a finger of scotch into a glass she'd added ice cubes to.

"Sure, help yourself," he said, stopping on the opposite side of the island, waiting for her to face him.

"Don't be so dramatic, Logan."

"Dramatic? Oh, don't tempt me," he said when she finally faced him. "What are you doing here?"

With her long fingers wrapped around his crystal, she brought it to her lips. After taking a sip, she lowered the glass to the marble top. "I told you I was coming."

"When? Memorial Day Weekend? That was months ago." Logan pinched the bridge of his nose and let out an aggravated sigh. "You need to call when you want to visit. I already had this conversation with you. Some people have lives, you know."

"So I see," she replied, raising the glass to drain the contents. She then aimed her gaze over his shoulder, and Logan knew that Tate must've come back into the living room by the devilment that lit her eyes. "My son is so rude. He hasn't even introduced us yet."

"I'm not being rude. I'm trying to work out why you're here. There's always a reason."

"Oh hush," she said, dismissing him with a wave of her hand as she rounded the counter. "What's your name, handsome?"

Logan looked to Tate, who was now standing in his living room with his hands in the pockets of *his* shorts and the newly added T-shirt. Tate looked over to where he was standing almost as if to gauge how he was supposed to be reacting, but Logan didn't have time to warn him one way or another.

Evelyn was Evelyn, and nothing he did or did not say would change that.

"I'm Tate," he offered in the end, and then he flashed that smile of his that made Logan's heart thump and his dick hard.

She took his hand, shook it, and then said, "Good taste, son. He's gorgeous."

When Tate chuckled, Logan rolled his eyes and

turned to pour himself some scotch.

"Have you two eaten yet? We should—"

"Yes," Logan lied just as Tate replied, "Not yet."

"You see what he's trying to do?" She tsked. "You shouldn't lie to your mother, Logan."

"It's late," he stated as he faced them, a glass in his hand. The last thing he wanted to do was go out to a restaurant, not to mention be stuck, with her. "*We* both have work tomorrow."

"You can go in late. That's the beauty of owning your own company," she retorted then aimed a "please say yes" look up at Tate, who was standing beside her. "What do you say? Want to have dinner with me and hear all about Logan when he was still sweet to his old mom?"

Tate smiled at him. It was obvious he wanted to go. It was also clear as a fucking bell that, once again, Evelyn had charmed her way into another man's life.

It all would've been amusing if her track record didn't make it so fucking tragic.

Chapter Nine

TWENTY MINUTES LATER, Tate found himself seated next to Logan in the back of a cab, while his mother was up front. After he'd finally given in, Logan had mumbled something about this being a "fucking disaster waiting to happen" and then had gone to his room to change. Tate had decided that a quick shower and borrowing Logan's clothes were in order since Evelyn had mentioned wanting to take them somewhere fancy.

Now they were in the cab, and he'd been smart enough to avoid engaging the volatile man beside him...*until right this second.*

As Evelyn started to speak to the driver, Tate leaned over and put his lips by Logan's ear. "I know what you mean now."

Logan faced him, a scowl of annoyance still firmly in place, but there was a definite question in his eyes.

"You know when you tell me how crazy it makes you when I scowl? This prickly, 'don't fuck with me' attitude you're throwing around? It's all kinds of sexy."

One of Logan's dark eyebrows rose. "Really? You're coming on to me here? My mother is sitting in the front seat."

Tate hummed and put his hand on Logan's leg, sliding it up his thigh as he flicked his tongue over his earlobe. "Do you want me to stop?"

Logan coughed a little and shook his head. "I didn't say that."

With a smile against Logan's cheek, Tate flexed his fingers into the material under his hands. "No, you didn't, did you? Did you—"

"It's so nice to spend an evening with family. We never get to do that, do we, Logan?" Evelyn's question broke through Tate's rapidly growing lust and reminded him that Logan was right—they *were* in a cab with his mother.

He shifted so he was sitting back in his seat, and just when he was about to remove his hand, Logan's came down over his to guide it farther up his leg.

"No, we don't. And I'm so distraught I can hardly speak of it," Logan said in a droll voice while he interlaced their fingers, locking his in place.

"Don't get sassy with me, young man. I'm still your mother."

Tate's eyes moved to Evelyn and then shifted back to Logan as he spread his legs a little wider and turned his head toward him—all the while carrying on a perfectly normal conversation.

Damn his ability to be so in control while turned on.

"I'm well aware of who you are, Evelyn. I'm just trying to work out what it is you want."

Tate bit down on his lower lip, thinking of exactly what *he* wanted in that moment, and Logan's eyes practically dared him to come get it. After making sure the other occupants in the car were facing forward, Tate glided their hands over to the growing erection under Logan's black pants.

"Is it a crime that I wanted to come and see my boy? I hardly think so. And it's a good thing I did. You never would have told me about Tate."

Tate wasn't even paying attention to the conversation. He was too busy squeezing his fingers around the hardness under his palm, and when Logan's lips parted and he pushed his hips up a little, Tate had to bite back a groan. *Goddamned exhibitionist.*

"You're right. I wouldn't have told you. Because it's private. If and when I was ready, I would've called."

"Which means I never would have known."

Logan closed his eyes then and pressed their hands hard against his groin. Tate's tongue almost rolled out of his mouth. He knew that, if the cab were to pull up at the restaurant right this second, getting out and walking inside would be a major fucking problem.

"And that would be a shame, right, Tate?" Evelyn finally

addressed him, but there was no way he could find the brainpower to talk. "You seem like such a nice boy."

The look that filled Logan's cobalt eyes was full of irony, and so was his positively immoral smile. "He is *very* nice. But would you stop calling us boys? We're not sixteen."

Knowing he didn't have the same control Logan possessed, Tate realized he needed to get his shit together—something that wouldn't happen while massaging Logan's cock. So he pulled his hand back and straightened in his seat.

Logan also sat up, and when their eyes met, he mouthed, "You started it."

Tate shook his head and stared out the window at the passing cars, trying to calm down. He couldn't believe he was sitting in a cab and going to dinner with Logan's mother and he had a fucking hard-on. *Who would've guessed?*

He'd borrowed a pair of dress pants from Logan and a burgundy, button-down shirt, which was under his jacket, and when he'd stepped out of the en suite earlier, he'd known Logan approved. Even with the surly look on his face, he hadn't been able to mask the heat in those eyes.

Logan had also cleaned up. Wearing all black, he resembled a dark prince as he sat there with his broody expression, which was now heightened by the flush of arousal staining his cheeks.

"This traffic is terrible tonight. Is it always so busy?"

Thankful for the question from the oblivious woman,

Tate managed to reply politely. "This is fairly slow compared to some nights."

"See, this is why I don't live in the city."

Logan shifted beside him and said, "That's not the only reason."

Curious as to what Logan meant, Tate was about to ask, but before he could, the driver informed them that they were almost there.

* * *

LOGAN GLARED AT the back of the headrest where his mother was sitting, knowing that that was a surefire way to get his body to cooperate as the car pulled up to the front entrance of—

"The Peninsula? Are you out of your mind? This place is ridiculously expensive."

"Logan," Tate said softly beside him, but he wasn't in the mood to be placated.

He clenched his fists as his mother, who hadn't even bothered responding, pushed the car door open and stepped onto the sidewalk as if she were royalty. Tate followed silently, probably realizing the sour mood he was fighting, and left him seated and fuming.

Why am I so fucking surprised? She does this all the time.

Taking a fortifying breath, Logan shoved his door open

and climbed out, coming around the back of the car and over to where Tate was standing beside his mother. He watched her carefully as she pressed something into the cabbie's hand before giving a little wave. And like every man under Evelyn's spell, he smiled like a true sap before he got back in his car and left.

"What are we doing here?" Logan asked as she started walking toward the revolving door, where a valet greeted them with polite smiles.

"We're having dinner. I've been here for a week now and thought it would be nice to invite you back to my place," she said with a flourish as she pushed the door and stepped in as it spun.

Tate glanced his way, and Logan grit his teeth. He was trying to think of a way to explain his mother, one that would make any fucking sense, but in the end, he figured that the best way for Tate to understand would be to just let things play out—after all, she never failed to disappoint in a spectacular way. It was only a matter of time.

"This place is insane," Tate said and whistled as he looked at the lights above.

"Yeah," Logan agreed and took his hand. "Evelyn never does anything halfway."

"Like you, huh?"

Logan stopped in his tracks and said more curtly than he'd intended, "Nothing like me."

"Okay," Tate said, narrowing his eyes at him. "I didn't

mean anything by that."

"It's fine," he replied, trying to brush it off, but his ill temper seemed determined to stay.

Tate released his hand and pushed his fingers through his hair. It was obvious he was getting annoyed, and Logan knew he was acting like an ass, but he couldn't seem to shake himself out of it.

"Look, I'm sorry," he started, but before he could continue, Tate was walking away.

Fuck…fuck, he thought as Tate shoved through the revolving door with a little more force than necessary.

Irritated at his own churlish behavior, Logan followed him inside and through the elegant lobby area. He didn't bother taking the time to observe. He wanted the night over with as fast as possible, which in turn meant no time for sight-seeing.

Once he'd spotted both Tate and his mother waiting for him by the elevator banks, Logan made his way over. When he stopped by the two of them, Evelyn ran a hand down the lapel of his black sports jacket.

"Give me a smile, Hot Wheels."

Logan saw Tate trying to bite back a grin, and he decided to try to loosen the fuck up.

"If you want to live," he told Tate in a most serious manner, "don't ever think about repeating that."

Tate pushed his hands into his pockets and gave a smug

look, and Logan knew that his tease would *definitely* not heed that particular warning.

When the elevator doors opened, Logan turned back to his mother and asked, "Where are we going? Please don't say your room."

"No, silly. We have a table up on the Shanghai Terrace."

As they followed her inside, Logan mumbled, "Of course we do."

"What was that?" she asked as she walked over to stand by his side.

Logan looked down at her and let his eyes search her face. He was hoping to see something that would indicate she'd changed, but so far, there was nothing.

"I said, 'Of course we do.'"

"Well, yes. Only the best for the Mitchells."

Logan leaned back against the wall of the elevator and felt Tate step beside him. He recognized the move for what it was—a silent show of support should he need it. Not that he really deserved it with the way he was acting.

As they were ushered out of the elevator and into the dimly lit waiting area, Logan scanned the dark, wooden furniture, stunning oriental silkscreens and paintings, and the large wall of windows letting in the lights of Chicago's skyline.

It was stunning. He had to give his mother that. Her taste, as usual, was impeccable.

"Good evening," the beautiful, young hostess greeted

them. “Welcome to the Shanghai Terrace. Do you have a dinner reservation?”

“Good evening, dear. Yes, I booked a table under Evelyn Mitchell for two. However, there’ll be an extra person dining with us. I hope that won’t be a problem.”

“No, certainly not, Mrs. Mitchell.”

They then followed her past several full dining tables to a nice corner one by large double doors that led out onto a terrace.

“Will this work for you this evening?”

Logan decided he should probably locate his manners and pulled his mother’s chair out as she told the woman that it was indeed okay. Then he took the chair opposite Tate. Once they’d ordered their drinks, he looked over to where his mother was shaking her hair back behind her shoulders.

As usual, she was immaculate, wearing an elegant A-line dress in crimson, the same color as her coat. It was amazing the way she never seemed to age—or not so amazing when modern medicine was to thank.

She sat forward as if about to ask state secrets and addressed Tate. “All right. Time to start talking. How long have you known this charmer over here?”

* * *

TATE GLANCED AT Logan, who was looking heavenward

probably hoping the night would hurry up and end, but he was out of luck. As far as he could tell, Logan's mother seemed determined to spend time with her son.

Tate had to admit, she was certainly more accepting of them than his mother had been, so that earned her points in his mind straight off the bat.

"That's a good question," he answered. "A few months. Right, Logan?"

"Yeah. About five now," Logan supplied.

"Wow." *Feels like I've known him forever.*

"You shocked you put up with me for that long?" Logan joked.

"Hardly. I'm just surprised it's not more. It feels like more."

Almost as if he'd forgotten his mother was there, Logan sat forward and took his hand where he had it resting on the table. "It does."

"Aww, you two are adorable," Evelyn gushed. "It makes me so happy."

"Oh, God," Logan said.

"What?" she asked with a romantic gleam in her eyes. "Am I not allowed to be happy that my son's in love?"

As the waiter appeared with their drinks, Logan immediately picked his own up and took a sip. "This night keeps getting better and better. Keep those coming please."

The waiter nodded and scurried off, leaving them to get back to their discussion. Tate smiled over at Logan's mother, who was looking between the two of them.

When her eyes stopped on him, she boldly asked, "How'd you two meet?"

"Would you stop with the twenty questions already?" Logan asked.

Tate found it extremely interesting that Logan seemed almost embarrassed about this part of the story.

"Oh, stop being such a bore, Logan. Plus, I wasn't asking you. I was asking Tate. What are you so worried about? Did you hunt the poor guy down or something?"

That was it. Tate couldn't hold back his laughter anymore, and the shocked expression that crossed Logan's face at his hilarity didn't help.

"Don't tell me…" Evelyn continued, picking her glass of white wine up. "He did, didn't he?"

Logan pointed a finger at him. "Shut it."

But he wasn't about to keep quiet. "Let's just say he was *very* persistent."

"In other words, I was right. He's always been like that, even as a kid. If he saw something he wanted, he went after it with the tenacity of a bulldog."

Logan took another gulp of his drink.

"To be fair, he had to be a bit more forceful than usual. I'd never considered dating a man, let alone wanted one before I met him."

Logan practically choked on the liquor he'd just

swallowed, and Tate gave his most charming smile as he raised his glass to his lips.

"Really?" Logan said as if he couldn't believe he'd just said that.

Tate lowered his drink back to the table and nodded. "Really."

"Good evening, and welcome to the Shanghai Terrace. My name's Julie, and I'll be your waitress tonight. Do you know what you would like to start with?"

* * *

FOR THE MOST part, the night went along smoothly, which was a minor miracle.

Logan decided to go all out after much coaxing from Evelyn and ordered the most expensive meal on the menu. The food was delicious, and after several drinks, Logan reluctantly admitted that the company wasn't too bad either.

He'd just excused himself, deciding to take a time-out to get the final round from the bar. All night, he'd been wary, waiting for the proverbial ball to drop, and he was both shocked and pleasantly surprised it didn't seem it would happen.

Maybe she is turning over a new leaf.

Resting up against the bar, he didn't see Tate approach until he felt a warm body behind him and heard a low voice whisper in his ear.

"Hey there, Hot Rod. Wanna come home with me later?"

A wide grin split Logan's lips at the change to his childhood nickname and he turned so he was only inches away from Tate. With one of his forearms on the bar top, he reached out with the other to play with the buttonholes on his jacket.

"Hot *Rod*?"

Tate's eyes lazily ran down his body, and when they came back up to his, the desire in them was obvious. "Yeah. I'm thinking that fits you better these days than Hot Wheels. Though you do still like fast cars."

Logan licked his upper lip, and when Tate's eyes followed his tongue, he cocked his head to the side. "Says the one who rides fast bikes."

Tate kissed him, and then said, "What can I say? I like sleek, sexy things between my legs. Makes sense since I fucking love having you there."

Logan placed his hand on Tate's chest and closed his eyes for a second. "Shit, Tate."

"You never answered. Want to come home with me?"

When Tate took a step back, Logan opened his eyes. "I'd love to, but I have a staff meeting first thing tomorrow and need several things from home. You could always come back and stay the night with me."

As the bartender came over with their drinks, Tate shook his head. "Nah, it's okay. I kind of need to go home and get into my own clothes anyway. Plus, I told Rachel I would meet with her before work with a list of potential areas."

"Excuse me, sir?"

Logan turned to see their waitress for the evening.

She softly asked, "Are you Mr. Mitchell?"

He nodded at the polite inquiry that also had Tate turning.

With a tight smile, she handed him a small, black bill folder. "Your wife told me she had to leave to catch her plane and that you'd be taking care of the tab for both the dinner and the hotel stay."

As Logan's fingers clutched the rectangular folder in his hand, he felt the blood drain from his face and all the sound around him ceased to exist.

No…she couldn't have…

It wasn't until he heard Tate's muffled voice disagreeing with the woman in front of them that he was aware she was waiting for him to respond. Like a robot on autopilot, Logan reached for his wallet, removed a card, and handed it over. All the while, Tate was still talking, saying words he couldn't quite decipher.

She'd done it again. Not only had she done it to him, but she'd done it in front of Tate.

Logan closed his eyes, willing himself to get a hold on his anger and not let Tate see how much he was fucking hurt. *Not like this behavior is unusual for her. This is her "thing." This is what she does.*

She'd accused him tonight of being a hunter, and it was no surprise he'd turned out that way. He'd learned from the best.

"Logan?"

Finally, Tate's voice broke through as he took his arm and ushered him toward the elevator. He didn't respond though; he had nothing to say.

What is there to say?

It wasn't until they were seated in the back of the taxi and Tate had gently touched his thigh that Logan turned his way.

"Hey."

As Logan stared over at the man seated beside him, he was numb. No matter how many times he told himself not to let her in, she always, *always,* managed to weasel her way inside to pull this shit again.

When will I fucking learn?

He looked away from Tate, unable to bear the sympathy in those beautiful, brown eyes, and decided to talk. Maybe, that way, the silence wouldn't suffocate him where he sat.

"When I was a little boy," he started, staring out at the traffic as they pulled onto the main street. "My mother used to tell me a story about the scorpion and the fox." He glanced over to Tate and asked, "Have you heard it?"

Tate shook his head and reached for his hand. Logan let him take it, but unlike earlier, there was no sexy flirtation here, no tension buzzing in the cab—just silence as Tate waited for him to continue.

"One day, there was a scorpion, and he was walking along the riverbank, searching for a way to cross. He looked around everywhere, but no matter which way he decided on, he knew it would mean instant death for him. That was until he spotted the fox. Casually, the scorpion walked over to him and struck up a conversation with the animal. He asked him to help him cross the river, but being a cunning and smart animal, the fox told the scorpion, 'No. Why would I help you? You'll only end up stinging me and then I'll drown. Sorry. I just can't do that.' The scorpion disagreed profusely, swearing his honest intentions. 'No, no, you have me all wrong. I'd never do something like that. I need you to help me cross the river. If I sting you and you die, then we both drown. So no, I don't want to harm you, fox. I merely want us to both get across the river.'"

Logan looked at Tate and saw that he was frowning. He was totally caught up in the story he was telling, but Logan knew he was also wondering *why* he was reciting an old fable from his youth—but he would soon understand, just as he eventually had.

"The fox thought over the scorpion's proposal and decided that maybe he had a point. Why would he endanger himself in such a way? So he agreed. 'Sure. Hop on,' he said, and the scorpion climbed onto his back. The fox then started across the river, believing that his leap of faith had paid off—until halfway over, when he felt the biting sting of a traitor at his neck and poison started to seep through his veins. Unable to comprehend why the scorpion would have done such a thing, knowing it would ultimately mean death for himself as well, the fox asked, 'Why? Why have you betrayed me in such a way? Now, you too will drown.'" Logan stopped and caught Tate's eyes as the tale ended the same way it always did. "'I couldn't help it,' the scorpion said, offering no apologies. 'It's my nature.'" As his words sank in, Logan took his hand from Tate's and ran it over his face. He then looked out the window and whispered into the night, "The only thing she failed to mention to the child was that he was the fox and she was the scorpion."

Chapter Ten

WHEN FRIDAY MORNING rolled around, Tate found himself sitting at Logan's kitchen island after he'd left for work, much the same way he had for the past several days.

Ever since the cab drive home on Monday, Logan had been different. He wasn't avoiding him or ignoring him in any way. In actuality, he'd been spending every moment he had free *with* him. But something had changed.

The usual arrogance that was always lying just below the surface, ready to be unleashed, had vanished. It was as if Evelyn's visit had snuffed out the spark that usually lit him up so vividly, and he just wasn't *his* Logan.

Trying to distract himself, Tate had brought over the paperwork he'd been putting off for the past week—Diana's divorce papers. When he'd finally finished filling them out, he placed them in one pile and then looked at a second piece of paper he'd received yesterday. One of equal importance.

All morning, he'd been looking at the two, undecided of when the right time to bring them up with Logan was, and it was starting to make him antsy. He'd thought that Logan would eventually bring up what had happened with his mother, maybe want to discuss it and get it off his chest, but instead of doing that, he'd moved right along as if it had never happened. Something that was not working.

Feeling frustrated, Tate picked up his phone and typed: **We need to talk.**

He stared at the text and waited impatiently for a response. When all he got was—**Logan: Okay**—he felt like hurling the phone across the room.

This was exactly the kind of thing that was driving him crazy. Logan would never send him some bullshit one-word answer, and if he thought he would let him get away with it for much longer, he had another thing coming.

You told me once that one-word answers don't work for you. They don't work for me either.

He put his cell back on the table and spun it around until it buzzed again.

Logan: Sorry. Just busy.

Busy, are you? Well, we'll see about that.

Tate shoved his phone in his back pocket.

If Logan was too busy to talk to him over the phone, then he'd wait in his lobby until he had two free minutes to work him into his *busy* day.

* * *

LOGAN LIFTED HIS eyes from what he was reading when

a knock sounded on the door. He had a killer headache and wasn't in the mood to deal with anyone, but when Sherry poked her head in his office, he mustered up a smile.

"You have a call on line one. Did you want to take it, or…"

Logan looked at the flashing light on his phone and gave a nod. "I'll take it. Just give me a minute and I'll pick up."

She smiled timidly as she left and shut the door behind her. She'd been a real trooper, considering his foul mood over the last few days—which, Logan noted, was still lingering like a dark cloud waiting to burst.

Every night this week, he'd gone home and tried to put on an "I'm okay" mood for Tate, but no matter how much he tried to run his feelings out of his system until he was so exhausted that he could barely move, he couldn't get his fucking head to cooperate, and it was obvious Tate was onto him.

Leaning back in his chair, he checked his cell to see if Tate had responded after the last text he'd sent, but no, it sat there blank.

What did you expect him to say, asshole? You told him you were busy.

Hating his inability to brush shit off and get over it, he sighed and picked the phone up, hitting the flashing button. "This is Logan."

"Oh, so you're *not* too busy to answer your phone."

Tate's voice at the other end of the line made his heart

thump. Usually, Logan would have some kind of smartass retort on the tip of his tongue, but instead, the annoyed voice he heard provoked the temper he'd been squashing for the past couple of days.

"I have to answer my *work* phone." Then he waited, wondering if Tate was going to call him out for being an ass.

"Invite me up to your office, Logan."

Yep, seems as if he is.

Logan closed his eyes and rested his head against his leather chair. "Tate—"

"Do you have time or not?"

Logan heard the bossy undertone in the question and replied in much the same way. "I do. There's nothing on the schedule this afternoon."

"So you lied to me."

"No. I'm busy doing paperwork," he was quick to clarify.

"Ask me up, Logan."

He reached for his tie and loosened it, remembering once again the pity in Tate's eyes on Monday night after the shitstorm with his wonderful mother. The mother who had cost him a fucking fortune, he might add.

"Where are you?"

"Standing in front of the elevator to your office."

Knowing there was no way out of it, Logan told him, "Fine. Come to me." Then he heard the chime of the elevator.

"Try to fucking stop me."

Well, shit. Guess the last text was a little too much. Tate was pissed. He could tell by the clipped words he was barking through the line.

"Oh, and, Logan?"

"Yeah?"

"Tell Sherry to take her lunch."

* * *

TATE WAS SILENT in the elevator as it climbed several floors before stopping on Mitchell & Madison's. When he stepped into the lobby, the woman behind the front desk smiled and greeted him by name.

"Good afternoon, Mr. Morrison."

Okay, that's new. "Hi. I'm here to see—"

"Mr. Mitchell? Yes, he's expecting you. He said to go straight back."

Tate wandered on past, but when he felt her eyes following him, he glanced over his shoulder and found her looking his way.

She gave a broad smile and shrugged. "Sorry. We've just been laying bets on when you'd finally be back, and with his mood this week…"

Tate reached for the handle on the large double doors, but before he pulled them open, he asked, "So he's being a real jerk to everyone? That's nice to know."

She pretended to zip her mouth. "You did not hear that from me."

"Don't worry. Your secret's safe with me. And please, the name's Tate. None of this Mr. Morrison stuff."

"Okay. I'll remember that for next time."

With that, Tate pushed through the doors and started to weave through the desks toward Logan's office. It was strange to be back here after the way he'd last left. A public coming-out, a yelling match with his ex and his sister, followed by a fight with Logan.

He could feel the eyes of Logan's employees on him when he finally came to a stop at the desk out in front of his office. Sherry, Logan's PA, flashed a grin as she stood and picked her purse up.

"You can go right in. He's waiting for you. I've been told to take the afternoon off, so before he changes his mind, I'm out of here."

Ahh, good, Tate thought. *He listened*. He said goodbye and watched her leave the same way he'd come in, noticing several heads rising. *Yeah, people are definitely looking at me.*

Trying to ignore the feeling of being under a microscope, Tate turned and knocked on Logan's door several times. As far as he was concerned, they better get used to seeing him around, because when it came to Logan, he was going no-fucking-where.

* * *

"COME IN," LOGAN called when a knock sounded on his door. He watched as it was pushed open and Tate walked inside.

Damn, it felt like years, not hours, since he'd seen him.

His tousled hair was windswept, and the dark-blue jeans and black V-neck sweater showed off a tan portion of skin at the base of his throat. He had his red helmet under his arm and his leather jacket on, and as he sauntered into the office, his stride was confident and full of arrogance—something that always made Logan's cock stand up and pay attention, even with his current mood.

"Afternoon," Tate said and shut the door, dumping his helmet on the couch.

Logan said nothing, just rolled his chair under the desk so he could rest his arms on top of it.

Tate shrugged out of his jacket then threw it by his helmet. "You don't mind if I lock this door, do you?" When Tate's eyes found his, they ran over him, and he added, "I don't want a repeat of the last time I was here."

Annoyed at the reminder of *that* shitty day and still riding his irritability from the most recent, Logan snapped out, "If you want to lock the door, then lock it."

"You know what," Tate said, doing just that. "I think I've changed my mind about this pissy attitude of yours."

Logan cocked his head to the side and pushed back in his chair as Tate walked across the office and rounded the end of his desk. "I haven't been pissy," he dared to say, knowing full well that his attitude this week really had been less than stellar.

So sue him. That was what happened when his mother left the state and stiffed him with a bill in the thousands.

"Anyway, I thought you said it made you hot." He swiveled in his chair until he was staring at Tate from behind his glasses. Then he sucked in a breath as Tate leaned down and placed his hands on the armrests of his office chair.

Tate then leaned in until their faces were only a whisper apart. "You're right. This week, you haven't been pissy. You've been absent. And yeah, usually, this irritated attitude does it for me, but when you're also acting like a dick, that makes me want to kick your ass."

"That's what you came here to say? That I'm acting like a dick? News flash: You're about the tenth person to tell me, and that's only today."

Before he could shove his chair back, Tate grabbed his tie and yanked him forward.

"I don't give a shit about other people," Tate barked. "You can act like the biggest asshole on the planet with them. But you better have a good excuse for acting that way with me, because that is about to stop right fucking now."

Logan wrapped his hand around the one clutching his tie and glared at the man fuming down at him. "I just didn't feel like talking today, okay?"

"Not. Okay," Tate growled. "You're the one who stipulated no silences."

"We've been together *all* week."

"We've been together, but you? Your head has been somewhere fucking else."

"Tate…" he warned.

"Logan," Tate said right back.

"It's just…Monday night," he started, dropping his eyes until Tate tugged the tie. "Would you stop doing that?"

Tate's eyebrows rose and a rebellious look entered his eyes as he yanked on it again, bringing him forward in the chair until he had to put his hands on the arm rest to steady himself.

"Oh, I'm sorry. You meant to stop doing *that*?"

Logan clenched his back teeth together and grated out, "Yes."

"Or else…what?"

"You're really fucking pushing it, Tate."

Tate's eyes glinted at him in a way that made Logan realize he knew exactly what he was doing.

"Am I? Or maybe you just need to work this mood out of your system."

"And how do you propose I do that? I've been trying to run it out all damn week."

Tate wound the tie around his hand and jerked it so he was forced to look up at him.

And yeah, fuck... The aggression pouring off him is unbelievably arousing.

Logan knew he could stand if he wanted to. He could push Tate away. But as his words and actions washed over him, Logan remained where he was. Maybe a good argument was exactly what he needed.

"You do realize that every time I've been in your office it's resulted in an argument of some kind."

"And?"

"*And,*" Tate said as he touched their lips together, "I think you need a reminder that you might be *their* boss and get to tell them what the fuck to do. But between *us,* you are not always the one in charge."

* * *

TATE DIDN'T DARE drop eye contact as he stared Logan down. It was imperative that he keep the upper hand here, even surrounded by the glaring reminders that in these offices, in this building, Logan was the boss.

But not with me. No, with me, he's—

"Remind me," Logan whispered.

—pliant.

Tate brushed a kiss across Logan's top lip, and when his

eyes slid shut, he crushed their mouths together in a savage kiss. Logan automatically opened for him, and Tate heard a groan escape his own throat as he slid his tongue between his lips.

It felt like an eternity since they'd last touched, and wanting to get back their usual connection, Tate pulled on the tie in his hand until Logan was standing from his chair so they were on the same level.

He felt a hand grab his waist and one push into his hair, and then he turned them so Logan's ass was against his desk and he could grind against him as he continued to devour the mouth moving hungrily under his.

Jesus. He loved that Logan never held back, always letting him know he was with exactly whom he wanted—and Tate couldn't get enough. Logan angled his head for a deep connection, and there was no way he wasn't going to give it.

With one hand still gripping the tie, he sucked and bit at Logan's lips as he worked the other between their bodies and cupped the erection he could feel pressing against his own.

"Oh, fucking hell, Tate," Logan cursed as he ripped his mouth free.

He put his lips to Logan's throat, just above the collar of his shirt, and asked, "Do I have your attention?"

Logan thrust his hips against the palm of his hand and tightened the fingers in his hair, yanking his head back with enough force to make him wince—but Tate didn't care. He knew what he was doing. Logan needed him whether he wanted to admit it or not.

He nipped at Logan's chin and then stopped what he was doing, and when their eyes met, he could see Logan's desire and annoyance that he'd stopped.

"You're going to come to me tonight. I finish at two. I expect your ass on a barstool, asking for a drink, at one forty-five, and not a minute late. Got it?"

Logan said nothing, but Tate saw his jaw clench and knew he'd heard.

"We're going to talk about what's bothering you. The same way you make *me* talk," he said and then tightened his fingers around Logan's erection, pulling a harsh moan from him. "Then we're going to work this attitude out of you."

Tate felt Logan's chest rise and fall against his own, as he released his hold of the hard cock in his hand and let go of the tie. Then he walked away from the man still frozen to his desk, unable to move.

When he got to the other side, Tate said Logan's name. He waited until he turned his head, and then he pulled a piece of paper out of his back pocket and slapped it down on the desk.

"Here are my results. Tonight, your ass is mine."

Yeah, Tate thought as he backed away, remembering what Logan had told him. *You're gonna go out of your fucking mind.*

He picked his helmet up, well aware of the wild eyes tracking him. Logan looked like a caged animal, and Tate couldn't wait to unleash him.

Chapter Eleven

LOGAN HAD TO hand it to him. Tate had finally managed to take his mind off his fucked-up week. With his parting line, the presumptuous bastard had firmly planted a new obsession in his head—one he was still thinking about now, hours later.

He looked himself over one last time. Navy-blue pants, a light-blue shirt, and a grey pullover that made his eyes appear exactly how he felt—stormy. He then grabbed his black, woolen trench coat from the coatrack by the door. Tonight, he'd dressed with one thing in mind: to bring Tate Morrison to his fucking knees.

With his keys in one hand, he shoved his and Tate's papers in his pocket and set out to find his bartender. It was time to remind him that, sometimes, things were more interesting when there was a fight for who was on top—*and I want it with the sexy fucker who left cocksure and victorious. Yes, it'll be real nice to get one up on him.*

It took him less than twenty minutes to get over to the parking garage attached to the building his office and After Hours were located in, and by the time he made it up the elevator and through the front doors of his local haunt, Logan was pleased to note he'd arrived with five minutes to spare.

There was a good amount of activity in the downtown bar, but that wasn't surprising since it was a Friday night. As he unbuttoned his jacket and walked through the tables, he let his eyes scan the interior, searching out his man.

Tate wasn't anywhere to be found, and as he settled at the far end of the bar, Logan saw Amelia making her way toward him. With a smile on her face and a towel tucked into the side of her pants, she gave a flirty wink and leaned up against the counter to put a coaster down in front of him.

"Evening, stranger. It's been a while."

Logan placed his arms on the bar top and clasped his hands together as his eyes shifted past her to see Stacy, another employee, push through the doors of the back room.

Where is he? he thought before he answered Amelia. "It has been, hasn't it?"

"Uh huh. So, how've you been?"

Logan brought his eyes back to hers and noticed a sparkle in them. "I'm just fine. How are you?"

She flashed him a mischievous grin. "I'm good. Looking for someone?"

"Pretty sure you know who I'm looking for."

"Pretty sure if you turn around you'll see him."

Logan swiveled on the stool and found Amelia to be right. Tate was standing over by the booths against the far wall with his back to him, but he'd know those shoulders and trim waist anywhere. The white towel that had been a fascination of his when they'd first met was hooked into the waist of Tate's pants and automatically drew Logan's eyes. He had one hand on the back of the seat he was standing by, talking to the women sitting in the booth, who were laughing up at him. When he bent across to take the glass from the blonde who was holding it out for him, Logan heard her giggle from across the room at something Tate must've said.

Logan put an elbow on the bar behind him and continued to watch the way Tate engaged the entire table before he walked to the next. At each booth he checked on, the patrons smiled, chatted, and seemed to genuinely enjoy interacting with the personable, not to mention extremely good-looking, bartender.

"He's really good with them, isn't he?" Amelia asked behind him.

Logan observed Tate as an outsider might. "Yeah, he's great. They really love him."

"Yep. They sure do. Not a hard thing, I imagine."

Logan chuckled. "Are you trying to weasel information out of me?"

"Me? Never."

"Sure."

Amelia placed a hand on her hip and shrugged. "I'm just

saying I bet he's easy to love."

"That better be *all* you're saying."

She rolled her eyes. "Please. Ever since you got your hands on him, he doesn't even flirt with the customers anymore."

Oh really? Logan thought, loving that particular piece of information.

"He's friendly, but that's where it ends. He's a good—"

"A good what?" Tate's voice interrupted Amelia's words and had Logan's head whipping around to see him standing in front of him.

Straightening on the stool, Logan took in the immaculate After Hours uniform and had a sudden flash of the last time he'd been up close and personal with it. *That* had him shifting on his seat.

Tate glanced at the clock on the wall, and then he brought his eyes back to meet his and gave a smile that just about melted Logan's insides. It was full of ego and sex as it screamed, *I know you want me—but you're gonna have to work real hard before you have me.*

"You're on time."

With a sharp nod, Logan told him, "I'm not the one with time-management issues."

That was when Tate shocked the hell out of him. He placed a hand on his chest right there in the middle of the bar and kissed the corner of his mouth.

"No, you just have an attitude one. You look seriously

hot tonight, by the way."

When he took a step back and walked down the length of the bar to the pass, Logan was left sitting on the stool with his mouth hanging open, thinking, *Oh, so that's how we're going to play… Challenge accepted.*

* * *

TATE COULD FEEL Logan's eyes on him as he lifted the pass and stepped behind the bar. He liked that, tonight, they were back where it had all begun. Back to the place where he had first met the compelling man currently sitting at the end of the bar.

Yeah, the only difference is I know exactly what's going on behind those blue eyes of his.

He made his way over to where Logan was watching him, and as he got closer, he pulled the towel from the back of his pants and ran it through his hands. Logan's eyes dropped to the movement, and Tate couldn't help the smug look that was plastered on his face. He knew that Logan was imagining what was planned for later—and damn if that didn't excite the hell out of him.

Stopping in front of the tense man, Tate leaned his hip against the bar and said, "The usual?"

"No, not tonight. I think I'll just have a water. Please."

Tate got a glass and some ice, and then aimed a look

back at his "customer." "A water, huh? I don't think I've ever served you straight-up water. I thought, after the week you've had, you might go with something a little stronger. You seem like you need it to *unwind*. If you know what I mean."

As the words he'd once said months ago lingered in the air between them, Logan licked his bottom lip, and this time, Tate had no problem watching the sensual move. What had once been awkward, strange—even a little taboo—was now hot as hell and making him hard as a fucking rock.

Those intelligent eyes behind the black, hipster frames were calculated as they swept over him, and Tate could tell that his words from this afternoon were now running through his lawyer's head—just the way he'd hoped they would.

Something that could be said about Logan: he could never resist an outright challenge. Especially one against anything authoritative. And ordering his ass to be in the bar at a certain time or else had definitely brought his competitive side out to play.

"I know exactly what you mean *this* time. But water will do just fine. As someone once said to me, I want a clear head for whatever is going to happen later."

Hell yes. There was his Logan—the smart-mouthed, witty man who never failed to get a reaction from him. He made Tate want to pull him across the bar and take that mouth in a blistering kiss. However, he held back and continued with the questions.

"Do you have a hot date or something?"

Logan nodded once as he reached for the glass he'd just handed him. "He's hot, all right, but he's playing games with me, and we need to get to the bottom of a few things. Or should I say, by the time we're done, *he'll* be at the bottom of things."

Tate's brow winged up as he started to wipe the counter down. All the while, he kept his eyes on Logan.

"Well, you seem confident, so that could help when you try to win your case. But I'm sure he has a good reason for doing what he did."

"He better have a damn good reason for what he pulled this afternoon."

Barely able to keep a straight face at Logan's irked tone, Tate managed to ask, "What did he do? I'm sure it wasn't *that* bad."

As Logan ran his eyes over him, Tate's heart started to pound in time with his stiff cock.

"He disclosed some information he knew I'd want to discuss further, and then he just up and left."

Tate clamped his teeth onto his bottom lip as he nodded with a serious face. "That is a problem. But I'm sure you're right. I bet he was definitely *up* when he left."

* * *

THAT TEASING ASSHOLE.

This whole exchange had Logan's hard-on aching between his legs as he drank in every move Tate made. If his goal tonight was to torture him into an apology for his behavior these last few days, then he was doing a spectacular job. All Logan wanted was to grab him by that vest of his and bend him over the bar.

But no…I can wait.

Logan was willing to take his punishment, especially when it was as delicious as this. He just hoped Tate knew exactly what kind of fire he was stoking.

"You think so?" he asked. "He was also rather…bossy."

Unknowingly, he'd struck a chord with that one, because Tate's mouth fell open and he informed him, "Maybe he wouldn't have had to be so *bossy* if you hadn't been such an ass these last few days."

Logan let his eyes wander to Tate's mouth. Tate was getting fired up. He'd played it cool up until this point, but now, there was impatience flickering in those eyes. *About damn time.*

"Did you miss me, Tate?"

"You know I fucking did."

"Hmm, I like that," he said, touching the hand Tate had on the bar.

"You like that I missed you? Fuck you. I thought we decided we wouldn't pull this shit anymore."

Logan took his glasses off and touched the end of the frame to his lips as if thinking over Tate's words. "We did. *You* agreed to no silences, and *we* decided that you would know where I was, and you did, did you not?"

"Don't use my words against me, I'm not on fucking trial. You know exactly what I'm talking about. You got hurt Monday night, and instead of talking about it, you decided to pretend it didn't happen and shut me out."

"Sounds familiar. Doesn't it?" As soon as Logan said the words, he wanted to take them back—but it was too late.

Tate lowered his voice then and asked, "Do you really think that being an asshole to me is going to make me leave you?"

Logan wasn't sure what he thought. For so long, he'd run from any kind of commitment that maybe he was, in his own way, testing the boundaries with Tate—pushing to test those extra bonds of trust.

"No."

"I think you do. I think you've been let down so many times, by so many people, you're intentionally provoking me to see what I do."

Logan shoved his glasses back on, always feeling a little more in control with them in place.

"But I've got news for you. Your shitty behavior this week doesn't make me want to leave. It just makes me want to pin you down until you open your mouth and start talking. I was there. I know how much she hurt you. Just like you know how fucked up my family is. So stop being such a prick and share it with me. I love you."

Well, damn…

He'd come down there tonight with one goal in mind, but after Tate's little "fuck you, I love you" speech, Logan didn't want to wait to continue their conversation. He wanted to get him alone and reconnect—the sooner the better.

He looked over at Tate, who was staring at him with such focus that he felt as though he were the only person in the bar. Standing, Logan fished out his key ring and checked the clock on the back wall. Tate's shift would be over in approximately five minutes.

Facing Tate, he told him, "I came to you per your instructions. Now, you can come to me."

As he put his jacket on, Tate's eyes narrowed on him.

"Meet me at the elevator to Mitchell & Madison in ten minutes."

"Why? Everything's locked up."

Logan adjusted the collar of his jacket and then slowly backed away, dangling the keys. "Not if you're the owner, it's not."

Chapter Twelve

TATE HAULED ASS out of the bar at two. After grabbing his leather jacket and helmet, he was striding through the lobby like a man on a mission—and his mission was to find the owner of Mitchell & Madison.

As he crossed the marble floor of the tall high-rise, the only sound he could hear was the echo his boots were making, which made what he was about to do feel even more risqué. He rounded a large, cement pillar, knowing the way to the elevator banks like the back of his hand, and then came to a stop when he saw the low lighting of the empty building illuminating Logan.

He was leaning against the wall by the elevators, his hands stuffed in his navy-blue pants. His coat was on and unbuttoned, the collar still flipped up around his neck, and when Logan saw him, he pushed off the wall and waited for him to do exactly as he'd requested—come to him.

No fucking problem, Tate thought, floored by how devastatingly handsome Logan looked tonight. There was no other place he'd rather be, and as he got closer, he let his eyes take in every minute detail of the man waiting on him.

As Tate advanced, he kept his face neutral and popped a piece of Big Red into his mouth, not willing to give the upper hand away just yet. It wasn't until they were only inches apart that Logan seemed to realize he wasn't stopping and backed up to where he'd just been lounging. But that wasn't enough. Tate wanted reconnection, and he wasn't going to stop until he got it.

When there was barely any space left between them, he asked, "So, how's that mood of yours?"

"Just fine."

Tate shook his head. "You're so full of shit."

Logan's eyes zeroed in on him, and the irritation simmering just beneath the surface—*Yeah, it's still there*—began to rise.

Logan was spoiling for a fight.

He had been ever since Evelyn had bolted Monday night. Tate got that. He understood the need to beat the shit out of something or disappear when someone let you down, but it was high time this was brought out into the open.

"You've been acting like you're 'fine' all week, and you know what?" he asked as he inched closer. *Jesus, he even smells fantastic.* "Time's up. You and I are talking this out. Now."

"Let it go, Tate. Let's just—"

"No," he interrupted. "I've given you time. Time to talk to me. Time to work it out of your system. Time to do whatever the fuck you need to to deal with the fact that your mother is just as horrible as mine—but you're not dealing. You're bottling this shit up."

Logan clenched his teeth together, and the red stain that hit his cheeks was a clear indication he was pissed. "So, we're just going to stand here and talk all night? That's disappointing, I had such plans."

Tate brought a hand up to Logan's chin, holding him in place. He ran his eyes over the face in front of him and thought, not for the first time, about how he'd ever doubted his attraction to this man.

"No need for disappointment. Once you open your mouth and start talking, we're going to take this elevator up to your floor, and I'm going to get you out of these fancy-ass clothes you put on to make me crazy. Then…then I'm going to fuck you until you've forgotten what a god-awful week you've had."

Logan arched an eyebrow. "Pretty arrogant there. Don't you think?"

Tate pressed his mouth to the stubble of Logan's cheek and then parted his lips to lick a wet path along his jaw. "So? You know you want it. You want me to strip you down in that office of yours and slide my cock inside you. Don't you, Logan?"

Logan's breath hit Tate's ear as he panted out, "Maybe."

Tate chuckled at the insolent response and pulled back

to reach for the up button on the wall. He pressed it, all the while holding Logan's gaze in a stalemate that was soon going to be fought over and won—by someone.

"I'm glad that's settled."

"Hardly," Logan muttered as the chime sounded.

It seemed so loud in the otherwise silent lobby that there might as well have been a marching band surrounding the two of them. Once the doors had parted, Tate lowered his hand and took a step back.

"After you," he told Logan, gesturing for him to step inside.

Logan brushed by him, and Tate took a deep breath before following. He was determined to stand his ground even though he wasn't sure how that would be physically possible if Logan decided to make a move on him. After Logan inserted the key into the wall panel, he turned it and hit the button of his floor. Then he stepped to the opposite side of the space and leaned against the brass railing as the doors slid closed.

"Okay, fine," Logan said. "Let's get this out of the way, because I don't plan to fuck around with anything other than you once we get up there."

Logan's ability to cut through all the crap to get to exactly what he wanted was, Tate had to admit, a welcome one in this particular moment.

"Go ahead," he invited as the elevator whirred and started its ascent.

Logan sighed and crossed his legs at the ankles. "*God,* you're tenacious."

"So are you. Now talk, Logan."

"Okay, okay," he said, rubbing the bridge of his nose between his fingers. "Ever since I was a kid, Evelyn has been pulling this sort of shit." He dropped his hand, focusing his gaze on Tate. "She's a leech. She uses people and then discards them when she's done. Exactly the reason my father never stuck around. Monday night wasn't the first time she's used me either, though I will say that it was by far the most spectacular and humiliating."

Tate nodded but remained silent as Logan lowered his eyes and continued.

"She's a master con. Beautiful and charming, and she knows *exactly* how to use it. And I knew…I fucking *knew* she was going to pull something. That's what makes it even more infuriating."

Tate walked across the space until he was standing in front of him and said, "Look at me." When Logan kept his eyes down, he repeated, "Look at me."

Slowly, Logan raised his eyes.

Tate told him, "It's not your fault."

"Yeah, I know that," Logan snapped.

"Do you?" Tate shouted right back. "Because it sure as fuck doesn't seem that way."

* * *

AS LOGAN GLARED into the frustrated eyes scanning his face, he knew that this was the attitude Tate had been talking about. All week, he'd been downright defensive every time Tate had brought up anything relating to his mother, and *fuck*—he knew he needed to quit. He just couldn't seem to help his explosive mood, even as he told himself to stop already.

"Can we drop this now? I talked. What else is there to say? That maybe, in some fucked-up way, I *want* it to be my fault? Because you know what? I kind of do. At least then I would understand why she does it."

Tate's eyes were so focused on him that Logan actually found himself biting his lips shut. He didn't want to think about that anymore. He wanted to move on, to lose himself in the man in front of him, so it was a welcome relief when the elevator hit his floor and the doors opened.

"Yes, we can drop it…for now. Get the key," Tate said before walking out into the dark lobby, leaving him to follow.

Removing the key, Logan stepped into the all-too-familiar space and felt a rush of adrenaline race up his spine as the doors closed, locking him and Tate inside. He could've sworn he heard the beat of his heart as Tate looked over his shoulder at him. The security lights were all that lit the lobby of the law offices, and as an illicit smile crooked the corners of Tate's mouth, all the blood that had been in Logan's head immediately detoured the fuck south.

Now that's *a dirty fucking grin.*

Logan swallowed back the groan that was threatening to escape and then strode forward to walk past Tate and head for the office doors. He wasn't even a foot past him when a firm hand took hold of his arm and brought him to a standstill.

Before he could even turn, Tate stepped up behind him and whispered, "Go into your office and take off your coat. Then I want you to sit on your couch and wait for me."

The warm breath teasing his ear just about made it impossible not to push back against Tate.

"Just my coat?"

"That's what I said, isn't it?"

Christ. A bossy Tate was his biggest weakness. Add in the slight edge of annoyance he heard in that last question and his dick went hard as a fucking steel rod.

However, he'd be damned if he gave Tate the advantage of knowing just how turned on he was. Instead, Logan kept his face forward as his arm was released. Then he made his way over to the double doors and unlocked them without looking back.

If Tate wanted to play it this way, then he sure as fuck was ready.

Logan wove his way back through the desks to where

his office was located, the lights from the surrounding buildings casting a soft glow over the desks. He'd been there many times after hours. In fact, before Tate had come along, it had been a habit of his to work late. But never had he *ever* felt the way he did right now as he opened his office door.

Moving inside, Logan removed his coat and hung it on the coatrack. He then fished *his* piece of paper out of the pocket. He still hadn't had an opportunity to share it with Tate—and he was waiting for the perfect time.

He walked over to his desk on the opposite side of the room and placed the paper down. After shifting the desk lamp to the far corner of the wide cherry oak, he also took a moment to push the trays to the side and move the fancy penholder and letter opener away from anything that they may cause…damage to, should he want to bend Tate over it. Once he was happy that his desk was clear, he leaned up against the edge, pressing a palm on the aching erection inside his pants.

As he thought about what Tate had in store for him, his temperature started to rise. Not that he was going to make it easy on the guy—and maybe that was what had him extra excited. He'd wanted Tate to push him, and as usual, he'd known exactly what he needed. Just as that thought entered his mind, the handle on the door turned.

Logan kept his eyes on Tate as he stepped inside and shut the door behind him. There was no need to lock it, but the fact that he did just meant that whatever Tate had planned likely required precaution—just in case.

And fuck me. That makes this even hotter.

The light streaming into the office was minimal, but it was enough to see the dark desire etched into the lines of Tate's face as he shrugged out of his jacket, hung it by his, and then walked over to him.

Logan wasn't sure why, but he took perverse pleasure in the eyebrow that rose as Tate asked, "Didn't you hear me out there? I said to wait on the couch."

Yeah, it's time to change this game up a little.

Logan straightened to his full height, and when they were toe-to-toe, he reached for the back of Tate's neck and pulled him in so their lips were touching. "I heard you, but if you want to bend me to your will tonight, you're going to have to *make* me." And with that, he took Tate's mouth in a fiery kiss.

He parted his lips as Tate's hands cupped his cheeks, aligning their mouths for a stronger connection. When Tate's tongue slipped inside, Logan sucked on it. He couldn't get enough of the taste. The cinnamon was strong after Tate had chewed that piece of gum earlier, but clearly, it was gone now, because *he* was investigating every inch of that delicious mouth and it was nowhere to be found.

His ass hit his desk as one of Tate's hands grasped his waist, and when he smoothed his palm up to tangle his fingers in Tate's hair, a low groan left him. Tate dragged his lips away, and the desire swirling in his eyes just about had Logan giving in and saying, "To hell with this. Take what you want." But then Tate reached between them and started to unbuckle his belt.

With their eyes locked, Tate got the buckle undone and was pulling it free of the loops. As it was dropped to the floor, the button on his pants was next, then the zipper, and before he had a second to return any of Tate's fast moves, that lecherous grin reappeared and Tate slipped his hand inside to wrap his fingers around his stiff cock.

"Jesus," Logan swore as Tate kissed his cheek, nibbling his way up to his ear.

"So you want me to *make* you do what I want? Does that mean you're going to put up a fight? Because so far, you're not doing so well."

Logan tried to remember exactly what his original plan had been, but when Tate's sharp teeth bit his lobe, he reached down to steady himself on the edge of his desk.

Holy shit. This was *so* not the sweet, Catholic Tate between his legs. *No.* This man was hell-bent on giving it to him hard and fast, exactly the way he needed it—and he couldn't wait.

A throaty growl escaped him, and Logan finally managed to regain some semblance of control. He grasped the back of Tate's head and yanked that teasing mouth from his ear, and when they were facing one another, Logan felt his lips curl as he slowly guided Tate down—down to his knees in front of him.

And fuck yes, he went.

* * *

TATE GLANCED UP Logan's body from where he was now kneeling, and when their eyes collided, Logan tore his sweater off and began to unfasten his shirt. Once it was free and he'd yanked it from his shoulders, Tate rose up to finger the material of his pants. He slid his fingers under the edge of the fabric and pulled them, along with his boxers, down, freeing Logan's thick shaft.

A strained sound came from above, and as Logan pumped his hips forward in an effort to get closer to his mouth, Tate circled the base of his cock with his fingers and used his tongue to tease the sensitive underside of the plump head.

"Tate, for fuck's sake," Logan cursed.

Raising his head, he caught Logan's intense look and tongued the weeping slit.

"Ahh…shit."

Tate lifted his mouth and rooted his nose in against his pelvic bone, kissing his way down to Logan's balls as he pushed his pants to his ankles. He figured that, if he ignored him long enough, then—

"Tate?" Logan growled and pulled his head up by his

hair.

Yes. There he is. The take-what-I-fucking-want Logan that I love.

"What?" he asked as innocently as he could manage with Logan practically fucking his cock against the side of his face. He loved the fierce restraint he saw in him, as if he were trying to hold back but was about to snap.

"Fucking suck it. *Now.*"

* * *

LOGAN COULD FEEL every pulse in his dick as Tate's stubble abraded his sensitive skin. Tate started to lick and suck at him again, but just like before, he continued to deny him the hot, wet slide of his mouth—*and hell if that rebellious side that fights me doesn't make me want him more.*

He still had a tight hold on the desk, but when Tate sat back on his heels and unbuckled his own belt, Logan asked, "Was I not clear enough for you?"

Tate didn't answer as he then sucked a finger into his mouth, and Logan swore he'd never seen a filthier look in all of his life than the one Tate was aiming at him.

"Turn around," he demanded from where he was kneeling, and Logan found it telling that, even when Tate was at his feet, he still had the ability to control his every move.

"Excuse me—"

"Turn around, Logan."

The order was harsh. It was raw and so goddamned sexy that he had to clamp a fist around his cock to stop himself from coming. The heat in Tate's eyes was smoldering, and Logan found himself turning the fuck around.

Instantly, Tate's hands were on his hips and ass, positioning him exactly the way he wanted, and then, without any more warning than his cheeks being parted, a warm tongue swiped across the top of his crack and flirted with the shadowed crevice in between.

Logan moaned and bent at the waist over his desk. As the tip of Tate's tongue touched his hot flesh again, Logan shoved back toward the tease. Then sharp teeth bit his ass and Tate told him, "Lift."

Logan lifted first one foot and then the other, and Tate freed him of his shoes and pants.

"Spread your legs," Tate ordered next.

He did as instructed and a thumb stroked down the crease of his ass and pushed against his hole. Tate was clearly determined to smash his resolve to smithereens, and he was going about it the right fucking way. "Oh, hell *yes…*"

The last word hissed through his teeth as Tate replaced his thumb with his greedy mouth. He alternated, using his fingers and tongue to stretch and prep him, until finally…*finally,* Tate was moving back to his feet and crowding in behind him.

"Don't you fucking move," Tate said, and then the warmth of his body vanished.

Logan was going nowhere, but if Tate didn't come back and get his cock inside him, he wasn't too proud to beg. But before he could find the right words, he was back and Logan saw him place a bottle and a condom on the desk beside his piece of paper.

Where the hell did they come from? But before he could ask, warm fingers circled his wrist and pulled him to his feet, turning him around.

Logan kept his eyes glued to Tate's, daring him without words to finish what he'd started, and the expression that flashed in Tate's scorching eyes was, *I fucking dare.* Tate shifted his body to reach for the condom, but Logan was quicker. He grabbed his papers on the desk, then slapped them against Tate's chest as he cupped the side of his neck. Then he pulled him forward to slam their mouths together in a bruising kiss, biting down on Tate's lower lip.

"You don't need a condom, you teasing motherfucker. I'm clean, and I want to feel you explode inside me."

Tate looked down at the paper and hesitated for only a second before he moved into action. He muscled him back, and as Logan stumbled, Tate smirked.

Smug fuck.

Logan got on the desk, thankful he'd shoved all the shit off it since it was now *his* ass lying across it.

"Lie back," Tate rasped, and without a word, Logan did

as he'd been told.

Everything, from Tate's expression to the stiff cock he was palming through his open pants, had Logan's arousal skyrocketing. Add in the thrill of being taken in his office and he was fucking positive that, by the end of this, he might need Tate to haul his bare ass out of there.

Either that or they could leave the door locked until they could both walk again—in a year or so.

* * *

TATE STEPPED BETWEEN Logan's legs and looked down at the fingers he had circled around the base of his erection to hold his orgasm off. He then grabbed the bottle of lube he'd brought in his jacket and tipped it over Logan's cock and balls, spreading it over his taut skin.

Fuck. The thought of taking Logan bareback had him so fucking ready that he was surprised he hadn't attacked him the second the words had come out of that frustrated mouth. But no, he could and *would* wait. *Even if it fucking kills me.*

Logan's eyes squeezed shut as he moaned, and Tate hooked his hands behind his knees and pulled him to the edge of the desk, pressing the head of his naked cock to Logan's hot rim.

As their eyes met, Tate told him, "Just so we're clear, this is me making *you* bend to my will," and then he surged forward with one deep thrust.

His name echoed around the empty office as it ripped from Logan's throat, and when his back arched off the desk, Tate grit his teeth together as the intensity of being inside Logan bare flooded his senses.

"Oh, God. *Logan,*" he gasped and leaned down to kiss his way up Logan's neck.

The feeling was unbelievable. It was hot, intimate, and sexy as all fuck. He was trying to get a handle on his control, but Logan wasn't about to let that happen as he wound his arms and legs around him, trying to get as close to him as he possibly could.

As he started to move his hips, he could feel Logan's tight channel clenching around his cock every time he pulled out—and it felt fucking unreal. And the erotic, guttural sounds coming from Logan when he tunneled back inside let Tate know he was feeling it too.

The mind-numbing pleasure he got from taking Logan without restrictions drove Tate's own orgasm closer to the point of explosion. His name was being chanted underneath him, and when he slowed down and took ahold of Logan's legs to push them back to his chest, a ragged sound left him.

Tate locked eyes on Logan's vibrant, blue ones, and as he pulled his hips away and then slowly eased himself back between Logan's cheeks, Logan growled out, "Deep, Tate. Get in deep. I want to feel it tomorrow."

He fisted Logan's flushed cock, and as the pre-come

slicked it up nice and good, Logan took over so he could do as requested. Tate shoved back inside, and Logan shouted, bucking up from under him in a way that could only mean one thing—*more.*

Logan was coming undone, and the sight was intoxicating. His cock was dripping with excitement, making one hell of a mess over his stomach and hand, and his inky-black hair stuck to his sweaty forehead while he chased his climax—and Tate was enjoying making him wait for it.

* * *

LOGAN LOOKED UP from where he was positioned on the desk, barely able to remember his own name. With one hand working his cock, he raised the other behind himself to the back of the desk, and Tate let him have it. He clutched the wood beneath his fingers when Tate's palms stroked up his thighs and over his hips to his ass.

"*Yes,*" he moaned, and Tate's lips tightened as his fingers flexed into his skin.

Tate's Adam's apple bobbed, and the veins of his neck stood out as his hair bounced on his forehead and he watched him through lust-laden eyes.

He was stunning. He held him completely enamored. And when Tate shouted out his name and a warmth flooded inside him, Logan exploded all over himself in a most spectacular fashion.

He had never felt more complete than he did in that very moment, and as Tate whispered, "God, I fucking love you," all Logan could think was, *He's all mine*

Chapter Thirteen

MONDAY MORNING ROLLED around, and as Tate opened the door to The Daily Grind, he was impressed that he was early. It wasn't often he was running ahead of schedule, but while making his way over to a booth on the far wall, he congratulated himself for arriving before Rachel.

"You do know the only reason you beat me here this morning is because I need to stop every five minutes to use the restroom, right?"

Tate swiveled in his seat to see Rachel standing beside the booth, smiling down at him. With a grin, he stood to give her a hug.

"Hey, don't try to steal my thunder."

She beamed up at him, and patted him on his chest. "Okay, you can have today. I promise not to tell anyone I had to stop three times."

As she took the opposite seat, Tate slid back into his and watched her pull a red folder out of her handbag. Placing it on the table, she looked at his widened eyes.

"I organized a list of places. We can check them out and then rate them accordingly on what you do and don't like about them."

When she opened the folder and he saw several different colored tabs running down the page, he laughed.

"What?" she asked.

Tate lifted his hips to fish *his* list of places out of his back pocket. He then put it on the table between them, and when Rachel eyed it, she started laughing also.

"Okay, so I'm a little anal about these things."

"Nah, it's great. I'm sure your system is much more efficient than mine."

Appearing rather pleased with the compliment, she sat back and grabbed the menu off the table that had several images of—

"Oh. My. God. Look at this chocolate caramel muffin." She turned the menu around and thrust it in Tate's face. "I'm going to get that. And you know what?" she asked with mischievous sparkle in her eyes. "I'm going to eat it *all*."

"As opposed to?"

"As opposed to my caramel-loving thief of a husband who would totally steal half of this from me."

It *did* look amazing. But he was more into the chocolate hazelnut bar he'd spotted when he'd walked in. "Do you know what you want to drink? I'll go order."

"Hmm..." she mused. "Just a cranberry juice please."

"You got it. Give me a second."

He got out of the seat, and as he made his way over to the line, his phone started ringing. After shoving his hand into his pocket, he removed it and answered, wanting to hear the voice of the caller at the other end more than he wanted his caffeine fix.

* * *

LOGAN SAT IN his chair Monday morning and studied his immaculate desk. With the phone to his ear and a smile on his face, he waited for the line to connect so he could start his morning right.

He knew that Tate was meeting up with Rachel, and he figured he was probably just strolling in now, so he was a little surprised when the call was answered.

"Hey. Can you hold a sec?"

Before he could say either yes or no, he heard Tate rattling off a drink order and then asking for a hazelnut bar and two muffins.

"Logan? Hey, sorry about that."

"No problem. I was just sitting here at my desk and wondering how the hell I'm going to get any work done, when all I can remember is—"

"Logan?" Cole cut him off as he stuck his head inside.

"*Is*?" Tate coaxed, eager to hear more.

Logan raised a hand and gestured for Cole to come in. "How *hard* I worked the last time I was sitting at it."

Cole walked into the office and shut the door, taking a

seat on the couch as Tate's chuckle filled Logan's ear.

"It's always important to work hard."

Logan turned away from his brother's curious eyes and told Tate, "Yeah, that's not a fucking problem right now. Thanks."

"Don't blame me. You started this conversation."

With a slight cough, Logan shifted in his seat. "Yes, well, your date's husband just walked in, so please give her our best regards."

"Are you trying to get rid of me?" Tate asked, and Logan could tell from his tone that he was enjoying himself immensely.

"Yes I am, troublemaker. Have a good day with Rachel," he said. When he turned back to see Cole frowning, he felt the devil on his shoulder. "But not *too* good of a day. That's from Cole, by the way. I'm more than aware you prefer my cock to her—"

"Logan," Cole warned.

He aimed a shit-eating grin at his brother and asked, "What? I'm just trying to reassure you. Tate's sexy and all, but—"

"Hey, smartass?" Tate interrupted. "Stop giving your brother shit and tell him to relax. I just bought him a caramel muffin."

"What'd you buy me?"

"I'm gonna buy you a muzzle if you don't watch it."

"Don't start acting surprised now. You knew I was this

way before you…" Logan caught himself when he realized he'd been about to finish with, "fell in love with me." He was comfortable enough talking about it with Tate, but with Cole's focus directly on him, he lost his nerve.

"My order's up," Tate said, inadvertently saving him. "I'll call you later, okay?"

"Before you go, if you find a place today, does that mean you'll tell me yes? Or do I have to wait another year before that happens?"

"Anyone ever tell you you're impatient?"

"Just when I know I want something."

"*Hmm*. We'll see."

"In that case," Logan said, sitting forward in his chair, "good luck today."

"Thanks. I'll let you know. Have a good day, counselor."

Upon hanging up, Logan pulled his chair in under the desk and looked at his schedule for the day. He had several meetings across town, and he'd told Sherry to let Lance Powell of LPCW Architecture know that, since he would be over that way, he'd swing by at three to pick up the forms they'd had to sign.

"Tate said to let you know he bought you a caramel muffin. So cool your jets over there, would you?"

Cole stood from the couch and walked over to take a seat in one of the chairs facing Logan's desk. "My jets are just fine. But since we're on the topic…how are yours?"

"Do I not appear fine?"

Cole's brow rose. "You do, which is suspicious in itself. All last week, you were acting like you wanted to murder somebody."

"You're one to talk. You've been in a foul mood ever since—"

"Your ex-boyfriend, who we've both had physical altercations with, showed up? Yes, I can't imagine why *that* would worry me. But you know what? Rachel told me it wasn't my business. So I've let it go."

"Have you?" Logan asked as he placed an elbow on the desk and rubbed his chin. "Don't let it bother you. Chris is the least of my problems or concerns."

"Really? Do you want to explain, then, why you were acting like a lion with a thorn in its paw all week?"

Sighing, Logan sat back and clasped his fingers over his stomach. "Evelyn was in town last Monday."

"Oh shit."

"Yeah, exactly."

Cole knew all about Evelyn and her track record. It'd been pretty hard to hide throughout college, especially considering Cole's father was her greatest mark.

Logan frowned at his shocked brother.

"What happened?"

"Let's see. She showed up, charmed Tate into dinner out. I played along, hoping she would behave herself for at least one night—"

"I'm assuming she didn't?"

"Let's just say I'm going to be paying off the dinner *and* her week-long stay at The Peninsula for the next few months."

"Jesus, Logan," Cole said, shaking his head. "That woman never ceases to amaze me."

"You and me both. I couldn't believe she would pull that shit on me in front of someone I fucking care about. I knew she had no problem screwing me over, but to do it in front of Tate… I've never been so humiliated."

"It's not your fault she's a damn parasite."

Logan gave a small shrug. "I know, but that doesn't really help when you're left with the bill your 'wife' left you."

Cole's eyes widened. "Damn. I'm sorry. I didn't know."

"Don't be. It's not your fault."

Cole was looking at him in a way that had Logan getting to his feet. The expression in his eyes told Logan he was feeling sorry for him, and he didn't want to go down that self-pitying path again. Tate had just dragged him the fuck out of it.

"Look, I have several things out of the office today. Is everything covered here?"

Cole stood and nodded. "Yeah. I have everything under control. Rachel won't be home until later. She's so excited about Tate's new 'adventure,' as she calls it. I wonder if he'll be able to get away from her before the sun sets."

Logan laughed as he picked his briefcase up and walked around the desk. "Tate's pretty amicable for the most part. I'm sure they'll be out until whenever Rachel decides to call it quits."

As they both moved toward the office door, Cole asked, "For the most part?"

"Yeah. He's only stubborn about certain things."

"Such as?"

Logan took his coat off the rack, and as he opened the door and Cole stepped out, he decided, *What the hell.* "Like…moving in with me."

Cole stopped in his tracks and pinned him with a "get the fuck out of here" look. "You asked him to move in with you?"

Logan closed his door and placed his coat over his arm. "I did."

"Wow."

"Why is everyone so surprised by this?"

Cole slipped his hands into his pockets and tried to fight back a grin. "You have to admit that it's a little shocking. You've gone from a man who wouldn't date one person, let alone—"

"*Yes*?" Logan asked, feeling perturbed.

Cole lost it then and started to laugh. Then he clapped him on the arm. "Nothing. I think it's great."

Logan eyed him as if he didn't believe him. "It would be

even better if Tate would hurry up and say yes."

"Did he say no?" Cole asked.

Logan was quick to tell him, "No. He said, 'Not yet.'"

Cole smiled, and as he turned on his heel to walk to his office, he called over his shoulder, "Give the guy some time to digest that he'd have to entertain your ass twenty-four-seven. Then I'm sure he'll give you the answer you want."

"Yeah, yeah," Logan mumbled and headed for the door. "Go do some work. I'll see you later."

* * *

IT HAD JUST turned three o'clock when Tate and Rachel walked through the doors of the final property on his list for the day. It was a corner lot with double doors that opened onto the street, and inside, there were three steps leading down to the main floor.

The space was large, and the bar was already built in, which, in his mind, was a plus. He didn't have the extra money for major renovations, so if they could find something in relatively good shape, he could definitely work with that.

Tate wandered into the center of the room, and the realtor came up next to him, rattling off numbers and figures on square footage—this one had 4,400. But what caught his attention this time around was the mention of an additional loft included in the rent.

He turned to see Rachel's grin as she nodded and walked over to the area off to the right, where a long wall of windows let in the afternoon sun and faced the side street where he'd parked his bike.

"The restaurant and bar scene has really taken off on this side of town," the realtor said. She'd been giving them handy little facts about each place at every new stop. "Owners have been investing in restoring and renting out their properties, and fortunately, that means a lot of business."

"And higher rent," Rachel murmured as Tate made his way over to where she stood.

"Yes, yes. In the end, you get what you pay for," the realtor told them.

Keeping his cards close to his chest, Tate remained silent as he walked to the long bar and ran his palm over the top of it. He didn't want to let on just how much he liked the place before he got to see more of it.

When he'd taken on his second jobs, he'd always done it with the intention that the second income went straight in the bank. He'd been saving every spare dollar he could since the day he'd started work for this very occasion. Even Diana had known not to touch that—he'd worked damn hard for that money, and this was the reason why.

"Can I see the loft area?" he asked.

As the woman hurried off toward the end of the bar,

Rachel came up on the other side of him.

"What are you thinking?" she asked.

Tate gave her a crooked smile. "I like it. Depending on what's upstairs, I may *really* like it. If that's included in the price, then I can get out of the place I'm in and take it."

"You think Logan would…" she ventured, but she trailed off as if she didn't think it was her place to ask.

"Would what? Move in here?" Tate asked as he walked to the end of the bar. "No. I'd never ask him to do that, but…"

Rachel followed, asking, "But what? You can't just stop your thought there."

He approached her, and she wrapped her arm through his.

"But maybe it's time to say yes to him. And this will be here for the really late nights if I need to just crash."

Rachel squealed and clutched his arm tight. "*Eek!* He's gonna die when you tell him! I can't wait."

"Don't get too excited. A lot has to happen first. I have to see upstairs. I have to like it. Then I need to go to the bank and see if this is all possible."

"I know. I know. But just hearing you say it… I'm so happy for you both."

Tate looked down at her infectious smile and saw tears welling in her eyes. "You're a romantic fool, Rachel Madison."

"No, just a hormonal one. Let's go and see upstairs."

* * *

THIRTY MINUTES LATER, he and Rachel were standing in front of his bike. He unhooked his helmet and shoved it on his head as Rachel continued to tell him the different baby names she was thinking about.

"And if it's a boy, Cole wants something proper like Thomas. Thomas Madison. But let's face it, then he'd get Tom his whole life and that's not bad. It's just… I don't know."

"Common?"

"Yes! I want something like Ignacio."

Tate stopped buckling the helmet under his chin. "Really?"

"Yes, *really*." She giggled and then slapped his arm. "Or I could just go through a fruit bowl and pick out a piece. Not an apple though."

Tate smiled. "Nah. That's so overdone."

"Oh look. Here's my taxi," she said and kissed him on the cheek. "Thank you so much for letting me come with you today. It was nice to get out and think of new possibilities."

Tate couldn't agree more. "Yeah, it was fun. I really like this last one." So much that he couldn't wait to pick up dinner and stop by Logan's to tell him.

After one last hug, she stepped back. "There are at least a dozen more for us to check out. But you definitely need to talk to Logan about this. Maybe even bring him by."

Tate nodded and watched her walk down the sidewalk to the cab behind him. When he was happy she was safely inside the vehicle, he got on his bike and started the engine.

Once he'd checked behind him, Tate pulled out into the street, unable to wipe the grin off his face. It wasn't until it was too late that he caught a glimpse of the red hood of the car hurtling down the wrong side of the street toward him.

That was the last thought he had—before time ceased to exist.

Part Two

Dependability: Being able to trust someone to do or provide what is needed.

Chapter Fourteen

AS LOGAN TOOK the elevator down from LPCW, he let out the breath he'd been holding the entire time he'd been in there. Thankfully, Chris had been out of the office today, and his meeting with Lance Powell had run on time and smoothly.

Not that it stopped me from watching the door like a fucking hawk.

He'd been paranoid the whole time that Chris would walk in and he'd have to deal with his passive-aggressive shit in front of his partner, but apparently, he'd inadvertently timed his visit well.

Thank God for that.

When the elevator came to a stop at the parking garage, Logan walked out to his car and climbed inside. After inserting the key into the ignition, he pulled his phone out of his pocket and shook his head. The damn thing had died about an hour ago.

He plugged it into the charger and sat for a minute with his head resting back against the seat, wondering how Tate's day with Rachel had gone. He figured he'd have a few choice texts or voicemails about being out of reach when his phone came back on, and when it finally lit up, he wasn't disappointed.

He picked the phone up and checked the notifications pinging across the screen. There were texts and voicemails, one every minute or so, that had started around thirty minutes ago until finally they stopped coming in.

Not one of them was from Tate though; these were from his brother.

What the hell, Cole?

Opening the texts first, he read the three that were several seconds apart.

Cole: As soon as you get this, call me.

Cole: Logan, you need to call me.

Cole: PICK UP YOUR PHONE

Frowning, he checked his voicemails and saw two in there, also from his brother.

Jesus. Is it Rachel?

He hit the first, and put the phone on speaker and held his breath as Cole's usually calm voice came through sounding unsteady. "Christ, Logan, why aren't you answering your phone? As soon as you get this, call me."

There was a second one, and before he called Cole back, he hit play.

"It's Tate. You need to call me. NOW."

As Cole's voice filled the empty space inside his car,

Logan felt his heart skip and stutter. He replayed the message just to be sure he'd heard it right.

"It's Tate. You need to call me. NOW."

What the… What about Tate?

His heart was racing in his chest as he hit redial and waited—still as a statue. He didn't dare move, and he wasn't sure he'd taken a breath in the last several seconds. As soon as the phone connected, he closed his eyes.

"Logan?" Cole said into the phone.

But Logan couldn't seem to find his voice to greet him. He was too busy trying not to jump to any kind of conclusion.

"Thank God. Where are you?"

Knowing he needed to actually speak, Logan managed, "What the fuck is going on, Cole? Your messages are freaking me out."

The silence that stretched across the line wasn't helping to calm him. Cole was never stuck for words, but whatever this was, whatever had happened, he was having trouble relaying it.

"Spit it out," he finally demanded, his anxiety hitting the breaking point.

"It's Tate."

"So you said in your message. What about him?"

"I need you to try to stay calm—"

"Fuck you and calm. Tell me what's going on." Logan

could hear people talking in the background of wherever Cole was, but he couldn't quite make out what was being said.

"There was an accident. Tate… He was hit when he was leaving one of the places he and Rachel were looking at this afternoon."

Cole kept talking but his words all started to jumble together. All Logan kept hearing was, *Tate… He was hit…hit…hit.* And before he knew he was going to ask, the words just tumbled out.

"Is he dead, Cole?"

Cole cursed through the phone, and Logan held his breath.

"*No*. No. He was just taken into surgery. But you need to get down to University Hospital now. The ER."

Biting his bottom lip to hold back the cry that was threatening to leave his chest, Logan remained silent.

"Logan? Can you drive? Do you need me to come down—"

"No," burst free of his lips, and then he placed a fist to his mouth.

"Are you sure?"

"Yeah. I'm on my way," he said and then hung up before he totally lost it.

As he gazed blankly out his front windshield, Logan's hands started to shake. He couldn't seem to remember how to put his car into gear, and he sure as fuck couldn't see through the tears welling in his eyes.

He swiped a hand over them and gulped in some air. He needed to pull his shit together and get over to the hospital. He just hoped he made it in time.

* * *

BY THE TIME Logan got across town, parked his car, and rushed through the doors of the emergency room, his state of mind was in complete chaos.

The entire way over, he'd berated himself for not asking more questions like, *Why is Tate in surgery? What did he come in with? What time did this all happen?* He'd been such a fucking head case when Cole had called that all of the important questions had disappeared from his mind.

After he'd marched through the automatic sliding doors, Cole was standing there to greet him. His face was strained, and his hair was a mess, as though he'd been worrying it all afternoon with his hands. But he took him in a hug and squeezed him tight.

Logan didn't have the will to do anything other than stand there as his eyes scanned the busy waiting area. It was a miracle in itself that he'd been able to function enough to get himself through the traffic and over here.

"You made it," Cole murmured in his ear, and when he released him, Logan merely looked at him. "Hey, why don't you come and sit down. Rachel's right over here."

As Cole turned to walk him over to the sitting area, Logan grabbed the arm of his jacket and stopped him.

"Tell me what happened," he said, his voice sounding foreign, detached, even to himself.

"Why don't you come and sit down first?"

Logan stepped in until only inches separated them and demanded, "Tell me what happened."

"I wasn't there," Cole explained as he clasped his arm. "I only know what Rachel has told me."

Logan's heart was working overtime as it tried to keep up, getting shock after shock. He looked beyond Cole's shoulder and found Rachel seated in the corner of the waiting room, her arms wrapped around her stomach and her bloodshot eyes glued to him.

"She was there?" Logan asked, not taking his eyes away from her.

"Yeah, she was in a cab about to leave. They just finished checking her for shock, but she insists she's fine. She wanted to be here when you arrived." Cole squeezed his arm, but Logan's eyes were fixated on the haunted ones holding his. "She saw it all happen. Called the ambulance and then called me."

Without a word, Logan pulled away from Cole and walked past the chairs filled with people to where Rachel was sitting. When he stopped in front of her, he didn't say anything, but as she stared up at him, her blue eyes brimming with tears, she finally lost it.

She got to her feet, tears falling over her blotchy cheeks. Then she wrapped her arms around his neck and whispered, "I'm sorry. I'm so sorry, Logan."

Logan mechanically wound his arms around her as she continued to cry. He felt numb as he listened to her weep.

"He…he was so happy. Couldn't wait to get home to you, and then…" She stopped and sucked in a breath, and when she pulled away, Logan swore he could see all of his worst fears in her eyes. They spoke the words she couldn't seem to manage.

What she'd witnessed was horrific. The pain and fear swirling in those usually sparkling eyes were gut wrenching. It was the kind of anguish one never forgets, and as she covered her mouth, fighting back a sob, Logan knew she'd been through hell. A hell he needed her to tell him about. One he needed her to walk him through so he could understand exactly what had happened to the man he loved.

He touched her cheek and somehow managed to speak. "Will you tell me?"

She took a shaky breath before replying, "Yes."

Logan took the seat beside her, and when she reached for his hand, he wondered if he was as strong as the tiny woman sitting beside him, because he wasn't sure he was ready to hear this.

"We had just finished for the day, and Tate… He was

getting on his bike to come and see you."

"That fucking bike," he muttered, his stomach knotting as he remembered all the times he'd joked about it with Tate.

Rachel nodded and clasped his hand in hers as if she needed the strength of another to get through the rest. "He had his helmet on, thank God, so it protected his head, but the car was going so fast. And before he had time to move, he... He was thrown so far, Logan."

She chewed her lower lip, and her chin started to quiver. Logan squeezed her fingers, fighting back his own emotions, unable to imagine what she'd seen—and not wanting to.

"I raced over to him as soon as it happened, and he was just lying there in the middle of the street. He wasn't moving. And I know you aren't supposed to touch someone, but I...I just couldn't leave him there."

Logan's chest ached to the point where he wondered if his heart could take any more. It physically hurt to hear what she was saying—as if it were splitting in two. But he needed to know more. He needed to know everything. So he clamped his teeth together and kept his mouth shut.

Hold it together, Mitchell. Be fucking strong.

"I took his hand and kept telling him I was there. But he wouldn't wake up. He just lay there—so still. Then I called the ambulance and Cole, and he said he'd call you."

When she raised her eyes to his, she shook her head as if she were still in shock. She opened her mouth several times before she said, "I'm sorry. I'm so sorry. I should've made him take a cab with me. Should've warned him—"

Logan couldn't get his tongue to work to tell her that it wasn't her fault, so he pulled her into his arms instead.

Tate. His gorgeous, stubborn Tate was somewhere in the hospital, unconscious and fighting for his life. *And what am I doing? I'm out here trying not to fall apart.*

He saw Cole watching them from the opposite chair and that's when Logan pulled back and managed to ask Rachel, "Did the paramedics or doctor say anything before they took him back?"

Rachel tried to focus on him through the blur of tears. "Not a lot. I heard them discussing possible broken ribs and a pneumothorax?"

Jesus. This can't really be happening, can it? Logan shut his eyes and tried to tell himself that everything would be okay. Tate was in surgery. He was in the best place he could be. But no matter how many times he told himself that, the reality was he was fucking terrified.

Letting go of Rachel's hand, Logan got to his feet like someone in a trance and made his way past Cole, who looked up at him with a question in his eyes. But Logan had no answers, and he wanted some. He wanted to know from the doctors what was going on.

He walked up to the main desk and waited for someone to see him standing there. After several minutes, a young brunette came over to find out what he needed.

"Can I help you, sir?"

Logan nodded and licked his parched lips. "I'd like an update on…" He tried to say Tate's name but couldn't get the words out.

"On who, sir?"

He was about to try again when Cole stepped up beside him and said, "On Tate Morrison. He was brought in a little while ago. They took him back into surgery."

The brunette sat down, and Logan turned to Cole with silent thanks in his eyes. Cole gave a nod of his head, and then their attention was drawn back to the woman in front of them.

"And who are you in relation to the patient?"

The question was so simple, yet at the same time, as it echoed around inside his brain, Logan knew that it was about to become extremely complicated.

"I'm his partner. My name's Logan Mitchell."

The woman narrowed her eyes and then lowered them to the forms in front of her. She ran her finger down several lines and then returned her gaze to him.

"I'm sorry, sir. You aren't listed as an emergency contact on the paperwork. You'll have to wait out here until you're further notified."

Logan shut his eyes and willed himself to be patient. He felt a hand on his arm and knew that it was Cole, and when he opened his eyes and faced him, Cole mouthed, "Let's sit down."

Yeah, not going to happen.

"Excuse me," Logan said as he turned back to the receptionist. "I don't think you understand. The man you have back there? He's with me, and I just want to know how he is."

She nodded and gave him a sympathetic smile that made Logan want to strangle her. "I understand perfectly, sir. But hospital policy states immediate family only, and until then, I can't give out any information."

Logan clenched his fists on top of the counter as a red haze clouded his vision. He was quickly losing any semblance of politeness he had, and as his temper started to boil, he reminded himself that losing it wasn't going to get him very far.

"I just want to know how he is," he tried again, hating the tremble he could hear in his voice. "Mr. Tate Morrison. Can't you take a look and let us know—"

"Sir," she interrupted. "I'm not allowed to tell you anything more. A member of his family has arrived, and when she is ready, I'm sure she'll come and tell you what you wish to know. Those are the hospital rules."

"Fuck the rules," Logan shouted.

Cole pulled him away from the desk. "Would you cool it? You aren't going to get any answers like that."

Logan glared at Cole like he wanted to murder him. "I'm not getting answers anyway." Then he realized exactly *what* the woman had just said. Marching back to the desk, he said, "You said when *she* is ready. Is his emergency contact Diana Cline?"

The pinched look on the receptionist's face made Logan think he wasn't going to get an answer. But she must have had an inner moment of compassion, because she glanced back down to the paper and frowned.

That was when it occurred to him— "I'm sorry. Diana Morrison."

"Yes." She nodded. "Mrs. Morrison was taken back around thirty minutes ago."

The temper that had been the reason for the blood pounding in his head drained in an instant.

As Logan took a step away from the desk, he heard Cole say his name, but he couldn't respond because his heart had finally shattered.

Chapter Fifteen

SECONDS TURNED INTO minutes, minutes turned into hours, and somewhere around three in the morning, Logan found himself in the exact same chair he'd fallen into earlier. He hadn't spoken a word since his conversation with the receptionist.

Cole had taken the seat to his left, and sitting beside him was Rachel, who had her head on her husband's shoulder. They both had their eyes closed. Logan envied the peace they must have felt in that moment because he would've done anything to be able to escape the all-consuming need to know what was going on behind the white double doors only steps away from him.

People had come and gone from the waiting room. Been seen, healed, and told to go home with a few pills—they would live to see another day. As for him, he was waiting in a room with his eyes fixated on a door in the hopes that the one person he'd thought he would never want to see again would walk through.

Diana. She was the only one who could get him access,

and he'd gone over every kind of conversation imaginable so he was prepared when—*or if*—she decided to come out.

Logan squeezed his eyes shut and brought a hand to his face. He rubbed his gritty eyes and then looked at the clock on the wall. Hours. It had literally been hours, and he knew nothing more than what he'd originally been told.

And really, what are the odds she'll come out here and tell me anything more?

If he was honest, she was the last person he'd want to engage with if the situation was reversed, and as that hard truth settled in the pit of his stomach, he felt bile rise in his throat.

"Logan?"

Not willing to take his eyes away from the locked doors leading to the inner halls of the hospital, he didn't bother turning his head. He remained silent and focused.

That was when a woman in a white lab coat and a black dress stepped in front of him, blocking his view of the door. He raised his head, ready to tell her to get out of the way, but when his vision cleared, the doctor turned out to be someone he knew. He was almost shocked out of his grief by *who* was standing in front of him.

"Logan?" she said again, bending at the waist to touch his shoulder.

"Shelly?"

She gave him a tight smile as he tried to work out what was going on. "Hi."

He blinked a couple of times, and when he couldn't think of anything to say, she offered a hand.

"Want to come for a walk with me?"

The bold blonde he'd met only weeks ago at game night was nowhere to be found. In her place was a sophisticated doctor. But Logan wasn't budging. He shook his head and turned away from her.

"No. I'm waiting."

She stepped in front of him again and crouched down so they were eye to eye, and as she gave a slight nod, she told him, "I know." She placed a hand on his knee and gave it a gentle squeeze. "I don't know if Cole told you, but I'm a pulmonologist here at the hospital." When it was clear he wasn't about to say anything, she said, "Come for a walk," and straightened to her full height.

When he looked up at her, the expression in her eyes finally had him getting to his feet quietly. Cole and Rachel were still resting, and he didn't want to wake them.

Shelly glanced at the two of them and smiled. "I'll tell one of the girls over there to let them know you're with me if they wake."

After Logan agreed, she approached the front desk, chatted with one of the women behind it, and then turned back to face him. He looked to the double doors one last time and then to Shelly, deciding that five minutes talking to her couldn't hurt, *right?*

He walked over to where she was standing and then followed her lead as she wandered with him down the hall toward the vending machines.

"I'm so sorry to hear about Tate. I hope you don't mind, but Cole called me this evening after you arrived here at the ER and were refused any information on his condition."

Logan still didn't have anything to say, so he remained silent until she stopped walking. Then he too halted his steps.

"I'm not supposed to do this, but"—she grabbed his arm and pulled him into a small alcove where there were two water fountains—"I know how much you care about him, and if I were you, I'd be going out of my ever-lovin' mind."

The slight Southern inflection that entered her feisty tone was the first thing that slipped through Logan's numb state, but still, it wasn't enough to get a verbal response.

"I spoke to the surgeon who worked on Tate when he was brought in and found out as much as I could. The first thing you need to know is that his condition is serious. They've listed it as guarded."

Logan took a step back and used the wall as a prop to hold him up just in case his knees gave out from what she was about to tell him.

"He suffered a broken clavicle and two broken ribs, one which punctured his right lung, causing it to collapse. Also known as a pneumothorax."

"Oh, God," Logan muttered, the words escaping without

any conscious thought, as he ran a hand through his hair. Gripping the back of his neck, he sucked his top lip behind his lower teeth, trying to keep the shout that was bubbling up inside him from slipping free.

"I know this is hard to hear. Do you want me to stop?" Shelly reached for his arm, a physical show of support.

Logan shook his head and tried to stave off the tears—he needed to hold it together.

"Okay. After they inserted a drain and relieved the air in the lung, his condition deteriorated and they had to place him on a ventilator. They thought that would be enough, that it would get him through the safety window and on the road to healing, but around thirty minutes ago, one of my colleagues was called to his room. Tate's condition…" She paused, and Logan didn't dare look away from her. "It's continued to deteriorate, and they've started differential lung ventilation."

He'd tried to keep up with all of the medical jargon she'd been throwing his way, and he'd understood most, but the last part… "What's that mean? Differential?" His voice was scratchy, and he knew it was from fighting back the emotional lump in his throat all day and his lack of actually speaking.

When Shelly stepped in beside him and ran her hand down his arm to take his hand, he looked at her sympathetic eyes and felt his entire body shudder.

Obviously, it meant nothing good.

"It means he's on two ventilators, one going into each lung. They're doing additional x-rays now, and we'll know more soon."

"Fucking hell," Logan cursed, unable to think of anything else that even remotely relayed every feeling he was having in that moment.

Tate was somewhere in here, with God knows how many tubes and needles going in and out of him, and he wasn't able to do a fucking thing. He was useless. Helpless. And the more he thought about it, the more enraged he became.

"Did you see anyone back there with him?" he grit out. "He shouldn't be alone through all of this, and since the guard dogs at your front desk won't let me back…"

Shelly winced, appearing uncomfortable, but then she said softly, "His parents are in there. And so is another woman."

Logan let the rage inside him boil over, welcoming the emotion, as he pushed off the wall and stalked away from Shelly.

Best to be nowhere close—he felt homicidal.

"His *parents* are in there? Jesus, no wonder his condition is deteriorating. I thought you were supposed to be around people who love you to heal, and he's stuck with his ex-wife and the parents who disowned him? Awesome job. This hospital is really on top of their shit."

"Logan?" Shelly said.

"What?" he snapped, rounding on her. He knew that it wasn't her fault, but at this stage, she was the only one around to let his anger out on. "The man *I* love is somewhere in this fucking building, surrounded by people who practically threw him out on the road like a piece of garbage. I'm not even allowed back there to see him. What a goddamn joke."

"I know this is frustrating."

"*Frustrating*?" he mocked. "No, you know what's frustrating? When you see someone you really want to fuck and can't because they keep saying no. I've *been* frustrated. This…this is agony. Torment beyond anything I've ever felt before." He paused and closed his eyes before whispering, "This is hell."

Shelly came over to him and clasped his hands. "Let me see what I can do about getting you in there, okay? Until then, I'll keep an eye on his progress. Hey?"

Logan looked at her. "Yeah?"

"He's lucky to have you."

Logan nodded as she stepped around him.

"Will you be okay getting back to the waiting room?"

"Yeah," he muttered, his anger having drained from him.

"Okay. I have rounds, but I'll be back before I go home. If anything changes, I'll let you know. Hang in there. He's going to need you when he wakes."

As she walked away from him, Logan was left with the one thought he'd been trying to avoid. *"If" he wakes.*

* * *

THE SUN HAD risen a little over two hours ago, and as the clock in the waiting room hit eight, Logan stretched his neck from side to side. He'd just finished telling Cole and Rachel what Shelly had said, and after getting over the initial shock of the severity of Tate's condition, Cole had volunteered to get them some real coffee.

As Logan bent over and rested his elbows on his knees, he rubbed his hands over his weary face. The day-old stubble scratched against his palms, and he realized just how unkempt he was. His jacket was a crumpled mess beside him, and his tie hung loosely around his neck. They all looked like hell, which was understandable considering the day and night they'd had.

Cole had tried to convince him to go home and take a shower, but there was no force on Earth strong enough to make him leave that hospital.

He wanted to see Tate. He needed to see for himself that he was still there—*still here with me.* And until he got that, he was going nowhere.

Trying to occupy himself, he undid the buttons at his wrists and started to roll the sleeves up his arms. When he was halfway done with the second, the double doors pushed open and the woman he'd ironically been hoping would walk out…did.

Diana Cline—or should he say, Diana Morrison—stopped just outside the doors and scanned the waiting room. Her eyes hadn't found him yet, and as Logan got to his feet, he noted that Tate's ex looked terrible.

Her hair was in a mess of a bun on top of her head, she was dressed in baggy sweatpants, and the sweater she had on looked three sizes too big. She looked like a woman who'd been sitting at home and had to suddenly drop everything and go somewhere.

Diana looked as bad as he felt.

When her eyes finally skidded to a stop and latched on to his, his palms started sweating and he had to move them to his pants to wipe them. This was it. This was the moment he'd been waiting for. The moment where, if he needed to, he'd grovel at her feet to see Tate—even if it was only for a second.

He took a step toward her, and when her eyes widened, Logan raised a hand, trying to convey he was…what? *Coming in peace?*

Diana's chin started to quiver as he continued to approach her. Her red-rimmed eyes blinked frantically, and Logan's pulse picked up. He was so close, but just as he opened his mouth to say something, she clutched her handbag across her body, turned, and ran out the automatic doors.

Fuck. "Diana!" he called out. *No. Damn it,* he thought as he watched her go.

He was two seconds away from chasing after her when the doors opened again and there, standing directly in front of him, was Tate's father.

"Mr. Mitchell, isn't it?"

Logan dropped his hand to his side and tried to get his mouth to work. But as he stood before Mr. Morrison, all he could think about was the last time he'd seen this man and that he had Tate's eyes.

Then he said something Logan had never expected to hear. "We need to talk."

Logan followed Tate's father over to an empty area in the waiting room. Rachel's eyes were on them, and Logan gave a small nod of his head, indicating that he was okay, before he took a seat opposite the exhausted-looking man.

"Is he okay?" Logan rushed out, not knowing what he was there to say but needing to ask someone who'd seen him.

"He's in rough shape."

"If you're here to tell me to leave, you can forget it," he said. "I'm not going until I see him. If I have to wait two days, two weeks, two fucking months—I'm not leaving."

Tate's father held his hand up and nodded grimly. "I'm not here to tell you to leave."

Logan swallowed back his next argument and instead asked, "You're not?"

Mr. Morrison met his gaze head on, reminding Logan so much of his son. There was no argument Tate would back down from, and Logan could see where he'd gotten his determination.

"No, I'm not. I'm here to tell you that *we're* leaving."

Logan narrowed his eyes and sat back. "I don't understand."

"In a couple of hours, I'm going to take Tate's mother and his sister home to get some food and get cleaned up. Then I'll bring them back this afternoon around four."

As what he was telling him sank in, Logan was at a complete loss for words. This was the last person he'd expected to show compassion. Never in a million years would he have guessed that Tate's father would be the one to let him in to see his son—yet that was exactly what he was doing. *Isn't it?*

Just to make certain, Logan said cautiously, "I can't get back without—"

"They have your name," Mr. Morrison said, and then he stood.

Logan looked up at the tall man towering over him, and in that moment, he felt the tears he'd been holding back since the moment he'd answered Cole's call slide down over his cheeks. The gift this man had just extended to him was…was…

"Thank you."

"Don't thank me. I'm still not on board with all of this, but Diana mentioned that, just before his surgery, Tate regained consciousness for a few seconds. The last thing he said before they put him under was, 'Tell Logan yes.'"

Logan brought a hand to his mouth and clamped it over his lips, trying to hold back the overwhelming heartache those words had caused. Even while lying on an operating table, in and out of consciousness, Tate had reached for *him*.

"I don't know what he was talking about, but this is my way of honoring his words. I'm telling you yes. You can go in there. See him, talk to him, but don't be there when I bring his mother back. If you can do that, I'm happy for you to try to get my boy to wake up."

Logan nodded, willing to take anything at this point. Tate's father gave a final nod, and as he walked away, Logan stood and somehow made his way down the hall Shelly had taken him to earlier that morning.

When he found the small alcove with the water fountains, he stepped into it and slid down the wall until he was crouched with his back against it. He wrapped his arms around his knees, placed his head on them, and finally let go of every pent-up emotion he'd had over the last twenty-four hours.

The wracking sobs that left his chest made his entire body shake and he clutched his knees tighter, trying to ground himself. The pain inside his heart was excruciating, as though someone were ripping it from his body, and as he opened the floodgates to release some of the strain, it merely intensified until it physically hurt to cry any more.

Raising his head, Logan looked up at the white popcorn ceiling above him. His eyes stung from the sheer amount of tears he'd shed, and as he thought about the man he'd *finally* get to see in a couple of hours, he sent a prayer up to the God Tate believed so strongly in.

"Please…" he started, wiping his cheeks. "If you're up there and listening, I know I don't deserve it, but he does. He really does. Let me see him today. Let me tell him how much I love him." He dragged the back of his hand across his wet mouth and could taste the salt on his lips before he whispered, "Please hear me…just this once."

Chapter Sixteen

SOMETIME LATER, LOGAN found himself being led through the double doors of the ER and down several winding corridors. He had no idea how he finally got to the ICU, but somehow, that's where he ended up.

The nurse who'd retrieved him pointed across the hall to room three and told him that Tate was just inside. With his jacket clutched in his hand, Logan took several steps toward the glass sliding door, petrified of what he would see on the other side, yet at the same time, needing to know. As he got closer, he reminded himself to breathe, but nothing could've prepared him for what he saw when he looked inside.

In the center of the room was a lone bed surrounded by mountains of equipment. But it was the man lying *on* the bed, flat on his back, with stark, white sheets around his waist, that had Logan reaching for the wall for support.

Tate's arms lay still by his sides. One had an IV inserted into the top of his hand, and the other had a small, blue clamp on his index finger that monitored his pulse. But that wasn't what had Logan gripping the jamb so tight that his knuckles were white. No, that was due to the drainage tube inserted below his purplish-colored ribs on the right-hand side and the tangle of them winding from the complicated machines by either side of his head to his mouth.

"It's hard to look at, isn't it?"

The quiet voice came from behind him, so Logan made himself turn, shocked to find Diana. She wasn't looking at him though. She was staring through the glass at the man lying in silent repose.

"I still can't believe it when I'm in there." She brought her eyes to his then. Logan saw the redness from hours of crying surrounding them. He supposed that his were much the same. "That it's really him, you know?"

Of all the ways Logan had ever thought he'd speak to Diana again, this was not it. He'd hoped, when he'd been outside, that she would see him, but after she'd run, he'd figured that was it.

"I know," he said, surprised when she stepped beside him. He looked at her side profile as she touched the glass.

"He really loves you."

Logan straightened and let his hand fall from the wall to clutch the jacket between both of them. So many things had gone through his head and heart over the last couple of days, but never had he expected to be standing here and discussing this with Diana of all people.

All the smartass comments or arrogant responses he would usually dish out in this kind of situation vanished in an instant, and he found himself…speechless.

"When I first came home from college years ago and Tate and I…" She gave a small grin that didn't quite reach her eyes as she glanced over at him. "When we got together, I begged him to tell his parents, and he wouldn't." She laughed a little and looked back at Tate through the glass. "He was worried about how they'd react since I was a friend of the family. It took him months…*months* to finally tell them. And with you—" She stopped talking and shrugged. "I thought if I threatened him, made him *have* to tell them, that he'd deny it. That he'd turn up at the house for Sunday lunch and tell me to never mention you again. But he didn't do that. That stubborn ass brought you home for lunch. A man. I never expected him to do that. Not to his very Catholic mother. And you know what?" she asked, fully turning to face him.

Logan looked at the woman who had caused them so many problems, and in that instant, he didn't feel any of the animosity he once had. He felt sympathy at the defeated look in her eyes.

"He never would've done that if he didn't love you with every fiber of his being."

When she placed a hand on his arm and stepped closer, Logan held his breath for whatever she was about to say.

"Love him," she whispered. "Love him, and don't ever stop—not even for a second. Because trust me—losing him feels much worse than standing outside this door right now."

Before Logan could respond, she moved around him and walked away.

* * *

BEEP... BEEP... BEEP.

That was the first sound that hit Logan's ears as he slid the door open, and squared his shoulders. Making sure to close it behind himself, he gathered his courage and walked into Tate's room.

Logan placed his jacket over the arm of the aqua-colored recliner in the corner and slowly made his way across to the intimidating bed Tate was stretched out on. He had a surgical cap on over his curls, likely to keep them away from his mouth and the tubes secured to his lips. His beautiful eyes were taped shut, and stuck to his smooth, tan chest were the pads connected to the heart monitor.

The picture he made was gut wrenching.

Logan came around the left side of the bed, glad for the chair that was there as he practically fell down into it and stared at the silent man in front of him. It was like looking at a stranger, because instead of the strong, obstinate, lovable man he was used to seeing, he was looking at someone who was a mere shell of himself.

He scooted to the edge of the seat and reached for Tate's

hand. Surprisingly, it was warm, and as Logan lowered his head and pressed his lips to Tate's fingers, he felt his body start to shake as the shock of seeing him this way started to overwhelm him.

The tears were starting up again as he continued to kiss Tate's knuckles. Then he glanced at his face and said the words he knew he would if Tate's eyes were open.

"You stubborn ass. I don't know if you can hear me right now, but damn it, Tate, I need you to wake up." Closing his eyes, Logan squeezed the fingers he was holding and asked, "Do you remember our first date?" He knew he wouldn't get a response, but thought about what Tate's father had told him.

"See him, talk to him… Get my boy to wake up."

"You know, the one where you tried to embarrass me by ordering a blow job? I don't think I ever told you, but that was the first time I thought about just how far I would go to keep you."

Resting his arms on the bed, Logan stroked a thumb over the back of Tate's hand.

"You were gearing up to tell me to stop coming by the bar, to stop seeing you, and I remember how angry I was that you were even suggesting it, but at the same time, I was grasping for anything—anything to make you stay. Then you did the one thing I can never resist. You dared me. You dared me to try something with you and *only* you."

Logan stopped and shook his head, not knowing if any

of this would work but willing at this point to talk for hours straight if need be.

"So I'm daring *you*. Wake up. Wake up and tell me that you were right. That you're the best thing that has ever happened to me." Logan sucked in a shaky breath and then let it out as he ran his eyes over Tate's body. "And that I never stood a chance. I love you, and I'm not letting you go. Not now, not ever. I can be stubborn too. Got it?"

When the only response he got was the beeping of the machines, Logan sat back in the chair and let his eyes wander around the room. It wasn't until they landed on the drawers on the far side that he noticed a plastic bag. He got to his feet, and walked over to it and saw Tate's clothes inside. Logan opened it up and removed his black leather jacket, noticing that one arm had a hole ripped into it from the accident. But other than that, it was as it had always been.

He turned back to the bed and brought the leather up to his face. He nuzzled into the collar of the worn material, and as the scent of Tate surrounded him, he closed his eyes and thought about the last time he'd seen him.

When he opened them again, he noticed the whiteboard behind Tate's head with the day, date, and time and was shocked. *I last saw him…Monday morning? And it's only Tuesday. Fuck.* It seemed like an eternity had passed.

With Tate's jacket in hand, he went back over to the chair

by the bed and settled into it. As he did, he pulled his phone from his back pocket so it wouldn't jam into his hip. Ever since he'd arrived at the hospital, he'd had it on vibrate, but as he sat there in the silent room, he had an idea.

He'd heard somewhere once that music was a good way to reach those who were unconscious, even bring back memories to those who had lost theirs—*so hell, why not try everything.*

As Logan scrolled through his music list on his phone, searching for the song he was after, he noticed a piece of paper that had fallen onto the floor. He bent down and picked it up, opening it.

Across the top, scrawled in Tate's handwriting, was: **Possible Bar Locations**

There were several listings underneath with check marks beside them or crosses through them, but what caught Logan's attention was the final listing. It was circled several times, check marked, and beside it, Tate had written: **Perfect location. Decent price. Show Logan.**

That wouldn't have been overly significant except for what was beside *that*—three simple words. The same words he'd been told earlier by Tate's father. **Tell him yes.**

For the first time in days, Logan felt his lips twitch, wanting to grin as he refolded the piece of paper and slipped it back in the jacket pocket.

Of course, he thought as he pressed play on his phone. *Even when you're finally ready to give me what I want, you're going to tease me a little first.*

As Peter Gabriel's "Solsbury Hill" filled the room, Logan stood, placed the jacket on the chair, and then leaned down until he was close enough to press his lips to Tate's forehead. "Come on, Tate. It's time to wake up and tell me yes."

* * *

LOGAN COULDN'T REMEMBER how he'd ended up in Cole's car, but when his eyes opened and he realized where he was, he sat up like someone had jolted him with electricity.

How the…"What the fuck, Cole?" he demanded as he glowered at his brother.

Cole took his eyes off the road and looked over to him with a frown of concern on his face. "You need a shower, brother. A shower, some food, and maybe, oh I don't know, ten minutes of uninterrupted shut-eye."

"Fuck you. Take me back."

"No," Cole told him, and Logan had the urge to punch him square in the jaw.

"Take. Me. Back."

"No."

That answer was really pissing him off, and as Logan unbuckled his seatbelt, Cole reached across and stilled his hand.

"Think about what you're doing. Do you really think you'll be any good for Tate if you can't function? If you yourself get sick?"

Logan wanted to tell him to go to hell, but the smart fucker had a point. Cole released his hold and brought his hand back to the steering wheel as he wove them through the quiet streets.

"I won't pretend to understand what you're going through, but I will tell you this: If that were Rachel in there and you were pulling this shit…I'd want to fucking kill you. But think for just a minute and you'll realize we're trying to help you."

Choosing to bite his angry words back, Logan glared out the front window and remained silent. Cole was right. He did want to kill him. He was furious that he'd taken him away from Tate. *What if something happens and I'm not there?*

"Shelly promised that, if anything changed… Hey?" Cole stopped talking and snapped his fingers.

Logan turned his head to look at him.

Then he continued. "If *anything* changes, she will call."

Logan didn't bother responding. He went back to staring out the window as Cole continued to talk.

"Rachel went home with Lena so she could watch her, and *you* are stuck with me."

"How wonderful," Logan muttered.

"What was that?"

"I *said*, 'How fucking wonderful.'"

"Logan..." Cole sighed.

"What?"

"You were like a fucking zombie when you came out of his room. You were barely coherent. You need to refuel."

Rolling his eyes, Logan shook his head and spat out, "How do you know what I need? I need to be there. With him."

Cole turned into the parking garage of Logan's condo, and as he punched the code in and drove into the visitor's area, he remained silent. It wasn't until he drew the car to a stop and pulled the keys from the ignition that Cole really let him have it.

"Listen to me for a second. I know you want to be there. But there's no fucking way I'm going to sit there and let your health go to shit. I have three people I'm currently worried about, and if I can get you remotely off the 'is he going to fall the fuck apart' list, that would be pretty damn awesome. You got it?"

Logan shoved the car door open and managed to get himself out, which was a feat in itself considering how shaky his legs were. Gripping the side of the car, he held on to it for a moment as everything started to spin around him. He felt like shit, and before he knew that it was going to happen, Logan grabbed his stomach, and threw up all over the concrete floor.

"Shit, Logan, are you okay?"

As Cole's words hit his ears, Logan's stomach convulsed a second time, and whatever was left inside him came out exactly as the first round had.

Jesus... What the hell is going on?

"You're a goddamned mess," Cole said as he wrapped his arm around his back and clutched his waist.

Logan's head hung down and his hair flopped in his eyes as the stress, the shock, and *fuck*, everything else finally took its toll.

"Upstairs. Come on. We need to get you upstairs." Cole pulled him up until he could sling his arm over his shoulders.

Logan brought bleary eyes up to his. "'Kay," he finally agreed.

"Can I just say how grateful I am that you waited until you were outside of the car to do that?"

Logan swallowed a gulp of air at the acrid taste in his mouth. He really did need a shower and, now, his toothbrush and toothpaste. After hobbling across the lot with Cole, he leaned on the wall and waited for the elevator.

When they got inside, one of Cole's eyebrows rose as he asked, "You going to be okay in here?"

Logan managed a small nod before the elevator took them up to his floor.

Cole got him down the hall and into his condo, and as the door shut behind them, Cole said, "Come on. You need a shower. Then, once you feel up to it, I'll take you back. I promise. You'll be there when he wakes."

Logan staggered into his dark living room, Cole's words repeating in his head. As he stopped and looked out his balcony doors to a view he thought would forever make him happy, he now found himself wondering if he'd ever know that feeling again.

When Cole had walked farther into his place, Logan finally voiced his biggest fear. "What if he never wakes?"

"He will."

Logan rounded on Cole and demanded, "What if he doesn't? You didn't see him, Cole. He's hooked up to so many damn machines it was hard to tell where they ended and he began. Fuck, I feel sick again."

Cole took a step toward him and gripped his shoulder in one hand and his chin with the other. "You okay?"

The question could've had many different answers, but all of them were summed up with his quiet, "No."

"We're all here for you, okay? For whatever you need. Work is covered. Food is covered. Lena and Mason are going to bring some by. We're going to get through this, and *when* Tate wakes up, we're all going to kick his ass."

Logan nodded as he sniffed back the tears that wouldn't stop forming. "Fucking tears. I've never cried so much in my whole life."

Cole pulled him into a tight hug and said into his ear, "You cry as much as you want to. You hear me? It doesn't do any good to keep shit bottled up. It just finds other ways out. Like through your damn stomach. Right?"

Logan thumped his brother's back. Cole was right—as usual. But that's not what truly terrified him.

"I don't know what I'll do if he doesn't wake up. I don't think I can do this. I mean, this… It's… It's—"

"He's going to wake up." Cole pulled back, and Logan was shocked to see that his brother's eyes were glistening. "That guy—he's a determined one, and he's a fighter. He fought for you, didn't he?"

Logan nodded.

"Exactly. So go and shower, lie down for thirty minutes, and then I'll take you back to him. Deal?"

Logan walked past him, and when he got to the door to his bedroom, he looked back to see Cole walking over to the balcony doors, running a hand through his hair. He'd brought his phone out of his pocket, and as Logan stood there, he heard his brother greet his wife.

"Rach? Hey, how are you?" He paused and then said quite reverently, "I love you so much. Please take care of yourself."

Yes, if ever there were a time to tell someone, it's now, Logan thought as he made his way to the shower—alone.

Chapter Seventeen

BEEP… BEEP… BEEP…

What is that noise? Tate thought as he tried to force his eyes open. They felt heavy as lead, and after several attempts, they finally decided to obey and everything around him came into view. *A white, blurry view.*

He blinked a couple of times, figuring he must've been in one hell of a deep sleep, then tried again. He heard the incessant beeping sound around him, and as the fog started to dissipate and the room came into sharper focus, Tate realized that something was definitely not right. In fact, it was very wrong.

There was a throbbing ache down his right side, and one of his arms was wrapped with a bandage, trapped across his chest, holding his shoulder immobile. In the other hand, he had an IV.

An IV… The hospital… The excruciating ache in my shoulder… What the hell happened? Where is Logan?

His eyes searched the room until they skidded to a stop on the back of a short, dark-haired woman—*Rachel.* He opened his mouth and said her name, but was shocked at the raspy sound that emerged. It didn't sound anything like him, and "Rachel" had come out sounding more like "Ray."

The woman standing over by the glass door turned anyway, and as Diana's face came into view, Tate's heart stuttered.

What the hell is she *doing here?* was his first thought, but he quickly pushed that aside as his eyes frantically shifted to the other side of the room.

Nobody else was in there with them. Just him and Diana—in a hospital room.

Jesus, did I fall asleep and wake up in the fucking Twilight Zone? And where is Logan?

"Oh, God. Thank God. You're awake." Diana sounded so stunned that it occurred to him that maybe she'd…what? Never expected him to be?

Tate swallowed, about to try to speak again, but his throat felt as though it were on fire—not to mention scratched to shit.

"No, don't try to talk," she rushed to say as she walked over to him.

Tate tracked her suspiciously as his pulse started to race and his anxiety level rose. *What happened to me?* He tried to remember how he'd ended up in the hospital, but he was coming up with nothing, and still…*no Logan. Where the fuck is he?*

"Your parents just stepped outside. They're going to want to see you. Oh, and the doctors," she rambled on.

But when she leaned down to kiss his forehead, Tate

managed to grab the wrist she had resting by his hand on the bed. He took it between his fingers, and as she stilled, their eyes connected. It was the first time he'd gotten a clear look at her, and she looked like hell—as if she hadn't slept for months.

Tate opened his mouth, and as his dry lips parted, he tried to speak. He didn't care where his parents were. He didn't even care about seeing the doctors. What he wanted—*no*. What he needed was to know where Logan was.

Why isn't he here with me? Did something happen to him?

When nothing came out, he shut his eyes, frustrated at his inability to voice his thoughts. And that was when Diana placed her mouth by his ear.

"Don't worry. He's here." When she raised her head, Tate barely recognized the soft expression in her eyes as she stroked her fingers across his forehead. "He's been here every day since you arrived."

Tate frowned, now wondering how long that had been—

"I have to get the doctors. You stay right there," she told him as she backed away to the door.

Her smile was so genuine that it reminded him of the girl he'd known a long time ago, and it left him thinking that maybe he really *had* woken up in the Twilight Zone.

* * *

A DAY. A week. Three had passed by in a haze, and every night, Logan had been ushered back to Tate's room to sit by his bed while his family left to go home.

It wasn't until a couple of days ago, somewhere in the fourth week, that Tate had finally started to show signs of improvement. The doctors had removed the drain on his right side and extubated him from the vents. Now, a full forty-eight hours later, he was breathing on his own.

Each day, Logan had been shuffled between the two rooms, refusing to leave except when Cole demanded it. He would sit and wait for any kind of information indicating improvement, but as the month had passed by, he'd started to believe that it wasn't going to happen—until this week.

With his head resting back on the wall, Logan sat in the far corner of the now familiar room and waited for the head nurse to let him know that it was time for him to go back. He wasn't exactly sure what Tate's father had told the staff of the ICU, but every time he entered the area, they all looked at him with curiosity.

"Mr. Mitchell?"

Logan sat up and got to his feet, making his way over to where the nurse was standing by the doors. As he started to wander down the hall with her, she turned in his direction and smiled.

"I don't know if anyone has told you yet, but Mr. Morrison woke up tonight."

Logan faltered and then stopped in the middle of the

hall. When the nurse realized he was no longer walking beside him, she came back over to where he was standing.

"What did you say?"

"I'm assuming no one *did* tell you." She placed a hand on his arm. "He's awake."

"Since when?" Logan asked, hardly recognizing his voice.

He'd barely functioned these last few weeks, other than to sit and talk to the silent man lying in the ICU. So this news—this news gave him hope. And it was the sound of *that* that he didn't recognize—because until right then, he hadn't realized he'd lost it.

"Around thirty minutes ago. His family was in there, but they just left."

Logan reached for the wall beside him. *He's awake… He woke up?*

"This is a good thing," the nurse encouraged, and finally he managed a nod. "Would you like to come and see him?"

More than my next breath, Logan thought and stood up straight. "Yes. God, yes."

He followed her down the hall, and when he stepped into the ICU area, three of the other nurses behind the station were smiling at him. Two of them he recognized, but the third was a tall blonde he'd never seen before, and as she made her way around the desk toward him, Logan looked behind himself to make sure she was heading in his direction.

"You're Logan, right?"

Logan shoved his hands into the pockets of his jeans and nodded.

She gave a cute little smirk and said, "Mr. Morrison has been quite adamant that he doesn't want to see any other person's face, including the doctor's, until he sees Logan."

A full-on smile stretched across his lips. *That stubborn shit…*"Is that right?"

"Yes. I was the first person to speak to him after Diana came to tell us he'd woken. He's having a hard time vocalizing right now due to the tubes that were down his throat. But he wrote this and gave it to me when I was in there getting his vitals with his parents."

Logan took the piece of paper from her, and when he opened it, he saw: **I want to see Logan. NOW.**

Logan clenched it in his fist as he brought it to his mouth and sucked in a gulp of air.

"Are you okay?" she asked, concerned as she touched his arm.

"Yeah," he let out on a relieved sigh. "Yeah. I've never been better. Can I see him?"

She walked over to Tate's door. "I think he'd like that very much."

When she opened it, Logan moved toward it, wondering if he'd ever felt such anticipation. The answer to that was easy—no, he fucking hadn't.

He couldn't wait to see Tate.

As he stepped inside and his eyes finally collided with the gorgeous, brown ones he'd so desperately missed, Logan shook his head.

"You, Mr. Morrison, are in *so* much trouble."

* * *

TATE HAD BEEN waiting for what seemed like hours for this very second. He'd been going out of his mind while the nurse had been checking his temperature, blood pressure, and every other fucking vital she'd needed to check. And then his damn parents had been fawning all over him, and he…he couldn't have cared less.

This was the person he wanted to see. The person he *needed* to see. And as Logan got closer to him, Tate found himself trying to sit up in the bed.

"No, no," Logan told him, wagging his finger back and forth as though he were scolding him. "You stay just as you are."

Tate watched him stop and take the seat by his side, and when Logan reached for his hand and entwined their fingers, he finally felt things start to fall back into place.

Damn, Tate thought. Logan was clearly trying to put up a strong front, but… *He looks a breath away from shattering*. As Logan's eyes roved over him and his fingers tightened around his, Tate's fluttered shut.

Yes, that feels familiar. It felt right. And when Logan brought their fingers to his mouth to kiss them, Tate opened his eyes and turned his hand so he could stroke his fingers over the dark stubble covering Logan's jaw. He traced them up and over his ear and then pushed them through his silky, black hair. The sound that left Logan was somewhere between pleasure and anguish as he leaned over and pressed his cheek to his thigh.

"Tate…God. Oh, God. These last few weeks…"

Logan's eyes were shut, but he kept talking, trying to explain what he was feeling. Tate stroked the hair away from his face and saw tears falling down his cheek. It was clear by the tormented words and trembling in Logan's body—he'd been through hell.

As Tate tried to soothe him, he opened his mouth and *made* himself speak. "Logan."

His voice was barely audible, but Logan's eyes opened. And when he told him, "Shh," Tate shook his head and forced his lips to move and get his words out.

"Love you."

Logan got to his feet then and pressed their lips together in a kiss filled with all the overwhelming emotions neither of them could put into words. Tate closed his eyes, taking in the scent of him, and when he finally pulled away and offered a shaky smile, Tate noticed that it didn't quite reach his blue eyes.

"I love you too."

Tate grimaced. "I'm sorry—"

"Don't," Logan said, cutting him off and brushing one of his curls aside as he bent back down over him. "Don't you dare apologize. You did nothing wrong. You did everything right." Logan brought his lips by his ear, and their cheeks were touching as he whispered, "You woke up."

When Logan straightened, Tate felt a keen sense of déjà vu, and he noticed that Logan was wearing his leather jacket. His lips curved as he nodded up at him and said, "You dared me to."

* * *

HOW DOES HE know that? Logan stared down at Tate's upturned face and couldn't resist the urge to touch him again. He ran his fingers across one of his eyebrows and down the side of his cheek to his chin. *Does that mean he heard me talking every night?*

"And how would you know that?"

Tate seemed almost as confused as *he* felt, and then he shrugged his non-bandaged shoulder. "Dunno. Will…" he started but coughed.

Logan looked around and spotted a pad of paper and a pen. He brought it back and gave it to Tate. "Don't try to talk right now. Write it."

Tate took the pen and scrawled on the pad: **Tell me what happened?**

Logan read the request and sat back in the chair. "No one has told you?"

Haven't asked. Wanted to see you.

"So badly you didn't ask why you were in the hospital? Have to say, you're doing wonders for my ego right now."

Tate wrote something else, and Logan peered over at it and chuckled.

"You don't look so great yourself, FYI. But I suppose that's acceptable after being hit by a car."

When Tate winced, Logan nodded. "Yeah. If you think for one fucking minute I'm letting you ride that damn bike of yours again, forget it."

Tate sighed and then wrote: **How long have I been here?**

"It's the third of September, so nearly a month," Logan answered as he crossed his arms over his chest.

Tate's eyes became so wide that, if it weren't so tragic, it would've been comical. Logan couldn't begin to imagine how he was feeling. He'd had a hard enough time waiting for Tate to recover. How must it have felt to be the one waking from pretty much a month of his life gone?

Trying to lighten the mood a little, Logan shrugged. "Yeah. And I never thought I'd say this, but you need a haircut."

Tate glanced down his body to the tabs stuck to his chest

and his bandaged arm then brought his eyes back to his.

"Yep, you went all out. Broken ribs, broken clavicle, couldn't breathe on your own. I mean…" Logan stopped as he remembered Tate lying there with tubes taped to his mouth and ribs and the machines surrounding his head, and he lost his ability to keep it cool. "Fuck, Tate, I thought you were going to die… It was…"

"Hey," Tate's voice rasped, and Logan looked into his solemn eyes before Tate lowered them to write on the paper.

Sorry you went through that.

Logan sat forward to rest his elbows on the bed and pressed his lips to his steepled hands. "It was worth every hellish hour just to see you awake and looking at me again."

When Tate reached out a hand to touch his, Logan took it. "My parents?"

Logan grimaced at that question and shook his head. "Have been here every day."

The scowl on Tate's face had Logan rubbing a hand over his own. He understood that reaction. It had been his at first too. But after having a month to comprehend the anguish they must've been feeling, he had—

Did you call them?

Logan rebuffed that with a shake of his head. "No. But that brings up a very important discussion you and I need to have. Your emergency contact is still listed as Diana."

"Shit."

Logan gave him a tight smile. "Yes. Getting in to see you was a fucking nightmare. I was going out of my mind. But…" He let his next words loop in his head before he said them out loud. He wasn't quite sure how Tate would react to them. "Your father gave permission for me to be back here in the evenings, but only after they would leave. Your mother still doesn't know."

A flush of annoyance colored Tate's cheeks and his jaw tightened.

Logan tried to calm him by saying, "He was pretty decent, all things considered."

Tate grabbed the paper out of his hand and furiously wrote. When he thrust it back at him, his eyes were alight with anger.

Permission? I'm not fucking ten. Where have you been this whole time?

Logan ran a hand through his hair then said softly, "Out in the general waiting room."

"For a fucking month?" Tate's voice cracked around the words.

"Hey," Logan said, and trapped Tate's hands between his palms. "I got to see you every night. That got me through."

Logan kept his eyes on Tate's, making sure he knew he was telling him the truth, but when Tate's eyes started to fill and a lone tear slipped free, Logan wiped it away.

"Don't you cry for me. It's time for you to get better. I

now have *your* permission to be in here whenever the hell I want, and you know what? There will be no slacking, Mr. Morrison. It's time for you to come home."

Tate blinked away the tears and mouthed, "Yes."

Logan winked back at him and said, "Just so you know, that doesn't count. And it won't until you're back on your feet, giving me hell, and then *telling* me yes."

And with that, nothing more needed to be said. The challenge had been issued, and the prize was now within reach.

Chapter Eighteen

"COME ON. IT'S all ready." Logan's voice echoed down the hall to where Tate was seated on the couch.

"You're really going to make me do this?" he asked as Logan walked into the living room and crossed his arms. He'd rolled the sleeves up on his black, knit pullover and was barefoot in his jeans as he stood there with his brow raised, tapping his foot.

"Yes, I am. So come on. Time to get up," Logan said, holding his hand out.

Tate took it and got to his feet with a wince.

"This will do you good."

It had been a couple of hours since he'd been released from the hospital and gotten a haircut, and ever since then, Logan hadn't stopped—until now.

"I don't remember the doctor saying anything about this," Tate pointed out.

"Everyone knows that a soak in a bathtub is good for sore muscles."

"Really? And how many times have you used this bath of yours after a long, hard workout?"

Logan wrapped an arm around his waist and smiled at him. "Never. But we aren't discussing me."

As Tate leaned against Logan's side, he rolled his eyes. "Of course not. You do remember the doctor saying I can walk on my own now, right? I'm also allowed to bathe myself."

Logan stopped them at the bathroom door and scrunched his face up. "Yeah, but where's the fun in that for me?"

Tate chuckled. Logan had been amazing since he'd woken up two weeks ago. Hell, from what he'd been told by the hospital staff, he had been pretty damn wonderful the entire time he'd been unconscious. Not only had he spent each night by his bed, they'd told him that he would play music, read to him, and even, at times, yell at him.

He studied Logan's side profile and smiled. Tate had no trouble believing that Logan would get frustrated at him while he was lying out cold, and every now and then, when he closed his eyes and really thought back, he almost remembered parts of it.

"Okay. I'll get in the bath if you—" His words came to an abrupt stop when he spotted the tub filled with… "Bubbles? You ran me a *bubble bath?*"

"Of course," Logan said. "That's the only way to take a bath, isn't it?"

"How would you know, since you've never had one?"

Logan's lips twitched as he looked from the tub back to him. "I watch TV?"

"Mhmm. And what kind of bubble bath is it?"

Logan gave a small shrug and helped him over to the sink, where Tate rested against the vanity. "I don't know. Lavender or some shit. The woman told me it was soothing."

"Did she?"

"Yep, she sure did," Logan said, examining the sling strapped around his shoulder. "So the doc said we could take it off for a little and then put it back on, right?"

Tate nodded. "Right."

"And you feel okay? You don't need to lie down?"

"Logan?"

Logan brought his worried eyes back to his.

"I feel fine. And I'd love a bath. Thank you."

"Okay," Logan answered, tapping his fingers against his lips in concentration. "We should take off your clothes, then."

Finding Logan's nerves endearing, Tate waited to see what he would do next, and when he didn't move, he asked, "Are *you* okay?"

"Yes. Of course."

"You sure? Because I can do this later. By myself." He didn't want Logan uncomfortable in any way, and if helping him take a bath crossed too many lines—

"No. That's not it. I…" Logan sighed. "It's stupid."

"Tell me," he coaxed.

Logan looked at the bath, a sheepish expression crossing his face. "I don't want to hurt you. That's all."

Tate took Logan's hand, and when their fingers touched, Logan faced him. It was high time to lighten the mood around them, and why not start here? He couldn't imagine the stress Logan had been under for the last month and a half, and as he stood in front of him, exposing his most vulnerable side, it just made Tate love him even more.

"How about we make this fun and concentrate less on all these ugly bruises and scars. I know something you never can say no to. Truth or dare," he suggested with a flirty wink.

Logan let his eyes run down over him, one of his eyebrows winging up. "Hardly fair considering I'd be the one doing all the dares."

"Not necessarily," Tate disagreed. "Who said a dare has to be something you *do*. It could be something said, something promised in the future… You're smart. You get the idea."

Logan's full lips came together as he mulled it over. Then the usual spark that filled his eyes was back. "Okay, I'm game."

"I'm glad. I would've been disappointed if you'd said no."

"How disappointed?"

"You'll never know. But since I thought of this, it's only fair that I go first."

Logan scoffed at his deductive reasoning, but then he raised his hand and crooked his fingers in a gesture that screamed, *Bring it.*

"Truth or dare?" Tate asked.

Of course, the first choice out of Logan's mouth was, "Dare."

Tate wondered what Logan thought he would ask. Probably something outrageous, maybe something sexual. "I dare you to stop thinking about how I looked weeks ago and start looking at me standing here and *now.*"

* * *

WELL, OKAY, THEN, Logan thought as Tate's words penetrated his brain. *Not what I expected.* "And how am I looking at you?"

"Like I'm still hooked up to—"

"Two breathing machines, a heart monitor, and around ten different IVs?" As Logan relayed the picture that would forever be imprinted in his mind, he took a step closer to Tate so their bare toes were touching.

"Yes," Tate said. "Exactly like that."

Logan reached for the buckle of the strap holding Tate's shoulder brace secure. After he gently unfastened it and slipped it from his arm, he placed it on the sink beside him and then fingered the red shirt Tate was wearing. "I don't know that I can do that."

Tate's hand covered his as he started to undo the top button. "I dare you to try."

Logan's lips curved at Tate's choice of words. "Talk about coming full circle."

"Mhmm. Come to think of it, I seem to remember a time in your bathroom just like this."

"Ahh, yes," Logan said with a sigh, slipping the first two buttons free. "But I was a lot more naked, and *you* were a lot more nervous."

"That's because I wasn't sure about you."

"And now?" he asked, and when he stopped what he was doing and waited for his answer, Tate looked surprised.

"Truth?"

Logan tugged on his shirt and gave a mock glare. "Of course. That's the game, isn't it?"

When Tate captured his lips, Logan's automatically parted. The feel and taste of Tate made him moan softly as Tate traced his tongue along his lower lip.

He said, "I've never been more sure of another person in all my life."

Logan's hands clutched Tate's shirt as he whispered his name reverently, and while they stood there in silence, the understanding of just how much they meant to one another was solidified.

"It's your turn," Tate said against his lips, finally breaking the connection.

Logan walked around behind him and helped him remove his shirt, and when he dropped it on the counter, he said in Tate's ear, "Dare."

Tate glanced back at him and gave that pearly grin he'd fallen for. "I dare you to get in the bath with me and smell like a lavender field for the next twenty-four hours."

Logan laughed at that, looking down at the tub before returning his gaze to Tate's. "I don't know. Do you think you can behave yourself?"

"Me?" Tate asked like he thought the question was absurd.

"Yes, *you*," he stressed, enjoying Tate's incredulity. He came around in front of him to undo the button of Tate's jeans, and as he slid the zipper down, he continued to talk. "The doctor said there was to be no…" When his words trailed off, Tate the tease came out to play.

"No?"

Logan narrowed his eyes on him and ended with, "No *strenuous* activity until you pass all the tests at your follow-up appointment and all the boxes are ticked."

The amusement stamped over Tate's face had Logan wondering how he'd managed to turn the tables on him. No one ever got the better of him—*well, no one except for Tate.*

Rolling his shoulders, Logan heard himself asking in a much more irked voice than he'd intended, "Is something amusing you?"

Tate clamped his lips shut and shook his head. "Nope. You going to take my pants off now, or do you think I should keep them on so I'm not tempted to do anything…strenuous?"

Logan slipped his fingers inside the waist of Tate's jeans. Then he mumbled, "Sure, laugh it up," as he crouched down, taking the denim and boxers with him.

When he was at Tate's feet, he sized up his naked body and was more than satisfied with the healing progress he was making. The horrendous bruising that had discolored Tate's ribs was starting to fade, and the incision where the tube had been was almost healed.

As he let his eyes continue up to the ones staring down at him, Logan tapped Tate's ankle. "Lift."

Tate lifted, and as Logan pulled the pants away and repeated the move with the other, he asked him, "Truth or dare?"

As he stood and faced Tate, who was now completely naked, he shocked him by saying, "Dare."

* * *

TATE DIDN'T TAKE his eyes off Logan as he continued to carefully study him. When Logan looked up at him from his feet and his eyes zeroed in on his bruises, he wondered what he was thinking. Would he ever see him the way he used to? *Enter my stupid decision of a dare.*

Really, when it came to Logan he should've known better. The guy would always find a way to come out ahead of the game, and of course, he managed to pick the most difficult of things—even when on the surface, it appeared to be the easiest.

"I dare you to keep your eyes open, and on my face, when I take off all my clothes."

That arrogant ass, Tate thought as he looked over Logan.

Considering that this was the first time they'd been truly alone for close to two months, *that* particular request seemed like the most impossible thing Logan could've asked.

But Tate was determined. He was the one who'd started this, and he'd be damned if he cracked first. "Easy."

"So confident," Logan said as he reached down and drew his shirt over his head.

Tate swallowed and watched him toss it on the counter.

"Should I tell you what I'm doing?" Logan asked, lowering his eyes over him. "Oh, would you look at that. I don't think you need me to tell you. You're imagining it all on your own."

Tate shut his eyes, but Logan was quick to say, "Uh ah, no cheating. Eyes open, Tate."

"Fuck you."

Logan removed his boxers and jeans, and when he was standing back up, he took a step toward him and grinned.

"That is exactly the kind of strenuous activity I was referring to. *See?* You are the one who needs to behave himself."

Tate grit his teeth as he continued to look Logan in the eye. This close, he could see the dark flecks of blue around his pupils. He really did have the most amazing eyes Tate had ever seen.

"I did it," he answered stubbornly.

"Yes, you did. So I believe it's your turn."

Tate let his eyes rove all over Logan, soaking in the sight before him. He was fucking beautiful, and Tate wanted to touch him. But the game was not over yet, so he asked, "Truth or dare?"

And quick as a flash, Logan answered, "Truth."

"Will you *ever* see me the way you did before?"

Tate held his breath as Logan's eyes darkened. He hadn't realized how important this question was to him. But ever since he'd woken up, Logan had acted…perfect. He'd handled him with the utmost care, and as he raised his hands to cup his cheeks, Tate discovered he was scared. Scared that Logan would forever see him as damaged.

"No," Logan finally said, and Tate felt his heart sink. "I'll never see you that way again. Because before this, I didn't know you were essential for me to feel alive."

Tate let out the breath he'd been holding and brought his hands up to cover Logan's as they stood there in the bathroom—stripped of their clothes and baring their souls.

He closed his eyes when Logan's lips caressed his in a kiss so sweet that Tate's toes curled against the tile floor. Then Logan's mouth curved and he said, "But don't think for a minute I'm not counting the hours until that follow-up visit. However, until then, you're off-limits. So quit being so fucking sexy, okay?"

Tate's laugh rumbled out of his throat, and Logan released him to walk over to the tub. He held a hand out for him to use and steady himself, and as Tate climbed in, he groaned. The hot water felt amazing.

Logan stepped in behind him, sat with his back against the tub, and invited him with a crook of his finger to sit down between his legs. "Come here."

He should've looked ridiculous amongst the mountains of bubbles, but as Logan smiled up at him, Tate thought he looked incredibly inviting.

Carefully, he lowered himself down and nestled between Logan's thighs. As he rested his head against Logan's shoulder, he felt him twine his legs over his. Then Tate closed his eyes, luxuriating in the safety of the body surrounding his.

Maybe he did like being looked after a little. He just wanted to know that Logan was aware that he was the same person he'd always been.

"Logan?"

"Hmm?"

"It's your turn to ask," he said, arching his head toward

the fingers Logan was threading through his hair.

"Truth or dare?" Logan asked and then kissed his temple.

Tate licked the condensation off his lips and replied, "Truth."

The silence that settled around them was comfortable and felt as warm as Logan's embrace—until Tate heard the question.

"If you told me yes today, would it be because you think you have to or because you want to?"

Tate's eyes opened, and he grasped the side of the tub with his left hand, pulling himself up so he could turn. He knew exactly what Logan was asking, and as he looked at him, his black hair slicked back from his face, Logan's eyes held his in a bold-as-hell stare. Logan wanted this answer, and he wasn't going to be put off.

Tate maneuvered himself as close as he could get to Logan in their positions and said just as boldly, "I wanted to and should've said yes the first time you asked. I didn't because I wanted to be able to give you something in return."

Logan started to speak, but Tate placed his wet finger over his lips. "Shh. This is my truth, remember?"

Logan silently inclined his head, and Tate continued.

"I want to say yes right now, but I don't think you'd believe me. Not in here," he said, moving his fingers down to Logan's heart. "I think you'd always wonder. So it's my turn to wait. Two, three days… Hell, Logan, I'll wait forever. But my answer will never change. So when you're ready to really hear me, ask. And I'll tell you."

Logan didn't say a word, continuing to hold his gaze until Tate decided he should let him off the hook and then turned around to settle back against him.

He understood Logan's showing caution—he didn't want a decision from someone who was feeling vulnerable and needy. He wanted it from a man who was strong and sure of himself.

I'll get better, prove to him that I'm the same—

"Tate?" Logan's voice cut into his thoughts.

"Yeah?"

He felt warm lips by his ear as Logan carefully wrapped his arms around him and asked, "Will you move in with me? I don't even care where. I've waited long enough, and I don't want to wait another second."

Tate turned his head, and as Logan looked down at him expectantly, he simply said, "Yes."

Chapter Nineteen

THE NEXT MORNING, Logan stood at the foot of his bed and tightened the knot in his tie. Tate was silently watching him from where he was lying with two pillows propped up behind him, and Logan had to fight the urge to climb back in beside him and call in one last day.

"Okay, I put my numbers on the side table next to you. There's the main office, Sherry's desk, my direct number, and my—"

"Logan," Tate interrupted with a grin.

"Yeah?"

"I'll be fine. I have your number in my cell. If I need anything, I'll call."

Logan dropped his hands to his sides and came around to sit on the bed. He took Tate's fingers in his hand and rolled his eyes at himself. "I'm acting like a moron, aren't I?"

"No," Tate laughed. "You're acting like you care."

He sighed, leaning forward to rub his smooth cheek along Tate's stubbled one. "Of course I care. And I want to know that you have every way imaginable to reach me if you need to."

"You're only going in for half a day," Tate reminded him.

"So? A lot can happen in four hours."

Tate turned his head, and when their eyes met, he said, "I'm going to get up, eat breakfast, and then watch some TV. Then I'm going to get in the cab you're insisting I take to meet you for lunch."

"Good," Logan said. "And then we're going to—"

"Cancel my lease."

Logan kissed his lips and then lightly nipped his bottom one. "See, that sounds like the perfect day."

"Of course it does, bossy."

"And?" Logan challenged.

Tate pulled his fingers away so he could touch his cheek. "And nothing. I kind of like you bossy."

"Do you?"

"Sometimes," Tate was quick to add.

"I'll have to remember that. For later."

"You do that. Now, go to work. Otherwise they're going to think you quit."

Logan got off the bed and walked to his closet. As he shrugged into his jacket, he looked back at Tate and asked, "Are you sure you're okay about moving in here? I don't mind if we look—"

Tate started to laugh then—really laugh.

"Okay," Logan stressed, knowing he was acting like a nervous shit. "I get it. You said yes. You meant yes. I'm going now."

He made his way to the bedroom door but stopped when Tate said his name.

"Yeah?"

"Don't forget to wear a scarf and coat. Weather said it was going to be icy this morning."

A wide grin split Logan's lips and he nodded. "Yes, *dear*."

"Oh, and Logan?"

Logan cocked his head to the side. "Hmm?"

"Love you."

Damn, Logan thought. *Every time he says it, my heart just about stops.*

"I love you too. See you at one, Tate. Don't make me wait."

* * *

AN HOUR LATER, Tate had already received two phone calls and one text from Logan. All under the guise of forgetting something when it was more than obvious he was checking up on him. It was cute, but he knew that if he said *that,* Logan would go from concerned to annoyed in the blink of an eye.

What had he once told him? *Oh yeah. Puppies were cute. Not him.*

Tate was still grinning over the last text when the intercom in the condo buzzed. Not expecting anyone, he made his way over to it and hit the answer button.

"Good morning, Mr. Morrison."

The fact that the doorman knew his name was the first shock Tate got.

The second came when he told him, "I have a man down here who says he's your father. Can I let him up?"

Tate stared at the black box in front of him and felt his hand start shaking.

How the hell did he know where to find me?

Things had been tense after he'd woken up at the hospital. His mother had refused to come into the room while Logan was there, so that pretty much meant that, from the moment he'd woken to when he'd been released, he'd seen his parents twice. And each time had resulted in close to radio silence.

He couldn't believe that, after everything he'd gone through, they still couldn't get past their warped views on his love life. Considering what they'd put him through, he thought they were lucky he'd agreed to see them at all. Just thinking about them making Logan wait outside every day had him—

"Sir?"

Tate closed his eyes and let out a breath, wondering

what the hell his father could possibly want. "Yeah. Let him up," he said and then released the button.

He rubbed his hand over his face and waited—waited for the inevitable disappointment that would come when he looked into the eyes he'd once trusted above all others.

* * *

IT HAD TAKEN a little over an hour for Logan to get through his stack of mail. As he leaned back in his chair and removed his glasses, he clicked on his e-mail and winced at the number of unopened messages that came up.

Placing his glasses on the desk, he pinched the bridge of his nose between his fingers.

"Um, Mr. Mitchell?"

"Yes, Sherry?" he said, spotting his PA standing just inside his door.

"Mr. Madison wanted to know if you had a minute to go and see him."

Logan glanced at the clock and nodded. "Yeah. Can you let him know I'll be down there in five minutes?"

"Sure thing," she said with a smile, and then she took a careful step farther into the office with a pad of paper in her hand. "Mr. Mitchell?"

"Yes?" Logan asked as he clicked open the first email.

"I just wanted to say I was very sorry to hear about Tate.

We all were. But we're so thrilled to hear he's doing well and back at home with you."

Yes, Logan thought as he stopped reading the e-mail. *I definitely like the sound of that. At home. With me.*

"Thank you, Sherry. I'll make sure to pass it along to him."

"Oh, well, that's the thing. We'd like to send him a basket of goodies or something. And the girls and I were wondering what he likes."

Logan felt a spark of mischief as he said, "He likes nuts."

Sherry rolled her eyes. "Really, Logan?"

Logan laughed at the use of his first name. It was rare that she used it, but when she did, it was usually because he'd said something outrageous.

"Sorry. I couldn't help myself, and it's actually the truth. He does like them."

She gave him a look designed to make him feel like a scolded little boy—and it worked. "What kind? And do not give me some smart-mouthed response, mister."

Logan picked his glasses up and stood, wandering around his desk until he stopped in front of her. "He loves hazelnuts. So I'm betting he'd love those roasted ones, you know—"

"From the confectionary store downstairs? Yes, I know the ones."

Logan nodded. "Also cashews and almonds, salted."

Sherry's brow arched as he stepped around her, and

then she asked, "What? No, salty nut jokes?"

Logan walked out of his office and placed a hand to his chest, his mouth falling open. "Why, Sherry, I'm appalled. I would never..."

Shaking her head at him, she went to her desk, and he saw a small smile curl the edge of her mouth. "It's good to have you back, Mr. Mitchell."

Logan chuckled and turned on his heel to head to Cole's office, telling her, "It's good to be back."

* * *

TATE ALMOST JUMPED out of his skin when three knocks sounded on Logan's—*no, their*—front door. *Wow, is that weird to think about.*

When he reached for the handle, he reminded himself that this was now his home. No one had the right to make him feel uncomfortable in it. But as he came face to face with his father, all of those confident you-can-do-it words went right out the open door.

"William."

Tate gave a curt nod and then moved aside. "Do you want to come in?"

His father's eyes shifted beyond his shoulder, and when they came back to his, Tate said, "If you're checking to see if Logan's here, you're in luck. He went back to work today."

"I know."

As those two words registered, Tate's eyes narrowed. "What do you mean you know?"

"He told me he was going back today when you were released from the hospital."

Tate wasn't sure why that piece of information totally pissed him off, but it did. He gnashed his teeth together and waited in stubborn silence as he faced off with the man who had essentially thrown him out of his life only months before.

"I asked him because I wanted to know if anyone would be caring for you when you left."

It shamed Tate to feel the way he did in that moment, because instead of the concern he should've felt for his parent's anxiety, he just felt rage. He was furious at them.

Angry for the way they'd treated him the weekend he'd brought Logan home. Hurt at the easy way they'd cut him off as though he didn't exist, and after he'd been lying in a fucking hospital room, *dying*—they'd dared to ban the one person who gave a shit about him and had taken it upon themselves to control his life.

Well, fuck that.

He hadn't had a real opportunity to relay his particular feelings about it all, but he'd be damned if he welcomed them back into his life as if nothing had happened. Not that his mother had even bothered to show up.

Before he exploded right there in the hall for everyone to

hear, Tate walked back into the condo, leaving his father to either come inside or leave. He wasn't going to beg him to stay.

When he reached the balcony doors, Tate turned and saw him standing in the living room. It felt weird to have him there. His father's eyes seemed to get stuck on the bedroom door, and Tate wondered what he was thinking.

"What do you want?"

"Son—"

"Don't," Tate interrupted through grit teeth. "You don't get to call me that. Not anymore."

His father had the decency to look ashamed. Tate wasn't sure, but he was almost positive that he was remembering the afternoon he'd told him to leave and never come back.

"Tate," he said, this time using his middle name, the one given to him from *his* side of the family. "I..." he trailed off as if he weren't sure what to say and then scrubbed a hand over his tired face.

Tate shoved his hand into the pocket of his jeans while he waited for his father to speak. When his eyes finally made their way back to his, Tate decided that enough was enough.

"Look, I'm fine, okay? You've seen me. I didn't die. Now you can leave."

"Stop it, Tate."

"Stop what?" he boomed back at him. "God. How dare you," he said and turned away, unable to look at the face so similar to his own. "Do you know how many days I've waited for you and Mom to call me? To maybe stop by my old apartment and see me since you kicked me out of your house?"

When his father didn't answer, Tate faced him head on and said, "Every fucking day. But you know what I'd tell myself when Sunday rolled around and I'd hear nothing? That *you* were the ones who got rid of *me*. You threw me out. Not only out of your house. But out of your lives."

"Tate—"

"I'm not done," he snapped, walking across the room to where his father stood. "You're standing in Logan's home right now, which, coincidently, is also mine. And you're standing here because he has the kind of heart that you lack, an open one. He invited you here to his place when you were so quick to throw him out of yours. That's one of the reasons why I love him."

When his father's lips tightened, Tate squared his shoulders. "It's not going to change. This isn't a phase I'm going through, and if you spent just five minutes with him without all of your bullshit prejudices, you'd see why."

The silence that engulfed the room was filled with tension, but Tate was not going to back down. He'd meant every word he'd said, and if his father didn't like it—*then that's too damn bad.*

"I have spent time with him."

If he hadn't seen his father's lips move, Tate would've

believed he'd imagined the words. "What did you say?"

"I *have* spoken to Mr. Mitchell."

"His name's Logan. And telling him to get out of my hospital room doesn't count."

His father rubbed a hand over the grey stubble on his chin and frowned. "I know what his name is, Tate. I also know he owns his own law firm with his brother, Cole."

Tate's mouth opened, but he forgot what he was going to say. His dad slid his hands into his pockets and glanced around the condo.

"This sure is some place."

"Dad," Tate got out, glaring at him in a way that screamed, *Start talking.*

"He was there every day you were in that place. Every night too. The first time I saw him, your mother and I were being taken back to see you. He was arguing with a woman at the front desk who was refusing him permission to go back to you, and he looked murderous. He was like a man who had fought through hell to get to where he was and was being held back in the final moment."

Tate tried to imagine how he would've felt in Logan's position and couldn't. All he knew was that, every time the topic came up, Logan looked physically ill.

"I couldn't do anything at that point because your mother—"

"I don't care about that. You said you spoke to him,"

Tate said, more interested in what had happened between his father and Logan than anything else.

"I did. Several times. After I finally got back to see you and realized how bad it was, I told myself that, when you made it through surgery I would go get him—the one person I knew you would fight for. It wasn't us—it was him."

Tate clenched his hand in his pocket as he looked away from his father, not willing to be that vulnerable in front of him.

"Tate?"

When he raised his head, he saw that his father was now down the hall.

When he got to the door, he said, "I was wrong to say what I did that day you came by the house. You came looking for your father, and *I* wasn't there. Just know that I am now, son. If you ever need to look again."

And with that, he walked out the door.

* * *

LOGAN WAS ALMOST at Cole's office when his door opened and Christopher Walker sauntered out.

"Well, well. If it isn't the illustrious Mr. Mitchell who takes off on a whim and drops his new clients in his brother's lap."

Not wanting to get into any kind of conversation with

Chris, Logan chose to ignore him and went to walk by.

"Not even a 'good morning'?"

Logan glanced over at the slick architect he'd once found so attractive and wondered what he'd ever seen in him.

Perhaps it was his back… It'd be nice if he walked the fuck out, and I could decide for myself.

"Good morning, Mr. Walker."

Chris laughed, and the sound grated along his nerves as Logan stood there acting the part of polite owner in front of a staff with curious eyes. It was bad enough they'd all witnessed Tate's public outing. They didn't need to see a replay of his past.

"So, where have you been, Mitchell?"

"None of your business," he said quietly enough that no one would overhear.

"I disagree. You were my lawyer. That usually means I can rely on you if need be. Not have to wonder if you're off on some two-month vacation fucking your latest boy toy."

As the words left Chris's mouth, all Logan heard was the final snide remark, and there was nothing that could've held him back. Quick as a flash, he grabbed Chris's jacket and shoved him up against the wall.

"You're going to want to shut your mouth right about now," Logan growled at him, two seconds away from going completely postal.

"Touchy subject, huh? What happened? Did the sexy-haired guy leave too? Just can't hold a good man down, can you, Logan?"

"Shut the fuck up," he snarled.

"Logan!"

Cole's voice cut through the anger that had boiled to the surface and heated Logan's face, and when he felt a hand on his arm, he turned and saw Cole giving him a polite but stern "let go of him now" look.

He released Chris's jacket and backed away from him, telling himself to calm down. But it was too late. He'd already shown his hand. He'd snapped, lost his cool, and as the cocksure prick in front of him smirked, Logan felt the urge to wipe it right off his face.

"I believe you were on your way *out*," Cole said, and the tone suggested that Chris do just that and get the fuck out.

"I was. It's a pity that a firm with such a good reputation could drop the ball so easily with no explanation as to why. But then again, it doesn't surprise me when it comes to you two. You were always better at using your fists than your brains."

Logan was about to say something along the lines of, "Fuck you," when Cole stepped between them and told him in a voice he hadn't heard for years, "I explained that Mr. Mitchell would be out for some time. It is you who chose to make it an issue to deal with anyone else. I suggest that you collect your coat and get the hell out of our offices."

Chris looked between the two of them with disgust

before turning and storming out through the double glass doors. As Logan glanced around at their employees, he noticed that they'd all lowered their heads and were pretending not to pay attention, but several seemed to be holding back grins as they worked.

Christ, working here is becoming as entertaining as a night at a fucking peep show.

Then Cole turned to him, smiled, and asked, "Ready to plan a party?"

Chapter Twenty

IF THERE WAS one thing Tate never got sick of, it was watching Logan when he arrived somewhere. That moment when he could observe him unnoticed—like now.

After the morning he'd had, he couldn't wait to push it aside for a while and be back in Logan's company. He'd taken a cab down to The Daily Grind early so he could face the windows by the side street, and now, he understood what Logan had told him that first night on their date. About how he got to watch him walk in. Because as he looked out the window, he spotted Logan striding up the sidewalk.

Dressed in his black, woolen coat and navy-blue scarf, Logan was sporting a look Tate hadn't yet gotten used to seeing him in. And as Logan pulled the door to the coffee shop open, Tate sat up straight to get a better view.

My man is sexy as hell, he thought while Logan unbuttoned his coat and scanned the shop from behind his glasses. The collar of his coat was flipped up, and his scarf… *Hell, who knew I'd love* that *so much?* But damn, that scarf around his neck suddenly had Tate's brain switching from how Logan looked *in* his clothes to the way he would look out of them.

The only problem was that he wasn't able to do anything right now because of his damn shoulder, and he wasn't allowed to do *that* until next Friday. And that was only if the doctor gave him the all clear.

As Logan's eyes skidded to a stop on him, his lips morphed into a sensual smile and he indicated with a tilt of his head that he was going to order. That was just fine by him; he was more than happy to sit there and watch.

With everything they'd gone through in the last two months, it was nice to finally be out of the hospital and doing something somewhat normal. While sitting there, Tate started to feel the need to do *other* things with Logan.

Maybe I can convince him to—

"Hey, you."

The voice came from behind his shoulder, and Tate didn't need to turn to know who was standing there. Robbie had a very distinctive tone—suggestive.

"I saw the curls and wondered if it was you."

As the blond barista stepped beside his table, Tate gave a reluctant smile.

Christ, I must be hard up for normalcy if I'm happy to see Robbie.

"No one has hair like— Oh shit. What happened to your arm?" he asked when he noticed the brace Tate had strapped on under his jacket.

The honest concern on his face surprised him, and when Robbie sat down and reached across the table, his eyes wide, a genuine smile crossed Tate's lips. He was about to answer when Robbie started talking again.

"I haven't seen you or Logan in forever. Oh wait... Are you two still...you know? Or did that end? Is he here?" As the final question tumbled from his mouth, Robbie swiveled in his chair to look around the café.

Tate laughed at the guy. "Let me answer the most important question first. Yes, we are still 'you know.' So stop looking for him, flirt." He hardly believed those were his own words.

When Robbie turned back to face him with a cheeky smile, it was clear he was shocked also. "Oh, so that's how it is, huh?"

"That's exactly how it is."

"I was wondering how long it would take you to finally tell me to back off. It was obvious you thought it, but...if you weren't gonna say it—"

"Consider it said," Tate said, chuckling at Robbie's audacity. "He's *still* with me, and I'm not letting him go."

"Well, if it had ever been an option, I wouldn't have either. Showoff." Robbie sighed as though he were totally put out. Then he gave an impish grin and turned to search behind him again.

This time, Tate knew he saw exactly what he did: Logan

walking toward them with two coffees and a brown paper bag in hand —and damn, he looked fine.

After Logan's eyes shifted to Robbie and then came back to his, Robbie turned around, slumped against the booth, and put a hand to his chest. Closing his eyes, he mouthed, "So fucking hot."

When Logan stopped by the table, he looked down to where Robbie was sitting with his eyes still closed. Then he turned to him with a question in his eyes.

"It's okay. He's having a moment," he explained as Logan took his lips in a swift kiss.

When he pulled away, he smiled. "So am I."

Tate licked his lips as Logan straightened. "Nice coat."

"You like? Some pain in my ass insisted I wear it this morning."

"Pretty sure I was nowhere near your ass this morning, but—"

"Don't finish that sentence," Logan interrupted. "There are children listening."

Both of them then turned their attention to Robbie, who had sat forward and was watching the exchange avidly. "Oh, come on. It was just getting good."

"Afternoon, Robbie," Logan said as he started to unwind his scarf. "I wasn't aware you were joining us for lunch."

With mischievous eyes, Robbie informed him, "I'd love to join in and eat you two any time."

"I'm sure you would," Logan said dryly while removing his coat. "You going to get out of my seat?"

Robbie stood and bowed before sweeping his hand toward the booth to indicate that Logan should sit. Then he turned his attention back to Tate. "You never said what happened to your arm."

Tate's eyes found Logan's as he shrugged his arms in the sleeves of his shirt as if trying to get comfortable—in his clothes or with the conversation, Tate wasn't quite sure.

"I was in a car accident," he finally said, glancing up at Robbie.

"Oh my God," he gasped, placing a hand to his mouth. "And your arm was broken?"

"His collarbone, among other things," Logan interjected.

Robbie's gaze ping-ponged between the two of them, and when he saw how grim Logan looked, it must've registered that what had happened was some serious shit.

"Yeah." Tate gave a tight smile and then stretched his legs out under the table on either side of Logan's. "But I'm getting better every day. So don't get any ideas about trying to steal my guy. Got it?"

Logan coughed around the sip of coffee he'd just taken.

"Hey," he said, running his eyes over Logan in a proprietary way. "I'm just letting him know you're off the market—for good."

* * *

JESUS. THE WORDS that had just come out of Tate's mouth and the look he was aiming across the table at him had Logan placing his coffee cup down just in case he dropped it. It was full of heat and arousal, and it had been so fucking long since he'd seen it that Logan's palms started to sweat.

"Yeah, yeah, I get it…" Robbie was saying, but as he continued to talk, Tate was busy rubbing his leg against the outside of his, and the small gesture was enough to have Logan shifting in his seat—"Logan?"

As his name was said with enough force to break through his sex-filled brain, he refocused on Tate, who smirked at him.

Tease. He knows exactly what he just did to me.

"Huh?" he managed.

"You need anything else?"

Tate to pass his fucking follow-up so I can… "No."

Robbie must've sensed the "go away" vibe he was throwing off, because he backed away with a small grin, saying, "*Ooo-kay,* then," and left him sitting there with the sexy, off-limits man opposite him.

"Stop it," Logan ordered and brought his coffee cup back to his lips.

"What? I'm not doing anything."

"Bullshit. You're looking at me like you want to—" His words ended as Tate chose that precise moment to press his leg back against his. Logan glared across the table at him. "And you keep doing *that*."

"I'm just stretching. I have long legs."

Logan narrowed his eyes and lowered the cup. "So do I, but I'm not rubbing all over—"

Tate did it again.

"Fuck you."

"Mhmm. I was just thinking how much I'd like that. I miss having you inside me."

Logan sat back in the seat with one arm resting on the table and used his other hand to discreetly push against his growing erection. "You have a sadistic streak. You know that?"

"Me?" Tate chuckled. "It's not my fault you look…" As Tate checked him out, Logan clenched his fist and waited for whatever sexy come-on he was about to throw his way. Instead, he got, "So, how was your morning?"

What? No way *is he changing topics now.* "Excuse me?"

"Your morning? How was it?"

Logan leaned forward. "Do you really want to get into that right now?"

"No. But you seem uncomfortable. So I'm trying to help you out."

"That's the point. You're not *allowed* to help me out. Not for another week. So keep your legs and sex face to yourself."

Tate shrugged and grabbed the brown paper bag in front

of him, pulling one of the sandwiches out. Once he'd handed it over, he sat back, got the second out for himself, and then said something that made Logan thankful he was seated.

"I've never known my lack of participation to stop you before."

Does he mean what I think he—

"And I'd be more than happy to provide you with visual aids while you work solo."

Yes, he fucking does.

"You know, to help you out, of course."

Logan methodically unwrapped his lunch and then pinned Tate with a look he hoped spoke volumes. If the way Tate swallowed and licked his lips was any indication, his intentions were coming across loud and fucking clear.

"And what kind of visual aids are we talking about here?"

"Any kind you like."

Logan shook his head. "You're going to have to be more specific than that if you want to convince me."

"You need convincing?"

"Hey, you're the one pitching the proposal. Give it to me."

Tate's expression told him exactly how he'd like to "give it" to him, but as he unwrapped his food, Logan could see the wheels spinning.

Yeah, come on. Tell me exactly what you want.

"Obviously, it would be somewhat limited," Tate started as Logan took a bite of his sandwich. He wouldn't have been able to say what was on it though, because he was too busy staring at the hungry expression that just flashed across Tate's face. "But my doctor did tell me I need to do exercises that maintain forearm and grip strength with my hand."

The answer was so unexpected, and so fucking spot-on, that Logan couldn't help his laugh. "That *is* a very persuasive argument."

Tate gave him his most serious expression and then, *yeah,* rubbed his leg again. "I think so. You wouldn't want to stand in the way of my healing process, would you?"

"No. I certainly would not."

"And you want to help me, right? They say if someone has a goal to work toward, they'll improve much faster than one who doesn't."

Logan took another bite, chewed, and swallowed. "Is that right?"

"Yep."

The arrogant way Tate answered, as if he already knew he'd won, guaranteed Logan's hard-on for the rest of their meal.

"Just so there's no confusion. You want me to 'help' myself in front of you to give you a reason to exercise the grip strength of your hand? Do I have that right?"

Tate finished chewing the bite he'd just taken and

nodded. "That's right."

"And the visuals? You never did tell me."

The way Tate shifted in his seat made Logan think he was imagining it already—then he shared his vision. "Me naked, on our bed. And you naked, kneeling over me."

"Fuck, Tate," he said, his breath now coming a little faster at all the depraved thoughts racing through his head. "Damn."

Tate raised an eyebrow. "You in or out?"

Logan grabbed his jacket and scarf and slid out of the booth. "Fuck going to cancel the lease. You can call them."

"Oh? Did something come up?" Tate asked, a victorious look crossing his face.

Logan kissed those provoking lips and whispered, "Yeah. I did. Let's go home. I believe you have a therapy session to go to."

Chapter Twenty-One

THE ENTIRE WAY home, Logan couldn't take his eyes off Tate. In the cab, walking through the lobby, and now, as they were standing in the elevator, he couldn't stop staring at him.

He was in his black boots and jeans today, and ever since he'd left the hospital, he'd started wearing button-up shirts, which were easier for him to get on—and made Logan want to rip them off. His good arm was in the sleeve of a warm bomber jacket, and the other side was draped over his braced arm.

God, it's good to see him upright and in front of me again, he thought as they finally reached their floor.

"This therapy session," Logan mused as they walked down the hall. "It doesn't need to start on a couch or anything, does it?"

When they stopped at their door, Tate's lips twitched and he answered, "I think it would be best to start wherever *you* plan to finish."

Logan turned the key and pushed the door open, and as Tate walked past, he told him in a lowered voice, "Then go to our bedroom. That's where we're *both* going to finish."

Tate's eyes dropped to his mouth. Logan thought he was about to kiss him, but at the last minute, he said, "I'm going to need your help. Is that okay with you?"

Fuck yes, it is. He nodded and shut the door, and then Tate continued down the hall, shrugging out of his coat. He threw it on the couch, and when he looked back at him and smiled, Logan wanted to clutch his heart.

He's something else. And that grin had him dumping his keys and removing his own coat as quickly as possible. Logan kicked his shoes off, and while making his way to the bedroom, he unknotted his tie and pulled his shirt from his pants. When he stepped into the room, he saw Tate by the bed, minus his shoes and socks, frowning and trying to unbutton his shirt.

Logan came around to him and brushed his hand aside. "You asked for my help, remember?"

"I didn't mean with this. I meant with—"

He knew what Tate had meant, but he cut him off by capturing his mouth and kissing him hard. As his lips parted, Logan slipped inside to taste the coffee on his tongue and groaned when Tate sucked on him.

Then Logan pulled his mouth away and whispered, "Let me help you." He unbuckled the arm brace before making quick work of Tate's shirt so he was left standing in only his jeans. "So sexy," he said as he drew a finger from the base of

Tate's throat down the center of his body to his navel, and then he touched the button of his jeans. "What do you have on under these?"

Tate's grin reappeared, but he said nothing.

"Have I mentioned how much I love that you"—Logan paused, unsnapped the button, and lowered the zipper—"like to run around commando?"

He took the sides of Tate's jeans and yanked them farther apart before kissing him again and sliding a hand down inside the denim. He kept his eyes on Tate's as he circled his erection, and then Tate's closed.

Nipping at Tate's jaw, Logan squeezed his fist around him. "I want you to keep these on and spread apart so I can see just a hint of you." He dragged his tongue up to Tate's ear and sucked on his lobe.

A strained sound left Tate as he grabbed his arm for support. "God, Logan. It's been too long."

Logan released him and wrapped his arm around his waist, pushing his hand inside the seat of his jeans. He dug his fingers into Tate's ass cheek and pulled him hard against him. "Yes, it fucking has."

He walked them backwards until the mattress hit the backs of his thighs, and Tate maneuvered between his legs, careful not to knock his arm. Pushing forward, he ground his hard-on against him.

"You're not to do anything strenuous," he reminded gently.

"I know."

Logan clutched his ass again and kneaded it. "I mean it. You want something, you ask. I have no problem with you using me."

Tate chuckled and took his face between his hands. He kissed him, biting his bottom lip before saying, "What if I want to lie down and let *you* use *me*?"

I'll probably lose my fucking mind.

"See?" Tate pointed out. "Even when you're being sincere, it comes out full-on sex."

"That was just an added bonus," he sighed as Tate ran his fingers through his hair. "But I mean it. You are to literally lie back and enjoy."

"Got it."

"Tate," Logan warned.

"I. Got. It," Tate reiterated. "Now, would you take off your clothes? There—that's me asking."

Logan stood, and when Tate didn't back up, their bodies brushed. "Everything?"

"Yes," was Tate's answer, and then he walked around him to get on the bed. When he was lounging back against the headboard, wearing only his jeans, he ran his eyes down Logan's body in a sensual invitation before confirming, "Everything."

* * *

AS LOGAN TOOK off his shirt, Tate couldn't stop the hungry way he watched the built chest that came into view. He loved the light dusting of hair across Logan's pecs and that sexy treasure trail of his. It led straight below, and when Logan unbuckled his belt, Tate brought his left hand to his open jeans and shoved it inside to adjust himself.

Holy shit. He was getting harder with every item Logan removed, but there was no way he was going to stop him. He wanted to see it all.

Last night in the bath had been cathartic. It was what they had needed after all they'd gone through—to be naked and vulnerable with one another.

That was definitely not the case here.

What he wanted right now was for Logan to show him that he was still desirable. That he was still the man he wanted. And when Logan's pants and boxers came off, Tate's fears were laid to rest. Logan's cock was rigid and thick, as it proudly proclaimed just how turned on he was.

"Come closer," he said, not looking away for even a second.

Logan was more than accommodating. He grabbed the bottle of lube from the side table and dropped it on the bed as he got up on the mattress.

While he moved closer, his eyes zeroed in on the hand Tate had in his jeans and he smirked. "I thought you were supposed to be exercising the *right* hand muscle."

"Yeah, I changed my mind. I really think I should rest it. Plus, it's not half as effective as my left."

"No?" Logan asked as he straddled his legs. "I think I should judge for myself."

* * *

LOGAN'S FINGERS FLIRTED with the open zipper of Tate's jeans before pulling them down his hips, which Tate lifted without hesitation, freeing his beautifully cut cock.

A low sound of approval came from the man seated in front of him, and as Tate pumped his pelvis up, Logan leaned down over him. The scents of arousal and Tate combined and had his own dick aching between his legs. It'd been too long since he'd been able to touch him this way, to even think about it, and as he let his mind relax and enjoy, he was engulfed by the eroticism of rediscovery.

Tate arched his body in an effort to get closer to his mouth, and Logan aimed his eyes up at him and tsked.

"Nothing strenuous, remember. Behave yourself." Then he slowly ran his tongue along the underside of Tate's cock.

Tate sucked in a hiss of air and let it out on a groan. "Logan."

Clearly, his patience was as precarious as his own today. Logan raised his head and caught Tate's ragged expression. "*Hmm*, I think I forgot..."

"Forgot?" Tate asked as he swiped his parted lips with his tongue, giving him a really difficult decision to make.

Do I go to his mouth or stay here at his cock?

Then Tate's erection nudged his cheek and Logan turned his head to lick a wet path up it.

Decision fucking made.

"*Ahh,* Logan… Forgot what?" Tate panted as he tongued his weeping slit. "God, that feels fucking good."

Logan sucked the swollen head between his lips and then felt a hand stroke the back of his head. As Tate teased the strands of hair under his fingers, Logan lowered his mouth and took him in deeper.

The groan that escaped Tate was tortured. He sounded like a man who'd been waiting years for someone to touch him, and as Logan grabbed his hips, he felt like it had been years since he'd been able to.

When he drew his lips off him and kissed the tip of his cock, his eyes found Tate's and he whispered, "I forgot how fucking gorgeous you are when you fall apart for me."

* * *

TATE LOOKED AT the seductive man straddling his legs and tried to remember a time when he didn't love him—*and hell if I can.* Logan had weaved some kind of spell over him, one he hadn't believed possible. But as he watched him rise up to his knees and stroke his own cock, Tate knew he'd found his person.

He reached out for him, and when Logan took his hand, Tate pulled him forward so he was kneeling over his hips.

"Kiss me," he whispered when Logan's mouth hovered over his. He lowered his head, and as their lips met, Tate closed his eyes, ready to savor the deep slide. When it didn't happen and that wicked mouth vanished, Tate's eyes opened to see Logan's blue ones shining down at him.

"Like that?"

"No."

"No?" Logan asked, rubbing his leaking hard-on against his chest.

Tate had his head tilted back against the headboard, but he could feel the sticky evidence of Logan's arousal as he looked up at the hedonistic vision kneeling over him. "No. I want more."

"Is that right?"

"With you? Always."

When Logan leaned down, bit his lower lip, and rasped, "Good," Tate groaned and let him in. The sexy sound that left Logan filled his ears as he cupped his face between his hands and devoured him.

He closed his eyes as Logan's hips writhed against him, making it impossible to think of anything other than the way he moved when he was inside him. It would be a fucking miracle if he made it through the next week alive to feel that again with the way his heart was thumping in his chest.

He pushed his hips up as Logan snaked a hand down between them, and when a tight fist pumped his dick, he let out a frustrated curse. "*Fuck*. I want… I…"

"Yes?" Logan urged, his voice barely a whisper and his hot breath shifting the hair by his ear. "What do you want, Tate? Tell me."

"More," he rasped even though he knew he couldn't have it—then an idea took root. One way or another, he was going to have Logan inside him. "I want to taste you."

Logan's eyes narrowed on him as if he were trying to get inside his mind, and then he gave him a look that was so fucking sinful that Tate knew he understood.

Silently, Logan backed away and tugged his jeans off of him. It wasn't until he threw the denim to the side of the bed and crawled back up to straddle him so his cock was inches from his face that Tate knew they were on the *exact* same page.

* * *

AS TATE'S EYES ran a hot trail down his body, Logan wrapped a fist around himself and positioned his body so he was nudging against Tate's chin and lips. *Yes, there's my dirty Tate. I know what you want.*

"Open your mouth," he ordered.

Tate moved his hand down to touch himself, and Logan

felt his blood pounding out a hard rhythm between his legs.

Oh yeah, I'm onto you.

"Tate," he said again, drawing his attention and his eyes back to him. "Open your mouth."

As he inched closer so his knees were flanking Tate's sides, Tate parted his lips and flicked his tongue out across the pre-come coating the swollen head of Logan's cock.

You've got to be fucking kidding me, Logan thought, placing a hand on the headboard to brace himself. Then Tate looked up at him, and his expression of longing made Logan think one thing only—*I can't wait to sink my cock between his lips.*

He guided himself to that waiting mouth, and as the tip of his erection ghosted over it, Tate tasted him again. His eyes lowered, and then he shocked the hell out of Logan by leaning forward to swallow him inside.

Logan ground his teeth together and flexed his fingers against the sturdy bed frame as he felt one of Tate's palms stroke up the back of his thigh to cup his ass.

"Oh yeah, Tate. That's it. *Suck* me."

He felt the suction around him increase as Tate's cheeks hollowed out and he moved his lips back and forth. Logan let go of his shaft and ran his fingers through Tate's hair so he could hold the back of his head as he slid his lips along his hardened flesh.

The hand on his ass pulled him closer, and as he used Tate's hot, wet mouth the way he'd asked him to, Logan felt his fingers dig into his ass cheek and then trace their way down to gently squeeze his balls.

Logan's curse ricocheted around the room, and his head fell back while Tate continued to work him over. His breathing was coming fast, and he was reminded that the man currently obliterating his control was the only person who'd *ever* made him feel that way.

Tate had the power to make him tremble from passion and from pain—and he trusted him with his very soul.

Looking down, he saw brown eyes full of desire staring back at him. He stroked his fingers over Tate's jaw, and when that expression morphed to one of love and gratitude, he felt his balls tingle and his body begin to shake.

His mind shut down to anything other than the explosive orgasm that then hit him while he was buried deep inside the delicious mouth surrounding him, and when Tate swallowed every drop and pulled his mouth free, Logan put both hands on the headboard to hold himself up.

Fuck, he thought. *He is so it for me.*

Tate had demolished any kind of thought he had, but when Logan peered down at the gorgeous face aimed up at him, he was determined to give as good as he'd just received.

He shifted down until he was lying beside Tate, and when he saw a particularly self-satisfied smile cross his lips, he asked, "Pleased with yourself?"

"Yeah, I think I am."

Logan ran a finger along the prominent erection still being massaged by Tate's hand. "Want to tell me why?"

Tate slid down the bed, and a shaky breath left him as Logan covered his hand and started to stroke him. "It's been too long since I've seen you that way. Wanted to make sure I didn't imagine it all."

That got Logan curious. Especially with the gleam in Tate's eye.

"Wanted to make sure you didn't imagine *what*, exactly?"

"The way I feel when we're together like this. And the way you go insane from my hands and mouth on you."

"Oh, do I?"

"Yeah," Tate groaned and closed his eyes. "I wanted you to get all hot and dirty just like you used to, and it worked. You were practically all the way down my throat. I drive you fucking crazy."

"Christ, Tate," Logan growled, burying his nose in the crook of his neck. "First, you *never* need to doubt that between us. Not ever. From the moment we met, I've been trying to get inside you, and I'll always want to be there. Second, I love to do everything with you, but when you say stuff like that…when *you* get all dirty and give it right back to me…"

"Yeah?"

Logan drew his tongue up Tate's throat and then kissed

his ear, where he whispered, "I can't decide if I want to love on you or fuck you until you're too weak to walk."

Tate turned his head toward him, panting from the solid hand job he was now giving him. "Both sound equally good to me. You're so…*God*…so uninhibited, and that makes me so damn hot."

Logan kissed him and gave his most demonic grin. Then he let him go and slipped down between Tate's thighs. He licked the straining flesh that greeted him, and dared, "Come on, then, Tate. Let me have it. Hot and dirty, just how we like it."

And as Tate's fingers twisted into his hair, Logan parted his lips and proceeded to drive *him* fucking crazy.

Chapter Twenty-Two

THE WEEK PASSED by uneventfully enough, though they seemed to be in a holding pattern of sorts. Logan would get up and go to work, and he would sit at home and wait.

But not today—today, the waiting would stop. Friday was finally here, his follow-up appointment was scheduled for three, and after that, Tate felt like he'd be able to finally move on with his life.

He was standing in the kitchen, eating his breakfast, when Logan came out of the bedroom fastening his watch around his wrist. Dressed for work, he looked polished, his black hair styled to the left as usual, and as he walked through the dining room, he picked up his glasses, which were resting on the newspaper, and made his way toward him.

"Seven a.m. I'm impressed."

Tate smiled around a spoonful of cereal as Logan put his glasses on and came around the kitchen island. He kissed his cheek and then walked over to the coffee machine.

"And coffee? Wow. You are full of energy this morning."

Logan reached into one of the top cupboards for his travel mug.

"I guess I'm just ready to get this brace off."

Logan glanced back at him. "I bet."

"Yeah. And it'll be nice to finally get back into a normal routine."

Logan poured his coffee and then screwed the lid on his mug before he came over to stand beside him. Placing a hand on his good arm, he squeezed. "I agree. But I still don't want you to rush things. Remember, Pete said you don't need to go back for another week. The temp is hired until then."

"I know. But I still need to move my things over here, and I also have to go down to the police station and deal with all of the accident stuff."

A frown pulled Logan's brow down, and he turned to get his jacket, which was draped over the back of the chair.

As he shrugged into it, Tate studied the serious expression on his face and asked, "What's on your mind?"

When Logan merely tugged on the sleeves of his jacket, Tate put his bowl down and made his way around the island.

"Logan?"

Logan looked at him and took a breath before saying, "Have you thought any more about pressing charges against the driver who hit you?"

They'd briefly discussed what options he had when he'd

been in the hospital, but at the time, he'd just wanted to deal with healing before he thought about all the legal crap he'd have to go through surrounding what happened.

"I think you should seriously consider sitting down with someone to discuss your options."

He really didn't like the idea of spending more money in an attorney's office, especially after Diana had switched their divorce proceedings between two. But he also knew that Logan was right. He needed to know what his legal choices were.

Logan pushed his hands into his pockets as he walked back over to him. "It's up to you, Tate, but you almost died that day. You were in the hospital for a little over a month, and you'll likely need physical therapy for some time, as well as follow-up appointments." He took his hand and brought it to his mouth, kissing it. "He needs to be held responsible for that. He was in the wrong, and he hurt you."

Tate slid his hand along Logan's cheek and leaned in to kiss his lips. "I know. I just needed to be back on my feet before I tackled it all."

"I understand." Logan nodded.

Tate could tell he wanted to say more but was, for once in his life, holding back. Which made him curious. "Did you want to do it?"

"I thought about it," Logan admitted. Then he let him go and walked up the hall to where his briefcase was sitting by the entry table. "But I think we should speak to someone who specializes in this sort of case," he called out.

"Hang on." Tate chuckled. "Are you actually saying there might be someone who's better than you? Because I think I'd like to document this moment."

"Aren't you funny," Logan said as he came back into the living room and handed him a white card embossed with gold.

Leighton & Associates. Tate ran his finger over the name and then looked back to Logan.

"They're a firm we've worked with a couple of times who specifically deals with personal injury claims. I've also come up against a couple of their employees. They're good."

"Good, huh?" Tate asked as he slipped the card into the back pocket of his jeans.

Logan shrugged nonchalantly. "Yeah. They're good."

"The best?"

"No. I said they were—"

"Good," Tate clarified with a smirk. He took a step forward so his toes touched Logan's dress shoes and ran a hand down his navy tie. "I'm pretty satisfied with the lawyer I have. And he's better than just *good.*"

One of Logan's dark eyebrows rose. "Yeah?"

He caught Logan's lips in a tease of a kiss before pulling back to nod. "Yeah. But maybe I should try these guys. My lawyer insists it's always good to try a little of everything."

Logan rolled his eyes and then stepped around him to

grab his coffee. "You *are* in a mood, aren't you, smartass."

"Maybe," Tate admitted with a laugh. "It's nice to finally feel better."

"Well, if you're up to it, there are a few people who would like to see you tonight. One very pregnant woman in particular."

Tate's palms dampened at the thought of seeing Rachel. She'd come by to visit a couple of times after he'd woken up, but every time she'd been in the room, she had sat in the corner, silent while Cole joked around with him and Logan. She'd barely said anything at all.

"I don't know. Maybe it's better if we wait. I don't want to cause her any more stress, and the last time I saw her…"

"Of course, it's totally up to you. But I think it would do her good to see you. You look like *you* again. Not all scary and in the hospital."

"Gee thanks."

Logan sighed and touched his shoulder. "You know what I mean. Plus, she asked to see you."

"She did?"

"Yep," Logan said before giving him a final kiss on the cheek and walking down the hall to the front door.

As he bent to pick his briefcase up, Tate enjoyed the way his dress pants fit perfectly across his firm ass.

"I'll be back at two so we can get going. We have a date with your doctor."

"A little impatient, are we?"

Logan's eyes swept over him, and then he flashed a smile that was completely sexual. "You don't know the half of it."

* * *

"OH, GOOD. THERE you are," Cole said as Logan entered his own office and saw his brother standing by his desk, writing on a piece of paper.

"Here I am. Leaving me love notes again? How many times do I have to tell you that it means so much more when you use your words, Cole?"

Cole flipped him off as he walked across the room and handed him the paper. "Rachel and I went through the restaurants you listed, and she agrees there are some great ones on here. But do you really think he wants to do a celebratory dinner with everyone asking how he is?"

"No," Logan laughed. "But we never celebrated his thirtieth birthday because he kept putting it off, and he deserves a glad-you're-out-of-the-hospital party. I know he's so sick of being cooped up, unable to do anything. He just wants to feel normal again, so I was trying to think of something."

"Since when have you done anything normal?"

"Good point," Logan acknowledged, and then he remembered a letter he'd received in the mail a couple of weeks ago but had been too busy to call about.

Hmm… Now that could work.

He looked down at the list in his hand anyway just to see which restaurants they'd agreed on, and his eyes latched on to the bottom one he'd written as a joke. Logan lifted his head, and a sly smile crossed his mouth.

"You dirty dog."

"Excuse me?"

He turned the paper around and thrust it in Cole's face. "Whipped? *You* circled that?"

Cole crossed his arms over his wide chest and scowled at him. "Just because I don't run around flaunting my sexuality quite as obnoxiously as you doesn't mean I don't enjoy certain things."

As Logan chuckled and walked over to his desk, Cole continued. "That's where I met Rachel, for your information."

Now *that* was an interesting detail he didn't know. Surprised, he turned to face Cole. "Really?"

Cole nodded as he moved backwards toward the door and opened it. "Really, really."

Logan's mouth fell open and then he laughed. "You've managed to shock me. Something I didn't think you had in you anymore. Bravo, brother."

Cole shook his head. "Unlike yours, *my* behavior remains a mystery to most."

Logan pretended to stifle a yawn. "Yeah, yeah. Well, either way, we're doing something right. 'Cause you got the girl, and I got the boy."

"That we did," Cole agreed with a smile Logan figured matched his own smug one.

Then he fingered the edge of the paper and thought, *What the hell.* "You're right. Normal isn't me. Do you think Rachel would be upset if we all catch up next week?"

"No, not at all. Actually, we all have dinner on Monday nights. You two should come."

Logan thought about it for a second and then said, "Let me talk it over with Tate, but I don't see why not. Meanwhile, I have a weekend to plan." Before Cole shut the door, Logan asked, "Hey? Leighton & Associates?"

"What about them?"

"Who's their best personal injury guy?"

Cole appeared to think it over and then snapped his fingers. "Finley. I've worked with him a couple of times."

"Okay," Logan said as he pulled his phone out to store the name in his notes. "Thanks. Oh, and Cole?"

"Yes, Logan?"

"Thank you. For everything."

Cole gave him an understanding smile and left the office, shutting the door on his way out.

* * *

TATE HAD JUST stepped out of the shower when he heard his phone ringing from the vanity. He grabbed a towel from the rack and made his way over to it to see Diana's number flashing across the screen.

Not exactly who I want to speak to right now, he thought as he wrapped the towel around his hips and picked the cell up. When it kept ringing, he looked at himself in the mirror and made himself answer.

"Hello."

"Tate?"

"Yeah, it's me."

"Hey."

He closed his eyes and told himself to have some patience. "Hi, Diana."

There was an awkward pause, and he wondered for a moment if she'd hung up until she asked, "How are you?"

Her question was almost timid, and when Tate opened his eyes, he asked himself, *What kind of man do I want to be?* He ran a hand through his hair and thought of the way Logan had extended an invitation to his father, which had him softening toward the woman at the other end of the phone.

"I'm doing much better," he told her, rubbing the back of his neck.

"Oh, that's good."

"It is. I go back to the doctor today."

"Good," she rushed out and then added, "I'm glad."

"Yeah," he agreed, and while the silence this time remained awkward, there was no simmering rage like there used to be.

"Okay, well, that was all. I just wanted to know… I—"

"Diana?" he interrupted, gripping his hair in a fist. *Fuck. When did talking to her become so difficult?*

"Yes, Tate?"

"I never got a chance before I left the hospital to say thank you."

"Oh," she breathed softly into the phone. "You don't have to do that."

"Yeah, I do. Thank you for relaying my wishes that day. I know it wasn't easy."

She laughed then, and Tate leaned against the wall as the sound that had once been so familiar filled his ear. "That's an understatement if ever there was one."

"I suppose it is, huh?" he chuckled.

"*Ahh*, yeah."

When their shared laughter dissipated, he waited.

Then she whispered, "Be happy, Tate. You deserve it." Right there in that moment, Diana sounded more sincere than he'd ever heard her before.

"I am. He makes me happy."

"Good. Okay. I don't want to hold you up any more than I already have…"

"Diana," he said again and thought he heard her sniff

through the phone.

"Yeah?"

"Thanks for calling."

There was a definite sniff this time as she answered, "Thank you for answering."

"Bye," he said softly, and she told him the same.

As he hit end on the phone and lowered it to the sink, he quietly studied his reflection. He liked the man staring back at him. The one he was when he was with Logan. He respected him, and as he lathered up his cheeks and his jaw to shave, he vowed to do whatever he needed to in order to always be that man.

* * *

DID YOU PACK your leather pants the last time we were at your apartment?

Logan smiled at the text he'd just sent. His day had flown by, and everything was set for the weekend he had planned. All he needed to do now was pick Tate up for his doctor's appointment.

Tate: No. There was no reason to. Why?

Logan shut his e-mails, closed out of the document he had open, and then picked his phone up to text back.

Wanted to know if we had to stop and get them on the way home from the doctor's. And we do.

He put his phone down and checked over the papers he'd just printed before he folded them and put them in his jacket pocket. Then his phone buzzed.

Tate: Why?

So nosy. Then he chuckled as he added: **Because.**

Within seconds, Tate responded.

Tate: Not a good answer, counselor.

Logan stood and hit call on his phone, and when it connected, he said, "You want to know why? Because I miss seeing your tight ass wrapped in them."

"I see. And am I taking my *tight ass* somewhere special?" Tate asked, his sexy laugh never failing to make Logan wish he were within touching distance.

"No. But I plan to."

"Hmm," Tate mused. "Where?"

"It's a surprise," Logan said as he grabbed his briefcase and walked to the door.

"Are we going to your cabin?"

"I just said it was a surprise. I'm not telling you," he said as he turned the lights off. "My lips are sealed."

"Now there's a first," Tate joked.

"Careful, Tate. I'm stealing you this weekend, and I plan to do *all* kinds of bad things to you."

"Do you? And what if I don't want to be careful?" Tate asked, the invitation clear in his voice.

"Guess you'll find out after your doctor's appointment, won't you? But don't say I didn't warn you."

"Threats, huh," Tate said, and the way his voice dropped made Logan's pulse race.

He mouthed a silent goodbye to Sherry and made his way toward the exit as he said into the phone, "No, Tate. That's a promise."

Chapter Twenty-Three

TATE COULDN'T WIPE the smile off his face as Logan weaved them through the afternoon traffic, away from the doctor's office. When he'd arrived to pick him up, Tate had figured he would text him to come downstairs. But Logan had come up, kissed him senseless, and told him to pack an overnight bag.

And he hasn't told me shit since.

But if the hot-as-hell way he'd watched him move around the bedroom to pack hadn't been incentive enough, then the way Logan kept accidentally touching him every chance he got was. It was obvious that Logan had plans—and he was more than happy to be the star in them.

Logan reached for the power button on the car radio and turned it on. Yes, good—maybe some music would help distract him from the man seated beside him, because as far as he was concerned, sitting next to Logan right now was an exercise in restraint.

The song that had been playing faded out, and the radio announcer came over the speakers talking of love and forevers as she promised that tonight, on her "Love Line," she'd deliver "the song that will make that special someone fall in love with you" —and it made him grin.

"What song would you pick?" he asked.

Logan briefly glanced over at him. "Song?"

"Yeah," he said, gesturing with a tilt of his head to the radio. "If you had to pick a song to make someone fall in love with you."

Logan smirked at him. "I don't need a song. The someone *I* want already fell in love with me."

"Arrogant." Tate laughed.

Logan winked at him and then shrugged. "Just being honest."

He scoffed and looked out the window as Logan exited the freeway. When he saw the sign they'd just passed, his mouth fell open. "The airport?"

Logan reached across the car and ran a palm over his thigh. "Maybe."

"What do you mean maybe?"

"You don't have an aversion to flying, do you? I'm not particularly a fan, but this afternoon, I'm willing to make an exception. Plus, I've always wanted to get on a plane with you. Ever since you made me think about it at the museum that time..."

Logan was still talking, but somewhere after *museum,* Tate had lost what he was saying, too focused on the fact that he was being driven to the airport.

It wasn't until Logan asked, "So, do you?" that he realized Logan had stopped talking and was waiting for him to respond.

He was trying to come up with some kind of answer, but they all got stuck when he saw a plane barrel down the runway, the nose lifting as it started its ascent.

"Tate?"

"What was the question again?"

Logan seemed extremely pleased with himself as he veered off to the parking garage on the left. "I asked if you have an aversion to flying."

"No," Tate managed, shaking his head. "What are we doing at an airport, Logan?"

Logan pulled the car into an empty spot and parked. When he took the keys out of the ignition, he looked over to him and said, "I told you I was stealing you for the weekend."

"In a plane?"

Logan reached across the console and took his chin. He kissed him so hard that Tate wondered if his lips would be bruised, and when he finally raised his head, he said, "Yes. In a plane. I don't think you understand how fucking happy I am to have you alive and well again. We've missed two months of our lives, Tate. This weekend, I want to make up for all of that lost time."

Tate's heart jackhammered at the intensity in Logan's eyes.

Then he added, "The only decision you have to make is whether you come quietly or screaming my name."

Logan's mouth took his in an intense kiss. *Jesus, yes.* This was the Logan he'd missed. He tasted him and sucked on his tongue, and Tate smoothed a hand up to Logan's hair to try to pull him closer. He ached to be with him again, naked and complete, and when the doctor had given him the all clear and he'd glanced over at Logan, he'd known that the feeling was mutual.

"*Ahh*, Tate," Logan breathed against his lips. "Let me do this. Let me spoil you, love on you, and then we can go back to being ordinary. I promise. But this weekend, I want to show you how extraordinary you are to me."

Tate swallowed as he stared into Logan's blue eyes, and when he silently nodded, Logan's lips tipped up at the sides.

"Okay, we need to get out of this car before I lose my fucking control."

Tate nipped his bottom lip. "Then let's go. Apparently, I have a plane to catch."

* * *

LOGAN SETTLED INTO the aisle seat as Tate buckled his seat belt beside him and raised the shade on the plane window. He really hated flying; it made him a nervous wreck. But he was willing to push that aside for a weekend away with Tate, and he was glad that he had.

Tate's expression had been worth his last-minute decision when he'd found out they were headed to New York, and the entire time they'd been boarding, he hadn't been able to get the grin off his gorgeous face.

"When was the last time you flew somewhere?"

Logan thought about that and realized, *Fuck. Wasn't it when I met Jessica?* "Umm..."

Tate didn't miss his discomfort, and when he turned in his seat and aimed a "spit it out" look at him, Logan swallowed and tried for his most endearing smile.

"A day before you and I met."

"And?" Tate pushed.

"And what?" he asked. Trying to misdirect Tate's focus, he glanced over to the flight attendant as she walked by. "Do you think she'd get me a drink *before* we take off?"

"Don't try to change the subject. Was that the trip you said was a tight fit—"

"Yes," Logan said, cutting him off.

He really didn't want anything to fuck this up, especially not a walk down memory lane with Jessica. So, when Tate put his lips to his ear, he tensed, worried he'd just ruined everything—but *that* was certainly not the case.

"Bet I'll be tighter."

Logan barely caught the groan in his throat as he turned his head, and when their gazes locked, he felt the desire radiating off Tate and wondered how he would make it through the next two hours and ten minutes without attacking him.

"Behave yourself," he said, loving the sinful glint that lit Tate's eyes. "I mean it. Keep your hands to yourself, William."

Tate chuckled and held his hands up, waggling his fingers.

"Ah huh," Logan grumbled. "Flying is stressful enough for me without trying to control the urge I now have to suck your dick."

That got a bark of laughter from Tate, and Logan turned to see the woman seated in the aisle across from them look their way. He smiled politely at her until Tate, *the handsy fucker*, stroked a palm up his thigh and nuzzled his nose into his neck so he could kiss his jaw.

"Would you—"

"Hmm?" Tate murmured in his ear, which had him sliding a little farther into his seat, trying to conceal what was going on between his legs. "Would *I*?"

"Quit, you goddamn tease."

"Why? You *love* it when I tease you. You probably also love that I'm doing it while that woman is watching us." Tate bit his earlobe, and Logan had to admit that he *did* love it—a lot. "You do, don't you? That's so fucking hot."

Logan bit the inside of his cheek as Tate continued to kiss behind his ear.

"You smell amazing."

"Christ, this is going to be a long fucking flight."

Tate tickled his lobe with the tip of his tongue and whispered in his ear, "Maybe so, but you're not thinking about the fact that we're about to take off, are you?"

As the engines rumbled to life, Logan's jaw clenched.

"I didn't know you were this afraid to fly."

He turned his head to face Tate's mischievous grin. "I'm not."

"Yes, you are."

The flight attendants were instructing them on what to do in case of an emergency, and as the plane taxied to the runway, Logan kept his eyes on Tate's. Maybe, if he focused on him, he wouldn't feel the intense sense of panic he usually felt when he thought about the sheer amount of trust he had to have in the jet engines propelling him into the sky. That was the plan, anyway, until he looked out the open fucking window.

"Hey?" Tate said.

Logan brought his eyes back to his. Tate's hand slipped into his own and gently squeezed it.

"When the engines start and we begin to move, count back from thirty."

Logan frowned at him, but Tate gave a somewhat comforting smile.

"The first thirty seconds of takeoff and landing are the most dangerous. So once you get through that, the rest is a walk in the park."

"Oh, yeah. That helps. Thanks a lot," Logan muttered, knowing he didn't sound thankful at all.

As the plane started to vibrate and power up, Tate brought his hand to his mouth and kissed his palm before aiming hot eyes at him and suggesting, "*Or* you can think about how good it's going to feel when you sink your cock inside me in approximately two and a half hours."

Logan's brain almost short-circuited at that visual, and he was about to respond when the plane began to thunder down the tarmac. Before he knew it, it shot up into the sky and they were thirty seconds closer to their weekend destination.

* * *

TATE COULDN'T BELIEVE he was in New York City. He'd been there once when he was younger and loved it, but being there with Logan guaranteed that it would forever be ingrained as a favorite, he was sure.

The flight had been smooth, and once they'd arrived, they had flagged down a taxi and were on their way to… *I have no idea*. That part was still a secret.

Logan wasn't giving anything up, and Tate wondered what he had up his sleeve. They'd just crossed over the East River and were told they were about twenty minutes out, and with every passing minute, he became more and more curious.

The city lights illuminated the streets as they traveled through the evening traffic and turned onto Fifth Avenue. The taxi maneuvered around several town cars and SUVs to finally come to a stop, and when he saw *The Peninsula* lit up across the front of the elegant building, he turned to Logan.

With a rueful smile, he shrugged his shoulders. "The benefits of spending an entire week at their Chicago location. A comped weekend at their New York one."

"Logan, this is way too much."

Logan grabbed his jacket and pulled him across the cab to kiss him. "It's not nearly enough. Plus, it's free."

Tate shook his head. "It wasn't free."

"Shh," he coaxed. "This is the first time I've ever been thankful Evelyn did what she did. Because of her, I get to be here tonight and tomorrow in this city with you. Let's enjoy it."

Tate touched Logan's cheek and smiled against his mouth. "Okay, let's."

* * *

AS THEY GOT out of the cab, Logan made his way around to the trunk to grab their bags. When Tate tried to take his own, he said, "Don't even think about it. You just got your arm brace off."

Tate stepped up to him, took his bag with his left hand, and told him quite matter-of-factly, "Yes. I got it off. As in it's better. You heard the doctor. He said I was fine. I just have to be careful with certain movements and positions."

Logan's lips twitched as he shut the trunk. Then he paid the driver. "Fair enough. I promise to be careful of the positions I put you in—and I'll be gentle."

Tate took his hand as he walked past and said, "Not *too* gentle."

Logan laughed as they made their way up the steps leading to the revolving door, and when they got inside, they stopped and Tate turned to face him, wide-eyed and clearly impressed.

"Wow."

Directly in front of them was a massive staircase that led up to a landing, and then it curved off to both the left and the right. An intricate chandelier hung overhead, and the marble floors were so well polished that Logan could see his own reflection in them.

"What do you think? You going to love it here?" He found the check-in area and tugged on Tate's hand.

Tate pretended to think it over as they got in line and waited. "That all depends. You're going to be here, right?"

"Mhmm."

"Staying in my room? In my bed?"

"Well, they only comped me the one room with a king,

but if you want to sleep on the pull-out sofa…"

"Yes?"

"Then I'll sleep on top of you."

Tate's eyes locked with his own as the woman behind the check-in desk called out that she could help them. Then he promised in a low voice, "I don't think a sofa will be necessary."

"No?"

"No. And I'm going to love it," Tate said as they approached the counter. "Because you're here."

They both greeted the woman, who welcomed them, and when Tate placed a hand on the middle of his back, Logan thought, *Perfect fucking answer.*

Chapter Twenty-Four

IT TOOK LESS than fifteen minutes for them to get checked in and travel up to the floor of their suite. When they entered their room, Tate wandered inside before him and gaped at their luxurious surroundings.

The space was large. On the far side, a wide window overlooked Fifth Avenue and the sprawling city outside, and in the center of the room was a huge king-sized bed made up with rich, cream covers. Black accent pillows were neatly displayed across the top of it.

Logan walked over to the vanity table that divided the bedroom from the bathroom and placed his bag on the small, rectangular stool as Tate dropped his on the end of the bed. It wasn't too late yet, just a little past nine thirty, and he figured they could settle in and get a bite to eat if Tate felt like it.

"This place is unreal," Tate said as he made his way over to the windows.

Logan took a quick glimpse through the only other door in the room and saw a massive whirlpool tub and a shower stall beside it. "It sure is. And if you want to go for a swim,

I'm pretty sure our tub has the capacity for laps."

Tate laughed as he turned around to look at him, and any thought Logan had about leaving the room disappeared. He didn't think he'd ever seen a more spectacular sight than Tate in that moment. He was dressed in black slacks, a red, lightweight sweater, and his black coat—and as he stood there with the backdrop of New York City behind him, he took his breath away.

"It's big, huh?"

Logan rested against the vanity, opposite the foot of the bed, continuing to check Tate out as he remarked, "Yes. Or so I've been told."

Tate laughed as he strolled over and stopped directly in front of him to graze his fingers down the zipper of his pants. "Whoever told you that wasn't lying."

Logan straightened off the table and pressed his palm over Tate's hand, flattening it against his erection—massaging himself. "Just wait. It gets bigger."

Tate's lips morphed into a grin that was full of mischief and sex as his fingers curled the best they could around the hard-on inside his boxers.

"I don't believe you," he said, and Logan decided that the time for waiting was over.

They'd been given the go-ahead from the doctor, and ever since then, he'd wanted nothing more than to get back inside his man.

He took ahold of Tate's jacket and tugged him forward

for a kiss before stepping around him. When Tate turned, his legs hit the small stool near the table, and he moved to the side of it. Logan then backed him up until his ass bumped the edge of the vanity and he could box him in and get between his legs.

"Maybe I need to prove it," Logan said, removing his glasses and placing them on the counter. Then he slid his hands into Tate's hair and tilted his face up. Since Tate was half seated, Logan found himself hovering over him, and he loved the position.

"Maybe you do," Tate dared him.

Logan lowered his head, and when their lips were only a whisper apart, he suggested, "Maybe you should take off my pants and see for yourself."

Needing no further invitation, Tate undid his belt buckle, and his eyes darkened as he then unbuttoned his pants. Tate's mouth curved at the edges, enjoying the tease, because this time was different. This time, they both knew—*I'm going to end up inside him.*

He looked behind Tate to the mirror and groaned at the visual he got. He flexed his fingers in all of those windblown curls, and it reminded him of that night months ago at Whipped. The night where Tate had danced up against him.

He also remembered the explicit fantasy he'd had of taking him that way—*naked, in front of a mirror.* A fantasy he was about to make a reality.

"Stand up," he said as he released Tate's hair and took a step back.

After shrugging out of his jacket, Logan threw it on the bed behind him. Tate was toeing off his shoes now that he'd removed his coat and tossed it on the floor. Then he brought his hands to his pants.

"No," Logan said. "Just the sweater for now."

Tate paused for only a second and then used his left hand to pull the sleeve down his right arm. The doctor had told him not to raise it unless need be, but other than that, everything should be working just fine.

Logan watched him pull the top over his head and loved the image of him in just his pants. Tate's olive skin always had him wanting to run his tongue over it, and the sight of him with no shirt had him springing into action to get as naked and as close to that body as possible. Kicking his shoes off, Logan finished undressing and then straightened to see Tate palming himself through his pants, watching him with hungry eyes.

He knew exactly what Tate was feeling. It'd been too long. *Way* too long since he'd been able to let go and take him the way he used to. He ached to sink his body inside Tate's, and Logan knew he was aching for it too.

"Do you remember that night we went dancing?" he asked, and as Tate nodded, Logan trailed his fingertips down his smooth chest to his navel. "You spent the entire time grinding all over my cock, and I promised myself that, one day, I'd see you like that. Naked and pressed up against me in front of a mirror. Then I could see *every* mouthwatering inch of you."

Understanding dawned in Tate's eyes.

Then Logan whispered, "Take off your pants, Tate."

Tate unfastened his pants, and Logan couldn't help but wrap his arm around his waist and stroke the crack of his ass, easing his finger down to graze it over his vulnerable hole.

"Today's that day. Turn around."

* * *

TATE FELT HYPNOTIZED by Logan's voice and the finger massaging him, but without question, he turned. He hadn't even thought twice about the mirror, which pretty much extended along the entire length of the dividing wall, but when his eyes found Logan's in it, he wondered how he'd overlooked the possibilities.

Tate watched avidly as Logan pulled him flush against his groin, fitting his ass exactly where he'd said it had been that night—over his cock. He then leaned back against his chest, feeling a shiver skate up his spine as Logan's warm breath ghosted over his ear.

"So sexy," Logan rasped, snaking an arm around his waist to dip his fingers into the front of his open pants.

"You're so *fucking* sexy, Tate."

When Logan's fingers wrapped around him and stroked, a groan of pure pleasure pulled from his throat.

"Like that?" Logan asked as he did it again.

"Yes," he sighed and caught Logan's eyes in the mirror. "Do it again."

"Or maybe like this?" Logan suggested, drawing his fist up to the tip of him, where he twisted his wrist in a way that had his toes *curling* into the plush carpet under foot.

"Oh, *hell,*" he cursed and grabbed Logan's forearm. He turned his head to capture Logan's mouth, and as their lips met, he pushed his cock back through the strong fist working him.

Tate wrenched his mouth free when Logan's other hand moved to the base of his throat, where he held him in place and started to press fervent kisses down the side of his neck to his shoulder. As he scraped his teeth along the top of it, Tate dug his fingers harder into the arm holding him. Logan raised his eyes to meet his in the reflection, and it was all he could do to keep his knees from buckling.

The expression in Logan's eyes was wild. It was proprietary, and as he continued to take in the rest of the picture they made, Tate watched those full lips curve against his shoulder.

"I'm going to enjoy this for *so* many reasons," Logan told him. "But one of them will be watching your face when you finally see how good we look together—fucking."

Goddamn. Tate knew how hot the gay porn had made him. Watching two guys going at it had been extremely arousing. So just thinking about how sexy Logan must look while fucking him had him really excited. It was a reaction he couldn't hide from the man behind him, because as soon as the idea had been planted, Tate jacked his hips forward, trying to get more friction on his dick.

"Oh, yeah. See?" Logan whispered, his voice husky. "You like that idea, don't you? Watching us fuck?"

Hell fucking yes, I do, he thought. But instead of saying it, Tate turned his head and kissed Logan's filthy-talking mouth, which was still issuing promises so hot they almost melted him to the ground. He heard an agonized sound of arousal that matched his own, and then his body and his lips were released. Logan's scorching, blue eyes found his and he simply said, "Watch."

* * *

LOGAN DRAGGED HIS eyes away from Tate's and ran them down the length of his spine. *The guy's skin is fucking delicious,* he thought as he smoothed his palms down his sides and placed a kiss at the base of his neck. Tate's hair tickled his nose, and Logan smiled as he started to trace his tongue down the long line of him. When he got to the curve of his lower back, he slipped his fingers into the black pants and crouched to pull them over the rise of Tate's ass.

As he dragged them and his boxers to his ankles, Tate's eyes found his in the mirror. He put a hand on the side of the vanity to balance himself and then lifted his foot without the need for instruction.

Once Tate's remaining clothes were gone, Logan let the connection between them be severed so he could focus on the ass he was now eye level with. He ran his index fingers up the insides of Tate's legs to behind his knees, and when he got to them, he flirted there for a moment, drawing invisible circles.

"Tate?" he asked, moving so he could rest his temple against Tate's hip.

"Yeah?"

Logan turned his head and nipped at the smooth skin of his hipbone. "I can't see when I'm down here," he explained, and then he turned back to Tate's heated gaze in the mirror. "So you're going to have to tell me what I'm missing."

One of Tate's hands circled his cock and he started to masturbate for him with a tense look of concentration on his face.

Oh, yes. He loves that idea.

Logan grabbed his bag from the stool beside him and unzipped it to get the bottle of lube he'd packed. He then placed it on the counter for later, shoved the bag aside, and shifted out of view. Tate's body rocked forward, slightly away from him, and Logan knew he was fucking his fist. But there was no sound in the room other than—*yes, there it is*—the ragged bursts of air that kept escaping Tate with every snap of his hips.

Logan grinned as he sank his teeth into the firm globe of Tate's ass, and when a feral fucking growl came from above, he said, "I don't hear you talking, Tate." He ran his hands over the rounded curve of Tate's behind and then gave it a sharp pinch.

"*Shit*, Logan."

Logan chuckled and then kissed the abused spot before saying, "Start talking. What do you see?"

* * *

WHAT DO I see? Tate thought as he continued to stroke himself and think about Logan kneeling behind him.

"I see me, standing naked in an expensive hotel suite. The curtain is open on the side of the room, and I see your clothes all over the bed behind us…which is fucking hot." He braced his left hand on the side of the vanity as Logan chose that moment to run his tongue over the dip of his lower back.

"What else?"

Tate felt his breathing speed up as his eyes took in the X-rated picture in front of him. "I see one of my hands against the vanity and one pumping my cock—" He abruptly stopped talking as Logan stood up behind him and drew his fingers lightly down his crack to his balls.

"Come on, Tate," Logan taunted. "Don't you know by now? I want *details*." His hand gently cupped his sensitive sac, and he blew a hot breath against his ear. "All the dirty ones."

Tate closed his eyes for a moment, trying to get ahold of himself, when Logan decided to make that a nearly impossible task.

"Mhmm. But while you're thinking about it," he said, and Tate opened his eyes to watch as Logan walked around the side of him and moved between him and the vanity, leaning *his* bare ass against the table. "Why don't you put your foot up on this stool and watch me suck your balls into my mouth before I swallow you down my throat."

Tate groaned as his eyes shifted to the mirror beyond Logan's shoulder, and then, without hesitation, he placed his foot on the small upholstered stool. The salacious smile on Logan's mouth as he dropped to his knees had Tate once again bracing himself against the vanity wall, ready for anything. His eyes took in their reflection, and this time, he found his voice.

"Fuck. Okay," he rushed out on a breath of air when he saw the back of Logan's powerful shoulders shift as one of his palms cupped his ass. "I can see you on your knees in front of me. The back of your head and hair, and every time you smooth your hand over my ass, your shoulder blades—

"

Logan leaned in where his leg was raised and dragged his tongue down his thigh to suck one of his balls between his lips.

"Oh, Jesus, Logan." Tate tightened a fist around himself and shut his eyes, fighting back the orgasm that was building. He squashed it down, knowing that, if he could hold it off somehow, the reward would be out of this world. He felt Logan's lips sucking the tender flesh scrunched high between his legs and *forced* himself to open his eyes. He didn't want to miss a fucking thing.

Tate could see the silky, black hair of Logan's head as he dipped down under him to torment with teasing licks and flicks of that rapacious tongue. He was relentless in his mission to have him on the ragged edge, and Tate knew when Logan lifted his head, sat back on his knees, and looked over his shoulder to the mirror at him that he'd just fucking started.

"You know what I see, Tate?"

Tate wasn't quite sure he was ready for this. Wasn't sure his legs would be strong enough to hold him up. But by God, he was willing to chance it.

"What?" he demanded.

Logan must've liked the bite to his tone, because his eyes darkened in the reflection and he licked his lower lip. "I see your fingers gripping the wall so hard your knuckles have turned white. Your left bicep is bulging, trying to keep you steady, and I see that thick cock in your fist that you want to shove in my mouth right now." Logan turned back from the mirror and looked up at him from where he was kneeling on the ground. "Don't you?"

Tate fucked his hips forward, and when the shiny head of him bumped against Logan's lips, he parted them.

"Give it to me."

Tate needed no further invitation.

He gazed down his body and guided his erection into Logan's waiting mouth. As his lips slid along his shaft, Tate glanced up to the mirror, balanced with the one hand on the vanity, and brought the other to the back of Logan's head.

Fucking hell, the sight of Logan Mitchell naked, on his knees, and sucking his cock down his throat made Tate feel like the luckiest fucker on the planet—he looked unbelievable there.

Tate pushed his hips forward, and with his leg still propped on the stool, he got a nice, deep slide. Luckily for him, Logan was practically a god when it came to giving head. He was so far down his throat that Logan's nose was in his pubic hair and his lips were touching the skin of his groin.

"Logan," he moaned and pulled himself free.

As Logan drew his lips off him, Tate twisted his fingers in his hair and tugged. When Logan got to his feet, the side of his mouth quirked and he walked around behind him, seeming to know he was ready for more.

"I've been thinking about fucking you ever since we parked my car at O'Hare."

Tate closed his eyes as Logan's palms smoothed down his sides to his ass and squeezed.

"You've been thinking about it too," Logan continued, using his fingers to spread him apart, and then he swiped his tongue along his jaw. "Haven't you?"

Tate clenched his teeth at the pleasure Logan was dishing out, and then sharp teeth nipped at his lobe when he didn't answer.

"*Haven't* you, Tate?"

Tate's eyes found Logan's in the mirror, and the feral fucking look swirling in them had him nodding fast. "Yes."

He didn't dare look anywhere but at the sinfully attractive man whose erection was rubbing a sticky, wet trail against the crack of his ass as he placed his cheek beside his own in the mirror.

They were both so incredibly different from the other, but as they stood there, rooted to their spots, they had one thing in common. The raw desire and emotion on their faces matched, and as Logan reached for the bottle of lube and opened it, Tate wanted to beg him to hurry.

"Wrap your left arm around my neck," Logan ordered when he put the bottle back on the counter and wrapped his lubed-up fingers around his aching shaft.

Tate's eyes closed at Logan's sensual touch, and as his head fell back on his shoulder, he heard him praise, "Perfection."

Chapter Twenty-Five

TATE WAS BETTER than any fantasy Logan could've imagined as he stretched back against him with his leg still propped on the stool. He glided his slippery fist up and down his hard flesh, and with every wet slide, Tate would punch his hips forward—he was beautiful to watch.

"Open your eyes and see how amazing you are," he said.

Once Tate's heavy eyes had opened and found his, Logan greedily drank in the sight of him. His curls were brushing against his cheek; his shoulders were pressed back against his chest.

As he continued to use Logan's hand as a hole to fuck, Logan growled in his ear, "Your body was made to be against mine."

Tate panted. "Love how you feel behind me."

Logan released the hold he had on him and placed his hands on either side of Tate's waist. He then ghosted them over his hips as Tate reached down to continue pleasuring himself.

"That makes me real happy to hear, Tate, 'cause you're about to feel a whole lot more of me behind you."

Logan began to rub himself over Tate's crack, and then he zeroed in on the image in front of them. He dipped his knees slightly, and when he saw the plump, wet head of his dick come into view between Tate's thighs, Logan gnashed his teeth together to hold back the roar he felt building. *Oh fuck, that's hot,* he thought as he repeated the sweet glide and felt Tate's balls against the top of his cock.

"You know what's about to happen here, right?" he rasped, running his slick fingers down Tate's crack to probe his tight opening. He could see Tate's chest rise and fall as he continued to jerk himself off, and Logan pushed the tip of his finger inside him.

"Yeah…" Tate managed, though the answer was so low that Logan was thankful for the mirror so he could read his lips.

"I'm going to slide inside you. Right here. And you're going to watch."

Tate's eyes were full of lustful challenge as he leaned toward the mirror, propped his arm up for support, and then bucked his hips back onto Logan's hand. When his finger grazed over Tate's prostate, Logan saw him grit his teeth and took the opportunity to enter him with two.

"*Fuck…*" Tate growled, and his head fell forward as Logan pushed his fingers all the way in so his palm was flat against the crease of his ass.

"*Yeah,* Tate. God, you're tight."

Tate lifted his eyes to meet his then, and the dark desire

in them had all of Logan's words skidding to a stop.

"I want it," Tate said, his voice husky.

"You want—"

"This," he demanded, using the hand he'd been stroking himself with to reach between his legs and touch the wet slit of Logan's cock.

Logan's breathing faltered as he removed his fingers, grabbed the lube, and took a hold of Tate's ass. He poured some cool liquid between Tate's spread cheeks then glanced down to look at what he wanted. Once he'd lined the tip of his erection up with the hole beckoning him, he raised his eyes to see Tate tasting the pre-come coating his fingertips.

Dirty fucker. Could he have found anyone more perfect for him? The answer was simple—*hell fucking no.* With that thought ringing through his ears, Logan dug his fingers into Tate's flesh and slowly pushed inside.

"Christ…Logan…" Tate moaned as inch by delicious fucking inch he slid in farther.

Logan lowered his head and sank his teeth into Tate's shoulder, muffling his own raw groan. He felt a streak so fucking possessive rip through him and wondered where it'd come from. He knew he loved Tate, that he wanted to be with and take care of him. But as he stood there with him like this—so open, so trusting in their connection—Logan had an intense need to make it known that he was his—and vice versa.

He could see a bead of sweat trickle down his own temple as he stared at their reflections. Then he smoothed a hand around to the one Tate had working his cock and instructed, "Brace yourself."

* * *

TATE DIDN'T THINK it was possible to dig his fingers any harder into the surface under them, but when Logan grabbed his hips and withdrew out of his ass only to slam back home—his fingers almost broke trying to keep himself upright. The unholy curse that ripped from Logan had Tate finding his eyes in the mirror, and the sight he saw just about made his knees buckle.

Logan's hair was plastered to his forehead, and the sweat running down his cheek made Tate want to taste it with his tongue. He soon shoved that thought aside though, as Logan's fingers flexed into the sides of his hips and he started to roll them.

The pace was intense as Logan drilled into him, and every time he bottomed out, Tate would hear a sound full of sublime ecstasy tear from him that made his cock pound. The man behind him—*and what a man he is*—owned him in that moment. He was not leaving any doubt about that.

Logan's eyes were locked on his, and his powerful jaw was clenched as the hand at the back of Tate's neck squeezed and pulled him up straight, aligning their bodies—head to toe.

As he rested back against him, Logan stilled his cock inside him, biting the curve of his neck and shoulder. Tate's hips arched, and he felt Logan jut his hips forward to get deeper.

"I don't think you know," Logan whispered in his ear, "just how hard I want to take you..."

"Do it," he urged, wanting Logan to lose control with him—wanting to *see* that.

"God, I want to."

"*Yes,*" Tate hissed, his ass pulsating in a hot throb around the wide intrusion. "I want you to."

In a voice he barely recognized, he heard Logan say, "The bed, Tate. Go and lie across it."

Tate could feel his breathing coming hard as Logan pulled out of him and stepped aside to let him pass.

That was when he heard him say, "I can't wait to come inside you and watch you take it all."

Tate was so fucking aroused. Between Logan kissing him, biting him, and promising the hottest fuck of his life, he wasn't sure he could remember his own damn name.

He walked around to the side of the bed and lay down across the king-sized mattress so he could see himself in the mirror along the vanity.

Logan came around to where his legs were hanging over the edge and moved in between, nudging his thighs apart.

Fully erect, he looked like some kind of sexual god come to tempt mere mortals, and Tate sure as hell was tempted. He'd *been* tempted ever since he'd dared him to try, and now, as Logan stood there, he was fucking thankful he'd given in.

"You're looking really fucking good, Tate," Logan said as he trailed his eyes over him.

Tate reached down to rub himself, trying to ease the ache that was now a constant throb between his legs.

"Put your feet up on the edge of the bed."

Breathing was becoming more of a challenge with every word out of Logan's mouth, but it was when he lowered down to his knees beside the bed that Tate thought he would *stop* breathing altogether. Quickly, he reached to the side for one of the small pillows at the head of the mattress. He shoved it behind his head, trying to see, but then he realized he didn't need that—he had the mirror.

Throwing the pillow out of his way, he laid his head flat on the mattress and turned just in time to see Logan's muscled thighs bunch as he knelt by the bedside. The hard cock that had been inside him only minutes ago was fully engorged and visible, and as Tate's eyes shifted farther up his body, he found his own bent leg in the way of his view and lowered it.

He wanted to see *everything,* and as he watched, Logan turned his head to the vanity and caught him spying. One of his dark eyebrows rose as if to say, *Caught ya,* and he reached forward, grabbed his thighs, and hauled him to the edge of the bed. The smile that stretched across Logan's mouth then was filthy as fuck, and when Tate arched his hips in response, his foot slipped off the mattress.

"That's right. Watch me," Logan invited, and then he turned, lowered his head, and dragged his tongue over the base of his cock.

The strangled sound that escaped his throat was loud, and he tried to put his foot back on the mattress so he could push up into Logan's face. But after a couple of failed attempts, Logan took his ankle and placed it over his muscled shoulder.

With his other leg lying flat and his hips angled up, the picture Tate was seeing was so fucking indecent that he couldn't believe he was in it. But as Logan's tongue drew a direct path to the tip of his cock and he saw his own hands reach down and grip all of that black hair to keep him in place, he remembered that the picture was his reality.

"*Logan,*" he cried out when Logan swallowed him back down his throat. He kept his eyes glued to the man who was bent over him, making a meal out of him.

"You taste so fucking good," Logan told him as he lifted his head and caught his stare. His eyes were so dark that Tate thought they were close to black, and Logan bit his swollen lip like he was trying to taste him again. "You love watching me suck your dick, don't you, Tate?"

Tate thrust his hips up, and Logan ran his eyes over him

in the reflection. Then his fingers were moving, trailing down to—

"What about this?" Logan asked, their eyes still locked as he slowly pushed his finger inside him. "You like watching me do this?"

* * *

AS LOGAN TURNED his attention back to the feast splayed out in front of him, he eagerly watched his finger disappear inside Tate, who looked as if he were about to pass out from what he was experiencing.

The sounds he was pulling from him were making Tate's voice hoarse, and they had him pressing his own cock against the side of the bed, needing to ease the ache in some way, as the man lying before him splintered apart under his hands and his mouth.

He tongued the strip of skin just above where his finger was penetrating, and as Tate shoved his hips up toward him for more, Logan trailed his tongue down and delivered. He removed his finger and licked over the tight pucker he was two seconds away from fucking, and when Tate's heel dug into his shoulder and his second leg came up to plant itself on the mattress, Logan knew he was close to losing it. He slipped his hands under Tate's ass and pulled him up to taste every part of him he could reach. When he slid two fingers inside him, a loud curse flooded his ears.

Pushed way beyond the limits of his control, Logan scissored his fingers apart a few times and then pulled them free of Tate's body before he stood. Tate's eyes had been fixated on the mirror until that moment, but he turned his head and locked gazes directly with him.

Logan grabbed the lube on the counter and poured some into his hand while Tate feverishly worked his palm up and down. He then walked back to the mattress, and when Tate scooted back, Logan placed a palm on his thigh.

"Where do you think you're going?"

Tate's eyelids lowered to half-mast as he touched the tip of his tongue to his top lip and widened his legs in invitation. "Nowhere. Was just making room for you."

Logan moved up his body so he could plant a hand by the side of Tate's head and then lowered himself over him. He ran his slick palm over Tate's cock before rubbing their erections together, and when Tate turned his head to the side to face the mirror, Logan did the same—and the picture they made was one he would never fucking forget.

Tate's beautiful skin was such a rich contrast against the cream of the covers, and with their long legs entwined and their brawny frames connected, Logan couldn't help but roll his hips at the erotic image he was seeing.

"Un-fucking-real," he said, never having realized how perfect they were with one another.

"I know. I can't stop looking," Tate confessed. "More. I

want to see more," he said, sounding desperate as he moved his hips under Logan's while they continued to eye-fuck one another. "I want to watch you take me."

Logan's entire body reacted to Tate's words, but when Tate added, "I want to watch us fuck," Logan thought he would explode.

He took his hand closest to the mirror and hooked Tate's leg under the knee, pushing it back and opening him wide. He kept his eyes on Tate's the entire time while he moved his hips up and the head of his bare cock brushed his hole.

"Feel me?" he asked, gently nudging against him.

Tate's lips parted as his gaze lowered to where their hips were connected and he nodded. Logan pushed forward then, and once the head of his shaft had slipped inside the tight ring of muscle, he squeezed his eyes shut and rested his cheek against Tate's.

His forearms were on either side of Tate's head, and when he said, "Open your eyes," Logan's stare met with his in the reflective glass.

He watched Tate's hands smooth down his back and cup his ass, and when he whispered, "Fuck me," Logan saw Tate's eyes dilate and his mouth part on a cry as he pulled out and did as requested.

* * *

HE WASN'T SURE when he'd passed the point of rational

thought, but when Logan slid back inside him, Tate's mind seemed to have lost the ability to focus on anything other than watching the man on top of him make him his.

Their bodies were so intimately fused together that it was hard to tell where Logan ended and where he began. But as Logan pulled his hips back and withdrew his delicious cock from his body, he watched like a voyeur at one of the filthiest sex shows.

His leg was hooked over Logan's elbow, and as he tunneled inside him, the dimples and muscles on his ass, hip, and thigh flexed. Tate couldn't help getting high off the visual he was witnessing.

If he weren't being so superbly taken, he might have thought he'd blacked out and was dreaming this. But the forceful way Logan was thrusting inside him left no doubt that he was most certainly the man on the bottom of that hot-as-fuck image. He couldn't even make out the words that were flying out of Logan's mouth as he continued to watch himself get pounded into the mattress. And somewhere in those euphoric seconds, he lost himself in the feeling of surrender. He'd never known such trust, such devotion in another—and he knew he never would again.

Tearing his eyes from the mirror, he looked up at Logan, and when he found him looking down at him, he wrapped his legs around his waist to pull him closer.

Logan buried his face in his neck as his hips sped up and

pistoned back and forth—his breathing coming in harsh pants. He sounded like a man about to fucking explode.

"Do it, Logan. I want to feel you come inside me. Make me yours," Tate demanded.

He bit his ear, and that did it. Logan stiffened inside him and came on a shout so loud that it reverberated off the walls. Tate turned his head as the warmth of Logan's release flooded through him, and the visual and mental snapshot of the entire act had his own orgasm right there, teetering on the edge.

Logan looked at him in the mirror and slowly pulled out. Then he reached down to take him in his hand. He held his eyes as he moved his fist up and down, and then he lowered his head to the crook of his shoulder and whispered, "You're so sexy, Tate. Fucking beautiful. Come for me."

Tate's eyes closed, and as he remembered the way they'd looked only a second ago, his climax slammed into him and had him arching up to come in a sticky, hot mess all over his stomach and Logan's hand.

He'd never felt so satisfied in all his life. His mind even felt foggy. And as Logan lowered down beside him and rolled to his back, Tate smiled up at the ceiling and let his eyes fall shut. Nothing that they hadn't already said with their bodies needed to be spoken.

They had already given to each other everything.

Chapter Twenty-Six

IT WAS A beautiful Saturday morning in New York City. The sun was shining, the air was crisp with the promise of winter, and Fifth Avenue was bustling with pedestrians. Hand in hand, they walked toward Central Park, and when they came to a stop on the corner of the street, Logan looked over at Tate. He was back in his usual jeans, shirt, and coat, and as the sun filtered through the buildings, it warmed them where they stood.

"Is there any place in particular you want to see once we get there?" Logan asked, waiting for Tate to look at him.

He thought about it for a few seconds before he smiled over at him. "Strawberry Fields."

As the light changed and they were able to cross, he tugged on Tate's hand and they started up again. "Really? Big Beatles fan, are we?"

"A little. Courtesy of my father. He used to listen to them a lot when we were kids, and I learned most of their songs on my guitar at school."

"I love learning these little things about you," Logan said. "Strawberry Fields it is."

"What about you?" Tate asked.

"Hmm?"

"What did you listen to when you were younger?"

Logan chuckled. "I didn't really listen to music."

"Seriously?"

"Seriously. I told you I was a nerd. Books were my thing, not music. Plus, you've met my mother. You can imagine her tastes weren't exactly what a young boy likes. Actually, that may explain a few things…" he mused.

Tate pulled him against his side, and when their shoulders bumped, he laughed. "That's kind of hot."

"What is? That I was a nerd?" he asked in disbelief. "Trust me. I was not hot. I was skinny and awkward."

Tate waggled his eyebrows at him. "Keep going. I'm getting a good visual here. The glasses, the books, that smart brain of yours, all wrapped up in…"

Deciding to play along, Logan answered. "I favored pressed polo shirts with my very proper pants."

Tate gave him a thorough once-over, and Logan rolled his eyes.

"Stop it. You never would've looked twice at me. I'm a guy, remember?"

"Perhaps not at first," Tate agreed. "But I bet if we'd spent time together…"

Logan scoffed at Tate's insinuation. "Oh, don't stop there. You're saying—if we spent time together in college, you think you would've tested the waters with me, huh?"

As they came to the entry of the park and wandered

inside, Tate glanced over at him and really seemed to be contemplating him before he said, "I think there's something about you that just…"

Logan pulled him to a stop. "That just?"

Tate touched his cheek and simply said, "Calls to a part of me. And I don't think it would've mattered what age we were."

Logan blinked at him, trying to think of something to say, but he had nothing. No one had ever said something so honest to him in all his life. As always, Tate continued to be the one person who could surprise him—just when he thought he'd heard everything.

"There's something about you," Tate tried to explain as he traced his fingers along his jaw. "In the way you *are*. It pulls me in, Logan. I can't imagine knowing you and not feeling it." He stepped toward him, right there in the middle of the park on a busy Saturday morning, and took his lips in a kiss so fucking sweet that Logan had to clutch his arms to keep from falling over. Then Tate raised his head and whispered, "It just took me a few days to see it."

Logan touched a curl by Tate's ear. "You *were* pretty stubborn. And angry."

"Do you blame me? You hit on me the first night we met. I was in shock."

Logan turned, and they started walking again, oblivious to anyone in the park but themselves. "I did not. I waited until the second day to do *that*."

"Sure. Your eyes were practically daring me to—"

"To?"

Tate's lips quirked into an ironic smirk. "To go home and think about you long after my shift was over."

"I like that. You going home to your apartment and thinking about me, curious. But you know what I love?"

Tate studied him and waited silently.

"You coming home *with* me—and being absolutely sure."

Tate winked at him. "I love that too."

And Logan felt his heart just about melt.

* * *

AS THEY STROLLED through the winding paths of Central Park, Tate couldn't imagine any place he'd rather be. The temperature was perfect for walking around town, and as he watched the couples stretched out on blankets and the children throwing Frisbees and chasing one another around the grassy fields, he felt the stress of the last few months lift from his shoulders.

This was exactly what he'd needed, and it shouldn't have surprised him that Logan had known that. He was extremely intuitive when it came to things like this.

They passed several people sitting under trees reading, and when they walked around the lake in the direction of

Strawberry Fields, he said quietly, "I've been thinking a lot about my family this past week."

He didn't say anything else as they continued, and Logan seemed content to wait for him to decide what came next.

"I know I haven't said much," he started, trying to work out how to say what he wanted to.

"It's okay to want to see them, Tate," Logan told him gently, saving him from actually voicing the words.

When his feet faltered under him, Logan tilted his face in his direction.

"Did you think I'd think less of you for wanting to?"

"No…I… Well, I didn't know if *I* wanted to see them."

"I can understand that," Logan said. Simple enough.

Tate walked over to lean on the side of the bridge they were crossing over. When Logan came up beside him, he rested his arms on the top and angled his body toward him.

"Tate, they're your family."

"But they were so…"

"Cruel? Judgmental? Bigoted?" Logan supplied, nodding as he looked out across the water. "Yes, they were all those things. And maybe they still will be, especially your mother," he pointed out. "But your dad? He's trying."

Tate ran a hand back through his hair and sighed. "Yeah, I know, and that's what I've been thinking about. Do you think… Nah. Don't worry." He stood straighter.

So Logan did also. "No, don't do that. What were you going to say?"

Tate shoved his hands in his pockets and chewed the side of his lip as he carefully thought over his next words. Then he looked Logan in the eye and asked, "Do you think maybe we could stop by their house on the way home tomorrow?"

* * *

LOGAN WASN'T SURE how he felt about going back to the scene of that long-ago Sunday dinner—the one that had resulted in Tate's leaving him. But as he stared into the nervous, brown eyes that were waiting for his response, he knew he had to get over his own fears in this situation and trust that Tate was at a different place when it came to the two of them.

This wasn't about him; it was about Tate. *And if he wants to reach out and try again with his parents, who am I to stop him?*

"Sure, I don't see why not."

"Logan?" Tate asked.

Logan leaned forward against the side of the bridge, and Tate crowded in behind him and put his hands on his waist. He pressed their bodies against one another and then put his lips by Logan's ear.

"It might be different this time."

Logan turned his head so they were practically nose to

nose and said, "It might not be also. Then what?"

"If it's not, then we'll get in your car and go home—*together.*"

There it was, his biggest fear laid out in front of him. The thought of Tate leaving him again or telling him to go away… *Fuck*, he wasn't sure which was worse. But by the pained expression that crossed Tate's face, he knew that his feelings must've been pretty obvious.

"I'm not going anywhere. You know that, right?"

Logan turned so he could place his hand over Tate's coat. "I feel like I should—"

"But you're worried anyway," Tate ended for him. "Don't you trust me?"

Logan frowned at Tate's annoyed tone, and then his own agitation rose. "Yes, I trust you, but damn it, Tate. I just got you back after a month in a hospital bed and the rehabilitation after. And the last time we went to Sunday lunch, you…you—"

"Acted like a dick afterwards?" Tate supplied.

"Yes," Logan finished on a rush of air. "You broke my fucking heart that day, and honestly, I don't think, after everything we've been through, that I can do that again. Not even if you need a moment to freak out."

Logan stopped talking, realizing how loud his voice had risen, and then he lowered his eyes away from Tate's. *Jesus, I hate feeling vulnerable.*

"Logan?"

When he didn't raise his head, he heard Tate say his name again.

"Logan, would you look at me please?"

With his lips pulled into a thin line, he glared at Tate, irrationally angry at the way the conversation had turned. When Tate's lips tugged into a full-on heart-stopping grin, it only served to make him surlier.

"Is something amusing, Morrison?"

"Oh, the last name. You *are* pissed."

"I'm not pissed. I'm—"

"Really cute when you're angry."

The glower he aimed at Tate then should have had him dead and on the ground. "Fuck you."

Tate laughed at that suggestion. "Stop trying to change the subject."

"I'm not."

"Yes, you are. But I'm not mad at your reaction. You have the right to be skeptical. I *did* act like a dick that first time. I pushed you away. That's what I'm annoyed at. Me, not you."

Logan's heart thumped in his chest as Tate placed his hands on his chest and kissed his taut lips.

"I would never do that again. Not ever."

Logan nodded slowly.

Then Tate took his chin between his fingers and asked, "Do you trust me?"

Swallowing, he looked at the earnest expression on Tate's face and knew he was telling the truth. "Yes, I trust you."

* * *

THEY SPENT A little over an hour wandering through the lush grounds of Strawberry Fields and taking photos. Then Logan suggested they have lunch at Loeb's Boathouse. It was obvious he'd been to the city several times because he knew his way around it like it was second nature, and as they strolled under one of the old arches covering the winding path toward the restaurant, Tate found himself backed up against the cool, stone bricks.

"I'm going to miss you when you go back to work," Logan said.

"Miss me? I live with you. You'll probably get sick of me."

"I actually think that would be impossible, but I meant that I'll miss you in the evenings. I like having you there when I get home."

Tate ran his hands down Logan's black, V-neck sweater, moving his fingers under the hem to run them along the waist of his cream pants. "I'll still be climbing in bed with you every night and waking you up in the mornings."

Logan laughed at that. "I'm pretty sure *I* will be waking

you up."

"Yeah, you're probably right," he agreed.

Then Logan asked something he hadn't even entertained. "Have you ever thought about not going back?"

"To work?"

Logan nodded. "Well, to After Hours. You're still looking into the bar idea, right?"

He'd thought about it when he'd been released from the hospital and wondered if maybe he should hold off—wait until he was back on his feet and all of this was behind him.

"Maybe this is a good way to start over?" Logan suggested.

Tate scrunched his face up and shook his head. "I have to work, Logan."

"I know. It's just something to think about. You'd be leaving anyway if you decided to go ahead with the bar. And that in itself would be work."

"I'll think about it, but I promise nothing."

"Okay. I can deal with that." Logan smiled and then kissed his cheek. "Did I remember to thank you for coming here with me?"

Tate moved his hands to Logan's ass and pulled him in between his legs. "If I recall, I didn't have much of a choice. You stole me."

"That's right. I did, didn't I?" Logan whispered in his ear. "I stole you away from everyone."

Tate had a feeling that Logan was referring to much

more than Chicago in that particular sentence. "Mhmm. But I wanted to be stolen, so there's nothing wrong with that."

Logan looked around at the dark shadows they were hidden in and then returned his attention to him. "This is the Riftstone Arch. Did you know that?"

Not having expected that, Tate's eyebrow winged up as he observed the jagged edges of rock arching across the top of them. "No. I didn't know that."

"Yep. It's made out of Manhattan schist."

"Schist?"

"Yeah. I read about it in an article the other day. It's a metamorphic rock that's found all around Manhattan. They blew them up from the outcrops in the park."

Tate chuckled at Logan's explanation. "You just happened to read that in an article?"

As he pushed off the wall and took Logan's hand, Logan shrugged. It was interesting to see that confident, cocksure exterior of Logan's vanish. It was rare, but when it happened, Tate always felt as if he'd been invited to see another side of him. A side he shared with no one but him.

"I may have done a little reading about the place."

As Logan kicked the rock in front of him, Tate thought, *If this is what he means about being awkward and nerdy, it turns me the hell on.*

They started walking, and Tate said in his ear, "See? Nerdy can most definitely be hot."

Logan's head snapped around, and his eyes zeroed in on him. "Excuse me? There's nothing wrong with being curious."

Tate couldn't help the laugh that boomed out of him at that. "I'm not saying there's anything wrong with *that*. But you researched this place, didn't you? What else did you research?"

"Nothing."

"Liar," Tate teased. "When we get back home, I want to see you in your pressed polo shirt, proper pants, and glasses with a book in your hand. All nerdtastic."

"You're really starting to push it, Tate."

"Oh yeah? And what are you going to do about it?" he taunted and then lowered his voice. "Don't tell me you didn't fantasize about the jock…*or* the broody music student who played his guitar."

Logan stopped just as they reached the steps that would take them to the front door of the boathouse and replied, "I had the jock, and he didn't live up to any fantasies I had in my head. As for the broody music student…"

"Yes?" Tate asked, loving the smile that spread across Logan's mouth before he answered.

"He far surpassed them all."

Chapter Twenty-Seven

IT WAS SUNDAY evening when Logan turned his car onto Tate's childhood street. It'd been around an hour and a half since they'd landed, and it had been bittersweet leaving New York behind. They both knew they had to come back to their real lives, but as he pulled the car to the curb in front of the two-story house, Logan thought, *Why do we have to start with the ugliest part first?*

Tate reached across the car to touch his thigh, and Logan glanced down and put his hand over the top of it. Bringing his eyes up to the concerned ones looking at him, he found himself smiling over at Tate.

"Shouldn't I be the one comforting you right about now?" he joked, trying to lighten the mood.

"Why? I'm not the one who's worried. Everything I want is right here in this car. That's not about to change."

Logan leaned his head back on the headrest and closed his eyes. "Sweet talker."

"It's the truth."

"Then remind me again. Why are we here?"

Tate let out a soft sigh. "Because I figure if my father can swallow his pride and apologize… then the least I can do is see where things stand with the rest of them."

Logan couldn't fault him for that. He was the one person who'd reached out to him during Tate's hospital stay. Logan hadn't seen him since, but he knew he'd visited with Tate, and it made him hopeful that maybe at least *one* of his parents would come around and accept his decision.

But will he accept us?

"All right, then. Let's go and see if the Morrisons are home."

Tate released his hand to open the door, and Logan climbed out also, rubbing his palms over the front of his jeans. He waited by the side of the car as Tate came around and held his hand out to him.

"Come on. I think it's about time you were introduced to my family the way you should've been the first time."

As Logan stepped onto the sidewalk and slipped his hand into Tate's, he marveled at the difference between now and the first time they'd stood here.

"And how is that?" he asked, curious of how Tate saw him—saw *them*.

He started to walk up the drive, making Logan have to follow or let his hand go, and once they'd reached the white steps leading to the wrap-around porch, Tate kissed him. "As my boyfriend and the man I love. The person I now live with."

"That's a lot of information right there," Logan said,

trying to hold back the smile he felt threatening to appear.

"It is. But they need to know that's the way it is. If they want to be in my life," Tate said as he backed up two of the steps, "in *any* way—whether it's on Sundays for dinner or in hospital rooms because I've been in an accident—then they need to know that *you* are going to be there. You're the only person I *want* there. Everyone else is just an added bonus. Got it?"

Logan took a step up, stroked Tate's cheek, and told him, "You make me so fucking happy. I had no idea I never was before."

Tate smiled broadly before capturing his lips in a kiss. Then he turned to make his way to the front door while Logan lingered just behind him, waiting for whatever the hell was about to take place. But he wouldn't have to wait long because Tate raised his hand and knocked.

* * *

AS TATE STOOD there with Logan's hand in his, he wondered what was about to happen. But instead of the apprehension he'd once felt about bringing Logan home to meet his parents, he felt proud.

I have a caring, successful partner. Hell yes, I'm proud, he thought as the door opened and his father stood before them.

He felt Logan's fingers tighten around his own, and Tate took a step back so he was standing directly beside him. His father's eyes went first to him and then over to Logan before they dropped down to where their hands were connected. He then raised his head and shocked the hell out of him.

"Tate, Logan... This is an unexpected visit."

It was the first time he'd ever heard his father speak Logan's name, and as it lingered in the air, Tate forgot what he'd been about to say.

"Do you want to come in?" he asked.

Tate wanted to answer, but before he said yes, he needed to know what they were walking into. "Is Mom home?"

"No. She's over at your sister's," his father said as he pushed the screen door open and stood aside. "Do you want to come in?"

This time, Tate took a step forward and felt Logan follow. As they passed by his father, Tate said, "Thank you."

They walked down the hall and into the living room where, months ago, they'd had their first spectacular showing, and Tate looked at his surroundings. It was strange to be back there after everything that had happened. It felt surreal. Like that Sunday had been a whole other life ago. And as his father gestured to the couch and he sat on it beside Logan, he thought that it really had been.

"I thought everyone would be here," Tate started, honestly surprised his father was here by himself. Sundays had always been a family day, and usually after church and lunch, Jill and Sam's kids would be racing around the yard into the evening.

"Yeah," his father said with a sigh as he walked into the kitchen. "Some things have changed over the past few weeks."

Tate looked over at Logan, who'd sat back on the couch and casually placed his ankle over his knee. He appeared relaxed, and for a minute, Tate bought it. Until he saw the way Logan's fingers were drumming out a frenetic rhythm on his thigh.

He reached out and put his hand over Logan's, stilling his fingers, and when he caught those blue eyes, he winked. He then turned back to the kitchen and saw his father watching them. He had the fridge door open, and when he saw Tate looking at him, he quickly averted his eyes back to the contents inside.

"Do you two want a drink? Soda? Beer? Wine, maybe?"

He's nervous, Tate thought, the idea never having occurred to him before. *Almost as nervous as we are.*

"Dad?" he said and then waited for him to look at him again. When he did, Tate let Logan's hand go, telling him, "I'll be right back," as he got to his feet. He made his way into the kitchen and got three glass tumblers from the cabinet. "You still got your bourbon stashed around here somewhere?" he asked his dad.

His father narrowed his eyes at him and then smiled.

The expression was so familiar that Tate felt tears prick his eyes, but he blinked them away as his father pointed behind him.

"In the flour container on the bottom shelf."

Tate took a deep breath and walked into his mother's large pantry. He grabbed the container, and when he came back out, he put it on top of the wooden butcher block and opened it.

"Thought you quit, old man," he said as he fished out a half pack of Marlboros.

"Life has been stressful lately."

"I totally agree with that," Tate said as he unscrewed the bottle of alcohol. "Dad?"

His father raised his eyes, which mirrored his own, and they encouraged him to continue.

"I want you to meet someone."

They both turned to where Logan had sat forward on the couch, and his father said, "We already met, Tate. I told you—"

"I know what you told me, but I want you to meet the man I know. Not the one you had to talk to because he was sitting in a hospital waiting room."

Tate poured the three drinks, and when he slid one across the surface, his father took it in his hands and lifted it to his lips.

"Fair enough."

He looked over to Logan and crooked a finger at him. As

he stood and walked their way, it was more than obvious to him that Logan was anxious. His shoulders were stiff, his hands were in the pockets of his jeans, and when he stopped beside him at the kitchen island, he made sure they were far enough apart that they weren't touching.

Oh no you don't, Tate thought, and moved over so their arms grazed one another. When Logan looked at him, he offered a drink with what he hoped was an expression that said, *Trust me.*

* * *

LOGAN LIKED TO think himself a pretty confident guy, but as he stood in Tate's family kitchen opposite his father, he had to admit that he was intimidated as hell. He'd been watching father and son from across the room as they stood side by side, intrigued by their likeness. It was almost uncanny.

The curls Tate wore messy and long had clearly come from his father, who wore them cut close to his head. But there was still a noticeable kink there. His weathered features were tan, just like Tate's complexion, and a moment ago, when he'd smiled across at his son, Logan had recognized the expression as the same easygoing one Tate would flash.

Tate was the spitting image of his father—and for a

minute, it had made Logan wonder how *he* would have measured up if he'd ever had a chance to stand beside his own father.

"I was just telling Dad I want you two to meet," Tate said, interrupting his thoughts.

Logan cocked his head to the side and eyed him. "Pretty sure we've met a few times now."

"That's what I told him," Mr. Morrison said before he raised his glass and took a sip of his drink.

"Okay, smartass," Tate said to his father. Then he faced Logan. "I meant it would be nice if he got to know you *outside* of a hospital."

"Ahh, I see," Logan said. He then turned to Mr. Morrison and extended his hand. He wasn't sure what he expected, but when he reached for it, Logan decided that it was about time to make his intentions crystal fucking clear. He clasped it in a strong grip and inclined his head. "I'm Logan, and I'm in love with your son."

He refused to look away from the man who still had his hand. When Tate's father shook it, his mouth twitched at the side. And he floored Logan by saying, "Yes. I can see that you are, son."

Logan wondered if he'd imagined what he just heard, but when Tate put a hand on his back and his lips by his ear, saying, "You can let go of his hand now," he knew he hadn't.

Did his dad really just call me son? he thought, and

released his hold.

When Tate's father chuckled, Logan reached for the tumbler in front of him and downed it. So Tate poured another glass for him, clearly sensing he needed it, and then started asking questions.

"You said Mom was over at Jill's? What's that about? She didn't know I was coming."

"No," his father agreed. "She didn't. But ever since..."

As his words faded, Logan lifted his glass back to his lips. He didn't think what was about to be spoken aloud was going to be anything good, and he wanted to be a little more inebriated before it was voiced.

"Dad?" Tate urged. "Just say it. Ever since what?"

Logan cleared his throat, hoping in some way to dissuade Tate's father from speaking—it didn't work.

"Ever since you woke up in the hospital and she found out Logan had been coming to see you—that *I* had been letting Logan in to see you—things changed."

Tate rested his hands on the counter and asked, "Changed? How?"

"Tate," Logan warned softly, not at all comfortable witnessing this conversation.

"It's okay, Logan. He deserves to know. Your mother... She's staying with Jill right now."

"What do you mean?" Tate asked, and then he looked over at Logan as if he knew what was going on—which he certainly did not. “She left because of a decision I made? That’s…that’s—”

“Not what happened,” his father interrupted, grabbing the bottle from Tate. He poured himself a much larger serving than before and then turned to Logan and added to his glass, saying, “He can drive you home. I think you need this as much as I do.”

Awesome, Logan thought and sat his ass down on the barstool at the kitchen island.

“Tell me what happened,” Tate said as his father reached for the pack of cigarettes on the table.

He held them out toward Tate, but he shook his head.

“I quit.”

His father turned Logan’s way and asked, “This your doing?”

Logan wasn’t sure if he was about to get in trouble or be praised, so he stammered a little. “I…ahh…may have mentioned something once or twice.”

Tate laughed at that, and when Logan glanced up at him, he caught him rolling his eyes.

“Do you disagree?”

“No. You just make it sound like you suggested it so nicely.”

“Didn’t I?”

“No. You told me to ‘do us both a fucking favor and quit.’ So I did.”

Logan thought about that and then, arrogant as ever,

said, "I don't see the problem. You quit, didn't you?"

Tate smirked at him in a way that made Logan feel like they were the only two people in the room. "I did."

"And I only mentioned it twice."

Tate poked his tongue into the side of his cheek and nodded. "Sure, counselor."

That was when Tate's father spoke up, reminding Logan that they weren't, in fact, alone.

"However you managed it, I'm glad for it." He then turned to Tate as he lit up. "These things will kill you, you know."

Tate shook his head and opened the window above the kitchen sink. The gesture seemed routine to Logan, as if the two of them had done this before when Tate had either lived there or visited.

"Dad, what happened with Mom?"

Logan looked between the two of them and then waited silently.

"She moved out a little while ago."

Tate's eyes crinkled up on the sides as if he were trying to understand what his father was telling him, and then he got his brain in order and managed to ask. "Why?"

When Mr. Morrison faced him, Logan raised the full glass to his lips and downed the third helping of bourbon. As it burned a fiery path down his throat, he felt a nice buzz start in his head and thought, *Yeah, I just love being the reason for families to split.* It seemed to be his specialty.

* * *

TATE STARED AT his father in shock as he waited for an answer. This was the last thing he'd expected when he'd walked in here tonight. He'd thought they would spend the evening trying to get his parents to accept them into their lives. Instead, there he was, sitting in the kitchen he had grown up in, asking where his mother was.

"We disagreed on something that was rather important."

Tate walked around the counter until he was standing in front of his dad and asked, "Me?"

His father raised his cigarette to his lips, took a drag, and then nodded. "Yes. You, son."

Tate said nothing as he placed his palm on the counter—he'd even forgotten he had told his father not to call him that. All he knew was that in that moment, the man standing in there was the same one he'd admired as a boy.

"When you first came to us with Logan, it was a shock. A big shock. It was hard to comprehend that you'd gone from being a married man to being—"

"*With* a man?" Tate supplied.

"Right. And we didn't react well at all," his father admitted as he turned away from him, almost as though it were easier to say it if he didn't have to face him. "I'm ashamed of how we acted that day, and I'm even more ashamed of the way I treated you when you came back to see me."

Tate glanced at Logan and found him sitting still as a statue on the stool as if he were afraid to breathe. He knew the feeling. He wanted to know where his father was going with all of this, but he was also terrified to hear the truth. So he waited patiently.

When his dad got to the sink and pressed the butt of his cigarette into it, he hung his head as if feeling the shame he'd talked of. "When I saw you lying in that hospital bed, I knew there was nothing that was going to stop me from having a relationship with you again." He leaned up against the sink, crossing his ankles out in front of him. "I couldn't believe that I might lose you, and the last thing I'd ever said was—"

"I was no longer your son," Tate whispered as he approached him. "Dad?"

"Yeah?"

"What happened with Mom?"

"She…"

Tate nodded and said softly, "She doesn't agree with you, I assume?"

"No. She and Jill still feel as they did before."

"But you don't?"

As his father stood tall, he reached out and clasped his shoulders. He wrapped his arms around him, and Tate felt his heart break a little as he said in his ear, "You're my son. And this man—he loves you." When he pulled back, Tate saw the tears in his eyes. "He wants you safe and happy. I may not fully understand it, but how can I not support that?"

He looked over Tate's shoulder, and when Tate turned to search out Logan, he saw that his blue eyes were glassy—from tears or the third drink, he wasn't sure.

"She needs to decide what's more important to her. But my family comes first, and Tate, you're family."

Tate hugged his father, and as he stepped away, he raised a hand and swiped at a tear that had managed to escape. Then he had a thought, one he knew would take not only his mind off all of this, but Logan's too.

"Is my guitar still upstairs?"

"Yes," his father replied. "It's in your room."

As Tate walked over to the island, he asked Logan, "Want me to show you the guitar I brooded over as a boy?"

Logan gazed past him to his father as if seeking permission, and the gesture was so unlike him that Tate thought that it was absolutely endearing.

When he stood, Tate snagged the bottle and said, "We'll be back in a minute, Dad."

"No rush. It's your house too."

Tate nodded, and when he turned back to Logan, he raised his eyebrows impishly and said, "Follow me."

* * *

LOGAN FELT AS though he'd had the carpet pulled out from under him. He'd come here expecting one thing and been totally blindsided by another. Tate's father had welcomed them into the house, given them booze, and then sent them upstairs with his blessing.

Okay, so maybe not the last part quite how I'm thinking it, but close enough, Logan thought as he concentrated on the tight ass in ripped jeans walking up the stairs ahead of him.

He was relaxed enough to acknowledge that the thought of being taken up to Tate's childhood bedroom was doing all kinds of inappropriate things to him. Add in the playful look Tate had aimed at him before they'd left the kitchen and, *yeah,* he couldn't wait to see Tate's old room.

When they were at the top of the stairs, Tate turned left and made his way down a narrow hall, past an old bookcase and several doors, to the one at the end, which was shut. As Tate reached for the handle, Logan made sure he kept his distance. He knew that, if they touched, he wouldn't want to stop, and considering they were in Tate's parents' house, he figured that it was best to keep his hands to himself.

Before Tate opened the door though, he turned to face him, and Logan wondered what the problem was.

"Wait a minute. Do you have your glasses?" Tate asked.

The question was so left field that Logan couldn't even

think of an answer. *Why do I need my—*

"Can you put them on?" Tate asked and then scooted around him.

Logan reached in the top of his sweater pocket, and as he put them on, Tate came back and stepped around him, pressing a hardcover book to his chest. He looked down at it and then back to the man whose eyes were full of devilry.

"You're almost exactly how I imagined you."

Logan's brow rose.

"I mean, you're wearing a sweater, not a polo shirt. And I'm pretty sure that, if you were shy, you'd be looking at your feet and not my lips. But the glasses, the book, the way your hair is perfectly done. Yep, you're looking pretty nerdy there, Mr. Mitchell."

Logan's mouth practically fell open at that, and as he took a step forward, Tate brought the bottle of alcohol to his lips and took a swig.

Fuck, he's hot. In his ripped jeans, black T-shirt, and jacket, Tate was anything but nerdy. He looked rebellious, sexy, and downright dangerous as he continued to check him out like they were standing in their own house—not his father's.

Loving his "broody musician," Logan chose to play his part the best he could and lowered his eyes. He pretended to drum his thumb nervously on the cover of the book in his hands, and when he looked up from behind his glasses at Tate, the devious smile that met him made his alcohol-hazed brain go into high lust alert.

Get it together, Mitchell.

"Come on, Tate. You said if I helped you with your homework today, you'd show me your guitar."

Tate didn't turn away as he twisted the doorknob to his room. He kept their eyes locked, opened the door, and waited for him to pass.

As Logan stepped forward, he made sure to give his best imitation of a "shy" look from under his lashes, and if the way Tate clenched his jaw and shut his eyes was any indication, he'd nailed that fantasy for him good and well.

Feeling pleased with himself—and somewhat buzzed—Logan stopped once he was in the middle of Tate's old bedroom. Over by the window was a narrow bed with a red-and-black-striped cover. The walls were plastered with throwbacks to their musical generation—as well as the classics, of course. And when Logan turned around to see Tate lounging back against his closed door, checking him out, he really *did* feel that rush of nerves mixed with excitement. The only difference here was it had zero to do with the fact that he liked a boy and was unsure if he liked him back.

No, this had everything to do with the boy he was looking at practically daring him to touch him—and there was no *way* he was going to do that with his father downstairs.

"My guitar is right over there," Tate told him, gesturing toward the foot of his bed with a tilt of his head.

Logan glanced over at it and was about to move closer when Tate pushed off the door and suggested, "Why don't you sit down?"

Logan looked for a desk chair, anything but the—

"On my bed."

"Tate…" he said, his pulse starting to race.

Tate regarded him as he picked the guitar up and came around to him. "Yes?"

Logan chewed his bottom lip and then pushed his glasses up his nose.

Tate chuckled. "Nervous?"

"No," he dismissed immediately, but when Tate took a step toward him, Logan backed up.

"I don't believe you."

Logan's legs hit the side of the bed, and as Tate brushed a soft kiss across his lips, Logan groaned. *Damn,* this fantasy was pushing every single button of his, including the one inside his chest.

When Tate raised his head and licked his lips, he moved even closer, and Logan had no choice but to sit down. Then Tate sat beside him, giving him an *oh-so-innocent* look.

"Relax, would you? I'm not going to make you do anything while my father's home. I'm a good Catholic boy, remember?"

Logan's eyes narrowed on the tease next to him, and

when Tate started to play the guitar, he thought how lucky he was that the cheeky flirt was his.

Chapter Twenty-Eight

MONDAY AFTERNOON, TATE found himself on the phone with Logan, trying to decide if he wanted to go out to dinner or have people over. He looked at the dining room table and scratched his chin. "Do you think we can fit that many people in here?"

"Ten? Yeah, I think we can squeeze them in. Adults in the dining room, and if they don't all fit, I'll just make Cole eat with the other kids by the coffee table."

Tate walked over to the new table Logan had bought a couple of weeks ago and agreed. "Okay. That could work. What about food and drinks? Do you need me to go and pick up supplies?"

"Rachel assured me that she is taking care of dessert, and Mason is bringing the food. If you want to go and pick up some drinks, I can't think of anyone more qualified."

Tate glanced at his watch and asked, "What time is everyone coming over?"

"We were thinking around seven or eight? What do you think?"

Tate laughed. "I'm good anytime."

"I agree with that most definitely," Logan told him, his voice dropping until it felt like a smooth caress over his skin. "You're good for morning, nooners, *and* night."

"Yeah, yeah. Get your mind out of my pants. I'll have everything ready by seven. You can decide on the time, but, Logan?"

"Yes?"

"Give yourself an hour leeway, okay?"

"Why's that?"

Tate walked into the bedroom to grab his wallet so he could head out to the liquor store. "I've been a little stiff today. I might need your help getting ready."

"Is that right? In that case I'll be there at five thirty and not a minute later."

"I think that's more than enough time," he joked.

"Trust me. There's never enough time for *that*."

"I'll see you at five thirty, then?"

"Yes, you will," Logan promised.

"Hang up the phone, Logan."

"*You* hang up the phone."

"I'm going. Goodbye."

"Bye."

Tate laughed and felt a stupid smile stretch his lips as he made himself hang up, and then he slid the phone into his back pocket. *Okay, I can do this,* he thought as he looked around the room. A night with Logan's family wasn't something that would generally stress him out. But the thought of seeing Rachel was making him anxious.

He just needed to get it over with, talk to her, make sure she knew he was okay, and then everything could get back to normal. *Right?* He grabbed his coat off the rack and made his way out the door to purchase some of his and Logan's favorite men.

* * *

"HEY," LOGAN CALLED out as Cole walked by his office.

He stopped and stuck his blond head in the door, his eyebrows raised.

"Eight work for you tonight?"

Cole glanced down at his watch and stepped inside. "Eight works. You sure he's up to this after the trip? If he's not, we can wait and do it next week."

Logan lowered the pen he was writing with to the desk. "He said he's fine. I think he's looking forward to it. Having friends around. Speaking of…" he began, and when Cole looked at him expectantly, Logan continued. "Is Rachel going to be okay with him tonight? He's noticed the weirdness going on there."

Cole wandered farther into the office and shut the door. When he turned back to face him, Logan sat back in his chair, this time waiting on *him* to speak.

"I honestly don't know how she'll be tonight."

Cole's expression was one Logan hated to see. It was also one he recognized—one full of worry. His brother sat on the couch and looked over at him for a few silent seconds before continuing.

"You know, day in and day out, she's the same Rachel she's always been. But the second I bring up the accident or you call or Tate's name is even mentioned, it's like she… Fuck, I don't know, Logan," he said, shaking his head and rubbing a hand over his face. "She zones out and gets this expression on her face. It's fucking heartbreaking. Like she's seeing it, reliving it all over again, and I ask her about it and she says she's fine. But I know she's not. I'm about at my wit's end over it."

Logan sat forward in his chair and suggested, "Maybe after she sees him, she'll feel better?"

"I don't know. She saw him before he was released and she still…"

"But that was different. He was still surrounded by all the medical stuff. He's great now. She'll see. Maybe then she can try to move past it. Then again, I don't think I'll ever be able to forget the way he looked, Cole, and that wasn't even the actual accident."

Cole grimaced. "I know. She's such a strong woman, and she's been through so much already. But I've never seen her like this, and she won't talk to me about it, which is completely unlike her. She skirts around the issue, and she won't tell me how she's really feeling. *Christ,*" he cursed.

Logan stood, coming around the desk. He walked over to where Cole was sitting with his head in his hands and sat beside him, putting a palm on his back.

"Hey?"

Cole looked over at him, and Logan tried for a smile.

"You need to throw up? I can get my garbage can."

Cole flipped him off. "No. But thanks for the offer. You *do* owe me."

Logan had never been more serious than when he agreed, "I know I do. Bring your wife over tonight. Let her see him, talk to him. Then we'll see how she does, okay?"

"Yeah, okay."

Logan clapped him on the back, and when they both stood, Logan adjusted his jacket and asked, "You still keeping the baby's sex a big secret?"

"Yes. So don't try to weasel it out of me."

"But you're usually so easy to crack. You don't even realize it until you've let it slip."

"I am not."

"Yes, you really are," Logan disagreed.

Cole opened the door. "That's only because you're a smooth-talking bastard. You circle the issue so much that, before a person knows it, you're back on point and tricking us into telling you everything."

"What can I say? It's a gift."

"A gift it may be, but you won't succeed this time. So get

back to work, would you? We have a business to run. I'll see you at eight."

Logan waved as Cole walked out, telling him, "Don't come early—got it?"

"I wouldn't dream of it with you. Just be decent by eight."

Logan cocked his head to the side. "I can promise to be dressed, but not decent."

Cole smirked. "As always, it's been a pleasure, brother."

Logan closed the door behind him and felt his smile drop from his face. He was trying to keep a good front for Cole, but he wasn't sure if seeing Tate *would* help Rachel. He knew how affected he'd been after everything that had happened. But Rachel? She'd been there.

How did you ever un-see something like that?

* * *

EVERYONE ARRIVED AT or around eight, and as Logan took their coats and showed them into the kitchen area to reheat food, grab a drink, or find a place for the dessert in the fridge, Tate surveyed the crowd of people who had somehow become part of his extended family.

Shelly was sitting on the couch with her daughter, Savannah, on her lap, and beside her sat Mason and Lena's little girl, Catherine. The girls were both dressed as princesses and giggling at something Shelly had just said. When she looked over at him, Tate was amazed that this was the same woman who'd been so professional in the hospital when she'd visited and, at the same time, the woman who'd been so outlandish at game night months ago.

Her husband, Josh, was chatting with Cole and Lena, who were both sipping on cocktails. Logan was standing with Mason in the kitchen, and Rachel, who was holding a piping bag arched up over a cake, had a fierce look of determination on her face.

So far, he'd been skirting the issue of approaching her, and he hated that. Every time they'd been left standing beside one another, she would give him a timid smile and then excuse herself, and he would do, well, something other than stand there trying to think of what to say.

But it was time to man up. *What am I afraid of? A tiny pregnant woman?* As he got closer, though, he rethought that. Okay, maybe he was a little scared of her.

"This is amazing, Rachel."

She was focused on what she was doing as she bent down to write his name across the cake in a cursive style. The apron she was wearing was black, and in white writing across her pregnant belly were the words, *Your opinion wasn't in the recipe,* which was so much like the fun, outspoken woman he knew. It saddened him that, each time he got close, she clammed up and fled the scene.

Once she'd finished his name, she glanced up at him and that sad look, the one she always got around him now, entered her eyes.

Tate tilted his head to the side and reached for her arm, and when she took a deep breath, he asked softly, "Do you think we could talk for a minute?"

She scanned the room, but when there was apparently no plausible way for her to say no, she nodded. Tate caught Logan watching them from across the kitchen.

"How about we go out on the balcony? Let me grab your coat."

"Okay," she said as she untied the apron and removed it.

Tate left to get the black-and-white-zebra-print coat she'd walked in with, and when he got back to the living room, he saw her standing over by the sliding doors, waiting for him. He spotted Cole sipping on his scotch, and when he gave a nod of his head, Tate held her coat up for her to slip into before he opened the door.

As they stepped out onto the balcony, the cool night air hit his cheeks, and Tate shoved his hands into his pockets. She walked over to the railing, and as he stood there, surrounded by the city lights, he wondered where on Earth to start.

* * *

"THINK THEY'RE GONNA make out?" Logan asked as he stopped by Cole and looked toward the sliding door Tate had just closed.

His brother turned toward him with a wry look on his face, and when he raised his glass to take a sip, Logan winked.

"Really though. How do you think that'll go?"

Cole shrugged, and Logan noticed Shelly watching the two of them. As a look of understanding appeared in her eyes, she ran a hand down the back of her daughter's hair and gave them a small smile.

"She's a contradiction, isn't she?" Logan mused.

"Shelly?" Cole asked as he leaned a shoulder against the wall. "Yeah, I guess she is."

"She was pretty fantastic when Tate was in the hospital," he said, stopping to look at the people laughing in his living room. "You were all pretty amazing."

Cole reached over and clapped his shoulder. "That's what family does, Logan. We come together in a crisis. Whether you want us there or not."

Having never really been part of a family, the sense of belonging that welled up inside him was overwhelming. He swallowed the rest of his drink, and as he was about to make up some excuse to leave Cole's prying eyes, he heard him say, "I'm really happy for you. You know that?"

Logan glanced over at him and tried to lighten the mood in his usual way—sarcasm. "I think Rachel's hormones are rubbing off on you. You've become very emotional lately."

Cole pushed off the wall and went over to put his glass on the kitchen counter. "I mean it, Logan. I had no idea if you'd ever, I don't know, settle down—"

"Okay, let's not get ahead of ourselves. There are no rings happening and no…" *Ugh.* Logan felt a shiver race up his spine. *Children for God's sake.*

Just as he thought it, the little blonde sitting on Shelly's lap started screaming at the top of her lungs. Cole started laughing, clearly at *his* expression, and Logan shook his head.

"Hell no. I am not settling down. I'm living with my amazing, sexy boyfriend—"

"Who you love very much and are in a monogamous relationship with."

Logan didn't balk, but instead nodded. "Yes. And your point is?"

"My point is, that *is* settling down. It doesn't always have to be a ring or a baby."

"Thank God for that. 'Cause I don't think I'm ready for a diamond ring just yet."

"You're such a smartass," Cole said. "All I'm saying is that settling down can be unique to whoever it's applying to. And I think you two are pretty damn close to entwining your lives."

Logan eyed Cole's empty glass and gave a false smile. "I

think you need another drink. And to go and talk to someone who has a baby and…oh, I don't know, ovaries?"

Cole rolled his eyes and waved his hand at him. "I'm going, and no more to drink for me, thanks. I'm driving home."

As Logan watched his brother walk over to sit opposite Josh and his wife, he thought about what he'd just said. About things being unique to certain couples.

The idea of settling down with Tate wasn't one that scared him at all, but when he caught himself staring at the glass door that led out to the balcony, he wondered how they could make that unique to just them.

* * *

TATE STOOD BESIDE Rachel as they looked down at the bustling street below. He was trying to decide the best way to start the conversation he wanted to have, and every opening line he ran through his mind felt wrong.

He wondered how, on the same day he'd lost a sister, he'd managed to gain someone who was just as important and helped to ease that void.

Rachel certainly had been a surprise in his life, and with the wind blowing the loose hair around her face, he finally opened his mouth and said the one thing that had been bothering him.

"I hate how you don't talk to me anymore."

Surprisingly, Rachel had tears in her eyes when she faced him. "When I first met Logan, I remember thinking how free he was. I also remember thinking he was an arrogant jackass, but mostly how accepting he was. Never judgmental…" she said.

Tate settled back against the railing and looked her in the eye.

"I married Cole pretty much a week after knowing him. Mason? He flipped his lid. I mean, he gave us such a hard time. And you know what Logan's reaction was?"

Tate could only imagine.

"He caught us on top of Cole's desk and casually wandered in, dropped a file on it, and told us to continue so Cole could get back to using it for its proper function." Rachel laughed at the memory.

"That sounds like him." Tate smirked.

She agreed, and then her lips pulled into a tight line. "He was always that guy. Totally carefree, someone different in his life all the time, and he never brought anyone to meet us—never spoke about anyone. Not until you."

Tate reached over to the hands she was wringing in front of herself and slipped them between his own as she continued to talk.

"He's my family, and I fully supported whatever he wanted to do with his life. Cole and I, we love him so much. And then you came along." Rachel smiled at him then, but it didn't quite reach her eyes. She turned her hands over to hold his and gave them a gentle shake. "And you're perfect for him, Tate. You're perfect *with* him, and that day..."

She swallowed and tried to fight back a soft gasp of air. "I thought I lost you that day. He'd sent you to me, trusted me, and all I could think was how could I ever face him if I lost you. How could I tell him I failed. God, Tate," she sobbed and brought a hand to her mouth. "I'd been so happy about everything, and then I watched you get on that bike, and before I could see the car or tell you...you..." Her rush of words came to a standstill as her body shook.

Tate pulled her forward to wrap her in his arms, and her small hands went around his waist, her belly bumping into him. He placed his lips to her head and kissed it.

"Aww, Rachel. It's okay. *I'm* okay," he whispered, rocking with her on the balcony. "It wasn't your fault. There was nothing you could've done."

"But—"

"No. There was *nothing*—do you hear me? You saved me that day. You got the plate number of the other car, got out of the cab, and came down and held my hand. You were extremely brave under the worst possible conditions—and you saved me *for* him."

Tears rolled down her wind-chilled cheeks, and Tate put his finger under her chin and lifted it.

"You need to stop punishing yourself for something that was out of your control. I'm fine, see?" he said, releasing her to hold his hands out to his sides.

She swiped the tears from her face and pursed her lips. "If I answer that, Logan will be upset with me."

Tate winked at her and looped an arm around her shoulder. "Well, we don't have to tell him." When they got to the door, he looked down at her and said, "And I heard that he used to call *you* Hot Cheetah Pants, so if anyone's going to get upset..."

Rachel laughed, and this time, her entire face lit up. That's when Tate felt the weight he'd been carrying around all night lift from his shoulders and disappear into the Chicago evening air.

* * *

A LITTLE AFTER midnight, Logan crawled into bed and felt Tate shift and settle against his side. He'd just finished cleaning the kitchen after having sent Tate to rest, and when he'd locked up, walked into the bedroom, and seen him already asleep, Logan made sure to be extra quiet undressing and getting in beside him.

Everyone had left an hour or so ago, and the night, as far as he was concerned, had been a success. Rachel and Tate seemed to have worked out their differences, and Cole's tense look from the past few weeks had disappeared with the reappearance of his happy wife.

Logan felt Tate's hair against his side as he rolled over in the bed and his warm breath ghosted over his chest. He brought his arm down around him, and as they fit against one another, Logan closed his eyes and said softly into the room, "I love you."

He wasn't expecting a response, but as he closed his eyes and drifted off to sleep, he was sure he heard Tate whisper, "Love you too."

Chapter Twenty-Nine

TATE RUBBED HIS hands together as he waited under the awning of his and Logan's building. The wind was really howling this afternoon, and as he pulled the collar up on his coat, he spotted Logan's silver Audi R8 making its way down the street toward him.

It was one o'clock, and they were scheduled to meet up with the lawyer, Finley, over at Leighton & Associates. Cole had recommended the guy as the best in the business when it came to personal injury claims, so he'd set up a meeting a couple of days ago. Since then, Tate had thought of little else.

When Logan pulled the car to a stop, Tate walked over to the curb and opened the door. He slid inside and brought his hands up to his mouth to blow on them as the locks clicked. Then he turned his head to see Logan as polished and put together as always in his business suit.

"Shit, it's cold out there today," he said, unzipping his jacket and putting his hands against the vents of the heater.

"And here I was just thinking how *hot* you looked."

Tate glanced over at him and winked. "Pretty sure that

would be you, not me. I feel like a fucking icicle."

"Why did you wait outside? I would've text you when I got here."

"I was only out there for a minute or two, but damn. I always forget how cold it gets here."

Logan put the car in gear and agreed. "I know. Why do we live here again?"

Tate snickered. "I ask myself the same thing every year. And this no-transportation deal is driving me crazy. I really need to get a car and soon. I can't keep having you drive across the city to get me."

"I don't mind coming to get you." Logan reached across the seat and stroked his thigh. "Not ever."

Tate sat back and buckled his seat belt. "Well, I care. You can't keep carting my sorry ass around the city. You have a job, and soon, I'll be going back to work. I need a way to get around."

Logan flicked his indicator on and checked over his shoulder before merging into the flow of traffic. "I know. And I have to say… I like that you said a *car*—a vehicle with doors and a roof. That eases my mind slightly."

"Slightly?"

When Logan ran his eyes over him and gave a rueful grin, Tate covered the hand he still had resting on his thigh.

"I'm pretty sure it's going to take years before I'm completely worry-free. Maybe forever."

"I can understand that."

Logan removed his hand to change gears as he slowed at a red light and then gave him a serious look. "Good."

As the light changed to green and they started up again, Tate looked out the window at the cars beside him and asked, "What do you know about this guy Finley?"

"Not a whole lot. Cole's worked with him a few times, and I trust him. Says he's a bit of a pit bull when it comes to winning, but that's what you want in this kind of case."

"Sounds good to me," Tate said and turned to study Logan's side profile. "Thank you."

"For?"

"Everything. I don't know. Choosing me."

"For *choosing* you?" Logan asked with a laugh.

"Yeah," Tate nodded, and then he raised his eyebrows suggestively. "You had a lot of…options. I don't think I ever thanked you for being such a persistent pain in my ass."

Logan turned the car into a parking garage and let down the window to take a ticket. When he gave it to him and clasped his hand, he shook his head and said so seriously that it made Tate catch his breath, "After I saw you, there *was* no one else. Now, put this somewhere fun for me to find later, would you?"

Tate made a show of lifting his hips and putting it in his back pocket.

As Logan drove in under the boom gate, he said, "See? No one else would ever do. You totally get me."

* * *

TWENTY MINUTES LATER, Logan sat beside Tate in the conference room they'd been shown into and unbuttoned his jacket. He looked around at the décor, and while it was elegant and comfortable enough for clients, he was egotistical enough to note that their office was much more impressive. As he turned his head in Tate's direction, he saw him watching his inspection.

"What?" he asked.

"Sizing up the competition, Mr. Mitchell?"

Logan rested an arm on the table in front of him as he angled his body toward Tate. "Always. Honestly, our relationship aside, would you want to do business in this conference room or ours?"

Tate let out a low chuckle. "You're so competitive."

"I am not."

"Yes. You are."

Logan arched an eyebrow and pointed a finger at him. "You didn't answer the question."

Tate rubbed his chin. "Putting our relationship aside and the fact that I have extremely vivid memories of the first time I was ever *in* your conference room?"

"Yes. Putting aside all of that."

Tate scrunched his nose up in mock disgust. "Then the truth is I never would've kissed you in this room. I was much more impressed by the *size* of yours."

Logan laughed and dropped his gaze to Tate's lips. He was about to speak when the door to the room opened, and Tate's new lawyer finally joined them.

"Sorry to keep you waiting, gentlemen."

Logan turned his head in the direction of the voice. When his eyes landed on the tall, good-looking blond who'd just entered the room, his mouth fell open. There, standing in front of them, was—

"I'm Daniel. Daniel Finley."

Logan felt his eyes widen in shock at the man who was currently looking between the two of them, and as he pulled the chair out opposite them, Logan tried to work out what the fuck was going on.

This *is Finley? The same fucking guy who was with Robbie that night at Whipped?*

He pivoted in his seat to face Tate and saw that he had the same shocked-as-shit expression. When he looked back at the man who was now sitting with a crooked grin on his face, he wondered if this was some kind of joke.

"Now this *is* a happy coincidence. I had no idea that the Mr. Morrison and Mr. Mitchell I was meeting with today were the two of you."

"The hell you didn't," Logan couldn't stop himself from saying, and he felt Tate sit up a little straighter in the chair beside him when he let out the obscene curse he'd been holding in.

* * *

DANIEL…FINLEY…*OR whoever the fuck he is,* Tate thought, opened the file, and as he ran his eyes down the information inside, he pushed a piece of his shoulder-length hair behind his ear. Tate shifted to see Logan pin him with a "can you fucking believe this" look of his own.

"Funny thing is, I didn't know that Cole had a brother," Finley stated without looking up from what he was reading.

"Apparently, there were several things neither of us was aware of."

Logan's tone was so frosty that Tate was surprised that, when he reached over and took his hand, it was warm instead of ice cold. Then Finley lifted his head, and when he locked eyes with Logan, Tate was torn between running interference and wanting to watch them lock horns with one another.

"I'm sorry. Are you implying that I just lied to you, Mr. Mitchell?"

"I'm not *implying* anything. I'm positive you knew exactly who Cole's brother and business partner was before you walked through that door today."

"And you? You didn't do a little background checking before you came in? I find that hard to believe."

Tate eyed the man who was holding Logan's stare, and

the air in the room thrummed with angry testosterone. He remembered the confident way this Daniel guy had practically invited them to his bed months ago, and so, apparently, did Logan.

"No. I didn't. I trusted my brother's judgment. Clearly, that was a mistake."

"What's the problem here?" Daniel asked. "That I'm one up on you? Because I'm not averse to *you* being up on me—either of you for that matter."

"That's it. Let's go," Logan said as he turned toward Tate.

Tate pushed back in his chair and got to his feet, knowing that the annoyance lighting those brilliant eyes had to be matching his own irritation.

Apparently, this guy isn't deterred by the word no.

Daniel also stood, placing his fingertips on the table as he studied both of them carefully. Then, as if he hadn't just blatantly hit on Logan, he dismissed him and addressed Tate.

"I read your case. Do you want to win or do you want to lose?"

Tate glared at him, trying to see past the urge to plant his fist in his smarmy face.

"If you do the smart thing here and hire wisely, you have a great chance of walking away with a substantial settlement. You were the victim in a horrendous motor vehicle accident—"

"Which is another reason we don't want to be fucked around with by you," Logan stated as he moved to stand behind his chair. "We've been through enough."

Daniel eyed Logan. "I don't believe I was asking you."

"Why don't you go fuck your—"

"I don't like you," Tate interrupted, finally speaking up. "I didn't like you the first time we met, and I don't like you now. But apparently, you're the best."

Straightening to his full height, Daniel slid his hands into his pockets and rocked back on his heels. "I am."

Tate looked over to Logan, whose jaw was ticking in frustration and annoyance. He knew he was raging mad, but Tate also knew that, if they wanted to win, they needed the smug prick standing in front of them.

"I want to win," he announced and faced Daniel. "And if you can do that, then we'll work with you."

A victorious smile stretched across his face.

Then Tate placed his palms on the table and lowered his voice to one he barely recognized. "But the next time you feel the urge to invite us to your bed, squash it or I'm going to put my fist in your face. Got it? We aren't interested. Not then, not now, not fucking ever. Am I being clear enough for you?"

Daniel's eyes shifted to behind him, where he knew Logan was standing, but he didn't dare look away. When Daniel's eyes came back to his, he gave a slow nod.

"Got it."

"Good. Now that we know who you are, your pricing, and your…practices, we'll be in touch," Tate said as he stood and found Logan glaring at him.

This time, though, there was something other than anger mixed with the fire blazing behind those glasses of his. *Arousal?*

"Ready to go?"

Logan didn't take his eyes off him as he silently nodded, completely ignoring the other man in the room. Tate took his hand, and as they made their way around the table and toward the door, he felt a deep sense of satisfaction settle inside him.

As long as Finley was clear on who belonged to whom, then he had no problem what-so-fucking-ever working with the guy—especially if he was going to win.

* * *

LOGAN REMAINED SILENT in the elevator as he and Tate traveled down to the parking garage. He was trying to calm his blood pressure, but every time he thought about that arrogant jerk upstairs, he wanted to—

"Hey?"

Tate's voice broke through his irritated musings, and when he looked over at him and saw the possessive way he was eyeing him, Logan felt the adrenaline that was riding him course through his veins. He wasn't a fan of being made a fool of, and he was even less of a fan of being cut off and not speaking his mind.

But hell, it was hot watching Tate tell Finley to fuck off.

"You okay?"

He didn't reply as the elevator hit the ground floor. Instead, he pushed off the wall and pinned Tate with a no-nonsense look. And when the metal doors parted, he strode out into the cement underground.

He knew he needed to mellow, but when he remembered the way Finley had sauntered into the meeting today, it pissed him off even more.

Conceited fuck.

As he continued to walk through the rows of cars, he wondered how long Tate would let him simmer until—*yes, there it is*—a firm hand clamped around his arm and pulled him off the road, backing him up to a large pillar.

When his shoulders and ass met the cool surface, Logan angled his chin up and made sure to keep his eyes connected with Tate's.

"I asked you a question," Tate said, placing a hand on the cement block just over his shoulder.

"I'm aware," Logan replied, and even though he knew that it wasn't Tate's fault, he couldn't seem to help himself—he was spoiling for a fight. "Am I allowed to respond or are you going to cut me off and speak for me?"

Tate narrowed his eyes on him as he took a step forward and fit his foot between his own. "You're pissed."

Logan bit his tongue to stop himself from saying something along the lines of, "No shit." It would be better for the both of them if he settled down before he spoke.

"Why are you mad?"

"I don't want to talk about it."

"Clearly," Tate acknowledged, and then he lowered his mouth to his ear and whispered, "But that's too bad."

A shiver raced up Logan's spine as Tate's lips moved to his neck and pressed a kiss there.

"Why are you mad?"

He let his head rest against the concrete and balled his fists by his sides as Tate rubbed his leg against the inside of his own—immediately, his cock reacted.

"Tate…"

"Hmm," Tate murmured as he brought his lips back to his ear. "Tell me, Logan. Why are you mad?"

Bringing a hand up to clutch at Tate's arm, Logan turned his head, and when their mouths were only a whisper away, he admitted, "I don't like the way he fucking looked at you."

Tate dropped his eyes to his lips, full of possession, and Logan felt his breath catch.

"Good, because I hated watching him hit on you."

Before Logan could respond, Tate crushed their mouths together under the flickering light overhead. He parted his lips, and when Tate's tongue slid inside and his leg inched higher between his own, Logan groaned and arched his hips forward, rubbing his erection against Tate's solid thigh. The hand that had been on the wall behind him speared into his hair, and as Tate lifted his head, Logan chased his mouth and recaptured his lips again.

Tate moaned and dived back in, this time pressing his entire body up against his own and grinding their hips together as the tongue-fuck continued to drive Logan wild. Grabbing a handful of Tate's ass in each palm, he pulled him as close as he could possibly get with their clothes on, and when Tate lifted his lips so he could kiss and suck his way down his throat, Logan's eyes fell shut and he continued to thrust his cock against the steely length pressing against him.

"Tate…" he said on a shaky breath as that determined mouth continued to destroy any coherent thought he had.

Tate's warm lips found the spot beneath his ear, and he sucked the skin there until a sting of pain had a curse falling from Logan's lips.

He knew exactly what Tate had just done, and when he lifted his head and stared him directly in the eye, Logan thought his knees might buckle from the possessive look on his face.

"I feel the need to make a point," Tate said as his hands moved to Logan's belt buckle and his fingers busily went to work undoing it. He then palmed Logan's aching cock and mouthed, "Mine."

* * *

TATE WATCHED LOGAN'S chest rise and fall as he tried to catch his breath, but that wouldn't do. He didn't want Logan calm. He fisted the engorged shaft under his palm and felt Logan's hips snap forward.

"I want you on my tongue."

"Fuck, Tate, what are you doing?" Logan asked as he looked from left to right in the quiet parking garage.

"If you don't know, then I'm doing it wrong."

He didn't give Logan a chance to answer as he quickly unbuttoned his pants and lowered to his knees on the concrete. He ran his palms up Logan's thighs, over the expensive material of his pants, and when he reached the zipper and drew it down, one of Logan's hands whipped out to grasp the back of his head.

Tate raised his eyes to the man above whose long, black, woolen coat was hanging from the broad shoulders he had pressed back against the concrete pillar. His tie was falling to the side of his body in a haphazard way that made Tate's temperature spike, and when Logan used his other hand to reach into his open pants and pull his thick erection free, Tate thought he might come in his jeans.

You're all mine, he thought as he dragged his tongue over

the underside of Logan's cock. As a guttural curse left him, Tate didn't play around. He circled the base and then sucked the tip of him between his lips.

"You're so fucking *dirty,*" Logan rasped and fucked his hips forward.

Tate swallowed him into his mouth and raised his eyes to see him staring down at him.

"On your knees. On the ground. Jesus, you look so fucking depraved right now."

He *felt* depraved kneeling there at Logan's feet. But he also felt full of adrenaline. This amazing man he had his mouth around, the same one using him in a deliciously carnal way, was his. *Mine, damn it.*

As that thought flashed through his mind, he closed his eyes and tongued the slit of Logan's cock, and when the sound of a car roared to life, Logan's fingers twisted in his hair—the chance of discovery ramping up the sexual high. This was not going to take long at all.

"Tate...fuck, *fuck,*" Logan panted as he really started to go at him, shoving his cock in and out of his mouth over and over, making his jaw ache in the most satisfying way. "Yeah, that's it... So good. You're *so* fucking good," he praised, and as he drove his hips forward, causing Tate to cough, Logan growled.

Tate greedily took him back between his lips and tasted the salty explosion of Logan's desire as his name echoed off the concrete walls surrounding them, and Logan came all over his tongue and down his throat.

* * *

WHEN LOGAN MANAGED to find the strength to open his eyes, he saw Tate getting to his feet with a wicked-as-fuck smile on his gorgeous face. Then he reached down to put himself back inside his pants.

"Still mad?" Tate had the audacity to ask.

He zipped his pants and pushed off the pillar behind him. "I was mad?"

Tate reached for his hand. "You were."

As they started to walk through the parking garage to his car, he said, "Funny, I don't remember that."

"No?"

He unlocked the car and opened Tate's door, shaking his head. Tate stepped forward, about to get inside when Logan said his name.

"Yeah?"

He took the back of his neck and pulled him forward to attack that dirty fucking mouth. After he tasted himself on Tate's tongue, Logan lifted his lips away and whispered, "You're mine too. Now, get in the car so I can take you home and make *my* point."

Chapter Thirty

THREE WEEKS AFTER their initial visit with Daniel Finley, they were finally making headway on the case. With Tate's physical therapy sessions having wrapped up, they were now able to file for the full amount they were seeking for damages, and Logan hoped like hell they could settle out of court.

As much as he hated to admit it, Finley was damn good at his job. He was a shark—a relentless one. But then again, in his business, he needed to be. After several meetings with him and Tate, Logan had decided to let the guy do his thing. He'd respected their boundaries since the day Tate had set them, and if he could get Tate what he deserved, then who was he to stand in the way?

He'd just grabbed a cup of coffee and was sitting down with the newspaper when Tate strolled out of their bedroom in his loose, grey sweats, scratching a hand across his lower abdomen. When he passed by behind him, he put his hands on his shoulders, and pressed a kiss to his cheek.

"Good morning."

As he continued into the kitchen, Logan turned his head

to watch him. "Morning."

Tate poured himself a cup of coffee and then moved to grab the hazelnut creamer that now sat in the door of Logan's fridge. Logan felt a smile cross his face, and Tate must've caught it, because he asked, "What's that about?"

"What?"

"The grin."

Logan closed the paper and put it down as he eyed the bottle. "I was just thinking how nice it is that things have changed around here."

Tate put the creamer back in the fridge. Then, after picking his cup up to take a sip, he took the seat opposite his. "Were you?"

"Yep. I sure was." Logan ran his eyes over the smooth skin of Tate's chest and down his ribs until they landed on the scar on his right side. "I'm glad I had a chance to *see* them change."

When he raised his eyes, Tate lowered his mug to the table and winked at him. "So am I."

Logan opened the paper back up and glanced down at what he'd been reading. The real estate section had caught his attention just before Tate had wandered out, and when he looked back to the listing, he saw the address and folded it over.

"Hey? This address… Isn't it the same street where the accident happened?" He slid the paper across the table to

Tate, and as he reached for it, Logan took a sip of his coffee, watching him carefully.

Tate picked up the paper and read over the article. "Yeah. That's the place Rachel and I looked at that day."

Logan said nothing as a reflective kind of silence settled around them, and when Tate sat forward and put his arms on the table, he waited for whatever he would say.

He hadn't pushed Tate about the bar since they'd last discussed it weeks ago, but when he'd gone back to work at After Hours, Logan thought that it was a shame he seemed to have pushed his dream aside…yet again.

"It's funny, you showing me this today."

"Oh yeah? Why's that?"

Tate's mouth curved as he raised the mug to his lips and took another sip. "You're trying so hard not to demand an answer from me right now, aren't you?"

Logan tried for his most affronted look, but he knew he hadn't pulled it off when Tate chuckled. "I can be patient."

"I don't know. It's not your finest quality."

Logan crossed his arms over his chest and eyed Tate, waiting for him to continue.

"Well, tonight…" he said, pausing as he thought over his next words.

"You're an asshole," Logan grumbled. "Spit it out, would you?"

"You know, you're right. You are so patient," Tate teased, a wide smile flashing across his lips. "Tonight is my last night at After Hours. If that's still okay with you."

Logan hadn't been expecting that—not at all. Sitting forward, he tilted his head to the side and heard himself ask, "Are you serious?"

Tate nodded. "But only if it's something you're still comfortable with."

Logan stood and walked around the table to rest his ass against it. "I know there's more. You'd never just leave your job to do nothing. So start talking, William."

Tate looked up at him and ran his fingers through his hair. "How do you know that?"

Logan placed a hand on the back of Tate's chair and gave him a lingering kiss. "Because I know you. You'd never be happy sitting around here. You're honorable, hardworking, and stubborn as hell. And by your own admission, you've worked two jobs most of your life with a single goal in mind." He kissed him again and then lifted his head. "They're also some of the many reasons why I love you."

* * *

TATE RAISED HIS hands to cradle Logan's face, and as he deepened the kiss, he stood up between his legs. He nipped at Logan's lower lip and then whispered, "I want to take you there."

Logan smiled, and then he joked, "You took me *there*

when I woke earlier. You should eat breakfast, restore your strength first."

Tate rolled his eyes and pointed to the paper by Logan's hip, indicating the advertisement for the restaurant and loft. "There. I want to show you this place."

Logan looked down at the paper, and then he backed away holding up his finger as if to say, *One sec.* He disappeared into their bedroom and, after several seconds, came back out with something in his hands.

When he put a crumpled piece of paper down on the table, Tate saw the circled address written at the bottom of the sheet with: **Perfect location. Decent price. Show Logan. Tell him yes.**

Tate took Logan's hand in his and tugged him forward, asking in a low voice, "You kept this?"

Logan swallowed, trying to keep his own emotions at bay. But when Tate wrapped his arms around his neck and kissed his ear, he nodded.

"Yes, and I've been waiting." When Tate pulled back, Logan smiled. "Show me."

* * *

AS LOGAN EXECUTED a perfect parallel park, Tate sat in the passenger's seat beside him, staring at the empty building on the corner of the block. The wall of windows that ran up the side of the property called to him just as they had the first time he'd seen them, and as he looked across the street, he was happy in that instant that he had no memory of what had occurred after he'd said goodbye to Rachel that day.

Logan turned the ignition off and faced him in the car. "This is the place, right?"

Tate nodded and reached for the jacket he'd thrown on the back seat before he passed Logan his burgundy scarf.

Logan unlocked the doors and asked, "Then what are you waiting for, Mr. Morrison? Show me."

Tate took a deep breath and then opened the car door. As the chilly air hit him, he pulled his coat on and zipped it while Logan came around the front of the car, wrapping the scarf around his neck. With his glasses on and his black coat buttoned over his dark jeans, Logan looked amazing. He reached for his hand, and Tate took it without hesitation.

They crossed the street and made their way around to the front double doors, where the same woman who'd shown him and Rachel the property the first time was waiting.

"Mr. Morrison. What a pleasure to see you again," she gushed, extending her hand.

Tate reached for it, and as they shook, she moved her eyes to Logan and smiled.

"And...?"

"Sorry, this is Logan," he told her. As she let his hand go, he added, "And please, call me Tate."

"Okay, then, Tate. Let's get inside and out of this brutal wind." She unlocked the doors and then pushed one open, holding it for the two of them to pass by.

The space was just as he remembered it—with the bar already in place and in great condition. The afternoon sun streamed in from the large windows, lighting up the seating area to the left.

Hand in hand, they took the three steps leading down to the main floor, and when Logan stopped, Tate turned to see him unbuttoning his coat.

"As you know, from your last visit, the space also comes with the loft area above. That's still included in the price, and since you last checked it out, the seller has dropped it a little."

While she continued to talk, rattling off facts and figures, Tate leaned his back against the bar and put his elbows on top of it, watching Logan wander around the space. He liked seeing him there.

Logan was clearly listening to everything the realtor was saying, as was he, and with every new piece of information, he'd nod his head with a look of concentration furrowing his brow.

Once she finished her spiel, Tate took a step away from the bar and asked if she could give them a minute to check out the loft. She agreed, gave him the key to the door, and then told them to take their time. She would do some work in her car.

Tate made his way over to the closed, wooden door with the square glass panel and rested his shoulder against the jamb, keeping a close eye on Logan as he silently made his way over to him. He was trying to gauge his thoughts, but he should've known better. Logan had a killer poker face.

"There's a loft?" he asked.

Tate nodded and unlocked the door to the little nook. He was about to walk through when Logan grabbed his arm and pulled him back.

"You aren't thinking of moving out, are you?"

Tate took the ends of Logan's scarf in his hands and wound them around his wrists. When Logan was close enough that his windblown hair was brushing against his forehead, Tate murmured, "Not in a million years. But…"

"But?"

"There'll be late nights, and I'd like a place close by for us if we don't feel like driving across town. This is close to Mitchell & Madison too." As Tate started to walk backwards, he unwound the woolen scarf, and then he tugged the ends, urging Logan to follow.

"For us, huh?"

"Yep" Tate agreed, and then he turned to make his way up the stairs. After two small flights, they reached the top and Tate stopped. "Something she forgot to mention down there…" he said as Logan walked around him, running his hand over the sliding metal door of the loft. "The builder made sure the loft was soundproofed to block out the noise below."

Logan turned toward him and arched an eyebrow over his glasses. "Really?"

Tate took a step forward until Logan's back met the door and nodded. "Really. When you step behind this door, you can't hear anyone, and they can't hear you."

Logan chuckled, and the smile he flashed was pure sex. "Well, I definitely like the sound of that. Not that I was overly concerned. It may have been a little uncomfortable for the customers to hear the owner shouting in pleasure while I blow his…mind, but I was willing to have earplugs for sale at the bar."

Tate raised his hand and slid the key into the lock of the old firehouse door. When he took the thick, metal handle in his hands, Logan stepped aside. Then he hauled it open and assured him with a wink, "No earplugs will be necessary. Feel free to *blow* the owner any time you like."

* * *

LOGAN LOVED IT. The space was absolutely perfect for Tate's ideas for the bar. Between the business area downstairs and the loft above, he was impressed.

They said their goodbyes to the realtor, and Tate told her that he would be in contact. But Logan wondered where his mind was at in the process.

"Well?" Tate asked. "What do you think?"

Logan slipped his hands into his coat pockets and walked over to where Tate was standing on the pavement outside the bar. Stopping in front of him, Logan smiled and looked at the locked double doors, which angled out to the street, and then back to him.

"I think it's great."

"You're being serious?"

"Of course I'm serious. It's a great location, and the building is in immaculate condition as far as I can tell. You'll need to hire an inspector for all the nitty-gritty, but the interior, like you said, is already remodeled. And the price—for this area? The price is insane."

Tate nodded eagerly like a little boy as he glanced back to the door and practically bounced on his toes. "I'm so happy you like it."

"I don't *like* it," Logan said. "I love it. I think it's absolutely perfect."

As Tate faced him, Logan stepped forward to kiss him and saw a white fleck of snow catch on Tate's eyelashes. He raised his gaze above them and watched as the first snow of the season fell down around them. Then he closed his eyes, letting the flurries hit his cheeks. When Tate's fingers slid into his hair and then pulled his face in close, Logan opened his eyes and saw snowflakes landing on those dark-brown curls he loved.

As the smile on Tate's face lit his warm eyes, Logan pressed their lips together and felt his heart pound—never could he have dreamed this for himself. Never could he have imagined Tate. But as he stood there in the snow, he realized that this man's future—*his* dream—had started to morph into his own.

Chapter Thirty-One

LOGAN SAT IN the waiting room of University Hospital, tapping his foot impatiently.

Of course it had to happen today. Of course.

He glanced at the clock on the wall and ran a hand through his hair to grip the back of his neck. *Why does shit always happen all at once?* He looked at the empty seat beside him and grit his teeth.

The coffee he'd been handed ten minutes ago was as thick as sludge—and the same color too. As he stared intently at the door leading back to the halls beyond, he cursed that he was even back in this hospital in the first place, but there was nowhere else he'd rather be at that moment.

He heard his phone buzz inside his coat pocket and pulled it out to read the message. When he saw it, he grimaced. *Not much I can do about that,* he thought as he opened it and typed back: **No, stay there. Text me when you can.**

After hitting send, he sat back and crossed his ankles. Tate was right; he had no patience. He hated waiting for anything, and as he looked around once again, he remembered Cole telling him that Rachel's contractions had started last night. It was now three in the afternoon.

Surely, that meant it would be over soon, right?

* * *

TATE PARKED LOGAN'S car in the garage of Leighton & Associates and picked his phone up. The text waiting for him made him chuckle. Logan was irked that he couldn't be at the meeting they'd been called in for today with Finley, but at the same time, there was no way he wasn't going to be at the hospital when his niece or nephew arrived.

Earlier, he'd given him a kiss, grumbling about timing and how it sucked, and then he'd handed over the keys to his car and said that he'd catch a taxi.

Tate hit call and unbuckled the seat belt as he waited several rings for it to connect.

"Hello."

He laughed at the bored tone in Logan's voice. "You've only been there an hour. Are you Uncle Logan yet?"

Logan let out a sigh. "No. And I know it's only been an hour. But all of this waiting is painful."

"Not as painful as it is for Rachel, I imagine."

"Hilarious."

"I thought so," Tate replied, checking his phone for the time.

"I assume my car made it there in one piece?"

Tate glanced around the luxurious interior of the vehicle and nodded. "It did. As did the occupant, who you seem much less concerned with."

"I figured if you can talk, you're fine. But that doesn't mean my baby is."

Tate opened the car door and climbed out, locking it behind him. "Your baby? I'm starting to worry about you and your vehicles. Your truck is female. This one, I'm assuming, is also female. Should I be concerned you might be wanting to switch sides here?"

A boom of laughter came through the phone at that. "Tate?"

"Yeah?"

"You *never* have to worry about that. I happen to love the way your crankshaft works. Your piston sliding through my cylinder."

Tate stopped in his tracks, his mouth hanging open. "A filthy mind—that's what you have."

"Around you? Fucking count on it."

He started walking again and then punched the up button on the elevator when he reached it. "You aren't worried about Finley, are you?"

"No," Logan answered a little too quickly, which had Tate's lips twitching.

"Good. Because there's nothing to worry about."

Logan mumbled something unintelligible through the phone.

Tate said, "Hey?"

"Yeah?"

"I'm going to get this wrapped up and head right over there, okay?"

"Okay."

He stepped into the elevator, and as the doors slid shut, he added, "Love you."

Without missing a beat, Logan replied, "I love you too."

* * *

"LOGAN?"

LOGAN OPENED his eyes at the sound of his name and found Tate striding down the hall toward him. He stood, smiling at the appearance of him and how damn good he looked. His cheeks were rosy from the cold, and snow was clinging to his hair in a way Logan was discovering he loved.

Tate gave him a solid hug and kissed his ear. "Before you feel the need to ask, your car is fine. She's parked outside in the covered lot."

"I wasn't going to ask," he said as they pulled apart and sat beside one another.

"Yeah, but not knowing would've killed you" Tate said with a laugh.

"I trust you."

Tate bumped their shoulders together and grinned. "I'm glad to hear it."

"Mhmm. So, what happened? Why'd he want to see us today?"

Tate placed his ankle on his knee and angled his body toward him.

Logan narrowed his eyes and asked, "Was it good?"

Tate nodded. "It's *better* than good."

"Better?" he asked as Tate took his hands in his.

"Yes, better. They settled. They gave us exactly what we asked for."

Logan's eyes widened at the grin on Tate's face. "You're serious right now?"

"I'm dead serious. The insurance company agreed to pay the full amount without us having to take it to court."

Logan sat up in his chair and grabbed his face. "That's fucking awesome!"

"I know," Tate said, laughing as Logan kissed him. When he pulled back, Tate lightly touched his chin. "Thank you."

"Me? Why? I didn't do anything. It kills me to say it, but we should be thanking Finley. He didn't let up for a second. He threw out a number I wasn't sure was even possible. And fuck, he got it for you."

The wide smile on Tate's mouth was so fucking

contagious that Logan found himself laughing.

"Happy?"

"I don't know. I feel..." Tate's words trailed off.

"Yeah?"

Tate leaned his forehead against his and said, "I feel like the luckiest person on the planet right now."

Logan was about to answer, but they were interrupted.

"Hey, you two? Think you could keep your hands off each other for a few minutes to give me a hug for having the most handsome boy in all of Chicago as of thirty minutes ago?"

Logan turned his head and saw Cole standing with his hands spread wide in front of him and a proud-as-hell look on his face.

"A boy?" Logan asked as they both got to their feet.

"Damn right," Cole boasted, walking over to them. As he embraced him, he asked, "Did you doubt it with my genes running through the child? Our stock produces men."

Tate reached forward to shake Cole's hand, and he pulled him into a hug.

"Glad you got here in time, Morrison."

"Me too."

"Where is the rest of the clan?" Logan asked as they followed Cole through the large doors.

"They're on their way. Rachel didn't want to call anyone until he was here. It was the only way to keep them out of the delivery room."

"You called me," Logan pointed out.

When they stopped at the door to Rachel's room, he caught Cole's "*Really?*" expression. "We both knew there was no way in hell you'd want to be in there."

As Cole pushed the door open and stepped inside, Logan mumbled under his breath, "You've got that fucking right."

Tate chuckled behind him.

"Like you weren't thinking it."

"Logan, Tate..." Rachel beamed at them.

"Well, hello there, Mrs. Madison," Logan greeted, making his way around to the side of the bed to kiss her forehead.

She looked beautiful, but the dark circles under her usually vibrant eyes showed just how exhausted she was.

As Tate moved to the other side, he took her hand and winked down at her. "If you didn't want to cook Thanksgiving dinner, you could've just said so. Fifteen hours of labor? That's one stubborn boy you have there."

She giggled at Tate's comment but gazed at her husband, who was standing at the foot of the bed. "What can I say? He wanted to be in control of things. Obviously a trait he gets from his father."

"Obviously," Logan agreed. "But don't worry. I'm sure his good looks will come from his mother."

She laughed up at him as Cole called him a not-so-nice

name.

"So," Tate said with a very serious expression. "I have a question I really need to ask."

"What?" Rachel asked, taking Tate's fingers in her own. "What is it?"

Then Tate's face broke out into a massive grin. "You didn't call the kid Ignacio, did you?"

"No," Rachel said with a laugh, gazing over at Cole. "We decided Thomas was a better fit after all."

Chapter Thirty-Two

A COUPLE OF days later, it was Thanksgiving, and with Rachel still in the hospital and Tate's family all over the place, they'd decided they would spend a nice, quiet evening together—or so Logan had thought.

It had just turned five o'clock when he looked down at the text he'd just received from Tate. He'd gone out a couple of hours ago, and all he'd said was that he wouldn't be long.

Secretive shit.

Tate: We don't have plans tonight, do we?

Logan typed back: **I thought we agreed to stay in.**

He settled back into the couch, picked up the book he'd been reading, and started again. He was halfway down the second page when his phone lit up.

Tate: Change of plans. Be ready in twenty minutes.

Logan frowned down at the text and wrote back: **Be ready for what?**

Not a minute later his phone vibrated, and he smirked at Tate's response.

Tate: Don't argue with me. Twenty minutes. Be ready.

Oh, I do love you all bossy, Logan thought as he put his

book beside him on the couch and sat up.

Okay. You have my attention. What should I wear?

He was on his feet and heading to the shower when the phone vibrated in his hand, and on the screen was a message that had him coming to a stop.

Tate: Doesn't matter. You won't be wearing it for long.

Logan groaned, and when the phone rang, he answered it and brought it to his ear. "You're being very demanding, Mr. Morrison."

"You now have *fifteen* minutes," Tate informed him in that spine-tingling way he had, all low and raspy.

Logan closed his eyes, imagining him there in the bathroom with him.

"Oh, and Logan?"

"Yeah?" he breathed out on a sigh.

"I haven't even *started* to be demanding…yet."

And before he could say a word, Tate hung up.

* * *

TATE WAS NERVOUS.

As he stood inside the silent space where he'd been waiting for the last thirty minutes, he looked out at the street. He was fiddling with the set of keys in his hands, trying to get his heart to calm the hell down. It'd been racing ever since he'd ended the call with Logan.

The snow was gently falling to the sidewalk, and with

every new layer, it hid the footsteps of the people who'd passed by earlier. There weren't that many out tonight, though, being that it was Thanksgiving, and he liked the solitude that seemed to have taken over the usually busy part of town.

He spotted the black car he'd hired pulling onto the street, and as the headlights brightened its way, he stuffed the keys into the pocket of his black dress pants. Running a hand through his hair, he watched as the car stopped in front of the windows he was standing by.

When the door opened, he held his breath, waiting for that exact moment. *And there it is,* he thought as Logan stepped out of the car—that moment when he would first see him.

As always, Logan looked sexy and sophisticated. He was by far the most attractive man Tate had ever seen, and all he could see of him was that long, black coat of his and a charcoal scarf with light-blue and black checkers on it.

The driver was saying something to him, and when Logan reached out to shake his hand, Tate saw black leather gloves on his hands.

Oh yeah. He dressed up for me.

As the driver got back in the car, Logan finally saw him through the window. He cocked his head to the side and let his quizzical eyes move over him from behind his glasses, and Tate wondered what he was thinking. When he pointed his finger toward the front doors, Logan inclined his head and then made his way over to them.

Tate took the three steps up to the entry, and as he unlocked the door and pushed it open, he knew that it was time—time to invite Logan inside forever.

* * *

AS TATE OPENED the door to the bar they'd looked at the other day, Logan ran his eyes over the gorgeous man in front of him, torn between being turned on and curious as hell about the outfit he was wearing. He had on a rich, burgundy dress shirt, a tailored, black vest and tie, pressed pants, and polished shoes—and he looked fucking amazing.

"Come in," Tate said, his voice low and inviting.

He stepped inside and started to undo the buttons of his coat when he heard Tate shut the door and lock it. Then he was behind him, running his hands over his shoulders and down to squeeze his biceps.

"You made it okay."

"I did. The driver you sent…he was very nice."

"I'm glad to hear it. It was my turn to collect you for a change," Tate told him, and Logan smiled at the sentiment. "You look…"

Logan caught a hint of Tate's cologne and closed his eyes to take it in. He smelled unbelievably good. "Yes?"

"Sexy as hell," Tate's voice was hoarse in his ear.

As he came around beside him, Logan opened his eyes and watched him make his way toward the bar, which he then moved behind. His eyes roamed the open space before he walked down the stairs and removed his gloves. He could smell something delicious cooking and wondered where exactly it was coming from since he couldn't see much in the low-lit area.

There were several candles along the wall separating the two main spaces, and there were more lining the bar, lighting the area with a muted glow. As he got closer, he noticed two tumblers on top of the bar and smiled.

"You planning to get me drunk tonight?"

Tate turned to the back of the bar, and as Logan stopped behind the lone stool in the place, he put his gloves on the counter. The silence in the building was ramping up the sexual tension humming between the two of them. Then Tate glanced over his shoulder at him, and Logan saw his eyes trail down the charcoal suit, light-blue shirt, and tie he was wearing, licking his lips as he went—it was obvious he approved.

Logan shrugged out of his coat, laid it across the counter, and then took a seat before zeroing in on Tate's firm ass. This entire scenario felt very reminiscent of...*me and my hot bartender.*

"Excuse me? Bartender?" he asked.

When Tate turned, he saw *a white fucking towel* tucked

into the side of his pants. Tate knew exactly what he was doing here. He'd set the stage perfectly, and as he came over to stand in front of him, he flashed that wide, friendly smile of his. Although, Logan noted, tonight, it was packed full of sexual invitation as opposed to the naïve charm it had held all those months ago.

"What can I get you to drink?"

Logan felt his entire body react to the question. His heart started to race; his cock took immediate notice. And when Tate pulled the towel from his pants and started to wipe the bar, he reminded himself, *I already have this guy. I live with him. So squash the fucking nerves of trying to get him, Mitchell, and enjoy him.*

"I don't know what I feel like tonight. Why don't you surprise me? " he suggested, and when Tate lifted the towel and started to slide it back and forth between his hands, Logan followed the gesture then saw a gleam in those brown eyes he loved.

"Surprise you, huh?"

"Yes," he said. "You can't go wrong. I'm positive that I'd be open to trying *anything* with you."

Tate gave him a mock frown and stilled his hands. "Sir, I'm talking about your drink. I'm not sure what *you* are talking about."

Putting his arms on the counter, Logan pushed up with his toes on the rung of his stool to get closer to the teasing flirt opposite him. "Oh, would you look at that. I've shocked and scared the man behind the bar…"

Tate placed his hands on the edge of the wood and moved in close so they were practically nose to nose. The one-time conversation from long ago was now taking the turn Logan had wished for that very night.

"No, you haven't. I'm just trying to decide how best to shut your inappropriate mouth."

"Well," Logan said, his lips twitching at the heat swirling in Tate's eyes. "Alcohol is certainly one way. Food, which I can smell somewhere in here, is another. But…I'm not very hungry for food, and I know a much more pleasurable way to fill my mouth."

As Tate angled his head and teased his lips over Logan's top one, he had a hard time staying where he was. *Hard* being the operative fucking word. The guy sure was testing his self-restraint.

"Do you hit on everyone you meet?" Tate asked and then—*fuck yes*—nipped his bottom lip.

"Not anymore."

"But you used to?"

"A long time ago. A whole other *life* ago."

Tate smiled against his mouth and straightened, their lips parting. "So that's why I've never seen you around here before."

Logan lowered himself back to his seat and shrugged as nonchalantly as he could. "Could be, or maybe it's because you're new here."

"You're right, I am new. But then again, so are you."

"Well, I used to frequent this one place. You may have heard of it—After Hours."

Tate's mouth curved up as he leaned a hip against the bar. "Yeah, I've heard of it. You say you used to, huh? What happened?"

Logan raised a hand to his chin and stroked it as he answered, "I got involved with one of the bartenders."

"Oh," Tate said with a false grimace and shook his head. "That happens, I suppose. Probably why it's not allowed here."

"Is that right?" Logan asked, looking around. "And where is *here*, exactly?"

"You mean you don't know?" Tate asked. "The owner wanted a catchy name. One that was…specific to him."

"He did, did he?"

"Yeah, but it's a secret right now because he was only given the keys this morning."

A massive smile stretched across Logan's mouth at Tate's excitement as he pulled a set of keys from his pocket and put them between them on the counter.

"I can keep a secret."

"I don't know. I don't think I should tell anyone yet who isn't totally committed to being involved."

Logan felt his breath catch in his throat as he waited for Tate to continue, hoping he was asking him what he thought he was. Ever since Tate had mentioned his idea for this, the dream he'd always wanted since he was old enough to know he had one—Logan had wanted to be a part of it. He just didn't know how much until right that second.

"I mean…" Tate started again. "He wouldn't have to be hands-on to be invested, and I don't want—"

Logan cocked his head to the side and asked quietly, "What don't you want?"

Tate reached for the keys and ran his fingers over them, making Logan think he was more nervous than he was letting on.

Logan placed his hands over the top of his, stilling them, and asked again, "What don't you want?"

"I don't want him to think he has to say yes."

Logan stared at the man across from him, the one who'd stolen his heart months ago, and knew that *this* was their way—their unique way to settle down.

"Ask me," Logan encouraged.

Tate chewed on his bottom lip then locked eyes with him, direct as always. "Do you want to be a part of this…with me?"

"As in?" Logan asked. He wanted to make sure he wasn't misunderstanding what Tate was asking.

"As in be partners with me."

Logan was about to speak when Tate rushed on.

"I don't want money or anything like that. I already have

the loan and down payment all in place. I just want you to do this with me. Be a part of it with me."

Logan rested his elbows on the bar and steepled his hands in front of his mouth, eyeing Tate carefully before he said, "I don't know, Tate. It all depends…"

"On?"

"Well, I'm not very good at being silent, and I definitely don't want to be a hands-off kind of partner with you. And there's one other thing."

Logan reached for his tie and pulled it from his vest. He ran his finger down the back of it before tugging him forward.

"I still don't know the name of *our* place."

Tate gave him a wicked smirk as he put his lips to the corner of his and flicked his tongue over it, whispering, "The Popped Cherry."

"The Popped Cherry?" Logan repeated, loving the witty reminder of Tate's first time with him. "And you think I'm fucking dirty," he said right before he yanked Tate close to taste his tempting tongue.

God, he'd been nervous tonight when the driver had shown up and requested he go with him. He hadn't known what Tate was up to. All he had known was that, if he wanted him somewhere special, he was going to be there. In fact, Logan wanted him to be a part of every decision he made from here on out, and when he pulled his lips away, he also knew he needed to tell him that. Before he could open his mouth, though, Tate spoke.

"I love you," he said, and as Logan looked at him, he reached for his hands. "I had no idea when you first sat down across from me that night—no idea what I'd been missing," Tate whispered. "It was you."

Logan's eyes started to fill with tears, and he blinked, trying to get them to stop as Tate continued to look at him as if he were his whole entire world—he hoped that was the case anyway, because it was never more apparent than in that moment that Tate was his.

"What are you thinking?" Tate asked. "Tell me."

Logan stood from the stool and placed his lips to the corner of his mouth. "Hmm, well. What I was thinking…just might terrify you."

Tate stilled against him, and then his body shuddered on a ragged breath as he stroked his fingers down his jawline.

Logan wound his arms around his neck and held on as Tate kissed a path along his cheek to his ear, where he nuzzled in against his neck. His curls brushed against the side of Logan's face as he repeated the words *he* had said back when this had all begun.

"Then, Logan, terrify me."

And with those four words, Logan knew he had found home.

Special Thanks

When I first sat down to write the story *Try,* I wondered if my readers would take a chance and follow me in this new direction. I was nervous but excited to jump into a genre I loved to read myself. So off I went into the great unknown—and I took you all with me!

Since then, I haven't looked back!

Logan and Tate's journey is one I have thoroughly enjoyed writing. These two men have been nothing but a blast. From Logan's lack of a filter to Tate's honest and forthright nature, helping these two find each other has been one of the highlights of my writing career.

Having said all of this, it never could've happened without the amazing team I've had working alongside me. Not only are they some of the greatest women I know, I am happy to call them all friends.

Candace ~ I literally could not have written this

series without you. It really is as simple as that, but I can't possibly leave it there. From the very beginning to the last word on *Trust*'s final page, you've been with me and the guys every step of the way. You kept Logan's mouth in line when need be and Tate's penchant for being a stubborn ass right on point. Your critiques are brutal, your feedback invaluable, but most of all, your friendship is essential. Don't ever change.

Mickey ~ My awesome editor. You are wonderful! Not only as an editor, but as a person and friend. Your positive attitude and outlook on life are truly inspiring, and your work is fantastic. You are a total rock star, and I can't wait to meet you in a few months' time. I feel extremely fortunate to have found you, and I'm so happy you took this journey with me.

Judy ~ You have worked with me on a couple of projects now, but I think this is the first one where you told me that I needed to go back and take someone's pants off. I appreciate someone who can write that as a serious note in the comments section! Thank you for dealing with my messy chapter reads and the frustration of waiting days for the next part of the story to come out of my brain.

Jen ~ One of my biggest L&T advocates EVER!!! I love the way you embraced my guys from day one, and ever since then, watching you fall more in love with them has been a total pleasure. You run my street team like a well-oiled machine, right alongside your partner in crime, Donner, and I am so fortunate to call you a friend. Thank you for beta reading each installment of The Temptation Series. Your opinion is one I highly respect and value.

Donna (otherwise known as Donner) ~ My mission here is complete, and you know exactly what I mean when I say that. Getting you to a) Read an m/m series and b) actually enjoy it is an accomplishment in itself. I fought tooth and nail to get you a certain someone's redemption, and by golly, I think I did it! THAT deserves a hug the next time I see you!! Just sayin'.

Stacy ~ THANK YOU! You gave me the best drink conCOCKtion out there! Even if I was vague as ever when trying to tell you-slash-not tell you what I needed it for! You did an awesome job!

The Bloggers ~ Too each and every blog who picked up *Try*, a HUGE thank you. I was fortunate enough to have you give me the benefit of the doubt, even though some of you had never read an m/m book before. I have been privileged to work with some amazing bloggers, and I thank all of you for taking a chance, and falling for Logan and

Tate, and helping me spread the word.

Finally, to you, the readers ~ Thank you for embracing Logan and Tate the way you have. I never could've imagined that these two men would resonate so deeply with all of you. My only hope from their story is that we each find a person who can make us feel loved and appreciated for who we are—and that we can open our eyes and see that sometimes we may just be surprised by WHO that someone turns out to be!

Xx Ella

About the Author

Ella Frank is the *USA Today* Bestselling author of the Temptation series, including Try, Take, and Trust and is the co-author of the fan-favorite contemporary romance, Sex Addict. Her Exquisite series has been praised as "scorching hot!" and "enticingly sexy!"

Some of her favorite authors include Tiffany Reisz, Kresley Cole, Riley Hart, J.R. Ward, Erika Wilde, Gena Showalter, and Carly Philips.

CPSIA information can be obtained
at www.ICGtesting.com
Printed in the USA
BVOW09s0102290417
482683BV00001B/2/P